Whasian

Joy Huang Stoffers

We express our gratitude for permission to quote **Chang, Diana C. Introduction by Shirley Geok-lin Lim. The Frontiers of Love: A Novel © 1994.** Reprinted with permission of the University of Washington Press.

Published 2015 by Harken Media.

ISBN-13: 978-0-9887757-6-3
ISBN-10: 0-9887757-6-X

Library of Congress Control Number: 2015941216

For Miaoli, Neal, and Will.
And for everyone who's ever felt in-between.

She knew suddenly that she had always been haunted by the doubt of her own existence. She felt a fraud, an illusion . . . Supposing she looked in the mirror and discovered her own face there? She was also afraid to be real—it would demand too much new courage of her.

Chapter One

Ava felt the stare pierce her like a fish feels the angler's hook. Curiosity no longer surprised her, but most people were subtler about it. Especially on the first encounter. When their eyes finished reeling their quarry in, they settled for whichever conclusion soothed them. Or, sensing that Ava resisted show and tell, they let her go. Neither applied this time. The stare dug deeper. Dropping her suitcase with more force than necessary, she stood with a jerk. The head rush awakened her.

"Where are you from?" the sophomore asked, inspecting her from head to toe before concentrating on her face.

Eyes fixed on the tiled floor, Ava rubbed her lower back. "New Jersey."

"No," the girl continued, "where are you *really* from?"

No. No? Who are you to tell me no? You're helping me move in, but I owe you nothing. Rubbing her bloodshot eyes, Ava retorted, "I'm *really* from New Jersey."

She barely waited for the sophomore to step out before letting the door to 102 fall. It automatically locked. She looked forward to tearing the door theme in half. Her name and Charlotte's had been typed onto clipart of winding yellow bricks. Above the road: "Follow your heart, wherever the path takes you!"

Ava trudged the way to her white Jetta. She popped the trunk.

"Thanks." Ava thrust her memory foam topper at the tall Asian girl. It obscured most of her view. Try playing twenty questions now.

But once they returned to the room, the prodding began again.

"Where's your family from?"

"About twenty minutes from here." Ava put her U-Haul box down, her backside to the girl. "Well, that's everything. Really appreciated—" she yawned "your help." Ava twisted toward the sophomore.

"Thanks again. I'm sure you've got loads more to move."

Instead of leaving, the girl took a seat on Charlotte's bare bed. "Your last name. On the door . . . it doesn't match your face. But then I saw the rest on the sign-in sheet." She made a show of redoing her long braid. "Ava Ling Magee."

"Glad you can read," Ava muttered, laying out her mattress topper. After bundling up her choppily layered hair, she bent over the clutter. Three boxes and one garbage bag later, she found her cotton sheets.

"Who's Chinese? Your mom or dad?"

Facing the grey wall, Ava shook out her fitted sheet. "Neither."

"Taiwanese, then?"

She smiled to herself, tucking in her flat sheet. "Nope."

"Japanese?"

"No." She shook her pillowcase until it completely covered the pillow.

"Malaysian? Filipino? You don't look Korean . . . "

"And what do Koreans look like?"

She sniggered. "Moon-cake faces."

Ava pursed her lips as she smoothed the wrinkles out of her ivory comforter. A perfectly made bed. She wanted to sleep it all away. Instead, she finally faced the sophomore. "Look, I don't know what you're on about. I'm white. My parents are American." She dug into her jean pocket to peek at her phone.

"But—"

"It's almost nine. My roommate's moving in soon." She waved at her containers and bags, which bled onto Charlotte's side. "I'd better rearrange things."

"Oh." The girl's fine eyebrows furrowed.

Ava almost felt pity. But then her parents walked in.

"No, Paul, she must double majors. Most impressive for future Ivies—"

Mei and Paul spotted the stranger.

She watched the Asian girl glance from them to her and back again. The girl raised her eyebrows as if to say, "I knew it." Face flushing, Ava avoided her eyes.

Her mother went for it first. "*Ni huibuhui shuo zhongwen*?"

The girl's round face lit up. "*Dang ran*! *Ni shi na li ren*?"

And they were off, chattering like chipmunks. At least, that's what they reminded Ava of. She exchanged a look with her father: let's leave them to it. She took her key and let the door sweep closed.

They loitered in the hallway, dodging the few others who had opted to move in early. Ava leaned against the plastered wall. Slate grey, like the doors. She inspected the rough carpet. Mottled grey, riddled with specks of white.

Her father cleared his throat a couple times. "They're talking about where they're from."

"Uh huh."

Paul shrugged apologetically. "You know your mother."

"Yup." She fought a yawn.

"She never misses a chance to brag about you. That's where the conversation will lead. Anyway, she's got reason to."

Ava clenched her jaw. Unclenched it. She pulled out her phone. If she texted Charlotte that'd be blatant disrespect. Think of safe places to look. She cleaned the screen with her shirt. Studied the carpet. Glanced down the opposite hallway. Going back in began to seem the better option.

"I'm—she and I . . . *we* are proud of you. I'm afraid we don't say it enough. You earned it. And I don't just mean the grades and the scholarship. You've got discipline and . . . and maturity." Her father chuckled weakly. "Probably more mature than most seniors. Can't imagine what you'll be like your last year."

The yawn withholding caught up with her. She covered her mouth and yawned successively, three times.

Her father yawned with her. "Trouble sleeping?"

"Exactly." One way to put it, anyway.

Her father nodded like they shared a moment. "I remember the night before moving to NYU. Finally, an opportunity to get away, to reinvent myself. Thinking about it made me so excited I pulled an all-nighter. No worries; you'll sleep it off."

Ava blinked, eyelids heavy.

"Although, I've got to admit . . . ," he said, surveying the dreary surroundings, further exposed by the harsh overhead lights. "No imagination in this design scheme. Institutionalized, if you ask me."

She shrugged, finding his struggle to engage her painful. But she required more energy to play along.

Undeterred, her father pushed up his glasses. He leaned against the door, mirroring her wide stance. She knew then; he planned on pleading his case in full.

"You're always welcome to visit the apartment. The train's right here. It's only an hour to Penn Station. And . . . and you could bring Charlotte."

"Probably not." She tucked escaping layers behind her ears. "We'd interrupt your work."

"No, if I needed to work late, I'd stay at the office. You'd . . . you'd be no trouble. No trouble at all. It'd be nice . . . I like company." He reached out to smooth back a tendril she'd missed.

Ava sidestepped him, rebundling her hair. Her father frowned but returned his hand to his side. "If you're so lonely, why don't you go home?"

"Well . . . you know why. Commuting's such a hassle."

"Then invite Mother for a visit. You could show her Manhattan. See your alma mater together. Think of all the opportunities available now."

"Er . . . right, true. But it wouldn't be the same . . . plus, there's no time limit for us. Once you're done with school, though, who knows where you'll be?"

She checked her phone. Ten minutes. Her mother had talked long enough.

"What about father-daughter time? We never talk—"

"Later," Ava said airily. "I've got to get unpacked before Charlotte arrives. Dad, could you move? You're blocking me."

"Oh, yes." He slumped away from the door. "Of course."

She unlocked the door and pushed it open. They sat on Charlotte's bed. Her mother and the Asian girl broke off mid-sentence.

"Mother, Charlotte will be here in twenty minutes."

"*Dui*." Mei reached out and gently squeezed the girl's fleshy arm. "Nice meeting to you."

The sophomore smiled back. Her smile evaporated when she nodded at Ava. "Guess I'll see you around."

Mei waited until they heard her take the stairs down to the lobby. She shook her head. "That one. Never stop talking." She fixed her black eyes on Ava. "Avoid her. She thinks you a threat. Never let those people get in way of your studies."

"A threat?" Paul asked, back straightening. "Who'd find Ava threatening?"

Ava sank onto her bed. "No matter." She rested her head against the plush comforter. "Mother, you said you've got some ideas about the room?"

"Yes. Paul, go check your car."

"For what?"

"I left my timer there."

"You need a timer? What for?"

Mei exhaled impatiently. "To be ready for Cha."

"For tea?" Paul asked, misinterpreting Chinglish for Chinese.

"She means Charlotte."

"Sometimes it's like you two share a language of your own," Paul said. When no one smiled, he shifted his weight.

"Dad, you know she likes her timer. We don't need you now. Could you just get it? Here, take my key."

Confusion marked his brow, but he went to do what he had been told.

Mei left Charlotte's bed and walked to the door. She removed the doorstopper. The door swung shut.

Her mother sailed into the center of the room, her pastel-flowered dress rippling. "Take note. You get the left side of the room. You must."

"But I've already made my bed here."

"*Ai*! Laziness always ugly. Move. Make it again."

Ava pushed herself to sit upright, envying her mother's self-possession. She saw no signs of exhaustion on her mother's face. "But . . . what about my say in this?"

"You want to pay? You own the thousands of bills to pay for the dorms?"

"Dollars," she mumbled, turning to strip the bed.

"What?"

"Nothing." Plopping her jumbled sheets and comforter on the left-side bed, she went back for the mattress topper. She knew better than to ask her mother for help. Besides, Mei had turned her attention to her iPhone. Probably monitoring her blog. Ava rolled the foam up and wrestled it onto her new bed. Finished undoing her handiwork, she leaned against a bedpost and crossed her arms.

Her mother slipped her phone back into her Dior python clutch. "Don't be bitch. Put your arms down."

"How's this bitch*y*?" Ava yawned, not bothering to cover her mouth. "I'm just crossing my arms." Your fresh start begins now. If you continually surrender, everything becomes a power struggle.

"Arms down, *now*," Mei said, stepping in front of her. She pointed an index finger an inch from her face, shaking it about like Ava was a dog.

Suppressing a flinch, she abruptly dropped her arms. She leaned back further, letting the bedpost dig into her lower back.

With the charm of an ingénue, Mei rocked back on her heels, hands behind her back. She smiled, but it possessed the depth of a raindrop. "No starting with your attitude. Sharpen your eyes. *Yin shui si yuan*. When you drink, where does water come from? I can take this all away from you, ungrateful. No dorming; you can commute. Think of all the times we can spend together . . . "

"But I got the full ride," she protested, voice small. "You promised I could dorm."

The sound of a key in the lock interrupted them. By the time Paul opened the door, Mei had tugged Ava into a hug. The scent of jasmine sheathed her like a shroud.

"No worry, I know this feels a lot. We handle it together. You be moved in before too long. You see." She held a rigid Ava and stroked her back. "You'll see *my* way," Mei whispered, lowering her voice so that only her daughter could hear.

Ava extricated herself from her mother's hold and edged away, sucking in restorative breaths.

Mei glided over to stand next to Paul. Only a couple inches above five feet, she should have been dwarfed by his height. But it seemed the other way around.

"Mei, I couldn't find the timer."

She scolded him in the tone used to discipline a puppy enveloped in toilet paper. "You must overlook. Like always."

"But I looked everywhere. Behind the seats, too. You sure you left it in the car?"

Mei sniffed delicately. "With my elephant memory? *Shen jing bing.*"

Her father stiffened. It must've been an insult.

"*Fen dan,*" Paul rejoined.

Ava's phone vibrated. A text from Charlotte: "Going to be a few hours late. Julia's such a diva." She frowned at her screen. "Okay, see you whenever."

Her mother refocused. "Paul, Ava wants the left side of the room. She thinks it better to place desk by window than by door, like on the right side. Less distraction when people passing. Or when Cha socials."

"Or when Ava socializes. But does it really matter? It's half and half. If she looks out the window she can also be distracted."

"Blinds easy closed. They've got two windows. Unlike sharing the door, see."

While they continued their discussion, Ava looked out the windows at the bustling campus. Plenty of friendly looking people milled about. School spirit displayed everywhere. Students helping with the move-in process wore "Davison U Crew" shirts. Red-and- white "Welcome Freshmen/Returning Students!" banners decorated buildings. Where grass existed, so did cultivated gardens. The flowers and grass seemed to shine under the sun. But she wouldn't care if rain and weeds greeted her. She would make a home. College provided a respite, and she'd let no one take this from her.

"She want it set this way, and that's her final decision. We must respect it," Mei said, shooting her a clandestine death stare.

Ava yawned. "Whatever. Let's just finish moving in; I don't want to be in Charlotte's way."

A good three hours later, she'd conceded on all fronts. Mei wanted Ava's shower caddy *there*, not there. Her pillow needed to be on the side of the bed furthest from the door, because *Ava* wanted to see who came into the room at all times.

From her desk drawers, to family pictures, to the composition of her closet, Mei arranged it all in a manner that suited her fancy while trumpeting the setup as Ava's preference. When Paul left to move his car, Mei warned her to change nothing; she planned on making surprise visits. If Ava showed Mei a room even slightly different from the original construction, she'd come home for a weekend of basement rearranging. Surely she wanted to avoid her "favorite" activity?

When Mei stepped out to leave, Ava heard Charlotte's family trouping down the hall.

"Mei, what a delight!" Mrs. Bell said, meeting Mei in the hallway. Ava moved to the doorway to watch the show.

"*E*ma," Mei replied, mispronouncing Ema's name as she had for the last five years. Tucking her python clutch under a toned arm, she kissed Charlotte's mom on the cheek.

"Emma but with one 'm,' Mei," Ema teased.

Mei giggled her apologies. She turned to beam at Charlotte. "Cha! So tall and beautiful."

"No, Mei, you're the beautiful one," Charlotte said, blushing. "It's like you age in reverse!"

Ava tried to see her mother through her friend's eyes. Slender Mei, lightly made-up, looking ten years younger than her fifty-two years. A twinkling laugh, ivory teeth, rosy lips. Pale skin because she avoided the sun. A chic dark bob with brown highlights, which framed her face and enhanced her delicate facial structure.

No one else saw the cunning beneath the coy. The way her smiles never connected to her eyes. Eyes capable of flashing, in one beat, from sympathetic to ruthless. If you stepped on her tail, she'd strike in the same breath—she always recovered faster. She wore impeccable camouflage, but she saw through your defenses like you'd displayed them as an offering at her feet. The China doll toyed with them all.

Ava's thoughts were interrupted when Paul called Mei. Other students needed his parking space. So the Bells finally became hers to enjoy. Ema entered, toting more than her plump arms should carry.

"Ava dear! How are you?" Ema cried, dropping her daughter's things in a heap on the floor. She rushed to enfold her in a tight hug.

Ava studied the floor until Ema released her.

"She was fine until you decided to squeeze the life out of her!" Charlotte said.

"Oh please, she looks fragile, but Ava's strong enough to handle a hug!" Turning back to her, Ema frowned. "You look lovely like always. But too pale. And too skinny." She held up one of Ava's slim arms for further emphasis. "You must come dine at my house so I can fatten you up!"

Ava blushed, laughing, but she knew better than to disagree.

Charlotte's sister stormed in, her dark purple hair a curly disarray. "Char, how come you've got so much shit?" Julia asked, tossing two black garbage bags onto the floor.

"Like you don't have twice as many things," Charlotte retorted with a small snort.

"Let's avoid fighting when we've got such nice company," said Ema.

"Oh please. Ava's not company. She comes over too much." Julia gave a garbage bag a kick for good measure.

"Hey!" Charlotte glared at her older sister. "When I help you move in, I never complain or kick your stuff. You probably made a mess of my folded clothes!"

"Ladies—though you two probably don't deserve the term right now—put a sock in it. We can literally make that happen, too. Charlotte's brought all her socks." Ema tied her thick black hair into a bun and put her hands on her wide hips. "Ava, you must be relieved you don't have any siblings. These two. Like rabid dogs!"

Ava restrained herself from shuddering. She couldn't imagine growing up with a sibling. She had no experiences she wanted to share. "Hey, why don't I help you guys? I'm moved in and settled anyway."

"Oh yes! We can totally use you."

"Now, Julia," Ema scolded, "Ava isn't required to do anything. You're official family, so don't think you can squirm out of helping your sister. Charlotte's right on one account: she always helps you move in. Ava, you sure? You must be tired after moving in yourself."

Ava smiled. "It's no problem, really. I've got nothing else planned, and I don't mind."

"Alright, then let's hop to!" Ema said, ushering the girls out the door.

Within an hour they settled Charlotte's things. Though still tired, Ava's spirits rose. The Bells always managed to make people smile and laugh.

The next order of business everyone decided: lunch at University Way's dining hall, albeit a late one. They swiped into Tobias and joined the winding food lines.

Ava passed a tray to Julia. "You live off campus, right?"

"Of course. I only dormed for a year. Now I just live with nine people total."

Charlotte butted in. "Don't start trying to lord over us. Living in a run-down house isn't special. Besides, you've still got a roommate."

"God, you're *such* a freshman," Julia retorted before moving away.

"What do you think, girls?" Ema asked, hovering by the lasagna. "Do I dare try it? I wonder if it'll make your nonna roll in her grave." She settled on a small portion.

"I know what you mean. I'm unsure if I should get stir-fry, but I think I'll try it."

She imagined her mother frowning at her plate, voicing her *ai* of disapproval. Mei never ate Chinese food out unless they went to select spots in Chinatown; she always bemoaned the Americanization of Chinese food. Restaurant owners pandered to Americans. They installed tacky décor and dim "mood" lighting. Menus were bilingual or English only. The sauces were too thick and sweet but never spicy enough. Eating family style was uncommon, and you needed to *ask* for chopsticks and tea. Some even dared to charge for the tea! Worse still, authentic restaurants were dying out. American- born Chinese or non-Chinese immigrants, lower-class races, took them over. Chinese-ness, steadily watered down.

Ava finally helped herself to three different stir-fry dishes. No mother around except in her head.

After getting drinks the group sat down at a round table.

Ema probed her lasagna with her fork.

"Mo-om. It's not gonna bite, you know," Julia said, looking around to make sure she saw no one she knew.

"How do you know? Maybe in between the layers lies the Flying Spaghetti Monster," Ema said, fluttering her fingers.

Ava and Charlotte obligingly laughed, but Julia grimaced.

Ema chewed a bite of lasagna. "Hmm. I deem it . . . acceptable! I definitely make better though."

Ava smiled while Charlotte and Julia exchanged a look.

"I think the stir-fry tastes acceptable, but I don't think my mother would. She'd go on a tirade about how traditional Chinese food is so hard to find nowadays. My dad would probably agree with me, but she'd say our taste buds are tainted because we're American. Apparently I don't know how to appreciate the 'real' thing."

But Ava knew that Mei herself hadn't escaped becoming tainted. Her mother had not returned to China since leaving thirty years ago, and she had studied at New York University for eleven years, almost getting a doctor of philosophy. Mei would never willingly admit it, but she had become more American than Chinese.

"Well, that's what you get for being Whasian," Charlotte joked.

"Being what?" Ema raised her eyebrows. "Help out an old woman now."

"You're not old," Ava protested.

"Brown-noser!"

Charlotte aimed a poke at her side. Ava dodged it.

"No, she has manners, unlike my children," Ema muttered in a stage whisper.

"Anyway. Ava's a Whasian—a half white, half Asian person. I came up with the term myself!"

Ema chewed a mouthful of chicken, shaking her head. "Kids these days. Coming up with ridiculous jargon."

Ava pointedly stabbed a mushroom. "I agree. It sounds so silly."

"Brown"—Charlotte fake coughed—"noser!"

"Why does it matter? I don't like to define myself and I don't like fake words."

"Who says it's fake?" Charlotte asked.

"It's not a dictionary-approved word. I realize that spell checkers aren't fail-proof, but there's a reason why 'Whasian' gets the squiggly red underline."

"I don't see why that matters," Charlotte countered. "We're not at a linguistics convention."

Ema eyed Ava speculatively. "Mei mentioned you want to be a neurologist. But are you sure you want to pursue a science major? Can't you can get a humanities BA and still go on to med school?"

"I'm supposed to major in cell biology and neuroscience. But I heard you're allowed to take nontraditional routes. Like major in philosophy and also take pre-med classes."

"But doesn't that defeat the purpose?" Julia asked. "What if you get really into your major and want to ditch the pre-med stuff?"

Ema chuckled. "Simple! She'd ditch the science and become a full-time philosopher."

"Ha. Yes, a simple solution," Ava agreed. Just inapplicable to her.

Julia didn't buy it either. "That'd be a waste. Overachieving Asians become doctors or lawyers. Who wants a person who'll contemplate the meaning of life instead of a brainiac who can save your life?"

Here we go. Yet another form of *You're half Asian, so you're supposed to be . . .*

"Just because I'm okay at math and science doesn't mean that I'm obligated to go into those fields."

"'Okay'?" Charlotte scoffed. "You got into all the Ivies you applied for. Davison pays *you* to come here. There's nothing you aren't good at." She ticked points off her fingers. "Straight-A student, pianist, piano teacher, perfect daughter of big-time lawyer and former Mrs. New Jersey. *And* you got a perfect score on your SATs—which I hate you for, by the way—so I'd say you're a bit better than okay."

Ava shrugged, looking down at her lap. "Just a little luck and a lot of studying."

Julia shook her head. "Nah, it's the Asian motivation. I mean, the motiv*asian*."

"I don't think so," Ava said, unsmiling. "It's not inherent. It's . . . instilled. I studied instead of going to the movies or hanging out. Anyone else could've done as well."

Noticing her red cheeks, Ema chimed in. "I must say, as a math teacher, if you aren't truly interested in math, there's no point in going into the field. The same goes for science and everything else. I don't understand why some parents try to convince their sons and daughters to become mathematicians, doctors, or lawyers. Interests and happiness come first. Parents just need to accept that."

Ava nodded, crumpling up her napkin. Realizing what she'd done, she flattened it out before folding it so that all four corners lined up evenly.

"I mean, look at me. I let Julia major in communications, knowing full well she chose it because it's one of the easiest majors and she wants more time to party."

Charlotte and Ava laughed while Julia looked guilty and then defensive.

"No point denying it," Ema said, eyeing Julia. "I accept it, and so long as you actually graduate with a communications degree, I'll support your decision."

Julia made a face, and for a moment Ava wanted to shake her. How could she be so ungrateful? Ava longed for such support, such logic. She knew that Mei only believed in her own logic, her own kind of consequentialism. Ava's feelings or desires never factored into her mother's equations. Mei believed these were her daughter's weak points, which needed to be squeezed into nonexistence, like water from a rag. *Hang hang chu zhuang yuan.* With the proper amount of devotion and toil, you will become the producer of outstanding achievements. Greatness must be earned. The end result needed to be strength, success, something to broadcast back to China . . . if any family survived. Whatever needed to be done, whatever unpleasantness needed to occur, it all existed for this purpose.

Chapter Two

"No. No!"

Panting, Ava ran down the hallway. But she slipped. Down she went, hands out to brace her fall. Get up, get yourself up—

Held by her hair, her head was wrenched back. Over their heavy breaths, Ava tried pleading. "I'm sorry. I didn't mean it."

No intelligible response. Only the scrape of the scissors as the blades opened wide.

"Don't," she sobbed, choking on her tears. *Snip. Snip.* "Stop! Please." *Snip . . .*

"No, no!" she screamed herself upright.

"Ava? Ava!"

Bending at her waist, she cradled her head with trembling hands. She took a few deep breaths before trusting herself to respond. "Charlotte," she said, eyes trained on her sweat-laced sheets. "What?"

"You okay?"

"Just perfect." Ava peeked at the glow-in-the-dark clock, 4:10 a.m.

Charlotte yawned loudly. "You sure about that? 'Cause you didn't sound okay."

"I'm fine," Ava said, throwing off her sticky sheet. The air in the room felt overused, stale.

"But you woke me up."

"That's never hard."

"With your screaming."

"So? Just a nightmare. A . . . monster running after me, that's all."

Charlotte yawned again. "Wanna talk about it?"

"Goodnight, Charlotte. Go back to sleep. Our floor meeting starts at 9:30." Ava lay back down, turning toward the wall.

"Okay . . . goodnight."

When she heard Charlotte flip onto her stomach, Ava turned over again. On her back, she stared at the white ceiling, following its many cracks. Fissures broke off from the main rift like creeks diverging from a parent river.

Would it be safe to fall back asleep? Not if you fall back into the same nightmare. Stay awake. Just stay awake. Watching the ceiling can't hurt you.

When Charlotte woke up to her alarm, Ava had already made her bed. She sat on top of it, reading.

Charlotte groaned.

"Morning. Waiting on you for breakfast, Lottie."

Ava turned a page without looking up. She approached the end of *Sula,* having quit ceiling watching after an hour. Novels were her solace. A book never judged her, never tortured her. She became an insider, capable of knowing all the author chose to reveal.

"Meh. Need coffee. Not all of us wake up singing 'I Feel Pretty,' y'know."

"Apparently. You're so groggy you're even letting me get away with 'Lottie.' Come on, hurry up. It's 8:15 already."

Over the top of her library copy of *Sula,* Ava watched Charlotte fumble her way to their small bathroom.

Five minutes later she emerged, her curly hair in a loose braid. "Put the book down," Charlotte demanded, throwing on a pink t-shirt and jean shorts.

Ava swung her legs over the side of her bed, slipped on her sandals, and continued reading.

Charlotte pilfered the novel and stuck Ava's bookmark in. "C'mon, back to reality."

Tobias Dining Hall teemed with students. While waiting in line, the girls tried to guess which of the students were also freshmen.

"Sitting at a single table in the Nirvana t-shirt," Charlotte whispered. "Total freshman. I hope we don't look that anxious. Poor girl."

"The raccoon makeup probably doesn't help her case either."

"Don't actually say what you're thinking aloud."

"My turn," said Ava. They were still ten people away from the main breakfast line. "Ah. Fairly muscular, shaggy-haired blond guy, tan, wearing chunky black frames. Sitting across from a pale guy with dark brown hair. The one who's talking loudly and wearing skinny jeans *I* definitely can't fit in."

Charlotte giggled. "Spot any Whasians?"

They enjoyed playing this guessing game.

"Any *Amerasians,* you mean?"

"Come on, 'Whasian' sounds more modern. Plus, who wants to go through the effort of saying A-mer-as-ian? Too many syllables."

"Fine," Ava sniffed. "If you want to be lazy with language, go ahead."

"Plus, some people think I'm saying 'admiration.'"

"Then you need to e-nun-ci-ate."

"Anyway, I think I spy a Whasian over there, by that ugly potted plant. What do you think?"

A few tables away, facing them, sat a girl with wavy, dark brown hair, pale skin, and almond eyes.

"Nicely spotted." Ava always pointed Amerasians out to Charlotte because it made her excited to find other "hybrids." Labeling others as Amerasian, whether she guessed right or wrong, gave her a sense of solidarity. Being too unique felt alienating.

"Oh, what about the girl two tables over, by the cereal bar?" Charlotte always asked Ava to be the final judge.

Ava frowned. "No, that's an Asian girl with dyed brown hair and blue contacts. Too unnatural. Even more so than me."

"You, unnatural?"

"Mhmm. When's the last time you looked at me?"

Charlotte scowled. "I'm looking at you now, obviously."

"No, I mean really looked."

"What do you expect me to see?"

Ava gestured at her face. "I don't know, my colorless eyes. The weirdly straight reddish hair?"

"You need to start watching *America's Next Top Model* with me. Different can be good. You've got greyish blue eyes. Like . . . I can't think of anything right now. You come up with something, you're better with words."

"Fog," Ava suggested.

"No, fog's whitish. Whatever. And your hair is *auburn*. Like Rita Hayworth's, except darker."

"Not her natural color. She was half Spanish and originally a brunette."

"Oh. Well, you get my point. There's nothing 'unnatural' about you. You were born out of love!" Charlotte put a hand to her heart and faked a swoon. "Nothing's more natural."

Ava couldn't agree, but she laughed all the same.

Finally they were able to get food. After loading their plates with hard-boiled eggs, grapes, and muffins, Charlotte and Ava found a table for two.

"I'm going to get orange juice. You want anything to drink?" Ava asked, standing up.

"Oh yes, coffee please! Two sug—"

"Two sugar packets or cubes and just a dash of milk." She raised the pitch of her voice to imitate Charlotte.

"I don't sound like that! Tell me I don't sound like that."

Ava smirked and went to get their drinks.

With a drink in each hand, she returned to the table. "You didn't need to wait for me to eat," she said, sitting down and breaking off a piece of blueberry muffin.

"I know. I decided I want cereal, and I didn't want to leave our bags unchaperoned."

"Lucky Charms?" Ava commented, raising a brow when Charlotte returned. "And you say I'm immature."

"Shut up."

"Why were you so concerned about our stuff? It's not like we've got flashy name-brand bags or anything. Plus, look around. Too many witnesses."

In between bites of colorful marshmallow, Charlotte asked, "Didn't you get your first crime alert this morning, from campus police?"

Ava sipped her orange juice. "That garbage? I deleted it. Julia told me to ignore those emails. She said they're useless."

Charlotte looked appalled. "Wait. First, you *listened* to Julia? The same girl who thought smoking weed while dyeing her hair a good idea? And you deleted it without even reading it? It said that a block from our housing someone got mugged."

"Oh please, calm down. Julia may not always come up with the best ideas, but this time I think she's right. A block away means it happened off-campus. We live on-campus, remember? Save your worrying for Julia."

"Still, you can't just dismiss it. Don't be naïve," Charlotte insisted, sipping her coffee.

"I'm not," Ava said, neatly peeling her egg. "I know the usual: walk in groups, don't wander outside at 3 a.m., etc. You know my dad works in the city; that's one of the first things he taught me. And besides, none of it applies to me. No chance I'll ever go out. Too much studying."

"Don't be cocky. And I'm sure you'll go out *some*time."

"Don't be ridiculous. I mean, come on, can you take an email from Bobby Constable seriously?"

"Of course. Why wouldn't I?" Charlotte furrowed her brow.

"Bobby Constable?" Ava paused. "No?"

"I don't get it."

"'Bobby' is slang for a British police officer. But wait, it gets better. 'Constable' is a Briticism for police officer. The emails from campus police are self-referential *and* the name they send them from is redundant. Basically their signature means 'police police.'"

"Oh, well that's just . . . "

Ava quirked a brow. "Ridiculous?"

"Anyway. What's up with last night? That dream of yours?"

"Of course, change the subject so you don't need to acknowledge my point. Typical Lottie."

"Stop calling me that! And *you* don't try to change the subject. Come on, stop the mysteriousness."

"No mystery here. There's nothing to discuss."

"You woke up screaming. How's that 'nothing'?" Charlotte tried to raise an eyebrow but failed, raising two.

Ava grinned. "I told you, only some of us possess the gift of eyebrow raising."

"Leave me alone. I'll get it someday. Never give up and all that jazz."

"Are you done eating?" Ava asked, checking the time. "Only twenty minutes before the floor meeting starts." Her phone buzzed. "Text from Dad," the notification informed her. She slipped her phone in her purse. Deal with it later.

"I'm done if you are." They got up and put their trays away. "I take it you're not going to tell me about this dream, then?"

"Stop glaring. Nothing to it, I'm telling you. I've seen too many horror movies. The usual monster-tearing-me-apart nightmare. But it realized I'm off-putting. That's when I woke up."

Charlotte studied Ava. "You never cried out when you slept over, but whatever. You know where to find me if you want to talk."

"Of course. In our room."

"Smart-ass."

"You know it."

They arrived in the common room ten minutes before the start of the floor meeting. Four other students stood waiting silently. Ava thought she recognized one other person, a guy with dark hair, but many guys had dark hair.

"Why don't we sit instead of standing awkwardly?" Ava whispered to Charlotte, who responded by relocating to the nearest red and white checkered couch.

"Hey look, school spirit," Charlotte said, noticing the colors of the couch.

"It doesn't look tacky at all."

"You can't be serious . . . oh wait." She noticed Ava's raised eyebrow. "You're just giving me a dose of Ava-casm."

A tall guy with short, floppy, dirty-blond hair walked in. He assessed the students in the room.

"Hey guys, I'm Dan, your resident assistant, or RA. Two, four, six," he said, counting students. "Looks like we're missing two of you so we'll wait a few minutes before starting introductions. Everybody excited to start college?" Dan flashed a smile worthy of a toothpaste commercial.

Silence, then a couple of shy mumblings.

"Lame. What kind of response is that? Ready to be away from your parents?"

Nods, grins, and a couple of small cheers.

"That's better. Ah, here come our stragglers!"

A couple of nervous-looking guys shuffled in, muttering their apologies.

"Okay, now we can really start. Why don't we sit on the floor and introduce ourselves?" Dan said, sitting pretzel style.

Ava gave Charlotte an annoyed look. Charlotte bit her lip to refrain from giggling. Ava hated sitting or kneeling on the floor, especially while wearing a dress, and a white one at that. Reluctantly she sat down, curling her legs to one side.

"Right. Can we move back to make this a circle? That way everyone can see each other. Great. As I said before, I'm Dan, your first-floor RA, and I'm a senior studying economics. It's my job to make your stay in the Lockhart honors dorm comfortable. You can come to me with any questions, concerns, whatever. I've got a single next to the boys' bathroom. I'll always post a sign on the door that'll tell you where I am, and later I'll give you my on-duty RA cell number. Why don't we go counterclockwise to change things up?" He motioned to the boy Ava thought she recognized.

"Uh. The name's Kevin. You can call me Kev if you want."

"Oh, right. So tell us your name, nickname if you've got one, potential major, and a hobby," Dan interjected. "Sorry Kev, go ahead."

Ava finally placed Kevin, recognizing his loud voice from the dining hall. The talkative guy wearing skin-tight skinny jeans.

"Yeah . . . I think I want to go for environmental science. You know, to save the planet and shit like that. Oh shit, we allowed to curse? I mean, or are we supposed to act like honors students 24/7?"

The group laughed.

"Nah man it's cool," Dan said, grinning.

"Sweet. Anyway, I like to write songs and play guitar. And smoke cigs," Kevin finished.

"Oh, that reminds me. Smokers must smoke outside, at least twenty-five feet from Lockhart's entrance."

A few students groaned.

"Even when it's snowing?" Kevin complained.

"Yup. If you really can't stand it, you'll need to take up a new hobby." Dan looked at the guy next to Kevin.

"Right. I'm Derek and I'm going to major in biology. I like to play basketball and other sports, so I'll probably join intramurals."

Ava discreetly studied Derek. If he'd eaten breakfast at the dining hall, they must've missed him during their spotting game. She glanced at Charlotte, who assessed him openly.

"Ow! What's that for?" Charlotte asked, rubbing her ribs, which Ava had attacked with her elbow.

"Psst. Your turn, roomie."

Charlotte's cheeks reddened. "Sorry. I'm Charlotte and I'm still undecided about my major. I like to um . . . sketch, and I like horseback riding."

"Nice," Dan said, nodding.

"I'm Ava. I'm going to major in . . . cell bio and I . . . I used to play piano." She tucked a strand of hair behind her ear. She'd always hated icebreakers. Too much sharing. Too many questions. Most of all, too many eyes fixated on her. Pressing in like needles assigned to each pore.

Kevin nodded. "Let's jam sometime."

Ava smiled politely. She felt no inclination to spend time with someone who smoked and thought "jamming" a good idea. At least only one person stared at her strangely: the biology major. But she'd expected that. When all eyes shifted to the next student, she let her spine relax a bit. Sinking into boredom, she waited for the meeting to finish.

"You can go now," Dan said. "At 10:45 the second-floor RA will be handing out donuts and juice in the lobby. If you don't have a car on campus, you can check out the other campuses by bus. Welcome to Davison U. and Lockhart Hall!"

"Dude, that took forever," Kevin said to Derek, his roommate.

"And I don't think he could flip his hair out of his face more," Derek replied, walking back to their room. He opened the door and put the stopper down.

Ava and Charlotte followed them. When the girls reached their room, they realized it faced the boys'.

Opening their labeled door, Ava gestured to their names. "I guess you were right to keep them. It's convenient. I've got a fifty-fifty shot of getting our neighbors' names right, but I'll probably get it wrong."

Charlotte glanced back at Kevin and Derek, who respectively opened the window blinds and took off sneakers.

"Wanna go over and talk to them?" she asked as Ava picked *Sula* up again.

"What, you mean be *social*?" Ava wrinkled her nose. Socializing meant answering questions, which potentially led to answering said questions with lies.

"Don't look so scandalized. We need to be *polite*. So put on a happy face and come with me to really introduce ourselves. We'll even have an excuse: we can go back to the lobby and eat donuts with them."

"I'm still digesting breakfast."

"So skip the donuts. Just drink juice."

"I'm not thirsty either."

"Don't have anything then!"

Ava nodded at the clock. "We've still got fifteen minutes to kill."

Charlotte finally let their door close. "What, and you're going to read till then?"

"What if I am?"

Joining Ava on her bed, Charlotte frowned. "You can't retreat into yourself now," she protested.

Ava put the novel down. "Why's that?"

"Because we just moved in. We're all new and awkward. Perfect chance to make friends."

"I've got a friend. She's sitting right next to me."

"New friends. More friends!"

"New isn't necessarily better. Quality trumps quantity."

Charlotte smiled. "But you sure you want to pass up a chance to compare notes?"

Ava's phone let out a reminder vibration. She ignored it. "Compare notes?" she asked, eyes narrowing.

"You're always pointing out Whasians. Now's your chance to commiserate with one!"

"But—"

Charlotte saw her waver and went for the kill. "Or I can talk to them and leave you alone to read. I could report back; but who knows, we might be having so much fun we completely forget about—"

"Alright, alright, you made your point. Give me a minute. I need to answer my dad's text."

"Oh. Okay." Charlotte smiled like a flickering light bulb. "Um . . . he still a workaholic?"

"Yes. Since making partner."

"He came back to help you move in, right?"

"Of course. But only because move-in day took place during a weekend."

"That's something. He tries! I'm sure he does." She perked up. "And now you're closer to the city! You can take the train to see him."

"Sure. Why don't you start talking to our neighbors and I'll meet you over there?"

Ava turned to her phone when Charlotte left. The text read, "Hope you've got nice floor-mates! Let me know if you want to talk." "Thanks," she texted back, and then headed across the hall. Making new friends . . . what a dangerous game, one fraught with potential slipups, diversions, and lies she'd need to remember. But she preferred that instead of reconnecting with her father. Because of her mother, Ava hadn't been able to look at her father straight—not for the last four years.

"It's Ava, right?" Kevin asked.

"Yes." She shook his hand and nodded at Derek.

"It okay if I invite my boyfriend Jason to our gathering?"

Ava and Derek didn't miss a beat, saying that they'd welcome Jason. Charlotte shot Ava a confused look. Kevin caught it.

"If you're wondering why I didn't room with Jason instead of Derek, I can clear that up for you," he told Charlotte.

Charlotte nodded, embarrassment dotting her cheeks.

"Well, we considered it, but frankly, what if we break up? That'd make for an awkward living situation, no?"

"You must be really open with each other. Most couples avoid those conversations, right?" Ava asked.

"Yeah, but we've been dating for three years," Kevin said, reaching for his cell phone. "We went to the same high school."

Ava watched him smile at a text. Of course, she didn't know what kinds of conversations couples had, having never been in a relationship. She wanted one. At least to try it. An experiment. A fling. Something, anything. But her mother deemed boyfriends a distraction. Not that it'd mattered. No one showed interest, anyway. No one even pitied her enough to ask her to prom. She'd had no choice but to go with Charlotte and their other single girlfriends. On the sidelines, she'd watched the couples in action. Observing, ruminating. Always the interloper.

A few minutes later, the party met Jason and headed back to Derek and Kevin's room, donuts and drinks in hand. They prepared to settle down on the floor.

"Sorry . . . but could we sit on the beds and chairs?" Ava smoothed the skirt of her white dress. "You know, to avoid stains."

"I hear you, I hear you," Kevin agreed, motioning for everyone to make use of the room's sparse furniture.

"This'll happen a lot," Charlotte explained. "For some reason, most of Ava's clothes are white. Of course she wears the color that stains the easiest. She likes being difficult."

Ava perched on Derek's bed. "That's not true. It's for . . . " It's for a reason. "White's my personal Goth color."

"Don't you mean 'anti-Goth'?" Kevin asked.

"Sure," she replied quickly. "How about napkins?"

Between bites, the students tactfully evaluated each other and learned about each other's lives.

"More, anyone?" Kevin asked, holding up the juice carton.

Jason shook his head. "Babe, chill out. We're fine."

"I'm just making sure everyone's got enough OJ," Kevin said, dipping his napkin in a cup of water. He leaned over to wipe powdered sugar off Jason's cheek.

Grinning, Ava nodded at Kevin's free hand, which floundered by his donut. "If you don't pay yourself attention, you're going to dip your napkin in your donut."

When they'd finished snacking, they decided to walk around University Way. The campus buzzed with activity. Freshmen explored; latecomer upperclassmen moved in.

They walked alongside the gymnasium, passing by a bus shelter. Three buses, leading to different campuses, lined up by the curb. The bus closest to them opened its doors, letting out a small crowd of students. They wore move-in crew t-shirts.

Jason and Kevin moved further up the sidewalk. Charlotte, Derek, and Ava tried to follow. Someone bumped into Ava, and in turn she bumped into Charlotte, who tripped over Derek. Ava nearly wrote it off as an act of clumsiness when she recognized the student.

The sophomore, the big Asian girl her mother had talked to. She stood next to an equally tall, but thinner Asian girl. She looked down at Ava. "So sorry," she said, with as much feeling as an automaton. Turning back to her friend, they began heading toward the student center—but not before she said, "Actually, that's the rice cracker I told you about."

"Rice cracker? *Rice cracker*?" Charlotte asked, turning to the group.

"Don't—" Ava warned.

Charlotte began storming off, but Ava used both arms to pull her back.

"Let go of me. I'm her height."

Derek winced. "But she's way wider than you."

"Dude, not a good idea," Kevin said. "No way you're gonna change her mind anyway. Let it go."

Jason frowned. "Guys, we're blocking the walkway."

They moved off and headed downtown. When the sidewalk cleared, they slowed their pace.

Kevin broke the silence first. "Um. Am I the only one who doesn't know what a rice cracker is?"

"Undoubtedly the most creative slur of them all," Ava said, noticing the study abroad office. A banner made up of diverse flags of the world hung down the edifice.

Derek cleared his throat. "A half chink, half cracker."

They looked at him in surprise.

"So I've been told by racists," he explained.

"Wait," Charlotte said. "Anyone else notice that? That girl acted like . . . Ava, do you know her?"

So much for shrugging it off as a random insult. "She helped me move in."

Jason caught Ava's blush. "What's she got against you?"

"Yeah," Kevin said. "How many boxes did you drop on her feet?"

"I . . . it . . . nothing I did, per se . . . "

"Maybe she's just jealous?" Charlotte offered.

Ava surveyed the faces of her new acquaintances. Logic told her to lie, to evade, to withdraw. But no one appeared ready to pin her to a noticeboard. She could test them, take a risk. Build trust. But she'd been disappointed too many times before . . .

"You're under no obligation to explain anything. Only if you feel comfortable," Jason said.

Kevin seemed curious, but he nodded. "You do you, girl."

They walked around an inconveniently parked DU ice cream truck.

"Why don't we cross here?" Kevin suggested. "I've heard it's nice to sit by the Nam memorial."

They settled on a "Class of 1922" bench, under the shade of the largest oak tree.

Ava looked over the lush grass at the marble pillars of the Vietnam War Memorial. If she squinted, she could make out the etchings, but the names were indiscernible. "I-I lied to her." Feeling Charlotte's eyes on her, she added, "For good reason, I think."

Derek scratched his dark brown goatee. "She ask you the origin question?"

"The origin question?" Charlotte asked.

"Any version of 'where are you from?'"

Jason shook his head. "Usually followed by questions aimed at your ancestry, am I right?"

"Y-yes."

Jason laughed. "Don't look so amazed. I'm also mixed."

"Touché," Derek said, grinning. "And here Ava and I thought we were alone among white people."

Ava smiled sheepishly. She'd never encountered this side of the wonder before.

Jason held out his muscled arm, the color of coffee splashed with creamer. "I can tan like this because I'm a *mulatto*. I'm half black, half Spanish. Dad's from Spain and Mom's African American. Anyone want to claim they see it now?"

"See what?" Charlotte asked.

"The defensive reaction," Kevin said.

"Typically used by white people," Ava added. "Like, 'oh yeah, now I see your racial mix. I knew it all along. You just confirmed it.'"

Jason snorted. "Like people have an innate racial gauge. What bullshit."

"What you see isn't what you get," Charlotte said, "but we tend to forget that."

"Deny it," Ava corrected. "People need to get over themselves."

"Well," Derek said, "glad we know better."

"If . . . if I may," Charlotte began, "what's your mix, Derek?"

"Chinese mom, from Shanghai, and a Russian American dad."

Kevin nodded. "That explains the awesome last name. Az-a-rov. That how you say it?"

"*Da*! That's about the only word I know in Russian."

They laughed.

Derek turned to Ava. "What about you?"

"My mother's Chinese. Originally from Beijing. My dad's Irish and Italian."

"Very cool," Jason said. "Where're your parents from, Charlotte?"

"Me? Nowhere exotic."

"We're not exotic," Ava interrupted. "We're just different from the majority."

"And that doesn't mean we aren't interested in you Caucasians," Jason added.

Charlotte raised her eyebrows. "If you say so. My mom is Italian. And my dad was Polish and Hungarian."

"Why the past tense? Has your mom converted him to Italian?" Kevin joked.

"He . . . he passed away."

"Shit, I'm sorry. I'd like to take my sneaker out of my mouth now."

Charlotte chuckled airily. "It's okay, you couldn't have known."

When the conversation returned to safe topics, Ava half tuned out. She still felt surprised. No one thought her and Derek freak show extras. No poorly hid looks of disgust thrown their way. No tones of condescension. Not even the "wow" response. And the other extreme hadn't happened either. None of that "I don't see color/race" nonsense. They'd just noted it in passing. Like they'd noted her name.

"She's inside her head." Charlotte poked her.

"I'm back, I'm back." Ava clutched her sensitive left side. "Hands off. Can't you get my attention in other ways?"

"Of course not."

"We're rating Dan," Kevin explained.

"Dan? Dan who?"

Derek smiled. "That's what I first said."

Charlotte sighed impatiently. "Our RA."

"Oh. Where did that come from?" Ava asked.

Charlotte nodded at the sidewalk. "He passed by a couple minutes ago."

"Well, I'd say he's a ten," Derek joked.

"Nah, more of a nine," Kevin said. "He needs to grow his hair out more, like Jason's, or just chop it off. It looks too much like Bieber hair now."

"Sorry, what's Bieber hair?" Ava asked, shooting a puzzled look at Charlotte.

The guys looked at Ava in surprise.

"If you didn't live in book-land all the time, you'd know that Justin Bieber is a teen pop star, adored by little and big girls everywhere," Charlotte explained.

"Even I knew that," Derek said.

Jason waved a hand in dismissal. "Enough on Bieber fever. Anyway, I don't like to judge with a numeric scale. He's easy on the eyes, but Kev's prettier."

Kevin smiled. "Yeah, you'd better think that."

Charlotte looked at Ava for her opinion.

"He's rather attractive."

"'Rather attractive'?" Kevin laughed. "You just outclassed us all."

"Ava's always prim and proper . . . unless she's goading me," Charlotte said.

"Psh." Ava yawned. "Anyone know what time it is?"

Jason patted his stomach. "Way past food time."

"It's . . . a quarter to six," Derek announced, surprising everyone.

"Holy crap," Charlotte said. "Time flies."

Ava shrugged. "Only when you're talking to interesting people."

They rose, shaking out their sleepy limbs.

"You guys want to grab dinner at Toby?" Kevin asked.

"Toby?" Ava asked.

"Yeah, Kev likes to shorten things," Jason explained. "He's too cool to say Tobias or just 'the dining hall.'"

"You're just jelly," Kevin countered.

"Jealous," Jason translated to the now-laughing group.

"Yeah, why not?" Ava rubbed her side. "We don't have anywhere to be."

"Alright, let's *do* this," Kevin said, swaggering down the walkway.

Jason shook his head. "No, just no."

"What, you think I can't pull off being cool? I am cool, man. Coolness personified."

"Points for figurative language, but I'm afraid I agree with Jason," Ava said.

Later that evening Charlotte and Ava returned to their room all talked out.

Catching the door before it slammed shut, Charlotte said, "See? We made new connections! Not painful after all."

"Better than getting dunked in a pool, I suppose," Ava replied, dropping her purse on her ivory comforter and then gathering her shower caddy and towel.

"You're ridiculous. My goal for this year: get you to climb out of your shell."

"Go ahead and try, but I'm a stubborn one."

"Yeah, tell me about it," Charlotte muttered. "You know what? I'm going to take a shower too."

"Copycat."

"Oh please, you wish. My shower stuff is better than yours. A white caddy and a dark blue towel? I think those are the only two colors you wear!"

"At least I'm not stereotypical. Half the things you own are shades of pink!" Ava gestured at Charlotte's light pink shower caddy and towel and her hot pink comforter.

They continued their friendly bickering until they went into the shower stalls.

After a few minutes of listening to falling water, Ava peeked out from behind her curtain, making sure that no one but she and

Charlotte were there. "So what do you think of our friends, if I may be so bold as to call them that?"

"Yeah, I'd say we made friends with the guys. They seem genuinely nice. Unlike Julia's bitchy party friends, the first college students I ever hung out with."

"I hope so. Real friends could be useful." Ava thought about comparing life notes with Derek. How had his Asian mom raised him? She wondered if she could trust him.

"What, I'm not real enough?" Charlotte asked.

"Oh shut up. You're my best friend so you don't count."

"That so? Ahem—bitch—ahem."

Ava sniffed. "You cut me deeply."

"Fine, fine. I know what you mean. Not a surprise, though."

"Why not? We were losers in high school."

"That's not true! Ava, you were the valedictorian. And I shared most of your smart classes. Everyone tried to beat our grades. We were competition."

"Um. I guess."

"There's no convincing you of anything you don't want to be convinced of," said Charlotte, "but things will be different here. We're in college now—"

"Hey look we're big learners now—"

"And no one cares how we scored on our SATs. We're in a freer environment. As my mom says, 'experimentation and questioning is what college is all about. Just don't do drugs and don't get a sex disease,'" Charlotte finished.

They laughed.

"Okay, I see your point."

"Look at you, acknowledging me. I'm impressed!"

"Don't get too excited. That's the last time I agree with you for this month. And technically, I'm agreeing with Ema, not you."

"There's no need to suck up to my mom; she's not here. Anyway, as I said, it should be easier to find friends in college because people are supposedly more open and friendly. If you aren't antisocial."

"Hey, you're just as introverted as I am."

"No way. I at least make an effort. Compared to you, I'm a freaking socialite! And I'm never a book-reading corner hog like you can be."

"Whatever. Moving on . . . "

"Of course. 'Cause you know I'm right," Charlotte said in a sing-song voice.

Chapter Three

The following afternoon the new friends ate brunch together.

"So I got a text from my sister Julia at 3 a.m.," Charlotte said.

"So?" Ava asked. Julia often drunk-texted Charlotte in the early hours of the morning.

"Give the girl a sec, Av," Kevin admonished.

"Thanks, Kevin. Anyway, she suggested we take advantage of Labor Day and go out tonight. What do you guys think?"

"Classes start tomorrow," Ava warned.

Charlotte scowled. "Don't look at me like that. I didn't forget. But I thought you also didn't have morning classes on Tuesdays."

"I don't . . . but what about Derek?" she asked hopefully.

Derek grinned. "I don't need to be awake for my first-year interest group. It's pass/fail. Let's go out."

Jason shrugged. "We'd like a date night, to be honest, right Kev?"

"Yeah. I mean, it's not like we don't drink or anything—"

"Shh!" Charlotte said.

Jason chuckled. "Oh please, don't be paranoid. Everyone knows most people under twenty-one drink."

"But that doesn't mean you should broadcast it," Charlotte whispered, looking around to see if anyone overheard.

"But lots of people party to drink and hook up. I'm already hooked up." Kevin held up a hand and Jason high-fived it.

"Fair enough. Well, Ava and I don't drink," Charlotte said, "but I think it'd be cool to experience a party before rejecting partying completely."

"You sure?" Ava asked. "That's not what you used to think."

"What do you mean?"

"How many times have you mocked Julia for 'going out'?"

The guys looked on with interest.

"'What's there to do, anyway?'" Ava said, mimicking Charlotte. "'Dance like an idiot and pretend to know the lyrics to trashy pop songs. Such a waste of time.'"

"True . . . but now that we're here . . . "

"When in college, do as the students do?" Derek offered.

"Exactly," Charlotte said, more confident.

Jason downed the rest of his milk before contributing. "But look at Ava's face. She looks like she'd rather swim in a snake pit." He chuckled at her deeper grimace. "Guess that's a bad analogy."

"Come on, Av," Charlotte pleaded.

Four pairs of eyes bore into her. Ava shifted in her seat. What to argue next? Oh, right. "But I could prepare for class. Build a normal sleeping schedule. Take my time in the big shower while everyone else parties."

"You can do that after tonight. Please? It won't be the same—no offense Derek—without my biffer."

"To be fair," Kevin said, "what's the harm in trying it, just once?"

"Isn't that what people say when they try heroine?"

Charlotte shook her head. "Come on, Ava. Dramatic, much?"

"Yeah, no harm," Derek agreed, "even if it's a bad experience. May be better that way. Then you're justified; you can really hate it with a vengeance."

Ava turned to Jason.

He shrugged. "Looks like we're outnumbered. But it is just one night. What's the worst that could happen?"

Kevin nodded. "At worst you'll be swarmed."

The French toast Ava had eaten began cartwheeling in her stomach.

"Swarmed?" Derek asked.

"Y'know. 'Cause they're fresh meat. It'll be less risky if they don't drink, but still. Freshman girls who are babes? You keep both eyes on them, bro."

Ava perked up. "See? A bad idea."

"Now who needs to quit worrying?" Charlotte countered. "I'll wear my heels. Derek's my back up. We've got this."

"So what's the plan?" Derek asked.

Ava slumped against her seat, unable to see a way out. No need for panic. Just one night. Just one night couldn't hurt, right?

"I don't have one yet," Charlotte admitted. "We've got options. We can go to the house party my sister will be at. We can house hop until we find a house we like. Or we can house hop and then end the night with seeing my sister get smashed. That's always an amusing sight."

"Julia is a super happy drunk," Ava explained.

"Oh, one of those." Kevin raised his eyebrows knowingly.

Charlotte looked at Derek and Ava. "So what do you want to do?"

Ava glared at her. "Why bother asking me? Clearly my opinion doesn't matter."

Charlotte blew her a kiss. "Don't be a killjoy."

"Let's house hop and then visit your sister," Derek suggested.

In the afternoon, Charlotte, Kevin, and Jason set off to locate their general psychology classrooms. Derek and Ava returned to Lockhart.

"You finalize your schedule yet?" Ava asked.

"I could take on one more class, but I wouldn't know what to take. You?"

They paused outside Ava's room.

Unlocking her door, she decided to invite Derek in. She watched him survey the room. Her side: neat and barren, pinkless. Charlotte's side: cheerfully overcrowded, a hodgepodge of posters, stuffed animals, and pictures—some with Ava, some of her family. Ava hadn't displayed any pictures. No decorations on her side either. No reminders. No sense of rootedness, of past.

She walked over to her desk and sat down. "Can you keep a secret?"

Derek raised an eyebrow. "Sure, but isn't it a bit early for you to be baring your soul to me?"

Ava began jiggling a leg. His joke possessed the truth. She hadn't told anyone yet, not even Charlotte. "Um. Well, never mind. I don't want to burden you."

"Burden me? Alright, now you've really got me interested." He took a seat on Ava's ivory comforter. "What's up?"

"So, here's the thing," she began. But as she reached for her laptop, she wavered again. She fixed her eyes on him. "Wait, you never answered. Can you keep a secret?"

Derek stopped smiling. "Uh, yeah, of course . . . from everyone, even Charlotte?"

Ava saw his eyes drop down to her leg. She stilled its movement. "No, not . . . not necessarily. From my m—parents. If you ever see them."

He seemed relieved. "Definitely, easily done."

She turned back to her laptop and logged in. "My parents . . . my mother, really, thinks I'm going to declare as a cell bio neuro major."

"But . . . ," Derek prompted, smiling.

Ava raised her chin defiantly. "I've got another plan. I want to—I'm *going* to major in English. Without her knowing. At least for this semester."

"That's it? That's the secret?" Derek chuckled. "How strict is your mom?"

"Sort of." She let out the rest of her plan in a rush. "Really it's that I'm going to drop the cell bio neuro prerequisites and take English classes instead." Logging onto Davison's web registration site, she pulled up the schedule she'd created the night before.

Derek whistled. "You rebel. And how're you going to keep this from your mom?"

"Davison has a student privacy policy. They can't disclose information to parents without student permission."

"Hmm. But won't she want to see your schedule? What're you going to do, doctor one?"

"I already did." Ava flashed him an impish smile. "And I emailed it to her. For the most part, I only needed to replace the class names. A couple CBN classes didn't match my new class times, but I told her my professors changed them."

"Sneaky." He paused, contemplative. "What about your science books?"

"I'm keeping them so she'll see them when she visits. I've already checked out the English books I'll need from the library." Ava pulled out her bottom desk drawer to reveal a stack of thinner books: a couple of Shakespearean plays, an anthology of poetry, and a few unfamiliar novels.

Derek stood to look at the contraband. He selected a novel with an interesting title. "*Native Speaker*. What's that about?"

This time she gave him a shy smile. "You really want to find out?"

He studied her curiously. "That depends on what the catch is."

She highlighted the class's title on the calendar view of her schedule. "Take the class with me and we'll both find out."

He moved closer to Ava, bending down to see her computer screen. "Asian American Literature in English," he read. Derek glanced sidelong at her.

"I know you're going to be a bio major, but this class will fulfill a general requirement, the one for global awareness. And don't you think it sounds interesting?" She turned to him in excitement, unaware of his nearness. They almost bumped heads. She smiled an apology, shifting away.

He straightened. "I'll sign up; no need to twist my arm."

Ava beamed. A friend in the class lessened her intimidation. Ava feared a class composed entirely of Asians would spotlight her as odd. But with Derek beside her, they would float between worlds together.

"Great! Let me know if you need help signing up. If not, Charlotte and I will come by your room later."

Derek stopped smiling, confused. "Come by for what?"

Ava looked at him quizzically. "So we can go out together, remember?"

"Oh right, right."

"What's the matter? You look a bit red."

"Yeah, see you then," he said quickly. He turned to leave. "I'll go sign up now."

Before long 10 p.m. rolled around, "getting ready to go out time" for many Davison University students.

Male students ran their hands through their hair once at most, either uncaring or believing they were already perfect. If they had enough hair to do so, some rubbed in a bit of gel. Many put on varying amounts of cologne. Regardless, guys were typically ready to go after ten minutes of prepping.

The majority of female students slaved to change their appearance. From painting their toenails to tweezing their eyebrows into sharp arches, they scrutinized and tried to "fix" themselves. Collectively, they spent a couple of hours teasing, straightening, or curling their hair, putting on all sorts of body-shaping material, followed by what they thought passed for outfits, and caking their faces with makeup.

Charlotte and Ava got ready in fifteen minutes with their natural hairstyles, enough clothing, and little makeup.

"I thought that'd take a lot longer," Charlotte said, looking at her confused expression in the communal bathroom mirror.

"That's what we get for taking your sister's advice. 'Getting ready's gonna take at *least* two hours,'" Ava said, mimicking Julia. "You call her 'Beauty School Dropout' for a reason."

Charlotte laughed. "That's true. Let's see what Derek's doing. We've got at least a half hour. Parties aren't supposed to start until elevenish."

Ava opened the bathroom door to find one of the other girls who also lived on the first floor, plus a gaggle of her friends. "Sorry." She held the door and waited for the six boisterous girls to troop in.

"'s okay!" the girl nearly yelled, clearly having lost her shyness and sobriety along with her glasses. She bumped into Charlotte, spilling her drink.

"Ugh!" Charlotte disgustedly looked down at her beer-splattered boots.

"Charge back in there and grind your heels on her feet," Ava offered.

"Don't tempt me. I'm going to clean this off in our bathroom. I'll be over in a minute."

Ava escaped to Derek's room.

"Hey. What's up?" he asked, combing his hair.

"Charlotte will tell you, but before she comes, you need to know something. And you need to pass it on to the guys."

"Uh oh. You're not going to drag me into drama, are you?"

"I hate drama." Ava walked over to Derek and dropped her voice. "If we see Julia tonight, avoid making comments."

"Making comments?"

"On her behavior. In December it'll be three years since their dad died. Julia didn't take it well. A year ago she stopped taking antidepressants, and we think she gets drunk to compensate."

Eyes wide, Derek abruptly put down his comb. "Holy shit. That's heavy."

"Yes, well so's life. Now act normal so she's not suspicious." Hearing the door open, Ava stepped back and turned around. "You manage to get it all off?"

"Uh . . . what happened?" Derek asked, combing again.

"One of the girls on our floor had the nerve to spill beer on my boots!" Charlotte bent down, inspecting the tops of her shoes. "And yes, I think they're clean."

"Welcome to college," Ava joked.

Charlotte grimaced. "The rest of the night better be more fun."

"Seriously," Derek said, shaking his head like a dog shakes off water.

"What's that for, and right after combing your hair?" Ava asked. "You just defeated its purpose."

"I comb it to make sure it's not tangled, but I shake it to make it look natural."

Ava smirked in response.

"Shut up! I have a system," Derek retorted.

"I didn't say anything."

"Anyway, moving on," Charlotte interrupted, "let's go find a party."

On this peaceful, late-summer night, the branches of the willow trees on University Way swayed to the breeze. A full, oyster pearl moon filled the sky. Flowerbeds forming the letters "DU" gleamed dully when the moon smiled down on them. Crickets and the rush of passing cars were the only immediate sounds that disrupted the peace. The lovely ambiance made it easy to overlook the neglected parts of campus. The worn-out brick buildings, the graffiti-scarred bus shelters, and the cracked sidewalks, the latter speckled with blackened gum and cigarette stubs.

The trio of friends made an interesting group. Charlotte towered over Derek and Ava in her silver, five-inch spiky boots, which matched the silver sequins that sporadically covered her black dress. Derek stood second tallest, blending into the night with a dark green polo and navy jeans. Ava looked delicate and even more slender than usual in her navy peplum top, black leggings, and black flats. She'd wanted to wear white, but

Charlotte convinced her otherwise: "How long do you think it'll *stay* white?"

Ava and Derek could've passed for cousins with their sleek hair, light olive skin tones, and "exotic" looks. Charlotte stuck out with her wildly curly hair and pasty skin, but they didn't notice; and if they had, it wouldn't matter to them. They were just three freshmen, working together to try to find their way through a foreign college world.

They made it to what students knew as "Frat Row." Fraternity houses held parties from Thursday through Saturday nights most weeks, which they usually opened to the student public.

"Anyone happen to know Greek?" Ava asked, clueless to what the three Greek letters they stared at signified.

Her comrades shook their heads.

"Let's try this one anyway."

The group walked up to the house. They felt the music more than they heard it.

"Six-to-one ratio, sorry babe," a tall, large guy in the driveway said, folding his arms impassively.

"Sorry?" Ava asked, confused.

"For the tenth time tonight, and it's only a quarter after eleven! Six-to-one ratio: six girls to one guy."

"Oh."

He leered at her. "Lose the dude and you girls are free to join the fun."

"Let's go then," Ava said, turning around.

The next house let them in with no trouble. Once inside the basement, where the loud music emanated from, Derek went over to the bar area to get himself a drink, leaving the girls to take in their dark surroundings.

"Appalling," Ava muttered, scowling at the sticky floor.

"WHAT?" Charlotte screamed, leaning down.

"I said, APPALLING." She didn't think that a strong enough word, but thought of nothing better. Her thinking faltered in this kind of environment. Then again, no one went to college parties to think.

When campus police pulled up, they decided to leave. Two houses later, they were again in search of a party.

"We're doing more party-hopping than actual partying," Charlotte complained.

"You don't say," Ava said, piling her hair up in a bun to relieve her sweaty neck. A few of her shorter layers escaped, brushing her cheekbones.

"Why don't we visit your sister's party?" Derek suggested, sidling up to Ava.

Charlotte, on Ava's other side, gave her a look.

"What?" Ava mouthed.

She mouthed something back, but Ava only made out "hot for." She wanted to ask Charlotte to repeat it, but Derek interrupted.

"Guys?"

"Yeah, let's." Pulling out her phone, Charlotte led the way down the street.

Ava resisted the urge to check her face in a car window. Maybe Derek stared a lot when he drank. "How many drinks have you actually had?"

"Just two Solo cups of diluted jungle juice. I'm not drunk though. Why, you see signs of Asian flush?" Derek put the back of his hand to his face.

She grinned. "Afraid so."

He shrugged apologetically. "I'm afraid I take after the Chinese side of the family when it comes to alcohol tolerance. My Russian dad puts me to shame, but my mom's whole face gets red after one glass of wine."

"Aw, no worries. I'll let you know if you get too drunk. That's what friends are for." Ava patted his arm.

Before long they reached the house at which Julia was partying. They'd left Frat Row behind a couple of blocks back. From the outside, this house appeared to be in better shape than the fraternity houses: its red shutters were intact and its porch light worked.

Derek rang the bell.

A voluptuous redhead swung open the door and inspected the trio. "Can I help you?" she asked in a bored voice, leaning on the doorframe and twisting a wavy lock of hair around a forefinger.

Charlotte stepped up beside Derek. "Yeah. I'm Julia Bell's sister. She said we'd be allowed in."

"Oh *you're* Belly's baby sis?" the redhead cooed, features immediately softening. "Then y'all can come in. Belly's the life of the party, as you probs know." She stepped aside to let the trio in. "Ima get some drinks. Basement's down the hall to the left."

"Why is your sister's nickname 'Belly'?" Derek asked before they opened the basement door and unleashed the music.

"She's known for doing belly shots."

"Julia's basically the polar opposite of Charlotte, if you haven't guessed it already."

Downstairs, the music beat loud, but not to the point of inducing a headache. The only visible lights sprung from a disco ball and a strobe light, so the room sporadically flashed most of the colors of the rainbow.

"Uh. Th-that her?" Derek asked. Eyes wide, he nodded toward the bar.

Ava and Charlotte turned to watch a blonde coed lick the belly button of a dark-haired coed, who lay back on the bar, shirt rolled up to her chin. She wore a neon orange bra. A small crowd of guys surrounded the pair, jeering and whooping. Someone took a picture and shouted "Facebook!"

"Um . . . no, thank God," Charlotte said. "Julia's got purple hair."

When they finally wrenched their eyes away, Derek hand-mimed that he wanted to get a drink. Charlotte scanned the room for Julia while Ava scouted out a corner to hide in. Just then, the pocket in Ava's leggings vibrated. Without thinking, she answered the call.

"Ava Ling Magee, where the *fuck* are you? Right now! Answer me, young girl!"

The raging voice shocked her silent. Obviously her mother heard the music and the sound of people. Frantic, she tapped the touchscreen until she managed to hit the red button. Call ended, her phone helpfully informed her. Had she actually just hung up on her mother—for the first time? Ava stared at her cell. Yes. You're screwed. So screwed.

What now? No, what later. What will you do? What can you say? She began composing a mental list: Explanations to Use During Next Phone Call. I'm sorry, I don't know what happened. Ha, like that'd work. I'm sorry Charlotte played a trick on me. No, then she'd flip because that'd mean Charlotte heard her curse. I'm sorry you heard the television. Okay, but what about the hanging up bit? I'm sorry I left my phone at Julia's and they threw a party and I went to get it back and you called and I panicked?

Her phone vibrated furiously. Five missed calls. She'd come up with nothing believable now. Trying to ignore the queasy feeling that continued building, Ava shut her phone off completely. She looked up, searching for Charlotte and Derek, but found neither. She felt surrounded, fenced in by sweaty gyrating drunk students she didn't know, who pushed and invaded her personal space as they stared at her staring at them, and, goodness did that guy just put his hand down her—

Easy now, deep breaths. Hyperventilating will *not* make the room stop spinning. Move. Find a new corner, some space to regroup. Sorry, excuse me, just let me, sorry, didn't mean to, ow, don't worry that's only my tibia, I hope *you* didn't mean that, a few more steps . . . made it!

She'd fought her way to a tall end table that rested against a wall. Hopping up onto the table, Ava struggled with her bun. When she'd freed all the choppy layers, she bent her head and ran shaky hands through her hair.

"Hey!" a male voice said. Someone grabbed her shoulder.

"Derek?" Ava asked, looking up, although she didn't recognize the voice. Sure enough, she found herself staring up at a blond male she'd never seen before.

He leaned down, brushing back her hair. "I can be Derek if you want me to be."

Ava shuddered. Shaking her head, she began edging off the table.

"Don't be like that," he coaxed, reaching out.

She looked down in disbelief. His entire hand encircled her arm.

He pulled her to him. Her head, she realized dimly, only made it up to his deltoid. She shook her head, harder. Maybe he had poor eyesight.

"Let's dance."

Ava tried to squirm away. "No thanks."

He brought her back like he pulled a piece of paper toward him. She tried to shrug off his other hand, which covered her entire shoulder, but the guy didn't loosen his leech-like grip.

"Come on," he coaxed, breathing beer breath down on her.

He's got more trouble reading social cues than you do! "No," she semi-shouted up at him, standing on her tiptoes.

"I like a challenge." Grinning wolfishly, he dared to grab Ava by the neck to pull her closer.

"Please stop. Stop."

He didn't appear to hear her.

"You're *repulsive*. Get off!" She struggled to push him away.

This only seemed to encourage the blond, who dipped down to her ear to whisper, "Don't be a fuckin' prude. Mommy and daddy aren't here. You scared to loosen up and live a little?" And with that, he leaned down further and licked the length of Ava's neck.

Enough. Enough! Ava never appreciated when others invaded her personal space, but she hated saliva, especially from an imposing drunken guy. Remembering what her ninth grade health teacher taught her, she swiftly lifted her knee and made him double over in pain. "No" really meant "no."

She turned to squeeze between the innumerable bodies in her way. Breathing through her nose stifled Ava. She opened her mouth to suck in more air. What were you thinking? Diverting Mother's attempts to keep track of you. Acting in self-defense. An unexpected night of firsts. But are you really that surprised? Didn't you want to instigate change? Aren't you looking for opportunities to burn brighter, to erupt into a new, irrepressible form? You know what happens when you boil four cups of rice in a three-cup pot . . .

Someone tapped Ava on the shoulder, and she spun around, grey eyes blazing in fury.

"What?" she hissed, ready to attack the next lout. But she only saw Derek.

He took a step back, startled. "Hey, you okay? I saw the end of that. Sorry, I should've stayed with you."

"Fine. Forget about it. Let's go find Charlotte." Ava held up a hand when Derek tried to inquire further.

On the other side of the room Charlotte found Julia. Or a semblance of Julia, anyway. She moved against a muscular, stocky guy, practically eating his face. Charlotte seemed to resist recognizing her sister, but everything indicated Julia: plum-colored curls, black-and-white-checkered fake nails, dark birthmark in the shape of an imperfect heart on the back of her left knee.

Ava saw Charlotte turn and start to say something to the stranger standing beside her. She watched Charlotte catch herself, probably realizing Ava had left her. When Charlotte looked through the crowd, she spotted Ava and Derek on their way over to her.

"Julia!" she poked the back of her sister's still-moving torso, hard.

Julia slowly extricated herself from the guy's tentacled embrace and turned around. Seeing her sister, she laughed and nearly tackled Charlotte in a hug.

"Oh God! Julie you *reek*." Charlotte tried to squirm away, but Julia long ago lost her ability to support herself.

Stocky guy pulled Julia back by the loopholes of her jean shorts, but Charlotte grabbed her sister's arms.

"Ha ha. Tug of Julieeeeee!" Julia giggled, her heavily outlined eyelids fluttering.

"Back. The. Fuck. Off!" Charlotte yelled at the guy, who took one look at her serious face, shrugged, and went off to look for the next girl he could tongue tango with. Dragging a deadweight Julia behind her, Charlotte met Ava and Derek.

"Let's drop her off and then go home." She eased some of Julia's weight onto Derek.

"Nothing like a stroll at 3 a.m.," Ava said grimly, helping the group navigate the streets to Julia's house, which they'd recently visited.

Julia's sporadic laughing fits, while amusing at first, quickly grew old. Fifteen minutes later, the relieved group handed Julia over to her unsurprised roommate, Kathy.

"What an . . . interesting night," Charlotte commented on the way back to their dorm.

"That's for sure," Derek said.

Ava felt his eyes upon her and closed off her expression. She hoped Derek understood that he shouldn't mention what he'd seen to Charlotte.

"Guess we're real college students now," Charlotte joked halfheartedly.

By the time they got back to Lockhart, exhaustion clamped a firm grip on them. They parted, relieved to see their beds. Derek felt sleepy from the alcohol, but the girls felt tired from the stresses of the night.

"Oh bed, I need you!" Charlotte tossed her wallet on her desk. "Screw showering; these heels are coming off and I'm diving under the covers."

"I'm going to shower," Ava said. "Don't wait up; I'm bringing my key." She promptly took her shower materials and left, glad that Charlotte knew better than to question her abruptness.

Ava turned the shower over to hot and watched her skin turn red. She scrubbed soap into her skin angrily, spending more time on her neck. While she could wash away the guy's saliva, she couldn't wash away what he'd said. *Fuckin' prude.* Prudish, are you?

What an idiot. But no—admit it—in his crude way, he made a valid argument. Okay, but how's that your fault? Sure, she'd never dated before, but how could she with her parents, schoolwork, and piano as obstacles? And then the lack of interest. Worse than that. People avoid you. But do you make them? Do you reject everyone before they can reject you?

No. So what if you're a bit rigid. A bit closed off. You couldn't expect anything else.

Being a prude doesn't make you worthless. Right? But turning into a slut . . . no, neither extreme made sense. What if you just act . . . slutty? How'd you go about that? Where do people draw the line between a fun girl and a loose one?

Mommy and daddy aren't here. But they lived in her. Unseen but felt. Get a firmer hold of yourself. Fight it, tame it. Try to ignore the unreasonable demands. You're a byproduct. You've risen out of an environment. It's normal for you to have adapted this way. Crying or complaining always led to more trouble.

Stop it! You're okay. Ava washed her torso, movements becoming softer. She'd continue to be okay. The Chinese way left no room for effusive emotion.

She learned this early on. Paul used to pick her up, swing her around in a circle and play active games with her. Ava used to look forward to Paul's comforting hugs. Mei never hugged Ava. Not on birthdays, not when she fell down and scraped her knees on pavement. Never. She touched only for instructive reasons. At the age of six Ava had talked to her father about some of her observations.

"Daddy, does Ma love me?"

"Of course she does, Ava." He pulled the covers up to her chin.

She sat up again, pushing the covers down. "Then why won't she hug me?"

Paul retrieved a poster-sized map of the world to prove his case. "See this big country labeled China, Ava," he said, pointing to the map, "that's where mommy comes from. That's where half of your family is from."

Though he'd told her this before, Ava nodded eagerly.

"In China, people are more reserved, which means that they don't display their emotions like Americans do. So while mommy loves you, she doesn't hug you because that's how she grew up. Her parents didn't hug her either."

Ava frowned, thinking. "But does Ma hug *you*?"

She noticed her father's hesitation. "Of course she does," he finally said. He got up from her bedside and called for his wife.

"What this?" Mei asked, taking in the map, the child sitting up attentively. "She supposed be sleeping already."

"She will be soon. She just had a question. I think it'll be better if you're here for it."

"*Kuai dian*, then."

"She wants to know why you aren't more expressive in your love."

Mei silently took the map from Paul and rolled it up. "If you know you're loved by family, no need to work for approval. Nothing to earn when you already have. *Sheng mi zhu cheng shu fan*. Cooked rice. Explain to her, Paul."

He bent down at Ava's bedside. Reaching over to the foot of the bed, he retrieved her Raggedy Ann doll. He handed it to her. "You've helped mommy make rice. When rice is cooked, it can't be uncooked. Sometimes there's no reversing what's done."

"Like how Ann's hair is red? And Ma's is black and yours is brown and mine's in the middle?"

"Yes," Mei said. "Paul . . . ," she warned. "No more keeping her up."

"Just a—"

Mei walked over to the switch and flicked off the light.

In the new darkness, Ava barely made out their shadowy figures. Her mother's loomed distant, partly blocked by the foot of her bed. But her father's remained by her side.

"Time for bed," Mei said.

"Daddy," she whispered.

"Yes?"

"I know when Ma hugs you. When it's time for bed. So no one can see."

Paul had chuckled quietly. "Exactly, sweetheart." He kissed her forehead. "Goodnight."

Ava opened her eyes to look at the water droplets that fell from her eyelashes. Did all of her experiences—and the experiences she'd never had—mean that the drunken blond spoke the truth? Did she not know how to "live a little"? *Yes,* a hateful part of her said. All this time she'd survived, not lived. Eaten husks instead of seeds.

She turned off the shower knob, her tingling skin raw and warm. Reaching out from behind the curtain, she plucked her towel from the hook. She cocooned it around herself. She'd been held back, but now *she* held herself back. Time for a change.

Chapter Four

That Thursday, at 7:20 p.m., Ava and Derek walked into the stuffy room where their Asian American Literature class in English took place. Class started in twenty minutes, so only four other people populated the room: two Asian girls and a Caucasian girl and boy. The Caucasians appeared to be friends; they sat next to each other in the back corner of the room furthest from the door. Ava believed the boy more interested in chatting up the girl than vice versa. One of the Asian girls sat in the center, second row from the professor's desk, and smiled at something on her phone. The other Asian girl sat back center. She'd propped her feet, clad in black patent leather Converse sneakers, on the footrest that the desk in front of her provided.

"Let's sit here," Derek whispered. He motioned to the front and made his way to the school desk chairs nearest the door.

He sat in the seat adjacent to an oversized bulletin board. Ava took the seat left of him. Unfortunately, this meant she had an optimal view of the blackboard instead of the classroom. So no way to look at her few fellow classmates discreetly; she'd need to turn around.

"How were your first two days?" Derek asked as students began filtering in.

Ava shrugged. "Preliminary. Going over the syllabus, getting to leave early."

She skimmed the many brightly colored flyers on the bulletin board. "STUDY ABROAD IN CHINA," one flyer exclaimed. "Join the 'Live Poets Society': first meeting next Monday," encouraged another.

Derek looked at her in disbelief. "Man, they let you English majors off easy. We worked on problems in calc. II, and I took a practical in my gen. chem. class."

Ava made a face. "Gross. I'm glad that I'm not missing out on anything."

"Rub it in, why don't you?"

She flashed Derek a grin. "Sorry."

"So what're you doing this weekend?" he asked.

"Nothing. Besides homework, I guess. You?"

"Wanna see a movie? Walter campus has a theater."

"Um. Sure. And it'll be perfect; Charlotte loves movies."

Derek gave her a strange look. "But do *you* love movies?"

"I don't mind them. I just prefer books."

"Let's do something else, then."

"Why don't we bring it up next time we eat? Jason and Kevin stay up-to-date on the recreation scene."

"Jason and Kevin? But—"

His blush bewildered her. But she hated when people stared at her embarrassment, so she looked away. "Let's talk later." She nodded at the clock above the door. "Class starts now."

"But where's the professor?"

Where, indeed? The desk at the front of the room remained unoccupied, and there weren't any bags or purses nearby. Ava twisted her body to look at the other chatting students, taking extra care not to stare. Twenty people composed the class, excluding her and Derek. A quick scan revealed that Caucasian females held the majority. Including the two girls she and Derek first saw, she counted just five Asians total. Besides Derek, there were two guys. Ava wondered why each student signed up for the class. Curiosity, or to fulfill a requirement? A bit of both?

Suddenly the Asian girl wearing Converse stood up. Hoisting her laptop bag onto her shoulder, she swiftly walked to the front of the room.

"Hi everybody," she said, placing her bag onto the desk before standing beside it. "I'm Professor Chen." She stood tall for a Chinese woman, 5′ 7″ and willowy.

For a moment no one said anything. The students stared. Jagged, side-swept bangs softened the severity of her high forehead. Her predominantly black, straight hair nearly fell to her waist. From her shoulders down, white, red, brown, and blonde streaks intermingled with her natural hair color. She regarded her students, unblinking, absorbing their stares like she'd been raised to be queen.

"When's the real professor going to show up?" a red-headed girl asked.

She inclined her head slightly. "I am the real professor."

Ava and Derek looked at each other, confused.

"You can't be a professor! You look like a badass," a guy in a Davison hoodie said, expressing everyone's thought.

Professor Chen laughed. "I'll take that as a compliment. But I assure you, I will be your professor. Unless you choose to drop the class, which I'm sure some of you will. Be aware of when the add/drop period ends." Her lips curved into a smile. "Or you might just find yourself stuck with a 'badass' as a professor."

"But if you're our professor, then why were you sitting in the back of the class?" a blonde girl asked.

Interlacing her hands, Professor Chen said, "Because it allowed me to observe all of you without being observed. Looking ten years younger than I am has its benefits, you know."

Ava felt convinced, but most of the students had trouble fully believing until Professor Chen began handing out and explaining the syllabus. She paced the length of the room like a caged wildcat, never needing to glance at her own copy.

"As you can see on the syllabus, we'll be reading a total of five novels: *Obasan, Native Speaker, Woman Warrior, Shortcomings*—which is a graphic novel—and *The Frontiers of Love*. There'll be one quiz per novel and you'll all take an in-class midterm. In place of a final exam, you'll write a paper, at least eight pages long, on a topic of your choice."

A couple of students groaned.

"Please," Professor Chen said with a grin, "wait until I'm done. That's not the worst of it." She momentarily stood still. "When we meet during finals week, you'll each have five minutes to summarize your final paper to your classmates. Okay, now you can groan if you'd like."

Some students smiled, but no one groaned.

Professor Chen sat back down on the front edge of her desk.

"Now that we've got logistics out of the way, why don't we introduce ourselves? List your name, class standing, potential or declared major, and why you registered for this class. I'll start.

"My full name is Li zhi Chen. In China family names come first, so it's really Chen Li zhi." She rose and began pacing again. "I finished my PhD not too long ago, and I'm an assistant professor of comparative literature. This is my second time teaching this course, and I love sharing Asian American literature with students and people in general."

Professor Chen glanced at her class roster, which included pictures of students. "We'll go from left to right. Your turn, Derek, I believe?" She halted in front of the door, a few feet from him.

Derek shifted in his seat and smiled sheepishly. "Yeah, Derek. I'm a freshman majoring in Biology . . . ," he trailed off, forgetting what came next.

She smiled encouragingly, withdrawing a gold-trimmed pen from her blazer pocket. "Why'd you register for this class?"

"Um," he began, looking at Ava out of the corner of his eye. "Because my friend suggested it."

Professor Chen nodded, scribbling key words under his picture. She went back to the rest of her roster, eyes roving. "Ava?"

Ava felt pressure to turn in her seat and address the other students. But there were too many eyes trained on her. Instead, she focused her attention on the professor.

"My name's Ava . . . and I'm the friend who dragged Derek to this class." Some of her classmates chuckled. "I'm also a freshman, and I . . . I hope to be an English major. I took this to fulfill a requirement." She nearly left it there, but Professor Chen's eyes seemed to be asking for more. "And I guess to also learn about my other half."

"If you don't mind my asking, is your mom or dad Asian?" Professor Chen asked.

"My mother," Ava said, feeling herself turn pink. Now everyone really stared at her.

Realizing this, Professor Chen said quickly, "Your turn, Anthony."

Ava gave her a grateful smile, which Professor Chen returned. She noticed that Professor Chen hadn't written anything down under her picture.

Chapter Five

Mei parked her maroon E-Class Mercedes Benz in her driveway. For a couple minutes she sat, unmoving, no longer listening to Chinese American Voice. Through the windows, the sunlight pressed in on her. She started the car again. Pressed the remote to the garage. Once enclosed inside, she basked in the darkness.

Ten days had passed since she and Paul dropped their daughter off at college.

Bai ban wu liao. Yes, exactly. She felt bored rigid. Time now stretched ahead of her like a road with no end in sight. Volunteering only took so long. She performed her daily routines too efficiently, leaving her with little else to do but imagine a bad return on her investment. What would Ava do without her guidance? The possibilities for losing face were endless. In college, bad habits never lurked. They paraded about. Students wore them on their chests like honor badges. Studies and the future, forgotten, all in the name of partying now. She hoped her daughter didn't even consider these options. No, Ava wouldn't dare undo the countless hours she'd toiled in childrearing. Better not undo values. The ones she'd fought to get her to accept.

She exhaled. But oh, she'd waited for this moment. Finally free. No longer subjugated by the burden of a child. Imprisonment over, she could live her own life. Seventeen years; she'd done her time. No, not that simple. Now she would collect her due.. Remember, Ava, young girl, *tuo er dai nu.* Family obligations. Yes. Now, more than ever, her daughter owed her. Turning off the radio, Mei stepped out of her car, locking it behind her.

In her house, the loud click of Mei's heels in the hallway reassured. After five hours of fundraising, of promoting for animal adoptions, she could relax. Finally, all alone. And she liked it.

A glass of red. Her heels, sheer stockings, off. The carpeted stairs, plush. She took her time walking up to the second floor, squeezing the carpet fibers between her toes.

She set her wine down on her computer desk. Today she'd skip a blog post. The Chinese didn't dwell on tragedies. No moments of silence on anniversaries. No bowed heads, commemorations. At least it'd been terrorism. And that of a focused kind, the loss of two towers and the workers within. Not mass starvation or inbred violence. Besides, that happened years ago. Americans never knew what to be grateful for.

Between sips of wine, she checked her social media accounts. Facebook, Twitter, Instagram, YouTube. Because of her pageant win, she had many followers. Nowhere near as many as Yao Chen, but much more than the average person. Her followers, mostly Asian but some adoring white men, mainly contacted her through Facebook message.

She scrolled through the messages, deciding which ones deserved answering.

The white men usually had yellow fever. Obsessed with Asian women, they learned a few Chinese phrases in attempts to claim a China doll. They offered too little and expected too much. Or, worse, they tried to lure her with faulty translations or Asian languages far different from her own.

She naturally took offense to the messages she received from the few Asians who misread her classical Chinese features. Those Koreans, Malaysians, Indonesians, Japanese, Thai, Filipinos, Vietnamese who imagined—in her!—a likeness with their native countries. She never knew what to make of the Taiwanese, so she ignored them and her dubiety.

Then those fresh-off-the-boat Chinese. Often spoiled, spoilt by their mothers and amahs. So controlling. Or needy. They never understood boundaries.

But Chinese Americans . . . Chinese Americans who spoke fluent Mandarin, anyway, were good to be around. Same cultural base, except they deferred to her. They looked to her to make the rules. The American Born Chinese didn't dare ask for her background. They just assumed she deserved respect. Unlike most women her age, her face showed no wrinkles. But her eyes spoke lives of experience.

Oh, this one wanted to meet for a drink. Tonight? She looked at her Cartier watch. Only 4 p.m. Wait, no need to get ahead of herself. How well did he know his idioms? She clicked on the message and began typing.

Yuan yuan liu chang.

This a test? he asked.

Yes.

The source of the water is in the distant past.

Close enough.

Looking for perfection?

Who doesn't?

Well, what about *shi shi qiu shi*? he challenged.

I am being realistic. People give up too easy. *Ji gong jin li*?

We look for instant gratification. Did I pass?

OK, we meet. Zen Asia Lounge? Give me your number.

But you won't give me yours?

No fun comes that way. I'll call.

At 6 p.m. she called from her car. "I'm right inside the lobby."

"You've got a nice voice," he said.

Mei laughed. "That's never original." She watched him approach the door. Not especially tall. But taller than she. Thin. Manageable. With a full crop of hair. He walked inside, uncertainty in his step. She eased out of her Mercedes.

"I don't see you."

"Wait there."

He nodded, unsurprised when she entered the lobby.

"Du shu yi zhi."

"Last test? You've got your own way of doing things. Shall we?"

They sat at a small corner table. Each took a drink menu. She decided. Putting her menu down, she openly assessed him.

Continuing to scan the menu, he spoke in Mandarin. "I feel your judgment like a downpour. What've you concluded?"

"Greying hair. Sleek suit, but untailored. I see your socks. Tie's off kilter. You're wearing too many dark colors."

Chuckling, he put his menu under hers. "All good, true observations. How old am I?"

"Younger than your body says. You don't take enough care of yourself."

"Ha! Forty-two. And you? Glossy bob, brown highlights. Bold lipstick, otherwise subtle makeup. Form-fitting dress. Manicure *and* pedicure. You care too much. You must be older than you look."

Mei smiled tightly. Snatching the menus up, she stuck them back in the wired holder. "I'll have a glass of plum wine."

"Knew you'd be slippery," he said, heaving himself out of the red egg chair.

She sat back and watched him saunter over to the bar.

"You want me to keep speaking in Mandarin?" he asked, setting their drinks down on the table.

Mei placed her glass on a napkin. "You aren't fluent, then?"

"I am. My parents came over before my birth, but I learned Mandarin and English at the same time."

She raised her glass. "Let's stick to Mandarin."

He put down his chili-pepper-infused tequila. "You miss the Mainland?"

"Yes. And no. I miss . . . it's the simplicity that I miss."

"Oh?"

"Life here is a series of choices. There are too many options. Not enough guidance and too much privilege. Too much taken for granted. It all starts with the children. Parents raise them into an inflated sense of self-worth."

He grinned. "When did you emigrate from China? You're sounding Communist."

"That's not funny," she snapped.

His grin faded. "I'm sorry. Didn't mean to offend."

"I . . . I knew people. In the Revolution. It wasn't—didn't seem like a good period."

"Right. Of course."

They quietly attended to their drinks, glancing at the lounge's other patrons. Happily chatting couples sat at tables. Friends bought each other drinks at the bar, glowing pink under the fluorescent lighting. A young, hip, mostly white crowd. They were probably the only two who wielded a Mandarin tongue.

"I work in advertising," he offered. "You, ah . . . what do you do when you're not online?"

She finished her drink before answering. "Volunteer. Check up on my daughter."

He raised his eyebrows. "Wouldn't guess you had children."

"No children. One child. One child's more than enough."

"I don't have any. But I've heard too many tales. Little demons, aren't they?" He gestured with his glass, empty except for the foam that had gathered at the bottom. "No ring?"

"Haven't worn it since—for a long time. He doesn't either."

"But you're still married?"

Mei shrugged. "Legally. He's my cushion. We don't . . . don't parent the same way."

"He American-born?"

"Yes. He's a foreign devil."

"Well! That does change things, doesn't it?"

Mei delicately snorted. "He isn't a real father. Has terrible parenting instincts. If he'd had his way, my daughter would've been given everything."

"And learned nothing."

"Yes, yes. I raised her to be like a tiger with wings."

He smiled. "I owe my success to my parents. Westerners baby their children. Too concerned with children's self-esteem. They never see the depths of potential for building character. Tolerance nurtures evildoing."

She nodded. "And children, the children! Act like they weren't born already in debt. They think they deserve a right to an opinion. A right to question. That parents—parents who teach, anyway—don't know best."

"American rebellion. Entitlement. No sense of filial piety, of gratitude."

"Well said! Everything I do to—*for* her, it's for her betterment. She doesn't appreciate it. Doesn't realize that I know what she's truly capable of. She can endure more than she thinks. But it's always a power struggle. Without me, she only sees leopards through constricted spyglass. I see near and far and can connect the two. I'm making her future full of possibilities. She'll receive the opportunities I only dreamed of. True independence."

"No need for marriage . . . or even a man?"

"No need. I want her to be better than that. She shouldn't need anybody. Self-reliance is perfection."

"How old is she now? Your daughter."

"Eighteen. She will be, soon."

"Ah. College freshman?"

Mei held out her empty glass. "Don't remind me."

He took it. "Alright. Whatever you want."

Chapter Six

With a red marker Charlotte crossed out October fifteen on their oversized school calendar. "Can you believe we're halfway into October already?"

"No," Ava said, raking a hand through her hair. "It's kind of freaking me out. And I don't know about you, but my assignments are definitely picking up. I'm reading three novels at the same time!"

"That's what you get for taking six classes and pursuing your major! Overachieving Whasian. I'm breezing through my five classes; they're all general."

"I hate you."

"Love you too." Charlotte threw her backpack over a shoulder. "Alright, I'm off to my Food and Culture class."

"Enjoy, I suppose."

"Not really. We're supposed to watch a boring documentary today. See you!" And with that Charlotte sped out the door. It locked shut.

Ava looked down at her watch; 1:10 p.m. Her Shakespeare class began in exactly three hours, and Asian American Literature started at 7:40 p.m. In three hours she'd easily read fifty pages of *Macbeth.*

She rarely completed an assignment on its due date, but time to complete schoolwork grew more elusive. Ava partly owed this to weekend partying with Julia, and sometimes with Jason and Kevin. But her mother had also made a comeback into her life.

She'd managed to explain away the loud partying sounds from the first time she'd gone out. She'd settled on the tenth excuse: "I'm sorry, I lost my phone and the person who returned it must've been partying. Of course it's the truth. When have I lied to you? Yes, yes I know, I'm terribly irresponsible . . ." But like the overseer of a recaptured prisoner, her mother made up for her "understanding."

Instead of a weekly call, Mei now called at least once a day. She interrogated Ava about her studies, but really just squandered time that she could've used for schoolwork. Each call lasted at least an hour and brimmed with disconnected ramblings. "You must go to sleep at 10 all nights and wake at 6 – it said on Sina; First semester hardest don't be cocky or like Cha's *huai dan* sister; Where were you? I call you pick up! Dare you do that again; What's that, passive aggression, your own mother; *Cong ming fan bei cong ming wu*, sharpen your eyes, don't reach over yourself; What's that noise? That laughter? Your windows open? I told you never to . . ."

If it were only calling, perhaps Ava wouldn't be so annoyed, but Mei also took to making in-person appearances.

Her phone rang. The screen read "Mother Dearest." "Speak of the demoness," she muttered.

"Ava Ling Magee, get over now and let me in this instantly."

She swallowed what felt like a wad of paper. Her mother only used her full name when she became really angry.

"What? You're here?" The rumpled paper lodged in her throat, half swallowed.

"Yes, *sha zi*. Come out *now*," Mei hissed before abruptly hanging up.

"Crap, crap, crap," Ava muttered.

She began repositioning her things in the manner that Mei ordered them to be set up at the start of the school year. Where had her mother put her alarm clock? Ava closed her eyes for a moment, trying to remember. Wait! She'd taken a picture on her cell phone. Scrambling, she pulled up the image. She took her pillow from the headboard closest to the door and moved it to the headboard closest to her desk. Then she hid *Macbeth* in the back of a lower desk drawer and threw *Organic Chemistry* onto her bed. She took her alarm clock from the top of her dresser and put it on her desk. Running over to her closet, she took the sparkly tops she'd bought with Julia and stuffed them in the back of a dresser drawer. Ava nearly headed out when she remembered: the ramen noodles! Avoid that confrontation. She threw her packages into Charlotte's food stash.

Grabbing her room key, she ran to open the lobby door.

Mei shot her daughter a scathing look. "You make me wait."

"I *made* you wait," Ava said under her breath, leading the way to her room.

"What did you say? You know I hate when you bumble."

"*Mumble*."

"Hurry up and open the door. I'm not a leisure lady, you know."

Ava bit her bottom lip to keep her conflicting emotions in check. Show no weakness, show no weakness. "After you."

Mei strode in and positioned herself in the center of the room, scouring her daughter's side. "Take out the doorstop."

With a falling feeling, Ava did so. She only disobeyed her mother in daydreams.

Mei stalked up and down the room like the lead dancer under the head of a lion costume. A few steps here, a pivot, a crouch. Springing back up for further inspection. Down again . . .

Ava almost expected to hear the accompanying drums. *Dongdong chang. Dongdongdong chang. Dongdong—*

The lion head stilled, eyes flapping. Open shut open. Mei turned. She smiled until the curve spread to her cheeks.

"Something different. It's a quiz. Tell me, you smart enough to know the answer?"

Dongdong chang. That falling feeling again—the one she got just before sleep sucked her under. No, she never measured up. Never smart enough, never good enough for Mei's impossibly high standards. Ava looked around the room, trying to see if she'd forgotten to put something in a position Mei had originally "requested." Nothing. She'd rearranged the room to match the picture she'd taken after moving in. It always started off a minute thing before mutating into a Big Thing.

Her mother continued to smile, black eyes burning. She strode around her in a circle.

"Can't tell a thing. Nothing in there, *ah*?" she jabbed Ava's temple with an index finger. Grabbing her arm, Mei pulled her daughter over to her desk. "Notice now?" She thrust her head toward the lowest of the three shelves that were above her desk. Before Ava could think, she continued, but in the tone used to discuss an unremarkable day of weather, "The picture, *nao can*. I can't believe I gave birth to you. You disgrace to my ancestors. Defectful girl. You don't have even common sense."

Dongdong chang. She bit her lip and tried to calm her skittish heart. You can't speak proper English and your definition of common sense is off-kilter.

"Close the blinds. *Now*." Mei shoved her over to the window.

No. No, I won't, and you can't make me, she wanted to shout. But she'd gotten used to this kind of treatment. It'd become her normal. And her normal reaction meant obeying and respecting her parents—in reality just her mother. Her father hovered on the outskirts of her life, never around long enough for her to respect. He never demanded it, anyway.

Palms sweaty, Ava took her time closing the blinds. Her mother didn't want any witnesses. Keep up appearances, no matter what. Like a well-tended garden. Except no one knew that worms lurked and thrived inside the produce. No one received the opportunity to take a bite, to free the unpleasant surprises.

Admittedly, Ava participated in the lie; she'd never told anyone about her childhood or how her mother really treated her because it would be too . . . too degrading. If she offered herself up, the blade of rejection would slice open a surplus of questions. *When? How? Why?* The unvoiced questions cut deeper. *You let it happen, didn't you? Are you a masochist? How can you be sure you didn't instigate it? What did you do to deserve it?* Shameful to contemplate answering. Shameful to admit. Even to herself, let alone Charlotte, and forget about her father. Secrets were easier, hiding easier. Mei had raised Ava on this style of being. It composed her foundation. Although, if she forced herself to be honest, she sensed its malignancy. But she never forced herself.

Dongdong chang.

"What's this?" Mei asked, still in a subdued voice, aware that people could be lurking in the halls and might hear. She waved the framed picture in front of Ava.

"What're you referring to?" Playing dumb always proved better than fighting back.

Mei used her other hand to brandish a fist by Ava's face. "You know, you know."

She bowed her head, barely resisting the urge to back away.

"The picture stood down so no one can see. Why you hide it? You ashamed of the family? Huh, huh? Ungrateful *sanba*! I'm ashamed to call you daughter—"

Ava braced herself, but nothing happened. *Dongdong chang.* Her heart began dancing faster.

"No, I didn't. It fell down," she whispered, looking at the floor. This time she told the truth. One day, when she'd reached for something else, she knocked it down and forgot to pick it back up. But she still felt the strike of shame.

"Say it again." Mei pulled on the shorter layers of Ava's hair. "You're my child. You always owe me. You give me respect, even if I need to choke it from you!"

Says who? Ava bleated in her head. "I said, it fell down. I-I forgot to put it up again."

"Excuses worthless."

Dongdong chang.

"What you owe me?" Mei laughed, a dangerous tinkle. "Besides everything."

Everything? Nothing. Some things . . . screw your moral actions! But she said without feeling, "I'm sorry."

"Sorry for what, bitch?" Mei jerked her face close enough for a kiss.

"S-sorry for not putting up the picture and for my excuses."

"Don't try dare . . . you don't dare to erase me again. I'm your mother! I will be recognized. I don't care that everyone sees you for a ghost. *You* will be recognized. You mine. You're a *zazhong*, but always you're Chinese. Don't forget it. Put the picture back."

"I can't . . . you've got me by my hair."

Dongdong chang. With a last yank, her mother let go.

Ava propped the picture up and stepped back, refusing to massage her scalp. She took a deep, restorative breath. "That all?"

Mei slapped her face hard enough to make her eyes tear. "Now, yes. Be grateful you have class."

Ava's eyes stung, but she wouldn't allow even one teardrop to fall. That's what she wants. Don't do it. Don't break. Whatever you do, do not break. Contain it! Hold it in.

Mei opened up her Chanel purse, withdrawing her matching wallet. She threw a twenty-dollar bill on Ava's desk and neatly adjusted her jacket, getting ready to leave.

"Buy yourself some makeup. You a plain Jane and you look washed out. Put in efforts and don't shame me. I held Mrs. New Jersey title, remember?"

With that stabbing remark, Mei swept away. She snapped the door shut behind her.

Ava hugged her sides. She grazed her smarting cheek and glanced at the mirror by the doorway. Red. On her cheek, the vague shape of a hand. The imprint would fade fast enough.

She walked over to her desk, sat down, and looked at the picture. Set in Disneyland. Next to Paul on one side and Belle on the other, Ava gleefully smiled in Mei's arms. The whole family looked happy. Even Mei, though her smile held no depth, not when compared to Ava's and Paul's. The last time Ava studied the picture, it had been displayed in the bathroom. Not this exact photo, but its duplicate. What had she been, ten? Yes, they'd recently moved into the big house . . .

"Ava Ling!" Mei had screamed up the stairs.

Looking up from her homework, Ava sighed. Could she pretend she hadn't heard?

"Ava Ling, get down here *now*!"

Of course not. Pushing herself away from her desk with her roller chair, she steeled herself to face the first floor.

"Taking your time," Mei said in English, and then switched over to Mandarin Ava didn't understand in the same sentence, "too good a life, aya!"

She reluctantly stepped off the last stair onto the first floor landing. "I had to climb down three flights of stairs; I'm sorry." She bowed her head. Her parents loved the largeness of the new house—at least her mother did—but she found it overwhelming. And there hadn't been a basement in the townhouse. Or a pool in the backyard.

"No good enough. No excuses!" Mei sang, shaking her index finger at Ava.

She continued staring at her feet.

Mei pulled Ava's even hair, bundled back in a ponytail that went halfway down her back.

"Pay attention, girl. You not listening. Look at me! What, you not want to see my smile?"

"You could just tell me that instead of pulling my head back," Ava mumbled, loud enough for her mother to hear.

"*Hun dan*, don't talk back. Now go. Go to the bathroom. You did something wrong there." Mei pushed her in the right direction.

Ava flicked on the bathroom light. Everything looked the same as it had since they finished moving in six months ago. In the corner, a shower stall with a frosted glass door. A few feet away lay a toilet. A sink perched on a cabinet, and on the wall hung shelves housing towels and decorations.

"I don't see anything different," she said, turning around to face her mother, who stared at her through slit eyes.

"Ha! Smart like stuck pig. You no see the toilet paper?" Mei pointed to the toilet paper roll, which harmlessly sat in the toilet paper holder.

She inspected the roll. "There's nothing wrong with it."

Mei cursed at her in Mandarin. Ava didn't know the language itself, but through her mother she knew its curses quite well.

Purposely bumping into Ava, Mei went over to the toilet paper and gave it a spin. "See? See this," she hissed, pointing at the stream of unfolded sheets, "it's upside down."

"What?" she asked, eyebrows drawing together.

After knocking her on the head with a fist, Mei impatiently explained, "It must be over, but it's under. You replaced this, you did it wrong. Admit it!"

"Um. I'm sorry?"

Mei's delicate features twisted into a snarl. A flush crept across her face. "*Guixia*! *Kowtow*! Always require disciplining. It's your white blood. You too wild!"

When Ava hesitated, Mei's voice caramelized. "Dear, you want the snake? We go down to the basement? I can make your life a real hell if I want. You no believe me? I say it once. You not listen I won't be so nice. Surrender arms."

Ava quickly kneeled down on the hard-tiled floor, placing her hands behind her head like she did during evacuation drills in school. She would've stood on her head in order to avoid the basement and the snake that lurked there.

A sixty-minute Chinglish tirade ensued, centering on her inadequacies and irresponsibility. No use in paying attention: her mother repeated the same complaints over and over, rarely varying her words. She supposed Mei fell back on repetitiveness because she resisted and groped for English. Ava spaced out. She alternated between staring at the picture of her family in Disneyland, on one of the wooden bathroom shelves, and the digital clock to the right of the photo.

Ava didn't know the age of the girl in the picture. She wore a miniature version of Belle's yellow costume, a red rose woven into her hair. Mei had made the dress herself, back in her sewing days. Little Ava's torso twisted in her mother's steady arms. She pointed at the Disney actress, eyes squinting with laughter. Mei didn't appear to mind the twisting, the pointing, the unrestrained excitement. Paul held one of her yellow slippers, smiling with his teeth.

But what would Ava's eyes say, without the squinting? No matter how hard she tried, she couldn't remember this moment. The costume long gone, the rose long dead. But what about the snapshot? This one, genuinely happy-looking moment. Had it all been staged?

"You insensitive about my needs," Mei continued ranting. "You don't care doing things best ways, right ways, and you never appreciate when I try to teach you lessons. You *mu wu quan niu*. I look at the ox and I know where to cut it to pieces. I see everything. For your own good, ungrateful *fei wu*!"

Ava shifted on her numb knees. The pressure in her bladder had been building for some time now, and it became unbearable. "I'm sorry. May I go to the bathroom?" she asked in a squeak.

"Dare you interrupt me? No!"

"Please? I really, really have to pee and the toilet's right there," Ava begged.

Mei flashed a smile. "No means no. You don't deserve it. Pee yourself."

"What? May I please go? Just punish me later!"

"No. I'm not allowing it. You want to be a childish? Go it all the way. Go in your pants."

Ava shifted her weight again and tried thinking about anything, everything else. How much homework to finish before the weekend ended? She multiplied in her head; she defined vocabulary terms and spelled them in preparation for her quiz on Monday. The minutes slowly passed and Mei stared down at her daughter, waiting for Ava to lose out.

Back to wind chimes and caramel. "Why don't I help." Her mother never cooed, but she knew how to pretend. She turned on the faucet.

After thirty minutes of water running, whistling, yelling, and taunting from Mei, Ava couldn't help herself. Her eyes glistened in humiliation when her pants became wet.

"So weak. Don't now cry," she warned, face full of revulsion. "Wet cheeks works on your father. Your tears mean nothing to me. You cry and I make everything worse! I give you something worth crying on."

Ava swallowed her sobs and blinked back her tears, wishing she could burn holes into Mei with the anger and hurt that she pent up inside. With no external release available, she added them to her feeling reserves.

"Stay like that for another half hour. Then wash your filth clothes." She flicked off the light to leave Ava in the dark. "Oh, and fix the toilet paper before that," Mei had called over her shoulder while walking away.

Ava jumped in her seat at the sound of a door slamming down the hall. With shaky hands, she put the Disneyland picture back on the shelf. She scraped away the wetness on her cheeks. Pathetic. Weak. It didn't matter that no one saw. Crying or succumbing to emotion meant that her mother won. That Ava proved her right. She turned the picture so that it faced the wall. On second thought . . . she struck it down. It deserved to remain unseen.

Her phone beeped, the reminder for her first class of the day. So much for getting reading done. She went to their small bathroom in an attempt to wash away the red handprint.

Half an hour later, she walked into class.

"Hey Ava, I saved you a seat!" Jason called from the second row of the movie-theatre-style seating in their Shakespeare class.

She sat down and tried on a smile. It fit like a right glove on a left hand. "Thanks."

She doubted she'd be able to handle talking to friends today. There should be enough time for her to calm down before Asian American Literature with Derek, but right now her hands quivered. And while Ava counted on Derek's inability to perceive her distress, Jason possessed a talent for reading emotional cues.

"You okay? Your eyes look a little red." He studied her while cleaning his eyeglasses with his polo shirt.

She took out *Macbeth*. "I'm fine."

"You sure?" He put his glasses back on and looked at her skeptically.

"Yes." Avoiding eye contact, she flipped to her bookmark.

"You look like you've been crying," Jason whispered.

"I'm *fine*," she repeated between tightly drawn lips.

"Well, despite what you might think, I'm more sensitive than I let on. I'm actually a great listener. And I get the feeling that you're one of those people who keeps everything bottled up inside. I've done that. *No es una buena idea*. Sooner or later you end up exploding."

Luckily for her, the professor called the class to attention at that moment. She settled into her seat and listened to the lecture attentively, even though she'd read *Macbeth* three times before. When the professor turned on the projector and dimmed the lights to play a clip from a film version of the play, she made a show of taking notes, knowing that Jason liked taking advantage of breaks in class routine.

Sure enough, a minute into the clip Jason gently poked her. "You want to grab dinner afterward and talk about it?'

Keep your eyes trained on the screen. "No."

"Okay. Want to grab dinner after this and *avoid* talking about it?" Jason saw the corner of Ava's mouth twitch. "Aha! An emerging smile! Come on." He switched to a Cockney accent and whispered, "What say you?"

"Your accent's terrible. You're not going to leave me alone, are you?"

Jason grinned. "Not a chance."

At 6:50 p.m. Ava left the dining hall for her Asian American Literature class. She knew she'd arrive early, but she didn't want to return to Lockhart and face Charlotte. And luckily, on Mondays Derek came straight from Walter campus, so they couldn't walk together as they did on Thursdays. She walked quickly, hands in her pockets, eyes trained on the damp sidewalk, stepping around broken glass and fallen leaves. Every few steps she'd look up to avoid passersby who'd been let out from class. Everyone else strolled. Jaunty. Heads up, bodies loose. Expressive, free. Chatting couples held hands or linked arms. Clusters of laughing friends spoke with their hands. Teasing, playfully jabbing, holding onto one another for balance, to tie shoelaces, to pick up a fallen book, just to touch.

True to his word, Jason hadn't pressed Ava during dinner. Instead, he regaled her with amusing impressions of the frazzled teacher's assistant who taught his introductory philosophy course. She found herself genuinely laughing. There were moments during dinner when she impulsively considered blurting out her earlier incident with Mei, but she turned down the flame and put the lid back on these feelings.

When she got to class she only saw Professor Chen.

"Hi, Ava." Professor Chen looked up from her laptop to flash her a smile.

She smiled shyly, sliding off her light jacket and dropping her backpack to the floor. "Hi, Professor Chen."

Professor Chen returned to her laptop, but looked up when Ava sat down. "Ava, you're a freshman, right?"

"Yes."

Waving Ava over, Professor Chen said, "Sit by me for a few moments. We've got some time before class and I'd like to talk about an opportunity."

She slipped into the seat that directly faced the front desk. Professor Chen had pulled her hair back into a bun today; the updo hid her multicolored locks. She wore pale pink lipstick, but the earrings on her helix undid the delicate touch. Three pink-gemmed studs led up to the fierce earring at the top of her ear.

"Is that a . . . dragon?" Ava asked, unable to contain her curiosity.

"A dragon? Oh, you mean this," Professor Chen said, briefly touching the small silver clip-on shaped and etched like a dragon. She turned her head so Ava received a better view. Its head curled around her upper helix and its body wrapped around to the back of her ear. Ava made out a small, bat-like wing on its body.

"Yes. I'm a regular dragon lady," Professor Chen joked. She turned back to encounter Ava's confused face. "The dragon lady stereotype?"

She shook her head. "My mother never . . . directly taught me about Asian culture." The phrase "dragon lady" sounded familiar and she thought it had negative connotations, but knew nothing else. She supposed her dad knew, but he hadn't taught her much more than her mother. Paul had suggested sending her to Chinese school, but Mei refused, determined to have Ava focus on piano instead. What little Mandarin Ava knew she'd picked up and pieced together during childhood.

"It's actually a Western stereotype for power-hungry, seductive Asian women. In the East, dragons are symbols of good luck. Don't worry; we'll talk about it in class. Anyway, I wanted to talk to you about a research opportunity. How would you like to be my research assistant?"

For a moment she couldn't say anything. She'd never seen friendly black eyes before. "Um. Sure!"

Professor Chen laughed. "You haven't even asked me what you'd be doing!"

Ava smiled sheepishly. "I trust . . . that you won't give me anything I can't manage." She'd almost said "I trust you," but felt she didn't yet have the grounds to say so.

"You've got good instincts, and I've noticed that you always make worthwhile points during our class discussions. I'm doing research for an academic book right now, but I'm also teaching a few classes. So really I'm teaching and neglecting the research."

She nodded. "I'd help you find the sources you need."

"Yes. And maybe go through some archives, spend some time at the library. Send off some inquires for me via email. Make a few phone calls, that sort of thing. I'm going to write about the commodification of Asian American women in the media, and how this has shifted to focus on mixed Asian American women. You've mentioned that you're mixed a couple of times, and I think you may have more interest in this than Derek."

Ava's earlier gloom momentarily lifted. How could she pass up the chance to do research that pertained to her, and with a professor she admired? "No way am I telling Derek about this. He might try to steal it from me."

Professor Chen smiled. "I'm afraid that this will be a volunteer position, but I'll pay for any meals you'll need while working. And if a source requires a fee for permissions, let me know so I can pay for that." The alarm on Professor Chen's iPhone went off. "Right. Class will start in fifteen minutes, so students should start filtering in. Why don't we meet for coffee to go over the details?"

A couple of students came in. Ava stood. "Okay. I'll send you an email with my availability?"

"Sounds like a plan."

She smiled to herself and returned to her seat.

Chapter Seven

Outside the Lincoln Tunnel, Paul waited for the clogged line of cars to resume flowing. He craned forward to look out his windshield. The clouds moved with rolling grace, grey but not menacing. A drizzle, probably, or intermittent rain.

With the help of E-ZPass he breezed through the tolls. When he'd merged onto the Garden State Parkway he eased up his grip on the steering wheel. A straight shot until exit 123 then he'd merge onto Route 9 South. If it weren't for the other cars, he could do this commute blindfolded. It'd become so effortless that if he relaxed into the habit, he became drowsy. Time to search for something invigorating on the radio. He flipped through his presets. Commercial, commercial, sports report . . . "And now my favorite from Rod Stewart, 'Forever—'" He jabbed the power button, silencing the DJ.

Any other day and he wouldn't be so irritated by his wedding song. He wished Rick had been available for dinner yesterday. Or tomorrow. Or the day after. Any other goddamn day. Or that he'd wanted to meet in the city. But his best friend made a living as a traveling salesman and his family resided in Old Bridge. Paul tried to ignore the insidious thoughts, but they kept creeping to the fore. Life had a way of finding the dirty laundry you'd buried and thrusting it under your nose. Why didn't you realize that the clothes were soiled? Why weren't you more careful? But not all stains are obvious. Specks of black ink don't appear on a black suit. Only when you soak the wool does the water turn cloudy.

His wife had seemed like a custom-made suit. Free from blemishes. Sleekly cut, made from the finest fabrics. Yes. At the start, Mei epitomized the definition of her name—beautiful—and with such energy that she'd swept his senses from him. They met at NYU in a Chinese language course. Mei took the class to fulfill an entry-level requirement for her Asian Studies major, but Paul took it for fun. He'd always found Chinese culture interesting and thought that knowing Mandarin could help him interact with Chinese clients he might have in the future. Regardless, he thought "fluent in Mandarin Chinese" would look good on his resume, which he needed to look as impressive as possible to get into a prestigious law school.

One day they were paired off to do a class project. He thought he'd impress her by formally introducing himself in Mandarin. She laughed at him, unabashedly proclaiming failure. "Mandarin is a tonal language; you must use the four tones good." Paul, surprised but intrigued, found himself saying, "Then correct me. I must use the four tones *well*." And so they struck up a mutual tutoring relationship that lasted beyond the class they shared. Once a week, for three-and-a-half years, they met in the library to tutor each other. After their third meeting Paul considered Mei "the one," but she always seemed to be in a relationship.

But when they finished their undergraduate degrees, she became single. She'd turned twenty-six, making her four years older than him. Paul heard that she'd broken up with her last boyfriend when he declined to marry her. Mei needed to get a green card within three months to prevent deportation to China, and she had depleted her savings. So Paul, known by his friends as "plan man," made the most impulsive decision he would ever make in his life. He proposed to her, in perfect Mandarin, over coffee. Sure, not his idea of romantic, but she'd only meet him at a café or the library, and proposing in a library felt wrong.

Over the intervening years Paul weaved together what Mei had really thought, beneath the coy smiles and laughter. She probably thought of him as a study buddy, but accepted his proposal to stay in America. Mei charmed Paul into loving her, and she took full advantage. A spineless white man, easily manipulated. Her ticket to freedom. His last name enabled her to stay in America, and with his ring she could bend him to her will. Nothing for her to lose. But Paul thought that she'd be an asset, a faithful lover, a wife with personality.

Though the ceremony had been understated—Mei wanted more money to be saved for a house—Paul's friends and family deemed it delightful. She, confident, radiant in her red silk dress. His parents and relatives flew in from Seattle and thought his new wife "such a doll." Mei hadn't contacted her relatives in years, and she disregarded his suggestion that they track any Lings down and invite them to the wedding. He should've asked more questions. Shouldn't have taken her at her word. He should've taken more time, for he didn't know her history at all, but he'd gotten swept up in her glamor, in the many preparations for the wedding and beyond.

At Mei's request, they skipped honeymooning to save more money. So after the wedding, the busyness continued. They went back to school. Paul went to Columbia University's law school, and she completed her MA degree in East Asian Culture at NYU. After getting his JD and passing the bar exam, Paul began working as an immigration lawyer. Wanting to teach like her parents, Mei went on to pursue NYU's PhD program. But then, at age thirty-three, she became pregnant for the first time.

Paul had been ecstatic. Mei decided to quit her PhD program, and he didn't protest. In the nineties, many women still stayed home and raised the children. But five months into the pregnancy, she miscarried. A boy. Of course, Paul felt distraught, but Mei displayed nothing. She abandoned her PhD program, though only a semester remained before her graduation. Mei cared only for "doing her duty" and trying again. Then, she told Paul, she would owe nothing to her in-laws. This isn't China, he'd replied. My parents just want us to be happy. You already owe them nothing. Still, Mei stood by her vow: next time, a healthy baby boy would be born.

One year later, on October 30, Mischief Night, 1994, Mei gave birth to Ava Ling Magee, six pounds nine ounces.

Having swaddled their baby, the nurse walked over to Mei's bedside. "Already so well behaved! Want to hold her, ma'am?"

Mei squinted at the nurse. "*Her*?"

"Yes, a beautiful girl."

Paul joined the nurse and looked over her shoulder. "*Ni kan*, Mei. She's got so many of your features!"

"Her. Her?" Mei asked, dragging her fingers through her sweaty hair. Strands stuck up in spikes.

Paul nodded. "*Nu er*."

The nurse held out the quiet baby, but her mother turned onto her side.

"She's tired," he said, trying to explain away the nurse's disapproval.

"Of course." But she seemed unconvinced. "Surely *you* want her?"

Beaming, he moved his arms into a cradling position.

"Yes, just move your arms slightly down. There, see? You're a natural. I'll give you two a moment."

Rocking their baby, Paul sat on the edge of Mei's bed. She stayed on the other side, her back to them, but he spoke so she'd hear his whisper.

"Mei, you'll see. My brothers and parents hoped for a girl; we're so lucky."

He felt a tiny hand reach for his forefinger. He looked down at their baby's Asiatic face and momentarily forgot about his wife.

"You're perfect."

And then she opened her eyes. Misty grey—his eyes. Joy took flight in his chest. He knew what to name her. Ava, derived from Eva; his life.

Ava Ling Magee: Chinese, Italian, and Irish. East blended with West. A product of transcendent love, love across racial and cultural boundaries. She'd be the new face of America.

As he pulled his Toyota Prius into their—his—*her* driveway, the clouds parted. Not a raindrop after all, and a clear twilight. A degradation of the brilliance of the sun. Its final appearance before bidding farewell, to be swallowed whole by the soft blushing colors and deep blues above it. When the sun finished setting, he walked up the pathway.

He knew she'd left, but he focused so hard on trying *not* to remember that he tripped. Tripped over the once tan doormat they'd taken from their first residence, the townhouse. "Bless this Home," it read in black cursive. He righted himself, slowly wiped his leather shoes on the mat, and then opened the door.

The world knew Paul as Mei's husband, Ava's father, and a respected man in and out of the office. But all of his success crumbled when he stepped into this large house. The house they were able to afford only because of the promotion. He walked over to the living room and sat on the couch, covering his face with his hands. Eight years. No chance of ever forgetting today's date, the date he'd been promoted. How could he? It'd also been the date his marriage turned bitter.

A partner at his law firm did almost anything, focused on almost any case. He could help so many immigrants get jobs, build new lives. Paul had called the townhouse to share the exciting news. They could now move into a single-family house. What his wife most desired.

"Mei?"

"Hi Dad," Ava said. "Mother's out shopping. I just got home from school. What's up?"

"We're going out to dinner tonight—I made partner!" He'd hoped to delight Mei with the news, but his daughter would be pleased for him. She knew that he'd been trying to get promoted for the last nine years.

"Wow! Congrats, Dad. I wish I could stay and talk, but I need to get ready for piano class. Steph's mom will pick me up any minute. Gotta go, see you later!"

"Bye Av—" But Ava had already hung up. Paul supposed this normal behavior for a ten-year-old. She already found her father boring. As he put down his work phone, a partner, now one of *his* partners, knocked on his open door.

"Hi Jeff," Paul said. Jeff, the youngest partner, had basically been handed the job when his father retired.

"Paul, I talked it over with the other guys, and we all agreed you should call it a day. Big promotion calls for a celebration, you know? Maybe some . . . afternoon delight?" He grinned, motioning to the framed wedding picture sitting on Paul's desk.

What you got away with saying when you were young and the son of the old boss, Paul thought. He shook his head and smiled, this time hardly annoyed at Jeff's cheek. "Well, if it's okay with everyone . . . "

So he arrived home early, especially pleased because Rod Stewart's "Forever Young" played on the radio during his drive back. Indeed, he felt young. Only forty, after all. The future welcomed him with open arms.

Whistling to himself and playing catch with his car keys, he didn't notice the unfamiliar Volvo parked nearby. Stepping onto their "Bless this Home" mat, Paul opened the front door, about to shout, "Mei, great news!" when he noticed sneakers by Mei's black heels. They looked new. Maybe Ava told her mother the news and Mei decided to surprise him with a pair of sneakers; she'd recently pointed out that his were getting old.

But something felt wrong. No, his paranoia arose from an overactive imagination. But then why quietly close the door? Paul set down his briefcase and slipped off his loafers. Instinct urged him to walk up to the master suite, though Mei should've been in her office by now, working on her Chinese blog.

The bed . . . unmade. Assorted clothes, male—not his—and his wife's scattered about the floor. Paul felt sick, but he needed to see to believe. Heart jumping, he approached the closed bathroom door. Sounds of cascading water. The shower. When he reached for the doorknob, he heard Mei laugh. Paul pulled his hand back. He couldn't. He did not want to see. No, he must. He needed to. After going back and forth for a minute—long enough to hear a male voice, Paul bit his cheek hard enough to draw blood. He finally opened the door.

"Get out." He flicked the lights off. For a moment, no sound but running water. And then that stopped too. "I said, *get out,*" he yelled.

Mei cursed in Mandarin, and then continued to speak in her native tongue, but not to Paul: "You need to go now."

The door to the shower stall opened, and an Asian man about ten years his junior stepped out, grabbing *his* towel. The man—no, in comparison, a boy—rushed past a stunned Paul to grab his clothes, and then sped down the stairs. When the front door opened, Paul flicked the lights back on with a shaky hand.

Mei stepped out of the shower like she'd just woken up. She wound her towel around herself before leaning against a nearby wall.

"Congratulations. You find me out," she said in a bored voice. "I'm glad. Now I no need to sneak around."

"Tell me something to stop me from throwing you out on your conniving ass and filing for a divorce."

Mei tucked a wet strand of her bob behind a delicate ear. "You not thinking right. We must think of our daughter. You want her devastated?" She left the wall and, spine stick-straight, began gliding her way to the bedroom.

He momentarily ignored her flimsy argument. "How could you? After everything we've been through together?" Paul angrily averted his eyes when his cheating wife nonchalantly dropped her towel and slipped on her undergarments.

"How can I? How can *you*?" Mei paused, shrugging on a sweater. "What you expect? No attention, no time for me. You think I cross my legs and wait for when you remember me?" One leg at a time, she pulled on jeans that showcased her slender legs.

"How dare you? I did it all for you, for this family! Who wanted me to make six figures so we could make *your* dream to move into a big house come true? And you repay me this way!" He pounded a fist against the wall nearest to him.

For a second this startled Mei silent. Then she smiled. "Cannot take the responsibility? Hui worships me! He shows me I'm beautiful."

"Who comforted you when we lost the boy?" Paul challenged.

The smile died. "Fuck you," Mei spat.

"Is it because you're forty-four? Does he make you feel young?"

"He no care how old I am!"

"I bet you lied to him. He thinks you're ten years younger, doesn't he?"

"*Ni, ta ma de*!"

"Leave my mother out of this," Paul retorted, dodging the tissue box Mei threw at him. "You know, I called earlier and told Ava we'd be going out for dinner. I made partner today, and you congratulate me by fucking another man. A Cantonese man! If I were Asian you wouldn't have the *nerve* to cheat on me!" He leaned on a bureau for support. Paul had never shouted like this before.

"What else I can do? Work now your wife! You come back only for sleeping. Don't blame me for finding support from other men! Men that *understand me*." Mei walked up to him, fiercely defiant. "And dare you bring up my people?" She jabbed a finger into his chest. "You know nothing; you just a *guilao*!"

"That's rich. So this isn't the first time or even the first man you *cheated* with? How do you have the audacity to stand there with your wedding ring on your finger? I studied your culture;

don't try to pretend I'm clueless! You've broken quite a few Confucian teachings. This is how you respect your husband?" He turned her language on her: "You know what you are? *Yinfu*!"

"Fuck you. Take back it. Take back!" Mei raised her arm to slap him, but Paul deflected her hand.

"I won't. You deserve it! You want me to take *it* back? I'll take everything back. I bought it all anyway!" He walked over to her bureau and roughly pulled open a drawer, intending to chuck the contents on the floor.

"Don't! Unless you want Ava to see. Yes, you and your *princess* daughter."

At the mention of his only child's name, Paul froze. Mei knew their daughter meant everything to him. He leaned on the bureau, panting heavily.

Mei guided her husband over to the bed and sat down next to him. "You never want to hurt Ava . . . right?"

Bending over, Paul rested his elbows on his knees. He held his forehead in his hands and stared at the cheap carpeting. Moving out seemed best. No way could *he* live in this townhouse, or any house with his wi—this woman. Not after what he'd seen.

Mei rubbed his shoulder like it preluded a massage. He shrugged her off.

She softened even further. Her voice drifted over him, lush but filled with dangerous promises. "If we got the divorce, I get her . . . "

"You want to drag up old ghosts? You try that and I'll do it."

"My words against yours. I can say you beat me."

"On what grounds? With what proof?"

Mei shrugged. She stood up and took her bottle of Jean Patou Joy off the dresser.

"Simple," she said, spritzing her neck and a wrist. "I get someone to bruise me." She rubbed her wrists together. "Or I make bruises myself."

He stared at her. Tried to refrain from breathing in the oppressively fresh jasmine notes.

"That's insane."

"Maybe, but what mothers can do? You threaten taking my child, my only *bao bei* from me."

"*You* just threatened to—"

She talked over him until he gave up. "What you mean to her? *Nothing*. Think of your childhood. What you do without your mother? Where you be without her guiding? With only your father? Fighting with your brothers for non-exist love?"

"How dare you use that against me! You want to play dirty? Should I mention . . ." But he couldn't say it. He wouldn't be able to stand the shame he'd feel later.

Mei switched to a different tactic. "Think of Ryan. You want to prove him right? You, become the only son to shame him."

Paul closed his eyes. "Shut up. Just shut up."

"Ava will be home soon. We finish this another time." She stood up to face him.

"No. We'll finish this now," Paul said tiredly.

He wanted it all to be over. Work meant work. Home existed in a separate sphere. A refuge. A place for security and comfort, to unload troubles, not pick new ones up. Not a place to be humiliated, exposed, attacked. "You suggest what, then?"

"You go get good apartment in New York. Come back on weekends. Unless you want Ava to wonder why we stop sleeping in our same room."

"Whatever it takes. Ava can't know about this. Tell her that with the promotion, it's easier on me if I sleep in the city." He knew what happened to split families. Held together by ripped fabric, they produced unraveling children. Paul would do anything to keep that from happening to his daughter. He shared nothing with Ryan; he saw when he hurt others, when his presence disturbed the tapestry. Only stable family structures reared healthy, well-rounded children. If he needed to suffer to make that happen, if he needed to adhere to pretense, then so be it.

They heard the front door open and close. Ava called up, "I'm home! Where are we going for dinner?"

Paul stood up and looked down at his wife. "I guess we're done here. If you want to cheat on me in the future, make sure you do a better job hiding it. The second Ava finds out about it, I'll drag you through the courts. I'll find a way to get custody of her. You'll wish you never married a lawyer," he'd said, leaving a surprised Mei to greet Ava downstairs.

His phone vibrated: a text from Rick regarding dinner. Paul sprang from the couch, still ruminating over the worst day of his life. Even Mei's miscarriage, which Ava still didn't know about, took second place. His marriage, now nothing more than a sham, appeared intact to the world, and, more importantly, his daughter. He didn't know if Mei still cheated on him, but he'd stopped caring about marital love. Paul texted back: "See you in ten." He picked up the tea-set gift Mei wanted him to give Rick. If she wanted to pursue a life of infidelity, so be it. He remained faithful to his vows. He lived by the dictates of integrity.

Chapter Eight

Forefinger on her lips, Charlotte ushered Derek, Kevin, and Jason into her dorm room. Ava still lay asleep; only five minutes remained before her alarm rang to life. Silently, she motioned for everyone to stand by Ava's bedside. One, two, three, Charlotte mouthed.

"Happy birthday to you, happy birthday to you—" they sang.

Ava jerked awake and nearly rolled off the side of her bed, but Derek caught her and pushed her back.

"Wha-what's going on?" she asked groggily.

"Happy birthday dear Ava, happy birthday to you!"

Using her arms to push herself up to a sitting position, she stared at them, mouth slack.

"I don't think she gets it," Derek said. "Let's sing it again!"

"No, no. Once is more than enough!"

The others laughed at her discomfort.

"Happy eighteenth! And I don't care that you don't like when people are touchy-feely. Today's extra special." Charlotte bent down to give Ava a quick hug. "Look, you're now an adult . . . though really, you've been one since high school."

Jason chuckled. "No way. Ava came out of the *womb* an adult."

Charlotte picked up a flat, square package wrapped in shiny red paper. "Anyway, we all pitched in and got you this."

"We were gonna wrap it in white paper, but Charlotte forbid it," Kevin said.

"You can't have plain wrapping paper on your birthday," Charlotte insisted.

"I suggested using Halloween-themed wrapping paper, because how many people have birthdays on Mischief Night, but she also shot me down," Jason said.

"So we settled on red because Derek said it's a lucky color in China," Charlotte concluded.

Ava shut off her phone's alarm and took the present, smiling sheepishly. She found birthdays awkward and in the busyness of school had forgotten hers. She began to open it.

"You really shouldn't have . . ." But then she got the wrapping off and opened the padded envelope. She stared at the book. A smile worked its way across her face.

"I told them about the book you'd checked out for Professor Chen," Derek explained. "And how you got really excited researching it."

Ava looked at the familiar cover. *Part Asian, 100% Hapa,* portraits by Kip Fulbeck, she read again. She touched the library-bound edition reverently. "You guys! Thank you!"

"We're glad you like it," Charlotte said, smiling at the gratitude apparent on Ava's face.

"Alright people, we'd better let the birthday girl get dressed," Jason said, leading the guys away. "She's still got classes today."

Charlotte shut the door after them and turned to her. "See, now you'll be able to look at pictures of other Whasians! Though if I were you, I'd just stare at the guy on the cover. That guy's really hot."

Before Ava could respond, her phone vibrated.

Charlotte sat on her bed, focused on smoothing out her pink bedspread. "Text from your dad?"

Ava nodded, reading the text to herself. "Happy birthday! Eighteen years ago we were blessed with you." If that's true, then where were you eight years ago, when you served me up to her? But she texted back, "Thanks!"

Paul quickly responded with news that made her stomach clench: "Mom and I are taking you out to dinner. When's your last class over?"

"What's wrong?" Charlotte asked.

"Oh nothing," she said, keeping her voice neutral. She didn't want to interact with her mother today of all days, but no way could she tell Charlotte that. "We'll be going out to dinner after my classes are over and I'll be tired, that's all."

"Oh, you've got a three-hour class today, don't you?"

"Right, followed by a regular one," Ava called from the bathroom, her voice distorted from the toothbrush in her mouth.

"Your Tuesday schedule sucks," Charlotte said when she reemerged.

"Tell me something I don't know."

"So Ava, what classes did you have today?" Paul asked, twirling his spaghetti around his fork. They were eating at The Prince, the same Italian restaurant where they'd celebrated his daughter's first birthday. And every birthday after that, until her sixteenth.

She paused, taking too long to sip her water.

Had he asked a dangerous question? Mei looked at her expectantly.

Ava turned her attention to him. "Organic Chemistry and Physics," she said casually. But she avoided meeting his eyes.

"You studied? When's your next exams?" Mei asked, back arching as she leaned forward.

He'd missed something, but what? He only knew that it made his daughter uncomfortable.

"We shouldn't talk about exams on your birthday. Especially not on your eighteenth." Paul turned to Mei. "She's now a legal adult. We can trust her." They could've trusted her years ago.

He returned his attention to his food, ignoring his wife's reproachful stare.

"I'll tell you later," Ava offered.

She shouldn't be the one making concessions, mediating in the dark. He'd made a promise. But he could break it for the right reasons. Because of the timing. Because it needed to be told.

"Yes, your father's right. *Shengri kuaile,* daughter." Mei raised her glass of wine in Ava's direction.

"Happy birthday," Paul translated.

"Thanks." Ava smiled tightly and returned to her chicken Marsala.

"How's the *zuppa di pesce,* ma'am?" asked the young male waiter. He looked a couple of years younger than his daughter, but that hadn't stopped him from flirting with Mei.

Admittedly, she'd started flirting first. Paul felt embarrassed but not surprised. Despite her imperfect English, Mei captivated in public. She'd been the volunteer spokesperson for the community's largest animal shelter since Ava's birth. Though she'd never allowed pets into her own household, Mei still convinced reluctant people to adopt needy animals. The workers and other volunteers at the animal shelter adored her. But who didn't?

Mei smiled coyly and crossed her slim, stocking-clad legs. "Magnifico, darling!"

The teenager blushed and smiled back. "Um . . . would you like to look at our dessert menu?"

Paul frowned at the boy, staring at his acne-crusted face.

Rubbing a thin hand over her obviously flat stomach, which her fitted red cocktail dress accentuated, Mei shook her head. "I got to watch my figure."

"No you don't." Seeming to remember his presence, the waiter hastily added, "Your husband's a lucky man." But he didn't look at Paul.

He tried to draw out his daughter again, but her attention remained on her half-empty plate.

"What about you, Ava? How about some birthday cake?"

She still didn't look up.

"Should I get the menus? We've got lava cake, carrot cake, chocolate-frosted—"

Mei laughed at the boy's eagerness. "You Americans with cake and pie. Chinese no serve sweet for birthdays. Sweets and birthday presents not custom in China. But how nice for you to offer." She took out her compact and made a show of reapplying lip gloss.

"The check, please," Paul said before Mei could open her glossy mouth again.

The dashboard clock read 8 p.m. when he pulled up to the house. He needed to head back to the city. Mei got out of his Toyota Prius with their leftovers. She drummed on his window with her manicured nails. Paul rolled it down. The scent of jasmine struck him.

Holding onto the window's edge, she kissed him on the cheek. Her lip gloss left a sticky residue on his stubble. His wife seemed big on showmanship tonight. "Safe drive home! Ava, say bye to your father and come inside. I got your present in the house."

They watched Mei open the door and slip inside. For a moment Paul and Ava stared at the house in silence. Elegant and charming, a product of Mei's planning. Surrounded by bright green lawns, well-attended gardens, and willow trees, the house possessed a bucolic allure. Though the same size as its neighbors, the Magee house stood apart. A pale yellow coated its exterior, and white outlined every detailed archway and border. Cheerful, grand, enviable. You wouldn't easily imagine the formidable vastness of its insides, the empty spaces, the dark corners that needed regular dusting. Or the backyard pool with a tendency of collecting algae. The roof was a slate grey. A turret with a round balcony extended from the third floor, the uppermost floor, where Ava's room resided. If you stared at the turret long enough, it looked grafted onto the rest of the house, like the architect added the protrusion at the last minute.

"She's a charmer, isn't she?" Paul said, more to himself than Ava.

She didn't respond. He shifted in his seat. Body mirroring builds rapport. But her hands hovered by her lap, fiddling with her phone. The gearshift divided them. He reached over, across it, to place a hand on her arm. She drew back like he'd scalded her.

He waited for an explanation, but she gave him none. Back to her phone. Did she hate him that much? Had his wife convinced her to do so? Maybe she hadn't needed to. Maybe the bonds between mother and daughter were that strong. Or . . . maybe he'd become more like his father than he'd hoped.

"Listen . . . ," he began. "I didn't get you a present, like you requested." He watched her closely for signs of disappointment, but she seemed to be relieved. "But I want to show you something. Sometime soon. As I said before, you're an adult now." He needed to stop seeing her as a child. "You'll be able to vote next Tuesday. You deserve to know things. About the family. Before you were born. About . . . about your mother's past, her childhood. I know . . . I know I've made mis—"

Ava's phone burst to life, crazily vibrating. She swiped the screen to pick up the call.

Mei's voice invaded the stillness. "Ava dear, let your father go." She sounded shrill. Wine either made her testy or tired. "He's busy and I want you to have your present."

"I'm coming in now." She hung up. For the first time that night, she looked at him. Still not meeting his eyes, but at least not looking past his shoulder or at his forehead.

"Are you memorizing my features for a sketch?" he joked.

"You look tired."

"I-I am. Ava—"

"I've got to go. Bye Dad," she said, hurrying out of the car.

"Bye. Happy—" His daughter shut the door before he finished.

Paul caught a glimpse of himself in the windshield's reflection. Grey hairs had cropped up in his short auburn hair. The frown lines between his eyebrows forever stood at attention. He didn't look tired. He looked haggard.

He refocused, just in time to watch Ava walk to the house he'd never considered a home. His daughter never looked back. But Paul recognized the vulnerable look in her eyes when she left. Helplessly, he thought of that rainy day in September of '96, back before the promotion, before 88 Pine Drive. Back when they lived in the townhouse. Unit 892, Magnolia Street.

He hadn't known it, but inside, in a small broom cupboard, his two-year-old girl hid, desperately hugging her sides. Paul of 2012 closed his eyes, unable to avoid recalling the confrontation.

"Mei sweetie? I'm home! Ava? Where's my doll? I've got a surprise for you!" he had called, fingering the package of gummy worms he had picked up on the way back from the office. Ava's favorite candy, a rare treat she enjoyed when his wife let her.

Mei came down the hallway, her red silk slippers pitter-pattering on the linoleum floor. "No surprises," she said, shaking her head so vigorously that her glistening hair hit her face. "She's *bad*."

He reached out, aiming to sweep the hair away from her line of vision. She slapped away his hand.

Paul frowned. "What do you mean?" He dropped the hand to his side, his other hand still holding his briefcase.

"She played with toilet water, so I had to punish her." Mei flexed the belt in her hands. The subtle movement attracted Paul's attention.

He looked down and noticed that she held a belt he'd never seen before. It looked . . . like a snake? Yes, no mistake. It had a metal head shaped like a snake's. Engraved, fierce eyes and a semi-open mouth completed the likeness. The body of the belt, curled in braided, thick brown leather; the rattlesnake tail forged of metal.

"What *is* that?" Paul couldn't picture his wife wearing that hideous belt.

"The one heirloom the Red Guards didn't find. Ma forgot she'd buried it under the patch of grass by our house. I used it to make Ava remember never to play with the toilet again."

"What? What do you mean?" Paul asked, confused.

"What that white saying? 'Spare the whip, spoil the child'? *Bu da bu cheng cai*."

"Do you . . . you mean to say that you used that *thing* on our *child*?" Paul released his briefcase onto the floor in shock. Out of the corner of his eye, he spotted his little girl. Ava and her Raggedy Ann doll peeked from behind a wall.

"I raise her like children must be. *Bai ban shun cong*. She must learn her place," Mei said, unfazed. "You know Confucian law. Children respect parents; she need be disciplined early."

Ignoring his wife, Paul looked at his daughter and quietly beckoned. "Ava honey, come here."

With a tremulous smile, she tottered over to him, keeping to the wall to stay further away from the belt. The back of the hand that clutched her red-headed doll swelled red.

"Ava, could you show me? Like this." He held his hand out, palm down. "You did this with that belt?" he asked, keeping his voice in check as he bent to examine his daughter's hand.

"I will show you," Mei insisted.

She seemed unable to understand why he couldn't understand. Sure, in China this might be accepted, in some cases common practice. East and West didn't always agree on what was right or legally actionable. But he couldn't fathom why she showed no agony over what she'd done.

Before he could stop her, Mei grabbed Ava's raw hand. She propelled her to the bathroom, passing through the brightly lit kitchen.

"Do it. Again! Show him!" His wife threw their daughter's hand in the direction of the white toilet seat.

"Stop this. This is crazy!" Paul looked on in horror.

"She must be taught. I teach. That's what parents for. If you were a *real* father—real man—you help."

Shock took any rebuttal from him.

Ava cringed and shrunk back, looking from the snake-headed belt to the cold ceramic toilet. In a fit of anger, his wife yanked their daughter's right hand into the bowl, splashing it around twice before withdrawing.

"See? Dirty! Don't touch, what I tell you?" Mei took the braided part of the belt and whipped it across Ava's hand. It made a resounding snap. Ava cried out.

"You want to cry? I can make you something to cry for!"

Paul lunged for his daughter. The belt whistled through the air before hitting his back. He stood up, sheltering Ava behind his knees.

"Stop it!" he yelled, feeling blood rush to his face. "*Shen jing bing*! Mei, you're acting crazy; she's two for Christ's sake."

He thought that the use of her mother tongue would help her remember to be a mother. Tearing the belt away from his wife, he stormed out of the bathroom. He didn't care if the emperor himself had passed that heirloom down to Mei. It belonged in the garbage can, along with such childrearing techniques. Paul threw it away in the kitchen.

"Now who crazy?" Mei shot back. "You're overreacting. I'm a good mother; toilet water's dirty! She put her hand there after I told her no. Paul! Why do that? That belt's an heirloom."

She lunged for the garbage can, but he blocked her. When she tried to push past him, he gently grasped his wife by her elbows. She pierced him with her black eyes.

"Mei, she's *two*. Of course she's not going to remember what you tell her; that's part of being a toddler! Don't you think this too extreme? Her hand's swollen and red. And . . . and *look* at her. You've obviously scared her! Why? I don't understand your . . . "

Little Ava silently watched them argue from the now darkened bathroom. She picked up Raggedy Ann, haphazardly dropped in the shuffle. As she bit her lip, her grey blue eyes filled with tears. But they refrained from spilling over.

Paul slowly shook his head, half-startled to find himself in his car. He returned to the present, but couldn't stop himself from thinking about the past. He felt like a boy again, rebuffed by Major Magee. *Outta my sight, boy. Take your figurines; I don't have time for games. For stupid sons playing at war. You disappoint me.* What time was it in Seattle? No, he didn't need his mother's assurance. You're a man. A grown man.

You're afraid. Of questions, of flaws, of yourself, of your family—that's why you trust. He shut the errant thoughts out. No. Mei had listened to him and never hurt their daughter again. He'd even made his wife promise by their son. Their loss made Ava more precious. If anyone doesn't fit in this family, it's you. Do you even have a right to watch from the sidelines? Admit it. You aren't needed—or wanted. Blinking back tears, he started his Prius and drove away.

Back at 88 Pine Drive, Mei continued berating Ava.

"You can't take my hint. So I got you a gift card to Sephora. No one's ever going to think you're pretty if you don't makeup. And your dad wired money into your bank."

"Thanks," Ava said, keeping all traces of irony out of her voice.

"Now upstairs, come to my study. You've got work doing for me. And don't be up the stairs slow. *Fen miao bi zheng*. No seconds to be wasted. Don't listen to your father. Just because it's your birthday not mean I can't be your mother. You still a child. *My* child." Mei momentarily paused on the stairs. "I brought you in this world. I can take you out."

This had become a sleeping threat. Ava heard it as often as most children hear mothers express maternal love. And with increased frequency after turning sixteen. So of course she felt no fear.

Mei woke her computer from its sleep and pulled up her blog. Chinese characters appeared, along with a pictorial depiction of what looked like an abdominal workout. In each photo, her mother demonstrated, imitating a model.

"Fix this," she said, tapping the screen.

"Fix what?" Ava asked, unsure of the glitch Mei referred to. The background of the blog remained pale yellow and the characters black, as always.

"*Taoyangui*. Look here! This shows just a link. I need the video to show on the blog. Fix it."

"You mean you want the video to be embedded?"

She stood next to her mother, who restlessly sat in a roller chair. She went to Google for the answer then returned to the blog.

"Whatever you call it, do it." Mei poked Ava's side, causing her to flinch. "No man will ever want you." She shook her head. "Ugly, fat, *and* stupid."

Ava blinked and bit the tip of her tongue between her teeth. She knew the latter insults weren't true, but no one ever called her beautiful. Unique, skinny, gifted, sure. But not beautiful. Everyone thought her mother beautiful, even at fifty-two.

"I fixed it." She clicked back to Mei's homepage to show that she'd embedded the exercise video below the pictures.

"About time. Now leave me alone. I meet you downstairs in a moment."

When Ava reached the front door, car keys in her fist, Mei grabbed her arm.

"Your gift card." Mei handed her the Sephora bag. "Makeup. You need it. No man wants an invisible woman, let alone the ghost girl you are. It's a shame you took to your father. I couldn't make you look like me if I tried. But you don't fit for him, too. Mongrel girl. You'll never be desired—not like me—but some makeup better than nothing."

Ava barely contained herself as she seized the bag and scampered out, nearly catching the top of her white cowl-neck sweater on the door. So much for being an adult. Where's your rebellious, fighting spirit? Suppress it. Forget it. You need breathing space. Just get out. Back to college, what she'd imagined would be the panacea to her troubles. This had yet to be the case. Still, Davison at least gave her the illusion of freedom. A place a safe thirty minutes away from home. Home? No—the prison with modern amenities.

By the time she got back to Lockhart, it was 9:30 p.m. She still needed to do homework, so she didn't even have time to enjoy the only birthday present that mattered: *Part Asian, 100% Hapa*.

"Did you have a nice time?" Charlotte asked.

"No," she revealed without thinking, dropping the hateful Sephora bag onto her desk.

"No? What happened?" Charlotte turned off Comedy Central and sat up in her bed.

"Sorry, knee-jerk answer. Repeat your question?" Ava composed her face before turning around.

"Whether or not you had a nice time at dinner."

She smiled, hoping it didn't look strained. "Of course I did." She sat down and turned on her laptop.

"Why was 'no' your knee-jerk reaction?" Charlotte rolled onto her stomach. Digging her elbows into her bed, she propped her head on her hands and stared at Ava's back.

"Stop staring at me; I feel your eyes." Ava laughed but refrained from turning around. She might crack and start yelling about how ugly her mother made her feel. "And I said 'no' to my mother all night. She kept . . . kept trying to feed me long after I finished eating."

Charlotte laughed. "Oh yeah, Mom does that to me all the time. Guess Mei took a page out of the Italian mom book."

Ava had neither the time nor inclination to explain to Charlotte that food giving was also a prevalent part of Asian culture. So she completed her schoolwork and Charlotte went back to watching *South Park*.

Halloween took place on the following night. Charlotte had gone home, so after Ava finished class, she returned to an empty room. Kevin went over to Jason's dorm to watch horror movies for the night, but Ava had enough nightmares of her own.

When she'd finished her homework for the rest of the week, the clock read 10:05 p.m. For once, she admitted to herself that she didn't want to be alone. She left her room and knocked on Derek's door—why bother texting when he was four feet across the hall? But no answer. Maybe he'd already gone out. What about texting Julia? No. It seemed like she always partied.

Ava tried to open her door and then realized her mistake. In her impulsive desire for company, she'd forgotten to take her key; the door automatically locked when she closed it. "Crap," she muttered. She'd have to bother Dan, her RA. And on the last day of October, too; no one was foolish enough to get locked out anymore.

Swallowing her shame, she walked to the only single room on the first floor. To her relief, she saw that he'd written "The doctor's IN" on the whiteboard attached to his door. She hesitated for a moment and then knocked. "Come in!" she heard.

Twisting the knob and peeking into his room, Ava found that she only recognized Dan from the neck up. He hadn't yet put on his mask, but a full-body Spiderman costume engulfed the rest of him. She entered in time to catch him struggling with the costume's back zipper.

"Um . . . let me help." She zipped him up easily.

"Thanks!" Dan turned, pushing his dirty-blond hair out of his brown eyes. "Ah, it's Ava with the unexpected assist."

"Right. Sorry to bother you, but I . . . I managed to lock myself out. Stupid, I know."

"Nah, no worries. That's easily fixable. Let me get my key and the one that'll open yours. I don't want to make your problem mine."

As they left the room, Ava couldn't help but notice the Marvel Comic posters that covered his walls. She smiled to herself, comforted that his walls weren't plastered with posters of scantily clad women, which she'd heard adorned many of the male dorm rooms on campus.

"So what are you up to for Halloween?"

She tried to hide her embarrassment with an apathetic sigh. "Nothing, actually. My friends are busy doing things that I can't or don't want to do."

"What?" Dan unlocked and opened her door. "We can't let your first Halloween at Davison suck!"

Walking past him, she shrugged. "There's nothing I can do about it. And I don't even have a costume," Ava said, taking a seat on her bed. Looking at him in the doorway, she decided that he made a nice-looking Spiderman.

"Actually . . . I think that can be solved. One of my frat brothers is throwing a party tonight—it hasn't even started yet—and my date just backed out on me. Wanna come?"

"What about the no costume problem?"

Dan grinned, looking boyish. "Got you covered. I just happen to have the costume my date was supposed to wear. I'd bet money you're her size."

An hour and a half later Ava found herself in black ears, a mask, and a cat suit at a frat house with her RA. Why's this suit so abrasive, right up against . . . ignore it. Blend, act natural. Make yourself fit. Fit? You can dress up like the rest, but you'll never be like them. All these costumed strangers . . . so stifling. Shut up! Watch, imitate. Pretend to belong. So while Dan talked to one of his fraternity brothers, she went to get a drink, completely forgetting that he could get her into trouble if he wanted to.

She peered down at the reddish liquid in her Solo cup. During her outings with Julia and the guys, she'd always abstained. But now . . . now she wanted to try the infamous jungle juice. Cheers, Derek, wherever you are. She took a huge gulp. Yuck! Too bad. It's what you wanted, isn't it? You can't complain. Force it down your throat.

"Easy there, soldier," Dan said, appearing next to her.

"I'm sorry, I just wanted to taste it, I swear I—"

He laughed. "Relax, I'm not going to rat you out. I'm off duty. Tonight we're just friends. I happen to be a bit older than you, that's all. Wanna dance?"

She'd wanted to "loosen up and live a little," right? What a perfect opportunity. She downed her drink and followed Dan into the living room. It warmed her insides. With her mask and costume on, she could be anybody, not someone composed of and limited by fractions. Fifty percent of her mother. Fifty percent of her father. Forever between two cultures. Ninety percent student, ten percent drunk. No, tonight she was any college girl, every college girl.

The night wore on. Ava and Dan drank and danced more. When they tired of both, they went upstairs, searching for a quiet space.

With a tipsy giggle, she pointed at his mask. "Aren't you hot under there?"

"Fuck yeah." Dan pulled off his Spiderman face and collapsed onto a sagging couch, prostrate. "God, those slits don't do shit. Can barely breathe under there!"

Ava whipped away her eye mask and took her cat ear headband off. She put them on a nearby table before sitting near him on the couch.

"Either your ex has a small head, or I've got a big one." She touched the tender spots behind her ears, where the headband had mercilessly gripped her.

He sat up and looked at her strangely, like he'd never seen her before. "What? Oh, I guess the manufacturer made them one-size-fits all."

"There something on my face?" She touched her eyes and then remembered that she'd elected not to put any makeup on, just to spite her mother.

He moved next to her and took off his red-and-black gloves, tossing them in the direction he'd thrown his mask. Dan began massaging the skin behind her ears. "Does it feel better now?"

"Whoa yeah." Ava closed her eyes. She felt him staring at her and shied from his gaze.

"You know," Dan said softly, "you're really pretty."

She snorted, opening her eyes. "We're drunk and your ex decided against getting back with you. Of course you'll say that."

They laughed.

"You're only half right, you know." He fingered some of the shorter layers of her reddish brown hair. "You've always been pretty to me."

Mei's voice echoed in Ava's head. *Ghost girl . . . couldn't make you look like me . . . you don't fit . . . mongrel . . . no man will ever want you*. Shaking her head, she let the alcohol take over. Her grey eyes boldly met Dan's. "Do you really mean it?"

He firmly kissed her in response, and pulled back to see her reaction.

"Do you want me?" she asked, staring at him.

"Isn't it obvious?" When it seemed that Ava wanted the words, Dan said them. "Hell yes."

She rose and went to the door, but instead of leaving, she closed and locked it. Ava walked back and sat next to him. "Then show me."

And for the first time, she felt—

Wholly desired.

Chapter Nine

Three days after Ava cast her first vote in a presidential election, she was researching for Professor Chen.

"You've got to be kidding me," she muttered under her breath. The printer in the comparative literature department had seized up. "System error," she read from the printer's screen. "Scanned documents lost. Please try again," it helpfully instructed. She'd have to spend yet another twenty minutes scanning the chapters Professor Chen needed. Ava usually handled the temperamental printer with aplomb, but the phone conversation she'd had with her mother the night before rattled her.

"Dare you call back so late," Mei had hissed.

"Class ended late," Ava explained, motioning for Derek to walk back to Lockhart without her. They'd just left Professor Chen's class.

"Shut up. All you say is excuses." Then, seeming to remember how she opened every phone conversation, Mei said in Mandarin, "You alone?"

"Not really. I'm heading back to Lockhart. There are lots of other students walking beside me."

Mei switched to the motherly voice she reserved for occasions like these. "English question from the T.V. What does 'p-a-n-a-c-e-a' mean?"

"P-a-n-a . . . oh, panacea. Cure-all." Without thinking, she asked, "Couldn't you have looked that up?" Mei owned an orange, bulky Chinese-English dictionary that Ava often flipped through for her. Mei kept it in the basement with the rest of the books she had brought from China.

Mei sucked in her breath and let out a stream of Chinese curses. "Who you think you are? I'm your goddamn mother. I owe you zero. You don't know shit, what I been through. You owe me your whole life. *Cao ni ma*!"

Ava heard that last curse enough times during her pseudo piano career that she'd asked a Chinese friend to translate: "fuck your mom." She shook her head and swiped into her dorm. Again, no way to contain herself. "You know that's an insult to you, right?"

For a couple of beats the sound of silence pervaded. Ava checked her touchscreen; her mother remained on the line.

She opened her mouth to apologize when Mei raked her nails into an old wound.

"*Cao ni ba*, then. You prefer to fuck your father."

Caught up in replaying last night's grisly phone conversation, Ava nearly attempted to scan the back cover of Professor Chen's library book. Blinking, she tried to focus on mechanical action. She sent the scanned documents over to Professor Chen's office computer and took the book off the platen. When she made it back to the room, she slumped into the desk chair, letting each limb slacken until she felt like a rag doll. Then she shut her eyes.

She wanted to imagine a different life, one in which her mother didn't strike with words. Didn't strike where it hurt most. She thought back to the last time she'd really spoken to her father. She'd been seven years old; Mei left the townhouse for a PTA meeting.

Young Ava cried into her sleeve. She had been teased at school again, during lunch. Always by girls, in front of other students. This time a girl with Barbie-blonde hair made up a stupid song, with gestures, and Ava now let it hurt her.

"Chinese baby," the girl sang, pulling the corners of her eyes up, turning them into slits. "White baby," she pulled the corners down. "Mixed baby, mixed baby," she pulled one corner up and the other corner down, and then switched directions, giggling gleefully over her un-crusted peanut butter and jelly sandwich.

Ava had eaten her stir-fried rice in silence, pretending to ignore the girl's taunts. Why had her mother packed her Chinese food for lunch?

Paul walked by her room but returned when he heard stifled sniffling. He walked in to find her crying in shudders. She was curled up on her side, facing the wall, hardly taking up any space on her bed.

"Ava sweetie, what's wrong?" He sat down to rub her back.

"D-dad-dy. I-I'm a . . . *freak*." Face streaked with tears and snot, she couldn't look at her father, so she continued to stare at the yellow wall. How she hated the color, how she hated the fact that she hated yellow because of the bullies at school.

"What? That's not true. Who told you that?"

"B-Beatrice, from school. Because I'm m-mixed." Ava's sob erupted into a wail.

"Come here." Paul gathered her into a light hug. Pulling her back to wipe the tears from her red face, he smiled.

She looked up into her father's eyes. They shared those eyes.

"You know something? She's got the green envy monster. You were born special, and she wants to be special too. I love you. Don't listen to those mean people, okay? Being mixed like you is a privilege. You know what?"

"W-what?"

"If we were in China right now, you'd be adored. The Chinese like the Chinese, of course, but they find Western culture fascinating. You're the best combination of both East and West. America is supposed to celebrate such diversity; your mean classmate's an exception. And how many people can have soda bread and fried noodles anytime they want? Love who you are. *I* love who you are, and I always will," Paul said, folding her into another hug.

Eighteen-year-old Ava blinked back tears. Her father had been her superhero. But then he'd left. And you'd helped him. You wanted to isolate yourself, didn't you? It's like you wanted to suffer. No, not "like." *Masochist*. She cleared her throat and moved on, shaking the computer mouse to get rid of the screen saver. Pulling up the documents on the computer, she noticed that she'd scanned a page Professor Chen didn't need. Ava nearly deleted it, but then the poem's title caught her eye. She began to read.

P.S. from an ABC daughter to her Immigrant Mother

Mother's tongue used to fork into me like an adder's.
It's 'cause we've got different mother tongues
and they're born from opposing cultures that
Wrested me from your China-first bosom, East versus
West of here you won't rest in peace, still haunt me
Grave, still hate my American *pengyoumen*, style, accent
When I try to piece together my broken Chinese . . .
How can I hate you dead? We never saw face to
Face it! Can I own my mistakes on the first anniversary
of the day you turned your back on me for the last time?
(Probably should've kept the bisexual thing a secret.)
I'm just a rebellious teenage daughter
didn't mean you no harm.
Stroke took you too soon but
I like to think you're happy, chillin'
with that Confucius man I never did understand.
I still don't understand you though you
won't leave my head
Alone I remember that unseen love united us
and I'm sorry it all went unsaid.

—Anonymous

"Ava? Ava?"

She tore her eyes away from the poem, which she had read three times, especially lingering over the line with the phrase "you won't leave my head." Ava found Professor Chen looking at her with concern.

"You look like you need a coffee break. And so do I. All this paper grading is getting to me." Professor Chen opened a desk drawer and pulled out two mugs. "It's five thirty; everyone's left. Come on, we can take over the lunchroom."

Getting up stiffly, Ava followed Professor Chen's colorful braid to the lunchroom. The clicking of her kitten heels on the scuffed tan linoleum chipped at the building's silence.

"Did I ever tell you about my parents?" Professor Chen asked after the machine began brewing fresh coffee. She plopped herself into the poorly padded chair closest to her.

Ava shook her head. She'd always found Professor Chen fascinating, but never dared to ask her personal questions. Until now, their research sessions had been strictly academic. They'd talked about Professor Chen's manuscript, Asian American literature, or Davison.

"They're dead," Professor Chen said simply.

"I'm . . . I'm so sorry." Her neutral tone made Ava unsure how else to react.

"Thanks."

Professor Chen got up and turned off the coffeemaker, which had finished brewing. She carefully filled their mugs and brought them over to the table.

"It's been a while. My brother and I made peace with their deaths." She paused to take a sip of coffee. "My dad died in a car accident coming back from work. I was nine and my brother six."

Ava sipped her coffee and stayed silent.

Professor Chen smiled wistfully. "My first name is Li zhi. In China, parents choose meaningful first names. They hope that a child will grow up to embody his or her name. My dad named me. 'Li' means 'clever,' and 'zhi' means 'knowledge.' It's like he knew I'd end up in academia."

Ava smiled.

"When he died, I had to help my mom run the Chinese restaurant my dad left behind. Without Dad, no one refereed our arguments. My brother couldn't do anything except hug Mom's leg; he'd always been her favorite child." Professor Chen drank more of her coffee. "But I guess that's not really relevant. You know that volume you were scanning for me?"

"Yes?"

"A friend of mine is the editor. That poem you read . . . I wrote it, years ago."

Ava cupped her mug, savoring the warmth of the coffee. Professor Chen's face became impassive. They sat silently for a couple of minutes. Finally Ava asked, "What's an ABC?"

Professor Chen cleared her throat. "An American Born Chinese."

"Your poem . . . I found it really moving."

Professor Chen wrinkled her nose in disagreement. "I'm lucky that I got involved in poetry after Mom's death. Poetry saved me from the things I almost got into."

"'I still don't understand you though you won't leave my head,'" Ava quoted softly. "That's . . . "

Professor Chen looked down at her mug. "Sometimes," she said carefully, "it's easier to exchange troubles than to reveal them by yourself."

She made no demands. Only a suggestion.

"That's exactly how I feel about my mother." Ava stared at the water cooler on the other side of the table. "When I was a child, she disciplined through force. It's not that bad anymore, but she's always trying to control and monitor me. I thought college would be my chance to run from her, to leave her behind. But she's found ways to follow me. It's only November and she's already made me go home six times, to clean and do things for her. Harassing me on the phone, daily. Ambushing me at school. I can't get away. Now my hopes are fixed on post-graduation. I can always go to Seattle, where my dad's family lives."

She shifted her gaze to her hands, gripping the mug until her skin grew taut. "But is physical distance ever enough? She's in my dreams, my head. The perpetual bad taste in my mind. That voice, so demeaning, repeating all the things she's said. I'm ugly, stupid, unwanted, a half-breed. An abomination. Rejected or ignored by both sides. That I don't count as Asian . . . or anything else. The worst part . . . sometimes I believe it all. That I'm nobody. Because I'm only half good enough. I'll always be an in-between. Maybe I deserve every curse, every . . . slap."

Ava continued absently looking at her hands. She lowered her voice so that Professor Chen needed to lean forward to hear.

"And I know, somehow I know . . . that she doesn't love me. I think she hurts me because I-I'm everything she's not. I don't think she loves my father either. Maybe she forgot how to love . . . she doesn't seem capable of loving. But still, still . . . part of me hopes to redeem her, to find something to salvage. If not now, then in the future." Ava chuckled darkly. "It's the part that hasn't grown up. Sometimes I'm still a little girl. Always, I strive for approval. Love can be too much. I get that. But can't she appreciate that I'm trying? Trying to be worth bragging about, at least. Surely she can see something in me worth claiming. Something in me that's worthwhile."

Professor Chen blinked away the tears in her eyes. "I'm sorry you feel that way. You shouldn't. No one's perfect. Your mother shouldn't hold you to impossible standards. But you can't control her. Every life is valuable. I'm not saying this as your professor. As a friend, I'm telling you—*you* are valuable. Unfortunately, only you can change how you measure yourself." She shifted in her seat to give her a loose hug.

Apologetically, Ava shook her head, leaning back in her chair, out of reach.

"I've never . . . I've never told anyone this before. Everyone who meets her loves her. Even if I wanted to tell, no one would believe me. She won the Mrs. New Jersey crown. She volunteers for an animal shelter. Even my best friend thinks she's perfect. You won't tell anyone, will you? Please don't." She focused on the floor. "I'm not ready," she whispered.

"You need to deal with her on your own. *Wo mingbai.* I understand."

Chapter Ten

Charlotte opened the door to find Ava on her laptop, furiously typing away.

"Hey," Ava said, eyes trained on her screen.

"What's up?" Charlotte asked, moving in to peer over her shoulder.

"Just finishing up this seven-page paper so I'll be able to party tomorrow."

"When did you start writing it?"

"This morning." Ava continued to type, only pausing to look up a quote in her poetry book.

"You're insane. Don't you have three classes on Thursdays?"

"Yup. I took notes on scrap paper in between my earlier classes and wrote most of it during the chunk of time before Asian American Literature."

"You know, normal people write papers over a longer period of time."

"I'm not normal. Never was, and never will be."

"Oh please. You enjoy being different," Charlotte said, sitting down on Ava's bed.

"There! Done." She hit save. "When you're automatically marked as different, you learn to deal with it. You try, anyway."

"Wanna paint nails?" Charlotte asked, getting out her nail kit from one of her desk drawers.

"Sure." Both girls set up paper towels on Ava's bed before settling down.

"Are you talking about being a Whasian?"

"No, I'm talking about being an *Amerasian*."

"Same diff.," Charlotte replied.

"There *is* a difference."

Charlotte stuck out her tongue. "Whatev."

Ava evaded racial discussions in high school. But in college, race became a bigger deal. It mattered in ways that it hadn't before. People of all backgrounds felt and acknowledged race's presence. Students and professors discussed it in and out of class. There were clubs for different groups and a sense of community for students with a whole ethnicity.

Refusing to be goaded further, Ava picked up a sparkly white nail polish. Take that, Mother. The Chinese considered white a cursed color, so she'd use it well.

"So how have things been so different for you, Ms. Downtrodden?"

"I feel like it's worse when you're racially mixed. For instance, Asians ask me why I'm tall, why I'm outgoing. But non-Asians ask why I'm short and introverted. I'm cursed, unable to fit anywhere."

"Red, pink, or green?" Charlotte asked, holding up the bottles.

"Red, definitely."

Charlotte shook the red bottle. "What do you mean, you 'don't fit'? Like you don't fit in? Fitting in is overrated."

"You know." But Ava supposed Charlotte didn't. The white students in Professor Chen's class sure were unaware. "In a group or nation. In a category. We love to categorize, and I think what makes some people uncomfortable is the fact that I belong in more than one category. It throws people off balance." She began to carefully coat her nails.

"So like 'Asian' versus 'White,' or something like that?" Charlotte asked.

"Exactly. It's far simpler to generalize. Because I'm 'only half,' I'm not Asian enough for Asians. To them, I'm practically blonde. If I contest their view, then their concession is to call me 'Asianish' or 'the halfie.'"

"And people who aren't Asian? What do they say, when they know you're mixed?"

"They label me as Asian. No other questions or complications. I'm never given a choice. I get reduced to one race." She reached for the word Professor Chen recently taught them. "Have you heard of the term 'hypodescent'?"

"Hypo-what? Did I miss that one on the SATs?"

Ava laughed. "I just learned it. It's also called the 'one-drop rule.'"

"One drop of what?"

"Blood, actually," she said, nodding at Charlotte's red nail polish. "In Virginia, at the beginning of the nineteenth century, people with 'one drop' of African blood were considered entirely African. By law. Whether or not you looked white didn't matter." Your blood did you in, stained you with indelible ink, and every ancestor counted.

"That's . . . really racist."

"We've come a long way since then, at least with laws," Ava conceded.

"Jason's always citing Obama's reelection as proof," Charlotte agreed.

Ava moved on to paint her remaining bare nails. "We're even more 'politically correct.'"

"I'm not so sure I buy that. Too many people are free with the 'n' word."

"True. Let me amend that statement. Most people *try* to be tactful. But I think the bigger issue now is implicit racism. People don't believe in it, or they pretend it doesn't exist."

Charlotte shrugged. "Okay, but we can't do anything about it."

She stopped painting a nail and stared at Charlotte. "Since when have you become so cynical?"

"I'm not cynical. I'm realistic. And why does it matter to you? You could tell everyone that you're white and they'd believe you."

Ava looked at Charlotte uncertainly. "What's gotten into you?"

"Nothing," she said lightly, blowing on her finished nails. "Just playing devil's advocate. I learned from Jason."

"Apparently." Ava closed her nail polish bottle and put it next to Charlotte's. "Let me tell you something I've only admitted to Professor Chen."

Charlotte raised her eyebrows expectantly.

"I'm—I used to be ashamed of my Chinese side. Taking her class helped me recognize my . . . self-hatred. I internalized white disdain for Asians. You don't know what it feels like . . . hating part of yourself, especially when it's the part you don't understand."

Charlotte frowned at Ava's profile. "But there are things—feelings—*you* don't know."

Guilt flushed through Ava. She quieted for a moment.

"I'm sorry. You're right; everyone has burdens to shoulder." She brought her knees up to her chest. Resting her chin on her knees, Ava stared at her ivory comforter.

"It's just . . . somehow I've grown to think like the people who judge me. I've got this shadowed side. This foreign half. It's alien. I don't know Chinese. I've never been to China. My mother's an immigrant, but she's so far removed from the China she grew up in. I don't know anything about her family. It's a taboo subject, so I can't even ask. Because I've been raised without knowing, without strong ties to her side . . . it's hard to associate with it."

"But what about Asian Americans?"

Ava shrugged. "What about them?"

"Where do you see them on the 'fitting-in' spectrum? Remember reading Amy Tan's 'Mother Tongue'?"

"I do . . . I'm sure we share many of the same feelings. Uncertainty, friction. Estrangement."

"But?"

"But we still endure different experiences. I think . . . I think Asian Americans live in the in-between. I *am* the in-between."

For a moment they sat in silence. Then Charlotte looked up suddenly.

"Remember . . . remember when we first met the guys?" asked Charlotte.

"Sure."

"The bitchy Asian girl. When she asked you during move-in day, did you tell her you were white?"

"Rice cracker girl?" Ava scowled. "I . . . basically. Yes. She'd just kept asking and asking. And she looked so complacent, so sure that she already knew the answer."

"Ugh. Hate people like that."

"I just wanted to move in. But she'd seen my full name, *had* to confirm her suspicions. So I told her the opposite of what she expected. I don't like being treated like a puzzle."

"Who does? But how'd she find out the truth? Or did she not believe you?"

"I don't know if she believed. She seemed skeptical. But then my parents walked in, and Mother addressed her in Mandarin."

They laughed.

Ava's phone buzzed. A reminder: "10pm WebReg!" "Wait, we need to register for next semester!"

"Shit! To the computers," Charlotte commanded. They had five minutes until registration opened to them. Each went to her respective laptop to pull up schedule wish lists.

Fifteen minutes later, they'd registered for the classes they wanted or needed for the spring semester. Ava especially looked forward to the identity class Professor Chen had suggested to her: U.S. Latino/a Literature in English. Jason also registered for it, so she'd have company.

"Alright, now that we've managed to live through that, I'm going to do more work."

"Sounds like a plan," Charlotte said. "I'd better get my work done too so I can go with you guys tomorrow night."

"You're . . . you're coming?"

"Yeah, you mind?"

"No, just thought you didn't like partying. You don't approve of the griminess."

"I want to give it another chance," Charlotte said, looking down.

Charlotte always looked at her feet when she lied. Ava just shrugged. She'd probably back out anyway.

But the next night Charlotte got ready with her.

"That's all you're doing?" Ava asked, pointing to Charlotte's light pink lipstick.

"Yup. Minimalist." She left their full-length mirror and went back to her bed, attending to her iPhone.

"Okay, suit yourself." Ava shrugged, giving herself a once over.

She didn't recognize the girl who stared back. This pleased her. Her auburn hair was half up, half down, and she had curled it to make large waves. As Julia had taught her, she'd applied eyeliner and mascara. Ava's glittery silver eye shadow matched her silver halter-top and metallic black jeans. She used to make fun of the people who made themselves up and partied during the weekends. But now she understood why. It became a masquerade. You weren't limited by your doubts or fears. Ava slipped her phone into her back pocket.

"Julie's outside. You ready to go?"

Charlotte nodded and they headed out.

"Look Julie," Ava said, pointing to her own and Charlotte's feet, "we traded shoe styles."

Julia giggled. Ava wore the heeled boots she'd bought with her birthday money; Charlotte wore flats.

"It's about time," Julia said, jovially elbowing her sister in the ribs.

Charlotte let out a quiet groan.

Julia and Ava settled on the third party they stumbled upon, a fraternity house. Once inside, Julia and Ava headed over to the bar for drinks, as they'd done at the previous two places. She knew Charlotte watched her every move, but she told herself she didn't care. Remember, on party nights, you're limitless.

Ava handed Charlotte a red Solo cup.

"I'm not going to drink it."

"I know, and I'm not going to make you." Ava lowered her voice. "Just pretend."

"Where are you going?"

"Back to the bar for something harder." She left before Charlotte protested.

Julia and Ava each accepted a lime and a shot of clear liquid. She glanced back at Charlotte, who stared intensely at the saltshaker. Ava smiled to herself. She probably thought it was cocaine.

A couple of guys stopped drinking their beers and nudged their friends.

"Tequila shots, baby!" one of them yelled.

"Girl on girl action, holla!"

Charlotte took a step forward, but an eager freshman boy blocked her way. Ava waved at her, knowing she'd be forced to watch the spectacle from the outskirts of the small, mostly male crowd.

Ava sat on a bar stool and bent her back over the edge of the bar. She put a slice of lime between her lips and tilted her head. Julia leaned down and licked the hollow of her exposed neck. A guy wolf-whistled. Ava laughed to herself. Julia sprinkled salt onto the spot she had licked. She licked the salt and then threw back her shot of tequila. Dipping down for the last time, Julia kissed the lime out of Ava's mouth. The guys shouted their approval.

Ava swapped places and downed her own shot with the help of Julia's neck. When they finished, they joined hands and bowed. Getting into the spirit, the crowd clapped. "Encore!" someone yelled. She and Julia turned to each other: why not? Ava liked this game. Theater. No. More like method acting. In makeup and costume, with liquid courage, she could get lost. Anonymous in the best way. Because she *chose* to be.

See? She wanted to tell Charlotte as she made out with someone new. It didn't mean anything, and yet it meant everything, all at once. She'd never see these people again, or at least out of this context. In the light of day, even if they did recognize each other, they wouldn't remember from where. Just a dance. Just saliva swapping. It'd end, it'd be forgotten, written over. But in the moment, everything became fine. She told herself that, and believed it.

The dark-haired guy she'd been dancing with left her. Alone, but surely not for long, she swayed by herself. He returned with a drink in hand. But just one. He held it out: what are you waiting for, can't you see this is for you? Ava took it. But you didn't . . . you didn't see him . . . you don't know what's in it. Shaking her head, she put down the drink on a nearby table.

He leaned down, breath hot in her ear. "It's a gin and tonic with a twist." He stroked her hair. "My buddy made it special for you."

"That's . . . that's nice. But see, I don't want another. Three's enough."

He took her hand, apparently about to lead her somewhere else.

Charlotte appeared from nowhere. "Sorry, she's with me, and like hell she's going anywhere with you!" Taking advantage of her height and his lack thereof, she glowered down at him.

"Wanna come with me instead then?"

"Fuck off." Charlotte tugged a limp Ava away.

"Ha ha. Lottie to the rescue. But. But I don't need saving!"

"Good God, another happy drunk. Let's go find Julie." Charlotte looked back at a still-giggling, vacant-looking Ava. "Okay, *I'll* go find Julie, and I'll drag you along too!"

After a bit of searching, Charlotte spotted Julia's plum-colored hair. She dragged them out of the house and into the nippy, late November air. Charlotte knew she'd be unable to manage both girls at once, so she walked them over to a sidewalk bench before calling Kevin. The call went straight to voicemail.

She tried Jason, but no answer there either. Charlotte looked at her iPhone's screen.

Ava looked too. "It's 2:43 a.m.!"

"Most helpful of you. Stop leaning on me, will you? I need to call Derek." Charlotte returned to her contact list. "Hey. Sorry, did I wake you up? You two, *sit down*!"

A pause on the other line. "Hi. No, just gaming. Lost track of time."

"Hiya, Derek!" Ava called. She poked Charlotte's arm. "Tell him we say hi," she urged before falling into giggles with Julia.

"Shut up. Sorry, that's not directed at you, Derek."

"What's up?" He sounded reluctant.

"I hate to ask you this, but Ava and Julia are drunk and I can't handle them on my own. Could you—"

"I'll be right over with my car. Text me the address," he said before hanging up.

"Derek's gonna help save your sorry asses." Charlotte plopped herself between Julia and Ava on the bench.

Ava giggled.

"How's that funny?" Charlotte asked, shaking her head.

"Alliteration!"

"What? Julie, pull your shirt down. There are still people passing by, and you're not flashing anyone in my presence!"

Ava ginned wildly. "Alliteration! 'Save your sorry asses.'"

"There such a thing as a smart drunk?" Charlotte wondered.

"Uh, duhhh," Julia said. "Raise your hand, Av!"

Ava did as told. Because you're an expert at that. "I accept! Valedictorian of drunks!"

Derek pulled up in his navy blue Honda.

"I've got Julie." Charlotte eased her sister up. "You get Ava in the car."

He stood in front of the bench, motionless.

"Derek?" Charlotte asked. "What are you waiting for?"

"Sorry," he said, and helped Ava up, looking at her strangely.

"Mmm. Sorry," she repeated.

"Come on, Derek. It's late and we're potential crime-alert victims. Literally throw Ava in the front seat, I give you my permission! She'll probably laugh anyway," Charlotte called from the back seat.

Besides the occasional giggle or nonsensical sentence from one or both intoxicated girls, silence dominated the ride to Julia's house. Ava sat, hands crumpled in her lap, dazedly watching Derek's hands. They clenched the steering wheel so tightly that his knuckles whitened.

After Derek safely dropped off Julia, he pulled up to Lockhart. "Can you take her in so I can park my car in the deck?"

"Of course. Thanks." Charlotte began helping her over to the front door.

"Shh. Shush. Sh, we must be quiet," Ava said in a pseudo-quiet voice.

"Put a sock in it before I actually do it," Charlotte ordered, guiding her to their room. "You're so lucky our RA isn't here right now, 'cause you're a sight to see."

"Dan?" she said, slightly more sober.

"Yes, Dan. Now get in and sleep it off." Charlotte closed the door.

Ava knocked on the door. "Wait. I need to pee!"

"Well, if you hadn't drunk so much, we wouldn't be in this situation right now, now would we? Also, dippy, we've got a bathroom in our room, so use it!" But Charlotte opened their door for her.

"You wanna watch?" Ava asked with a giggle.

"Of course not. I just want to make sure you don't pass out or go for a swim."

Later that night, Ava shifted in bed to lie on her back. She twisted to see the clock on her bureau. Four in the morning. Excellent: more time to sleep the alcohol off. Peeking over at the bed next to her, she saw that Charlotte had fallen asleep.

Ava pressed her fingers to her side, trying to dull the ache. She slipped into a half sleep. The water. It clogged her. Close your eyes and hold your breath! Had enough yes I've had . . . It burned, felt aflame, like . . . all over again. If you could change would it be the same? Mother, at your side. What did you do? How much trouble you cause . . . The bright lights, the white walls. Father, waiting with you. It's going to be okay. Mother, standing over you. Don't dare you get up stay seated stay down. Clean your plate clean your bowl. No until you finish every last drop it's good for you want to go downstairs? I thought so . . . *shagua – naozhong – ren zha – jianhuo – si san ba – qu si – cao ni b –*

Curling up, she pressed her fingers to her temples, digging in with her nails. Stop stop *stop*. In, out. Out, in. Repeat. Slowly. In out in out in out. They went away. Her dorm room returned. Charlotte slept six feet from her. Ava pulled her comforter further up before slipping her hands under the sheets and resting them on her stomach. Within five minutes she fell back to dozing, and finally to sleep. She slipped into the fog of forgotten memory.

Ava dipped her head back, dunking her long, even hair into the warm bath water. Baths were the only times she really relaxed, especially since she recently started locking the bathroom door. She needed to create privacy for herself, to combat the constant invasions. Ava massaged her scalp, rinsing out the conditioner. Invasion. An assault. An intrusion, a violation. Thinking the word . . . knowing its meaning only half formed the reality, only cracked an egg in two to spill the yolk. But *feeling* the word. Invasion. Invaded. Feeling made it hatch, made it give birth to a fully formed chick. A chick at the mercy of its hen.

Her mother knew no concept of privacy. She barged in on her wherever and whenever. So far Mei hadn't attempted to open the bathroom door when Ava locked it. She timed her baths well, taking them whenever her mother watched Sina news. Mei participated in a trickle of activities that allowed Ava some time to herself: speaking on behalf of the animal shelter, reading her hoard of Chinese scholarly books and magazines, updating her Chinese blog, working out, and watching Chinese news programs. Ava constantly monitored Mei's whereabouts. She snatched and savored every chance to get away from her mother.

She'd just finished washing off soap when the doorknob jiggled. Uh-oh. The doorknob jiggled harder. Then came an angry rap on the door.

"Ava Ling! You have some of nerve! Who you are to fucking lock the door?" Mei yelled.

She didn't respond. Anything she said only made matters worse, so why bother?

"Young girl, you open the door, now! I must teach you lesson; want me to make it two?"

"What did I do wrong?" she asked, refusing to unlock her sanctuary.

The door shook with more angry rapping. "Many things, fucking whore."

"What are you talking about? You're making unreasonable assumptions," Ava called back.

"You supposed to go to dinner with Cha last night, not fuck around."

It annoyed Ava when her mother shortened words she had trouble pronouncing. Speak English, or ask for help, she thought bitterly. Can't be that hard to say Charlotte. No need to rely on the immigrant act. Especially since Mei prided herself on her ability to learn. Stupid, how she hid behind laziness. But what really pissed off Ava? When Mei accused her of outlandish things.

"I did go to dinner with *Charlotte* last night. And I'm a single fourteen-year-old student who plays the piano religiously. I rarely see the sun. How am I a whore?"

She breathed in deeply to keep her temper in check. Don't you dare sink to her level. She wouldn't throw around profanity. Ava shared nothing with her mother. Nothing with her, nothing like her.

"Open the door, fucking *jian nu*."

"What are you accusing me of? Where's your evidence?"

Mei tried the doorknob again and again.

"Found a love note for you. Open this door before I break it up!"

"What? What do you mean? What did it say?" Ava pulled her knees in, resting her chin on them. Her fingertips pruned in the water.

"Quoting, 'Ava,' and then two dots—"

"You mean a colon?" she blurted out.

"Shut the fuck up! Two dots, then 'thanks for last night.' Then a heart."

What? Ava blanked. Did you ever receive such a note? Wait, yes, yes you did. "Charlotte wrote that! She thanked me for dinner. And she always ends notes with sappy hearts."

Silence descended. The doorknob stilled. Maybe Mei had gone away. Maybe she believed her. Crisis averted, right? But Ava didn't trust the eerie stillness. Her mother never accepted being wrong. Blame must be placed on someone—someone other than herself. Situations like these made Ava wish her dad didn't work at his law firm so much. The reward of his long sought after promotion hadn't resulted in Paul working fewer hours. In fact, he stayed away more often, spending all weekdays and nights in the city. No, it's better this way. You've no right to feel abandoned. She wished she could go back to sometimes staying at his apartment. But her mother had ruined that for her.

She jerked her head up at a small sound. A definite "click." Mei found the bathroom key. Ava's heart thumped.

Mei threw open the door, revealing herself in red-faced rage. Her typically polished mother didn't look so attractive now. Ava stood and reached for her towel, but Mei snatched it out of her hands. Opening the toilet's lid, she hurled the towel in the bowl.

"You fucking whore bitch! See what you make me do?"

Ava felt no surprise. She knew this area of her mother's thought process well. Mei wanted to teach her daughter that she held control. Ironically, Ava made Mei lose control.

"How did *I* make you do that?"

Mei closed in and slapped her. "Shut up, *xia jian*!"

"Crazy bitch," Ava snapped, outraged, before clapping a hand over her mouth. Where had that come from? She'd never cursed aloud in front of her mother before, let alone cursed *at* her. So much for not sinking to her level.

"You dare? Who you are? You the crazy bitch!"

Ava's gaze shifted to her mother's neck. Her veins bulged like they too wanted to escape. Rage consumed Mei; Ava watched her shake. Chinese custom dictated that a mother cleanse her chi, purge her body of parental anger. Ava unwillingly offered herself, becoming the perfect receiver.

"S-sorry."

Too late to repent. Cursing at a parent—more than just unfilial. Sacrilegious. She was Chinese enough to know she was in for it.

"*Dan da bao tian*! I'm going to nail you, young girl. You must be tamed! Fourteen and still a bratty, ungrateful child. *Qian jin xiao jie*. Lucky you I'm dedicated to your *education*." Mei suddenly grabbed her wet hair. She started walking out of the bathroom.

Ava cried out, tripping over the ledge of the bathtub. She fell down, kneecaps banging against the tiles.

Staring down with cold black eyes, Mei bared her teeth. She resumed walking, pulling Ava by her hair.

Ava screamed, feeling her hair rise from her head. In the dragging from the bathroom to the carpeted hallway, she'd been turned over. Unable to crawl to make the hair pulling less painful, she felt its full force—in addition to the burning from the carpet on her shivering body.

"Stop, stop!" she half screamed, half sobbed.

"You want to cry, *hu li jing*?" Mei asked, pausing momentarily. She breathed hard, but steadily. "Go ahead. Rebel like Americans." Her voice became light, like weak tea. "I can make you still, bag you again. I need to get the loud timer? Need to remind you of learning piano Scarbo movement?"

Ava's chest seized up, her extremities tingled, remembering. The echo of her uncertain repeated notes, her faulty double-note scales. Again, again! So far from perfect. Her turgid hands. The wax. And then the ticking hours. Being trapped, frozen. Back to those keys that gleamed like teeth. More failure. The cycle beginning again.

"N-n-no. N-no," she said, struggling to even her ragged breathing. "This . . . this is fine." Swallowing her hiccups, she went limp. "Con-continue."

Halfway down the hallway, Mei stopped dragging Ava. Spotting the small dents she'd made when she'd kicked the bathroom door, she changed directions and dragged Ava up to the door.

"See? See what you make me do?"

Mei pulled her hair harder. She changed her grip, this time holding Ava's hair by her scalp. Her mother jerked her neck back, making her tear up in pain.

Then, as abruptly as Mei had seized her hair, she dropped it. Ava suppressed a moan of relief. Violence, she supposed dimly, became tiring.

"Now clean up the mess you brought yourself."

With tears still slithering down her face, and a runny nose, Ava quietly murmured, "Brought upon."

"What? You asking for it? Want more?"

"No! N-nothing," she whispered, folding into the fetal position.

Mei kicked her daughter in the ribs.

She walked away, saying over her shoulder, "Next time I won't be so gentle. You get the bag in the basement. Don't try ever locking doors on me again. I'm your fucking mother, understand? With me, you have no rights to privacy. And clean up good. I'm going to blog. I'll check to see if you did a perfect job, half-breed *biaozi*."

After Mei disappeared down the stairs, Ava took clothes from her room and went into the bathroom. The mirror reflected her pathetic state, exacerbated by bruises and rug burns. Her skin flared a violent red. She put on clothes and then inspected the hallway. Small clumps of her reddish brown hair were scattered on the carpet. After picking up the loose strands and clumps, she grouped the hair together on the bathroom counter. Taking a brush, she carefully went through her thick hair. By the time she had finished, the cluster of hair she'd lost grew to the size of an orange. She looked down at the auburn mass and then at the mirror, at her tired and tear-streaked face. Ava stood there for a minute before breaking into a sob. She put half of her fist into her mouth. Make no sounds.

Ava woke and silently sobbed into her pillow. She drew the comforter over her head. Under the covers, she cradled her head toward her chest. Get away, get them out, get out, leave me alone! Escape. Still too much to ask for? A new start, a thorough cleaning, a purge. The change, college—both inadequate. Instead of liberation, she continuously circled, hovered, returned. The miles weren't distant enough. Too many ties, too many threads. Go ahead, cry. Because that definitely makes everything better. You're vindicating her. Empowering her. Stop being vulnerable! Stop it . . .

But, another part of her argued, crying felt cathartic. A hidden torrent of tears brought no shame. Tasting the salty wetness solved nothing. It only provided a paltry release. But fine. Cry—if you must. If you can't contain yourself. But never make a sound.

Chapter Eleven

The next day, Charlotte and Ava awoke at noontime.

"How about brunch?" Charlotte asked.

"Sounds good. Give me a second to get changed," Ava said, rifling through her dresser drawers.

"No rush."

But there were things Ava wanted to do, reading to begin. She selected her favorite white blouse and a pair of jeans. "Why don't we go to Dana's Café?"

"Sure; it'll be a nice change from dining hall food."

"Want to walk?" Ava asked after they'd put on their jackets and headed out of Lockhart.

"Why not. Um. So how—"

"I love how we can just be silent together and it's never awkward."

"Uh. Yeah. Totally."

Suppressing a shiver, Ava watched people casually mill about campus. She sensed that Charlotte wanted to bring something up. And Ava had foreboding feelings about whatever that something involved.

Fifteen minutes later, the pair reached Dana's Café.

"Hi, I'm Stacy. What can I get for you?" asked a dark-skinned woman with wildly curly hair, chomping on a piece of gum.

Ava smiled. "French toast and scrambled eggs for me. Oh, and a glass of orange juice, thanks."

Jotting Ava's order on a pink notepad, the woman turned to Charlotte expectantly.

Charlotte pulled her curls into a ponytail. "Uh. Water's fine. And I guess I'll go with pancakes. Could you put the butter and jam on the side, please?"

Ava shook her head, smiling at Charlotte when the waitress left. "Typical Charlotte. Why bother? Your food all goes to the same place, you know."

"Whatever. It's a free country."

The waitress came back with their drinks and straws and then hurried away to serve other tables.

"So," Charlotte began after a short pause.

Ava eyed her warily. "Uh-oh. You've got the look."

"What look?" Charlotte asked, widening her eyes. She sipped her water.

"You know. That uncomfortable, worried look you get just before giving well-intentioned advice. Is this going to be a 'what are you doing with your life' talk?"

"You're imagining things," Charlotte said, waving a hand in dismissal. "But I have wanted to talk to you. I feel like we haven't had a real conversation in weeks. How've you been? How're classes?"

Though she remained guarded, Ava projected composure.

"Fine. The usual. Lots of reading, a good amount of writing. It feels a bit overwhelming at times, but I'm managing."

"And the research for your Asian professor?"

Ava frowned. "She has a name."

"Of course. I just don't remember it."

"So? That doesn't mean you need to resort to identifying her by race."

Charlotte seemed startled by the firmness in Ava's voice. "I didn't mean to be offensive! You can't spend your life walking on eggshells and being politically correct."

"I know, I just . . . sorry, I'm a bit raw this morning. I guess I want to make everything universal. Human, I mean—the concepts and interests that we all relate to." Ava drummed her fingertips on the table, frustrated. She stopped to drink some of her orange juice.

"We're never going to live in a level world, Ava. You know there can't ever be a utopia. Surely you remember reading 'Harrison Bergeron' in high school."

"Yes. I get it. Hierarchies make the world function. I'm not asking for perfection. Just slow changes. Why does it have to only exist in fiction?"

Charlotte shrugged. "Beats me. How did we even get onto this topic?"

"You brought up Professor Chen and I derailed the conversation."

"Then you never answered me. Is the research going well?"

Ava smiled suddenly, realizing how comfortable she'd grown around Professor Chen. "She's like my mentor. I know it's early yet, but I think I want her to be my honors thesis advisor."

Charlotte raised her eyebrows. "Then it's settled, you're going to be an English major? Is Mei okay with it?"

Ava winced. "I haven't told her. I can't."

"How can you keep it a secret from her? She'd support you in the end! Your mom's nontraditional anyway. How many Chinese moms speak for the animal shelter, instead of, I don't know, music prodigies? I think Mei is proud of whatever you do."

"No, nothing's that simple, trust me. Privilege comes with responsibility. I'm supposed to do better than the last generation. To 'keep family face,' which means obtaining a well-reputed job.

Engineer, doctor, lawyer, astrophysicist. Something prestigious and complicated that offers a generous salary."

"Tell her on your own time, then. But I still think she deserves to know. Oh, and I keep forgetting to ask you. Did you read that book yet?"

Ava paused in the middle of reaching for her glass. "What book?" she asked cautiously, returning her hands to her lap.

"The one we got you for your birthday. Called *Part Asian*, at least the first part of the title."

Ava relaxed. "Yes, not too much to read. A lot more pictures of what they called 'hapas.'"

"Whasians, you mean?" Charlotte teased. To her surprise, Ava grinned.

"Sure, Whasians."

"Why the sudden change? I thought you hated that. Not a legit-enough word for you."

"Used to," Ava corrected. "To be fair, Amerasian isn't in the dictionary either. Professor Chen says that dictionaries aren't definitive. They can't be. Words change. Context changes. We change. Even slang can make us more visible."

"I guess intention matters most—how and why you're using a word."

With a nod, Ava went back to her orange juice.

"But what about you? Have you settled on a major?"

"I'm actually really interested in my psychology class. Maybe I'll even major in psych."

"Going to practice your mind techniques on me?" Ava asked, arching an eyebrow with a smile.

"Only if you ask for it."

The too-made-up waitress returned, expertly wielding a tray with their orders on it.

"Pancakes with butter and jam on the side." She slid the plate in front of Charlotte. "And French toast with scrambled eggs." She put Ava's order down next. "Let me know if you need anything else." The waitress bustled away.

"Thanks."

"Poor girl. Dealing with the brunch rush with a face bathed in makeup." Ava picked up her fork to stab one of the strawberries atop her French toast.

"Ava," Charlotte chastised, looking around in a paranoid manner, "how many times do I have to tell you? Normal people don't actually say the mean thoughts they're thinking aloud!"

She shrugged. "I believe someone once told me that it's a free country."

"Jerk."

Ava smiled sweetly.

"You know, I don't mean to sound like your mother or anything," Charlotte began.

It took some effort to prevent herself from visibly stiffening.

"Don't worry, Charlotte. You're nothing like my mother."

"That's a shame. Your mom's awesome!" Busily cutting up a pancake, Charlotte missed the dark look on Ava's face.

"Right, awesome," she echoed. "So what advice do you have to give me now?" She studiously added pepper to her scrambled eggs.

"Don't sound so gloomy. This isn't going to be a sermon. I remember that you're an atheist."

"Good, because then I'd fully tune you out."

"If I didn't know better, I'd say your mama never taught you manners," Charlotte teased.

Frowning, Ava stabbed some scrambled eggs and took an unenthusiastic bite.

Sipping her water, Charlotte furtively glanced at Ava.

"Um. So why have you started drinking?"

Ava looked up, surprised at Charlotte's directness. "Seriously?"

"Yeah. I wanna know." Charlotte put a bite of pancake into her mouth and avoided eye contact.

"I'm partly Irish; it's in my blood."

"No, seriously."

Ava shifted in the booth, trying to ignore her headache.

"You forget. About things. Things in the past, things looming in the future. It puts you in an uninhibited, present state of mind. Everything seems manageable. No worrying, remembering. No real thinking, so you fall back on your instincts. It's . . . liberating."

Ava stared into nothing. And it remained that way . . . for about five minutes. Then you crashed, and everything seemed so much worse than it had before, *plus* you had to deal with the effects of the hangover. Nonetheless, drinking provided her with a brief period of oblivion. For Ava, real life meant hyperawareness: it meant feeling divided, confused, indeterminate, undefined, unsure—a continuous struggle in limbo.

"So a lot of people just don't have good instincts, hmm?" Charlotte asked, watching her carefully.

But Ava sensed the monitoring. She kept her face impassive.

"Ha. I'd say so, considering the amount of stupid things people do when they're drunk."

"You're not even supposed to be drinking."

"Charlotte. Look around you. We're on a college campus. Everyone's doing it. There's a reason why DU is nicknamed Drunk University." She conjured excuses to hide behind.

"Oh, so just because 'everyone's doing it,' it's okay?" Charlotte scoffed. "That why you did body shots with Julia? 'Cause all the girls are doing it?"

"Considering your sister's party nickname, neck shots are tame. You sound like a freaking book of maxims. Save it for Jason; he loves arguing about ethics."

"Fine, then let's ignore ethics. Answer me this: would you say you drink a lot?"

Ava tried to stab her toast, but it'd become soggy. Her fork sank in and syrup spurted out.

"And by 'a lot,' you mean too much, am I right?"

"You can't answer a question with a question!"

"According to whom? I don't see the conversation police anywhere, so I think I'm good."

Charlotte's hurt look confirmed Ava's belief that her roommate had the most effective, guilt-inducing "sad look."

Ava sighed, her anger subsiding. "I hate when you go all ASPCA commercial on me. Fine. I guess I drink more than I should, but the next day I always remember everything that happened. No blackouts."

"I believe there's a hidden 'yet' in there."

"I don't recklessly drink, which is more than what at least sixty percent of students at Davison can truthfully say."

"Oh? And where are your stats from?" Charlotte fired back.

She massaged her temples, unable to continue suppressing the signs of her hangover. "Could you keep it down? And you know what I mean. It's a guesstimate."

Charlotte lowered her voice. "That's not good enough, Ava. I'm worried about you." She tried to look her in the eyes, but Ava resolutely stared at a spot on the table.

"Why? You went out with us last night. Nothing bad happened."

"Are you serious? You're lucky no one took pictures of you doing the shots. And nothing bad happened because Derek and I helped you and Julie. Must I remind you that I pulled you away from some drunk guy leading you God knows where?"

"We'd have managed without you. And who said I needed saving? Ever consider that I could've *chosen* to go with that guy or not? I'd decided to pull away, actually."

"Who are you and what've you done with Ava?"

"I'm the same person in a different context. This is college. Lighten up, will you? I'm just trying new things and not being an uptight prude, that's all." Ava signaled for the check.

"That's what you think of me? Five years of friendship, and *that's* your conclusion?"

"No. No, of course not. I'm sorry, that was downright bitchy of me. I didn't mean it, really."

Charlotte shook her head. "That's not even what I wanted to talk to you about. I'm sorry for bringing it up the way I did. Mind if we finish this outside?"

"Let's. Want to take a walk through the park?" Ava said as they paid the bill.

"Yeah. I think that'll help both of us clear our heads."

The girls walked down University Way in silence, each caught up in her own web of thoughts. They passed by a Dunkin' Donuts, the dining hall, and the red-bricked School of Communication before starting on the cracked sidewalk that led into Millcreek Park. Only a few joggers braved the overcast November afternoon. The trees were bare and the grass, while overgrown, looked sallow. No flowers could be seen; they were either dead or in hiding.

When they walked by empty wooden picnic tables, Ava finally spoke. "You want to say something."

"Well . . . promise you won't get mad?"

"Great start," Ava said, putting a hand to her face in mock distress.

"I mean, you can get mad at me. Just don't get mad at Derek."

"Why would I . . . what did he tell you?" she asked suspiciously as they passed dormant rosebushes.

"Stuff about Halloween." Charlotte studied her scrupulously for any passing reaction.

Ava kept a composed, expressionless face.

"What about Halloween?"

"I'm so not playing this game. I'm just going to tell you what he told me."

"Okay." Ava shrugged. That gave her the upper hand. She could contrive her responses to best combat Charlotte's explanation. "Let's talk on the swings though. No kids are there, see?" She had fond memories of swing sets. Before the promotion, while they still lived in the townhouse, Paul used to take Ava to the nearby park and push her on the swings.

Charlotte shook her head but followed.

She sat down and Ava hopped onto the flexible, black swing seats. For a few moments they swung without talking, admiring the peaceful, deserted park.

"Derek told me you went to a party on Halloween. Want to tell me about it?"

"Not particularly. Just your average party, except people dressed up like fools, that's all."

Ava looked straight ahead while pumping her legs hard to go higher. Her love of swings went beyond memories with her father. In grammar school, she swung during recess, pretending to sprout wings and fly away from the judgmental kids at school. Away from the white kids, who rejected her. Away from the Chinese kids, who also rejected her. Fly with the birds—they knew no difference.

"Yeah, I thought so. Guess I'll lay it out and you'll have to confirm or deny it, hmm?" Charlotte easily matched Ava's height with gentle use of her legs.

"Guess so, long-legged jerk."

"Anyway. So Derek went to this house party with two other guy friends, dressed up as nerds. Amusing, I know," Charlotte said, agreeing with Ava's smirk.

"Okay. So?" Ava hadn't seen him during the actual party, but the house had been crowded. Lots of people came and went.

"Derek noticed a girl dressed up in a cat suit at this party. He thought this girl could be you but didn't know for sure, so he left you alone. He also noticed that the girl came with Dan, our RA." Charlotte paused to look at a swinging Ava, but her face remained inexpressive. "Some time later Derek saw cat woman come down without her mask, with her suit zipped a bit more than halfway up her back, and it turns out to be you! Outside, after you fought Derek for a bit, you let him walk you back to Lockhart, and then he even held your hair when you threw up. Agree or disagree?" Charlotte concluded, shooting her a penetrating look.

"I'd say that's a fair assessment of that night," Ava said nonchalantly. At least Derek had omitted details. Like how messy she'd looked. She remembered looking into the mirror after Derek assisted her. Her hair, a nest of tangles. Her face, flushed. Cheeks scratched from Dan's stubble. Cloudy, uncertain eyes. In the process of spiting her mother, she spited herself.

"How can you be so callous? Can't you see that we're worried about you? Give me something here!"

Ava continued to swing. "Thanks for your concern, but really, I can manage myself just fine."

Amazed, Charlotte abruptly stopped her own swing.

"Tell me something, Ava," Charlotte said quietly, "are you still a virgin?"

About two weeks had passed since Halloween. She supposed she shouldn't keep that from Charlotte any longer. "No."

"Were you raped by our RA? Because we can bring that rapist down—"

"No! Dan's not a rapist. No rape. That's the brilliant conclusion you and Derek came to?" Ava asked incredulously, letting her swing slowly come to a stop.

"I don't know! You're so closed off, so hard to read. We're only left with visual clues, and you know how misleading those can be. Is it too much to ask for a bit of direct communication? Some straightforward honesty? I thought we were close!"

Ava finally let an emotion slip: a guilty look flitted across her features.

"I want to, really. I don't go out of my way to keep things from you. It's just . . . " Charlotte believed in the illusion her mother had created for the world to see. Mei and the Magees were perfect.

"Just what?" Charlotte demanded, eyebrows furrowed.

" . . . I don't want you to judge me," Ava finished weakly.

"Judge you? Seriously? How could I do that? You've put up with my problems for so long; don't you think it's about time that I return the favor? Have faith in people, at least in me."

Ava stared at the sand, making an indentation with a booted foot. If only it were that simple: yellow or white, lies or truths.

"Basically, I hung out with Dan before the Halloween party. We talked and flirted, no big deal. At the party we had a bit more alcohol than usual, and . . . I don't know. He dressed up as Spiderman and I dressed up as a cat and we somehow went from talking to having sex."

Ava looked up at Charlotte and shrugged. She didn't know if her friend would be more or less forgiving if a couple of white lies hadn't been thrown in. But Ava definitely couldn't say that she'd used Dan in an attempt to nullify what Mei had told her on her birthday. Dan had wanted her, even with no makeup. She'd used him, not the other way around. The guilt belonged to her.

"Just like that? That spontaneously?"

"I mean, the transition felt smoother, but yes. Alcohol can take the awkwardness out of socializing." Her self-revulsion only hit her later, when Dan went sweet—when he realized she'd been a virgin. Yes, she regretted that night. But she refused to tell Charlotte.

"Did this have something to do with your birthday? What, did you want to prove that you were really an adult?" Charlotte accused.

"Of course not. You know I don't believe in that 'woman of the world' jargon any more than you do."

"I don't know what to believe, Ava. And that's all you've got to say about losing your virginity?"

"It's no big deal. We were safe about it and we were consensual; those are the things that matter. Simple facts." She'd long forgotten their fifteen-year-old promise to uphold the conventional wisdom of teen-girl magazines.

Ava wanted to use college to become a completely different person. But so far nothing turned out like she'd envisioned. She remained split, groping for footing. Her mother still hung over her. She'd always seen herself through others' eyes, but for the first time she tried to see herself *by* herself. And Ava didn't know what she saw, but she disliked the person in the mirror.

"Not to mention the fact that Dan's our RA and a relationship with him is probably against housing policy. Is he your boyfriend? Are you dating now? You see him at least once a day!"

"I don't regret it." Blatant lie, but maybe if she said it often enough the lie would become truth. "No, he's not my boyfriend, and we're not dating. Sex doesn't entail a relationship, you know. In both cases you can have one without the other. We've agreed to just be friends and pretend it never happened."

"But . . . you were *intimate*. And you can't deny that sex and relationships are inextricably related," Charlotte argued.

"Trust me, you can have sex without intimacy. Just because two things are related doesn't mean that they're a package deal. This isn't the nineteenth century, Lottie. My reputation isn't ruined, and even if it were, there's no village gossip to label me a whore."

"Have you slept with anyone else?"

Ava smiled wryly. "No, don't worry. I'm not whoring myself out."

"Good. I hope you don't ever. Because then I'd have to kick your ass."

Chapter Twelve

The lychee disappointed her. Too soft. Too bruised. Mei picked up the tenth bundle. The tie holding the red net began to unravel. She immediately put it back on the heap.

She pushed her cart onward, inspecting the Asian pears next. They were on sale. It only took her four tries to find a pack that had firm pears. Baby mangoes sat nearby, but a mere glance told her to forgo feeling them. Far too small and shriveled. Too yellow, and probably mushy inside. Sometimes she wondered if the packers threw all the produce in the crates, and then the crates into the truck. It seemed that all Asian supermarkets sold imperfect produce. Probably cheaper for them. She knew her people's tricks well.

"*Xin xian de*?" she asked the middle-aged seafood processor, pointing at the sea bass.

He smiled, revealing crooked yellow teeth. "*Gangdao, gangdao de*."

His accent hurt her ears. His skin, marred with age spots, hurt her eyes. Must be Cantonese. He looked like it. Mei eyed the fish. She doubted it *that* fresh and clean. Drawing her spine up even more, she switched to English.

"Do you charge extra to scale it?"

That rotten smile again. "For you, *shao nai nai*, no."

Humph! Middle-aged but attractive? Rude, stunted peasant. She flashed a bright smile. "I'll come back later." Mei nodded at her half-full cart. "At the end."

"*Dai hui jian*."

You'll be looking forward for a long time, then. She shook out her sales flyer and moved on.

Mei stopped in the dried pork section and took inventory. Scallions, green mustard, loose spinach, yu choy tip. Check. Young coconut, Asian pears, oranges, dried longan meat. Pork long feet. Salted duck eggs. Seasoned seaweed, dried squid. GeXianWeng Gan Mao tea, bitter gourd tea, Tan Ngan Lo medicated tea. Tong Ren Tang Fritillary and Loquat Syrup. Hericium Shark's Bone Soup for detox, Qing Bu Liang soup mix. She just needed one more item. Well, two in order to fulfill the "2 for $2.98" special.

In the soy sauce section, she found what she looked for. Lee Kum Kee black bean and garlic sauce. Oh, but Beauideal Superior Pickle Sauce was just $0.98 for 16.9 fluid ounces. Get that, too.

"Mei, is that you?"

She turned around, pickle sauce still in hand. Charlotte's mother.

"Ema! Surprise to see you here." Placing the sauce in her cart, she allowed herself to be enfolded into Ema's thick arms.

"I've meant to come here for some time. This is the first weekend I've had free. I'm determined to learn how to cook Chinese food."

"Oh?"

"Yes. It's one of Charlotte's favorite cuisines." Ema peered into Mei's cart. "But I'm hopeless. I've no idea what half the things you've bought are."

Mei checked her watch. 2 p.m. She had enough time to kill.

"I'll be help."

"Are you sure?"

She smiled. "Come, we'll get you basics."

Ema brought her empty cart over. "You're such a doll; thanks for doing this."

Guiding Ema to the beginning of the aisle, she began with vinegars.

"Black vinegar a must. It has a unique taste, make any dish pop."

Ema dutifully placed the bottle in her cart.

"Lee Kum Kee Plum Sauce is sweet; use with bitter veggies like spinach or asparagus."

They moved along, Mei teaching, Ema collecting.

She placed a bottle of soy sauce in Ema's cart. "Know where they come from. Japanese soy sauce my favorite, less salty. Korean sauces are popular. But I try to buy Chinese."

"Shouldn't be hard to do; almost everything's made in China these days, no?"

Mei frowned. "Food and ingredients isn't iPods. We cut corners to make some product cheap. Especially for foreigners. But these things," she continued, gesturing to the quarter-full cart, "are different. They are by us, for us. We grew up on these flavors. We take pride on them. Chinese cooking is an art."

"Like for Italians, our balsamic vinegars and regional wines," Ema concluded.

"Yes," she replied, though she had no idea.

They began making their way down the spice aisle. Tired of explaining, Mei began pulling items off the shelves. Down came five-spice, ginger powder.

"How often do you talk to Ava?"

"Every . . . every now and again. You?"

"Once a week. If it weren't for my book club and my friends, I'd feel so alone! It's terrible."

Mei looked up sharply. "Why terrible? What's wrong with alone?"

"Oh, hun, you wouldn't know; you've got Paul. You don't really have an empty house."

"Use powdered garlic and ginger sparing," Mei said, eyes on the shelves again. Dare she look at her with pity. "The real thing's better. Cut up and preserve in oil or wine, put in the fridge."

Ema squeezed her arm, consoling. "I know. It's hard to admit. We have no control over our children's paths. Can't shield them from mistakes. You want to hold on, but we've got to be strong. College is where they're supposed to experiment. It's a safer place to do so. And Charlotte and Ava have got each other, don't they?"

"It's good to keep shiitake mushrooms, dried, in pantries. When you ready to cook them, soak in water for an hour minimum. Great stir-frying veggie. Don't overcook or they get soggy."

"They've got to be just right," Ema agreed. "Can't force your timing on them."

"That's why you must watch close."

"But surely you've got to let them breathe. Let them cook on their own? You can check in now and then, but staring won't make them ready faster."

"Chinese cooking all about monitoring," Mei said, exiting the aisle. "Constant assessment."

"Now, what's that about?" Ema asked, nodding at the nearby hanging, roasted poultry.

Mei led the way toward the barbeque station. They stood off to the side, watching Asian customers rapidly talk to butchers and vendors. "That's Peking duck, and chicken."

"Why are the heads still attached?"

"We never waste food. Nearly everything is edible. If we able chew it, we eat it."

Ema appeared unconvinced. "Even . . . even the eyes?"

"Especially eyes. And fish eyes. They're good for you."

"Uh huh. To each his or her own." Ema stared at the roasted birds. "Don't you feel bad for them? Strung up like that, ankles tied together, wings forced back?"

"'Course not. I mean—we have to eat. Tying them this way is best for roasting, even cooking."

"Still . . . I sure wouldn't want to be on display like that."

Mei shrugged. "Buddhists say you could be, next lifetime. But no one knows. We make work with lives now."

Next they walked down the cooking-utensil aisle.

"Why are we here?" Ema asked. "I've got cookware."

Arching an eyebrow, Mei replied, "You need right kinds. Unless you own a wok?"

"Oh. Guilty as charged."

Mei scoured the woks that were on sale. With the concentration of a lab technician, she sampled four of them.

Ema watched her hold a wok in one hand and then sway her arm back and forth, like she tossed and caught invisible ingredients. "Why are you doing that?"

"We Chinese have many saying. *Qiao fu nan wei wu mi zhi chui*. Even smartest housewife can't do cooking without right equipment."

"How true," Ema said, accepting the wok Mei decided on.

They weaved through families, many multi-generational. Cane-supported, non-English speaking grandparents clogged the pathways that led to the registers.

She checked out after Ema. The grey-toothed woman with dyed brown hair complimented her food choices. "Good see you, Miss-is Ma-gee."

"Good see*ing* you, *mei mei*," she replied. The woman might be younger than her, but she wore her years poorly, like a grape that'd seen too much sun.

"*Zai lai*. Come again!"

Mei and Ema rolled their carts out to the car-ridden parking lot.

"Goodness, is it always so crowded on Saturdays?"

"Yes. Especially after Chinese school let out."

"I see. Well, my car's on the other side."

Mei paused, intending to kiss Ema goodbye.

"What are you doing tonight? My girlfriends are coming over for a movie night. Why don't you join us?"

"It's okay."

"You sure? There'll be wine. And I'm cooking Italian. Spinach risotto."

"I . . . I can't."

"Doing anything tomorrow? You could come over for lunch and tell me what I'm doing wrong when I try to cook Chinese."

Mei smiled. "I have one appointment. If not, I—"

"No worries, dear. Don't feel obligated. I look forward to bumping into you again, even if it's just at Davison. Ciao!"

After settling in at home, Mei called her daughter.

"*Yi ge ren*?"

Ava cleared her throat. "Not . . . not really."

"Charlotte's there?"

"Yes."

She shifted pitch, letting her questions trickle like juice from a ripe plum.

"How it went? Your chemistry exam?"

"Um. That's tomorrow. December first. Organic chemistry hourlies take place on Sunday nights."

Mei pulled up her Facebook page. He'd messaged her. She held off reading it. "Are you prepared?"

"Of course."

"You'll do good?"

"I'll do well."

"*Nu er,* you know why I bring pressure?" she asked, leaning against her chair.

"Family honor."

"Wrong. *Wang nu cheng feng*. I have hope for your success. I don't want slipup, regret for you. *Gong bai chui cheng*. College is not for resting. Education, best education, is career investment. But you can't pressurize yourself never enough. You stop before potential. You stop when it's hard, don't know how to push through. My job as your mother, I remind you to keep the focus. *Gao zhan yuan zhu*. I see the future like you can't. This for your life! Life lessons. More than staying better, smarter than everyone. You need to beat yourself. Success mean no less than best. No mistakes. You can stop mistakes. Struggle for the perfection. You must dedicate yourself."

"Right."

"Study with stress on repeating."

"Emphasize rote studying. I know."

She kept her voice level. "You think I notice nothing? You don't know. Every day, every talk, I translate. Constant translation in my head! I must fight to word my voice. Everything not straight. *Cuo zong fu za*. Always twisted, complicated. You don't know better! When I have failed you? *Shang wei*. Never. I am both parents."

Mei took on the voice of a woman stabbed in the front. "You take me granted. What I do to deserve so cold treatment?"

"I'm sorry." Ava's voice became small. "I—I'm really grateful for your efforts. You're . . . you're the most constant thing in my life."

Mei's call waiting went off. "Good. Remember that," she said, hanging up and switching over.

Chapter Thirteen

Back from dinner with Kevin and Jason, Ava finally found a chance to open the package she discovered while cleaning Paul's home office. For almost an entire month, circumstances prevented her from opening it. Either Charlotte or one of the guys hung around, and then Ava had been inundated by papers. But Charlotte had gone home for the weekend, and Ava had tamed her coursework. Now the perfect opportunity arose for some personal reading—in private.

She settled on her bed and pulled the padded manila envelope onto her lap. Ava had inspected the envelope so many times that the corners wrinkled and begun to tear. She'd memorized the notes that her father had made on the back. Ava thought she knew what to expect, but still she hesitated.

What if her questions remained unanswered? What if—and this perhaps troubled her more—she uncovered the truth? Mei always accused her daughter of not knowing what she'd been through. True. But, in these diary entries, Ava could unearth long-concealed truths. And this frightened her. Breathing deep, as if she were about to go underwater, she broke open the sealed flap. Inside lay a small, stapled packet of paper. The sheets, half the size of standard paper, felt thick and seemed of good quality.

She found a Post-it note, no longer sticky, paper-clipped onto the first double-sided sheet. Paul's handwriting rushed across the note: "Lao lao's translated diary during the Cultural Revolution." Flipping through the stapled, half-sized sheets in her hands, Ava felt disappointment rise. No more than thirty pages—this looked nothing like a diary. The front of the package promised more: "Lao lao/Mei diary, 1966–1970." Where was her mother's diary, and why was it missing? She supposed she could call her father and ask. After all, he'd written on the envelope that he'd show her the sections of the diary that survived. She planned on examining what she now had and dealing with the rest later. Putting aside the Post-it note, Ava began to read.

Foreword

Dear Mei,

My only daughter, I've started this journal for your sake, and for the sake of your future children. It's hard to even imagine a future during this tumultuous time, but the thought of new generations is what brings me strength. I will fight the Party through words. I'm writing in this little red book to write over the propaganda. My observations speak volumes for those who endured more injustice than we have. This is for the friends and relatives I felt too scared to help; I beg forgiveness for my inaction. I've written elusively in the hopes that at least some of these pages will be preserved. This being said, burn this book if you believe it will be confiscated by those affiliated with the Red Guard. Learn from my experiences, and share them with my grandchildren. I'm uncertain of what lies ahead, but I know you will survive. I'll survive through you.

I've never had a journal; words have never fascinated me the way science has. But my job as a biology professor has been suspended indefinitely at Peking University, so I must turn to writing to express myself. My parents used to push for my education, even though I'm female. They taught me that words can be powerful and freeing, especially in a time like this, a time of terror and oppression. I don't believe in this Cultural Revolution, especially after what's happened. If this diary is found by a party member, I will meet my death. But I will go mad if I don't write down my experiences. I must write them. I must make them real, at least for you, Mei. You're so young, which I am partially grateful for. Whatever happens should sweep through your memory like wind. My only wish is that your father and I will remain rooted in your memories. Besides, if I keep this bottled up inside me, I'll slowly poison my mind. Aya, I don't even know where to begin; it's all so terrible and overwhelming.

Beijing, China, 1966

While I fear that those damned Red Guards may return to search the apartment again—what's left of it, anyway—I don't think they will. With Guo gone and my baby dead, and with me lying low as a dumb dog, I think Mei and I can survive basically undisturbed.

Oh Mei. My only child. They've closed all the nearby urban schools so children can become little Red Guards. This infuriates me. How dare they deny the importance of a true education? They are terminating the intellectual growth of a generation! Luckily Mei is too young to be recruited. I will do everything I can to teach her properly. To protect her, to shield her. Everything. Already, I must make up for all that she's seen. Too much needs to be unseen.

I know now that I was complacent, thinking that my husband and I, both distinguished professors at Peking University, had done well for ourselves. We were respected by our peers in academia and by our neighbors and community. Guo's engineering knowledge and his opinions were so valued that they always asked him to attend weekly salon meetings. We'd built stable, prosperous lives for ourselves. And Mei, our darling only daughter, who looked so much like my beautiful grandmother, rest her soul, continued proving to be equally bright and beautiful.

Then, in May, Chairman Mao ruined it for us, practically declaring war on intellectuals. He told everyone through his propaganda that we represented "The Four Olds": Old Culture, Old Customs, Old Ideas, and Old Habits. He announced that the Four Olds needed to be purged. We, the sudden dissidents, needed to be purged. And then, to our horror, the propaganda led to action. First high school students went on rampages against their teachers. I heard stories of students forcing teachers to crawl on their hands and knees, eat grass, wear derogatory signs, clean toilets and eat feces. Surely, our students were above such ill-disguised brainwashing. No, our students respected their professors too much to viciously lash out against their venerated elders. Things would be different at the universities.

We'd thought wrong. Our college students soon caught the Red Fever. They destroyed old literature, classical paintings, ancient and precious Chinese artifacts. Irreplaceable treasures of history, trashed. They considered nothing sacred. So much Chinese culture eviscerated, our ancestors' spirits must have howled in fury. Then the professors were targeted. I had a friend, a professor of aesthetics. The students went after her first. She was a younger woman, with glossy, thick hair that fell to her waist. Some female students, jealous I'm sure, forced her down and sat on her back. Then they shaved her head completely, laughing at her cries for help and spitting in her face. I saw it with my own eyes, like my colleagues. But, like my colleagues, I didn't do a thing. I only watched, horrified. Then they forced her to pick up garbage in front of the student dormitories; I and others worked alongside her.

Day after day the students grew bolder, experimenting on us. We heard about a professor of literature whom they forced to drink pesticides. Some held him down. Others wrenched open his mouth. After the last drop, he instantly became sick. He died that night, only thirty-five years old, leaving a wife and two small children behind. Of course we wanted to fight back, but they vastly outnumbered us. That could've been me, we each thought to ourselves. That could've been my family. Best to play their sick games and try to go unnoticed.

And then, one balmy day, on the way back from the market, Mei and I stopped by my cousin Jiao's apartment. Jiao lived on our street, a couple apartment buildings down, and I'd grown up with her. She's two years older than I, but she had married young. When Mei was three years old, Jiao's older husband died of heart disease, leaving her with two sons and his vast wealth—he'd been a successful dye factory owner. In the years since his death, I'd noticed that Jiao had taken to vanity: makeup, stylish Western clothing. During the build up to the Four Olds campaign, I'd warned her to downplay her wealth and Western interests. "You'll be labeled black; branded a capitalist. Make yourself invisible, if not for your safety, then for the sake of your sons," I'd urged her. "You worry too much, An-xiang. This fervor will soon pass," she'd assured me.

"What's that?" Mei asked me, tugging on my free hand.

I didn't need to follow her small pointing hand to know what she meant. A small crowd drew around Jiao's lawn, surrounding the spectacle. I pulled Mei back a few feet, to the cover of a nearby tree. Though we were a safe distance away, I made out Jiao's frightened face, her slouching posture. Eight junior high school students—too young to be in the Red Guard—were in control.

"See what Western extravagance Jiao Ling indulges in!" the leader shouted. He looked no older than Jiao's second son, and he theatrically gestured to the mound of dresses in the center of the lawn. Another student, a girl with short hair, stepped forward and threw something onto the clothes. Flames leapt up and the crowd cautiously took a few steps back.

"Look Ma, fire!" Mei said gleefully. She pulled my hand again, and in my shock, I let go of the bag holding groceries. Vaguely I sensed it fall, produce rolling onto the sidewalk.

Jiao looked ready to faint. But they wanted more from her. Another student struck a gong, and yet another beat a drum. The students began chanting.

"Revolt! Revolt! Down with bourgeois Jiao Ling! Praise be Mao Tse-tung Thought! He is the Four Greats: great helmsman, great commander, great leader, great teacher."

The girl who'd lit the match stepped forward and raised a poster in the air. Red characters had been painted on the white background. From our vantage point, the angry red strokes looked like splattered blood.

"Jiao Ling," the leader said sternly, lifting his voice over the murmuring crowd. "We command you to post our *dazibao* on your door."

He motioned for another student to come forward. A bucket and a brush were both shoved toward Jiao's unsure hands. She took them silently, head slightly bowed. I gripped Mei's hand fiercely and she squirmed. We both watched Jiao painfully paste the defamatory poster to the front door. Everyone knew that her upstairs neighbors, who used her entrance to reach their apartments, would constantly be reminded of her black category. And the people who passed by would read her shame; the red characters demanded attention.

I shook my head and gathered the spoon vegetables and scallions, shaking off dust and dirt and returning them to my bag. Holding Mei close, I crossed the street and kept my head down, briskly walking toward our apartment. Mei ran to keep up with me.

"Ma," Mei said, her head turned, looking at Jiao as I propelled us along. "Auntie's crying." I cautiously glanced up. Jiao bent into herself.

"Start over," I heard the leader yell. "Read it aloud without stumbling, capitalist widow!"

Shaking Mei's hand, I said urgently, "No dawdling; Baba's waiting for us at home."

After that incident, I made sure to visit Jiao less. It was wrong of me, distancing myself, but I didn't want our family to be associated with her. When I visited Jiao, I did so at night, when Mei slept and darkness shrouded the *dazibao*. I only needed to read it once: "Black witch, trying to seduce everyone with your bourgeois ways. The more you paint your face, the more your heart decays. We proletarians know you for the evil fox spirit you are! Sycophant, parasite! Repent, remold yourself. Renounce your capitalist tendencies and honor Chairman Mao's teachings!"

Yes, Jiao lived a bit free after her husband's death, a bit self-indulgent. But she hadn't deserved such humiliating treatment. No one did. Nature seemed to agree. A month after Jiao had been forced to post the *dazibao* to her front door, a ferocious thunderstorm came with nightfall. I lay awake, watching Guo sleep, and imagined what happened outside: the wind shaking the trees, the pouring rain drenching every *dazibao*. Those outside schools and universities, outside shop doors. Outside Jiao's front door. I pictured her *dazibao*. In the rain, the red characters bled together, becoming illegible. In the morning, I knew, Jiao's shame would be a dull red blur on soggy, pulpy paper. Not erased, but lightened. If only we too could be washed clean, given an existence outside of class backgrounds, free of the lives our forefathers had lived.

Then came August. The nights were sticky. Falling asleep became a tedious affair. One night Mei came to our bed, complaining. "It's too hot!" Guo began to comfort her when we heard a ruckus outside. A voice. No, voices, screaming piteously. Mei climbed over to the window before we could stop her, and looked down. We lived on the third floor and had a wide view of the street. "That's Rich Widower!" Mei exclaimed. I pulled Mei away, exchanging a worried glance with my husband. While Guo continued to watch, I held Mei firmly in my lap, distracting her with an adventure from *Journey to the West*. Mei fell asleep just as the Monkey King encountered trouble.

I wiped the sweat from her forehead before looking out the window myself. Eleven Red Guards dominated the street. Rich Widower, the man who owned a mansion a couple blocks from us, nowhere to be seen. I saw a woman dragged by her hair. There was an unmoving body, with awkward legs, at the base of a tree, soaking in a pond of blood. Two members of the upper class, old money, beaten. Five Red Guards clubbed one gentleman, and six beat the other. Blood gleamed in the streetlight. Cries of agony, still clearly discernable, grew weaker.

"An-xiang. An-xiang!" My husband drew my arm away and firmly shut the blinds.

"No more salon meetings," I said, looking at his sorrowful face, my shoulders shaking.

"Don't look again," he whispered, drawing me into his arms, stroking my hair.

I pulled back, holding back my tears. "Promise me," I whispered fiercely.

He sighed. "Alright, I promise."

I collapsed into his chest, silently sobbing. Through my blurry vision, I watched Mei's small torso rise and fall. I tried to focus on her gentle breathing. I tried to block the screams outside.

So I thought we'd been relatively lucky. It seemed that we would escape true persecution. They'd only shaved most of Guo's head; the students, thinking themselves clever, formed an *X* with the remaining hair. He'd been assigned janitor duties, like others in his department. They made us wear heavy signs around our necks that labeled us, in bright red paint, "counter-revolutionaries." Guo told me that one of the professors in his department had chastised the students, demanding that they recognize the wrongness of their actions. First they laughed. Then they beat him and forced him to sit on a chair that they'd driven knives through, blades up. The other professors heard his cries but were powerless to take action. No one spoke up after that. We're all out to save ourselves, to minimize the impact the destruction will have on our families. And who can blame us? We didn't start this war.

Then we began hearing about the searches; they took place at any hour, unannounced. I heard from friends that we must rid ourselves of anything deemed one of the Four Olds. Jiao urged me to discard anything that could be considered bourgeois or capitalist. So with my six-year-old daughter watching with curious, innocent eyes, my husband and I sadly burned old artwork and our parents' wedding pictures. I made sure that we only owned nondescript clothing. We sold engraved mahogany furniture, a porcelain stool. We replaced the sofa with a humble-looking armchair. I cut my own and Mei's hair into "revolutionary" bobs.

All this will save us, I thought. It's for the best. In a constant state of uncertainty and fear, we waited. Maybe they wouldn't even come. But they did. When they came to search us I'd just entered my fourth month of pregnancy. We'd been having dinner; I'd managed to save enough to treat the family to a whole trout. Mei had been so pleased, still young enough to consider such simple pleasures her world.

"Open up, by order of the Red Guards and Chairman Mao!"

Our time had come. My hands started shaking and sweating. I rushed to throw the fish out, fearful they'd consider it a sign of opulence. My husband went to the door, and five of those devils stomped in, chests puffed out like they were soldiers in Chairman Mao's personal army. Four young men and one young woman made up the group. The woman sneered at us with the same vindictive spirit that dominated the men. Their distorted faces, still plump with baby fat, almost looked comical. They pushed us out of the way and ransacked our house, overturning tables, smashing dishes, confiscating objects without explanation, and insulting us along the way. They found the fish in the trash and threw it in our faces.

And then they found the one thing I'd forgotten about: a genealogy book that my grandmother had given to me while on her deathbed. They gleefully burned it, and when I protested, they beat me and my husband. My Mei, powerless, cried out and tried to reach me, but the female guard slapped her and pushed her away.

Somehow I'd been thrown to the ground, and I begged, I pleaded for the life of my unborn child. The woman walked over to me, possessed with imagined authority. My husband dove in front of me, a shield. But the four men pulled him away, taking out a copper-buckled belt and whipping him. The young woman cursed me, her flapping mouth revealing many cavities. She took to viciously kicking my small baby bump. And when the fat witch jumped on my stomach, multiple times, ignoring my pitiful cries for mercy, I knew that the baby would die. Only when they left, laughing, triumphant in their self-righteousness, did Mei and I cry. My husband, bloody shirt sticking to his back, held us stone-faced, anger eating him up inside. In our dazed, beaten state, we hardly noticed the vandalized state of our apartment. It looked like a typhoon had swept through.

A couple hours later, after I could move without severe pain, my husband and I took inventory. Half of my clothes, gone. The fine china, wedding gifts, all smashed. I didn't allow Mei into the kitchen until my husband thoroughly swept the sharp shards up. It took us three days to clean everything else.

A day later I miscarried, and Mei saw it all, though I'd told her to stay away. I think she meant to help because she brought towels to clean, but she strangely showed no fear of the body tissue and gushing blood. So, so much blood. Clotting, sticky and warm. The growth of life, ripped out far too soon. My husband and I sobbed for our lost child, the sibling Mei would never know.

I'd thought that it must be over, that we'd now be left alone. A baby miscarried, a home destroyed. A family shattered.

But it seemed like we couldn't shake away the black mark. Two weeks later other students of the Red Guard came, this time with a loading truck. A crowd gathered around our lawn.

"Rise up, proletarians! Tear down the bourgeoisie!" the students shouted, running up to the third floor.

Unable to ignore their thunderous knocking, Guo opened the door. They invaded. They confiscated our "capitalist" bed, our armchair, much of our clothes. Our radio. I kept Mei by my side, away from the upending, the overturning of chairs, stools, the throwing of notebooks. The foolish, power-hungry kids, I thought angrily. They treated this like theatre. But they ruined our lives in real time.

"Guo Ling," the familiar-looking leader declared, "admit that you're a rightist and xenophile!"

My husband shook his head but didn't say a word. I couldn't believe my eyes and ears.

"Feng Wu?" I asked in disbelief. I'd taught him once; he'd been a troublemaker and a terrible student, but I couldn't believe him capable of orchestrating such destruction.

Feng flicked a glance at me and sneered. The cruelty in his face stunned me silent. "Not so scholarly now, An-xiang Ling!" He turned away from me and announced their intentions.

And then my nightmare became reality. They were going to cart my husband away for "reeducation." I begged them for leniency. When that didn't work, I demanded an explanation. I received several paltry ones. His colleagues had betrayed him and confessed to Guo's involvement in salon meetings. Guo's best friend had even abandoned him, revealing the well-kept secret that his father had been a landlord. Finally, they pronounced Guo an anti-revolutionary capitalist, simply because he'd taught "Western" engineering classes. So all Mei and I could do was watch, weak with fear and silent anger. With Mei clutching my leg, Guo swore to return to me. He begged me to wait, to keep silent, and to take care of our only child.

"We'll start again when this revolution is over, I promise. Just hold on."

Ava reached for the next entry when a strong knock on the door shocked her back to the present.

"Floor meeting!" Dan said through the door. "It'll be a quick one if you get to the common room in the next minute or two."

Wanting to avoid an awkward one-on-one exchange, Ava yelled, "I'll be right there." She carefully put the diary entries back into the envelope, slipped it underneath her pillow, and left to hear about the latest Lockhart news.

Chapter Fourteen

On the evening of December 10, Paul pulled his tan Toyota Prius into the driveway at the Maplewood Estates Complex. He checked the garage, cursing his remote when it revealed his wife's Mercedes Benz. Nothing he could do. Facts were facts.

Before he finished turning the key, the front door swayed open. The scent of jasmine assaulted his nose.

"Good to see you," Mei purred. "*Li bie qing geng shen.*"

Paul stepped inside, brushing by her. "No. It's the opposite for us." He shrugged off his jacket and threw it over his arm. "What the eye doesn't view makes the heart swell in relief."

She sidled up to him. Tendrils of jasmine crushed his throat closed. "I can take your coat?"

He coughed and backed away. "No. I'm not staying long. I just need a few things."

Her black eyes glittered. "Leave so soon? Not even staying to toast? No need pretending you forget what today is."

Paul turned to head for the stairs. "How about we pretend we've both forgotten?"

Mei slunk ahead of him, blocking his way upward. "Come, no hug, no kiss?" She laid her manicured hands on his chest and looked up, eyes wide.

He pushed her hands away. "Quit playing around. You know how I feel. *Wu ke yao jiu.*" Yes, he resented her for falling so far below his expectations. He knew she felt the same toward him. These overpowering currents flushed away what had ever been good between them. Only dregs remained.

She put a hand to her rosy mouth like he'd said that her lipstick had faded. "Twenty-seven years! What you will say ten years more from now?"

"*Zi zuo zi shou, zi shi er guo*. Or have you forgotten that cheating has consequences?"

Mei licked the inner rim of her lips and smiled when she saw his repulsion. She placed her hands on his waist like she was about to pet the sides of his sweater. "Happy anniversary—" she dug her nails into his sides "*hus-band.*"

Paul flung her claws away. "If you don't leave me alone at once we won't be married for ten more days, let alone ten years."

She let him pass. But when he started up the first flight, she called after him: "*Liang hu xiang zheng, bi you yi shang.*"

A logical statement, but she'd started this war, and he resolved to prevent her from finishing it.

He resisted slamming the door to his home office. What had he come here for? For a moment he worried that his brain was failing him. Get it together! Forty-eight, not eighty-four. No, his brain, only momentarily fogged by anger, still fully functioned. He just needed some paperwork.

Paul opened the bottommost drawer to his oak desk. He paused a moment, about to take the photocopies of client contracts he had originally come to the house for. His office looked . . . neater. Dust free. Straightening up, he discovered a Post-it note attached to the monitor of his desktop computer. "Freshly cleaned by Ava," it read. Nice of her. He hoped she'd kept things in order; he didn't want his filing system to be muddled. Paul went through his desk, drawer by drawer, confirming that everything remained the same. He took the contracts out, and flipped through them, eager to leave.

Underneath the contracts, in the back of the drawer, was supposed to be an envelope he'd marked "Lao lao/Mei diary, 1966–1970." A partial copy of the incomplete diary he translated so long ago. Paul intended to take *Lao lao*'s sections back to his apartment and reunite them with Mei's, but it slipped his mind every time he returned to the house. Had Mei found it? His stomach roiled; he feared what his wife would do if she knew. No, impossible. Mei didn't remember showing him the original entries, and if she'd found it she'd surely let him know. She couldn't check her temper.

This meant only one thing. Ava had found it while cleaning; the maid never entered his office. The circumstances under which she'd found the diary were less than ideal; Paul had wanted to give her the complete diary and do some explaining. Her eighteenth birthday had passed and she needed to know about her mother's traumatic childhood. Paul had planned to use *Lao lao*'s miscarriage as a prelude; Ava deserved to know that she'd almost had an elder brother. He brushed away the thought that Mei only wanted a son.

But, like everything else he wanted to talk with Ava about, there never seemed to be the right time. Maybe it'd be better that she found out this way. He had originally wanted to hand over the diary on her birthday, but what kind of present would that make? Besides, he didn't know how to talk to Ava anymore. He turned his back for what felt like a second, and his daughter became a stranger. She rebuffed his attempts to communicate with her, and over four years had passed since she last visited him in the city. To be fair, Paul knew he'd also become a stranger to her. And he let that happen. But surely Ava wanted space? Maybe Paul would've been closer to his daughter if he'd taken risks. Ignored his experiences, gotten the divorce, and fought for her. Had he done the right thing?

Chapter Fifteen

By mid-December the frosty air had become more than a whisper. Snow dusted the landscape but melted under sunbreaks. Like an ellipsis following the words of winter, finals week arrived at Davison University.

University Way's honors dorm, Lockhart, fell into a silent panic. Those able to study in the lobby buried their faces into books that may or may not have been used all semester. The honors students ignored all distractions except the occasional text, to which they replied, "Leave me alone!" With room doors tightly shut, occupants cocooned themselves in pajamas and bathrobes to read or solve problems until words and numbers ceased making sense. Tensions roiled, loomed, and erupted over a roommate's music or television show that "couldn't be missed." College finals weighed upon freshmen with the added pressure of proving themselves for the first time.

Charlotte spent most of her time at University Way's library with Kevin and Jason. This left Ava and Derek camped in their respective rooms. Ava felt particularly strapped down, forced to juggle her studies, deflect inquiring texts from her dad, and endure lengthy calls from her mother. She lectured Ava about her expectations. Nothing Ava said, whether obedient or argumentative, was acknowledged, only denounced peremptorily and angrily.

Halfway through Ava's finals, she received one of these phone calls. She had been in the process of writing her final, eight-page paper for Asian American Literature when the insistent ring of her phone interrupted. Reluctantly putting down the article she had been skimming for a good quote, Ava pattered over to her bed, where she had left her phone. Maybe her dad called to give her encouragement, but probably not. Surprise, surprise, Mother called. Mother. The name seemed too indicative of a healthy, emotional attachment. How can you have a healthy relationship with someone you obey out of fear? Still, the label endeared less than "Ma," "Mom," or—worst of all—"Mommy."

She forced her fingers to accept the call. Ignoring the calls always led to more trouble.

"Hi Mother," she said tiredly.

"Why aren't you studying?"

"Well I was, until you called."

"No excuses. I expect A pluses, no less, you hear? You keep your scholarship or else you move back home."

Ava resisted a shudder at the thought of commuting. "Do you want something?"

"Already an attitude, what gives you the right?"

"What are you talking about? I need to finish writing—" a paper, Ava almost said before catching herself in time—"an answer to an Organic Chemistry problem; my exam is tomorrow afternoon." She bit her lip anxiously. Close one.

"You dare? Put your mother first. You so unprepared for your exams, I can feel it. Every exam counts. Think this hard? This is med school prep. You got any grades back?"

"Of course not! I won't get my grades back until a week after the semester officially ends." And I'll be forced to lie about my classes then, too. She needed to write all the lies down or she'd end up slipping.

"Such a loose tongue, the way you talk to the woman who gave birth to you. I raised you, ungrateful *zazhong*. You know, I could've been something. I could've been a professor like my parents!" Mei raised her voice so that Ava's phone echoed.

She thought of *Lao lao*'s diary. You could never be like your parents. "I can't deal with you—this now," she said, brushing her choppy-layered hair away from her face. Yet another reminder of her mother.

"What." Mei dropped her voice to a caressing whisper.

Ava's stomach clenched. Mei spoke softly before striking like a typhoon. So Ava felt no surprise when her mother's voice ripped through the phone. Ava held it away from her ear. She turned the speaker on in the unlikely case she needed to respond. Putting her phone down on the side of the bed closest to her desk, she returned to her article and laptop.

She expertly blocked unwanted noises. Besides, Mei's tirade was nothing new. The usual nasty concoction of curses and name-calling in Mandarin and English, with some more elaborate Chinese curses thrown in: "illegitimate half-breed," which Ava could only half argue with; "dumb egg," and an unrecognized slur that her father probably knew, "you are shameless and a thing, not a human." But as Ava had grown inured to such insults, she let the curses blow by.

The storm quelled. Mei's voice candied ginger again, sweet laced with spice. "Are you listening, girl?"

"Yes," Ava lied. She continued typing, integrating the quote she needed into her paper.

"You lucky to have me. I take all your abuse and shit. If I can go back I wouldn't have you. I gave up everything for a boy; you just a worthless, problem girl. You bring shame to me, shame!" Mei finished, abruptly hanging up.

Resisting the urge to reach across her desk and chuck her phone across the room, Ava rose to place it on the top of her bureau. Maybe she should take a break from her paper and read the next entry in *Lao lao*'s diary. After that one-sided conversation, she lost the desire to write about her chosen paper topic, "Eurasian Identity in *The Frontiers of Love*." Reading about a situation that's irrefutably worse than yours always makes you feel grateful for the relatively minor crap you have to deal with.

But before she retrieved the envelope, someone knocked on the door. Taking a deep breath and exhaling in a gush, she saved her essay and opened the door.

"Hey Ava," Derek said, hands in his pockets.

"You look guilty. What's up?"

"Uh, yeah." He sheepishly touched the back of his head. "I kinda heard the end of that conversation."

"What . . . what exactly did you hear?"

"Something about you bringing shame—to I guess your mom? I didn't eavesdrop, I swear. I planned to knock on your door to see if you wanted lunch when . . . "

"When you couldn't help but listen." Relief surged through Ava. He hadn't heard the worst.

"Sorry. Uh . . . can I come in?" he asked, shifting his weight from foot to foot.

"Not until after I come in," a familiar voice called.

Ava mentally groaned when Charlotte stepped in, followed by Derek. No chance to read anything now. Resigned, she climbed onto her bed.

Derek and Charlotte sat down on Charlotte's bed. Ava turned to face them. These days they spent more time together than Charlotte spent with Ava. She wondered if they were dating. If not, she felt tempted to join their hands and say, "Whom are you kidding? Just get together already!" From the way they strategically positioned themselves on the bed, carefully avoiding physical contact, she sensed she'd have to fight her temptation.

"So I was just about to ask Ava if she's okay," Derek informed Charlotte.

"Why wouldn't she be okay?"

"I'm fine." Ava carefully kept a level voice. What was this, an intervention?

"Bullshit," he said, surprising them. "'I'm fine' is code for 'things are going to hell.'"

Charlotte laughed but Ava didn't. "What makes you say that?"

"You know, he's got a point," Charlotte said. "How many times have you been greeted with, 'how are you?' and you respond with 'fine' when the day's been shit and at the very least you're feeling stressed?"

The not-couple appeared ready to tag team this conversation.

"Right, I see what you mean," she acknowledged, hoping to end it there.

"I know what you're going through," Derek said.

Charlotte looked at him curiously. "What do you mean?"

"Uh, being a—what's the word we learned in class? Amerasian?"

Ava got the hint but somehow doubted that he really knew her situation. From what Charlotte had told her, his mom was normal.

"I know it's hard, being an Amerasian," he continued, trying to get Ava to open up. "There's constant conflict between two cultures, and it's worse because both my parents are immigrants. Just your mom is, right?"

"Mmhmm." Ava picked an imaginary piece of fuzz off her sweats.

"Well, isn't that true for most immigrant/nonimmigrant relationships?" Charlotte asked. "My mom's an immigrant; at age four she came over from Italy. But . . . not my dad. And you can go beyond that to say that there's constant conflict between wives and husbands."

"What are you trying to do, widen the scope of this convo?" Derek asked, giving Charlotte a playful push, which made her giggle.

Sickeningly cute. Ava wished she could video record how silly they were acting. She better start talking before they began making out for her viewing displeasure.

"How do you answer the origin question?"

Derek stopped teasing Charlotte to look at Ava. "What do you mean? You know what I am," he said, confused.

"How would you answer that question to someone like Charlotte, for example."

"Hey! What are you trying to say?" Charlotte protested.

"That you're a racist, obviously," Ava said. "No, a white person who hasn't been exposed to an Amerasian before."

"I guess that it depends on how I'm feeling that day. I usually go with 'New Jersey—'"

"But then you get the 'no, where are you *really* from,' right?"

Charlotte just listened, unsure of how to contribute.

"Exactly, like I lied the first time," Derek agreed. "If I find the person annoying, I'll just repeat myself. Then they either give up or try rephrasing the question. Playing dumb is a great way to get back at insensitive people."

"Seriously? People actually say these things to you?" Charlotte asked.

"Are you kidding? When I was younger and looked mostly Asian, I got 'what are you?' so many times I can't remember who asked," Ava said. It felt like opening up a talking Hallmark card and being attacked by a chorus of people, all shouting, "What are you?" One pesky, multi-layered voice that constantly demanded the right to know her racial identity. No one cared about how she saw herself. They just wanted to know what percent of this, and what percent of that, all to satisfy their curiosity and get on with their lives. Ava wished that self-definition could be that simple for her.

"How do you usually answer?" Charlotte asked.

"As Derek said, it depends. If I'm feeling snide, my go-to response is 'an alien from outer space. Crap, you've found me out!'"

They laughed.

"But now people just assume you're white, right?" Derek asked.

"For the most part, yes," Ava replied. "When I get questioned now, Asian people ask. It's like they have better Amerasian radar."

"What, like gaydar, except for Whasians?" Charlotte asked, amused.

Derek looked at Ava again, studying her features. "Yeah, it makes sense for someone who doesn't know better. To assume you're white, I mean. Do you think you've got an advantage because you can pass?"

"Probably. Maybe I'd feel different if no one called me a chink in grammar school— "

"What?" Charlotte asked. "Why didn't you tell me?"

Ava shrugged. "You never asked."

"It's not like 'Have you ever been called a chink?' is a common question," Charlotte said defensively.

"Do you think it's fair to participate in the passing?" asked Derek.

Rice cracker. "I've done it before," Ava admitted. "You know it's not. It erases part of you. And it perpetuates Western ideals."

"What, so you bring it up yourself?" he asked.

"Ideally. Then I get to direct the conversation."

"No wonder you're so angsty all the time. You've got all this pent-up resentment toward all the racists you've encountered!" Charlotte said. "You know what you should do? Make a Facebook group. 'Whasians unite: teaching ignorant crackers that mixing is okay.'" She moved her hands in the air as if talking about seeing her name in lights.

"Because that'd solve all problems," Ava said.

Derek grinned. "You can be our enlightened spokesperson, Charlotte."

A knock on the door interrupted, followed by Jason's voice. "Open up, we've got a warrant to search your room for a Charlotte Bell."

"She's not here," Charlotte called back, remaining on her bed.

They heard Kevin next. "C'mon Char, we're going onto round two of studying. You won't want to miss out on all the fun. Who's going to hold us to task? You know how easy I get sidetracked. Please!"

"Ugh. The *children* need me to lead a psych study session. I'm afraid I must leave you to it," Charlotte said, heaving herself off the bed.

Derek and Ava heard Charlotte say, as the trio left, "And I don't want to hear any more talk about last week's episode of *Dancing With the Stars*, okay?"

"And so that leaves the hybrids alone together," Derek joked.

Silence.

"Are you . . . are you still ticked at me?"

"For what?" asked Ava.

"You know . . . telling Charlotte about Halloween."

"To be honest, that annoyed me."

"I didn't do it maliciously, you know. She freaked out with worry, and—"

"I know, I know."

"So . . . you're okay? Dan didn't . . ." Derek shifted uncomfortably on Charlotte's bed.

"That's what you've been thinking this whole time? No, it was consensual. I can't believe Charlotte didn't tell you that."

"Oh. Well . . . good." He ran a hand through his hair, inadvertently spiking it up.

She felt sorry for him. He seemed to care, but his concern faced the almost insurmountable obstacles she threw in his way.

"You know, it's funny how things change," Ava finally said, eyes coming to rest on the downward-facing Disneyland picture.

"What do you mean?"

"I used to look obviously Chinese," she explained.

"When did you stop?"

"By the fifth grade. I'd caught the flu, which had been going around at school, and my mother came to pick me up . . . "

When Mei greeted her, the nurse immediately went into the back room and brought out the Asian boy who had been lying on the cot across from Ava. Not sick enough to experience a lack of curiosity, eleven-year-old Ava peeked at her confused mother.

"Here's your son, Mrs. Chan." The nurse tried to pass the equally confused boy to Mrs. Magee.

"I have no son," Mei said, annoyance seeping from her voice. "I'm here for my daughter."

"She's not my mommy," the boy weakly agreed, trying to wriggle out of the nurse's firm grasp.

The nurse joined the confusion. "What? But there's only Ava Magee back there."

"Yes, yes," Mei said impatiently, her intolerance for incompetence flowing through the split in her genial veneer. "Ava, time to go home. You're eating *xi fan.*"

Though she dreaded Chinese rice gruel, she made her way over and stood next to Mei. The nurse looked from the now-still boy, to Mei, and then from Mei to Ava and vice versa.

"But—" she protested, settling a disbelieving set of eyes on Ava.

"I am Mrs. Magee. See? Mei Magee. Not so hard to believe. Give me the form. I need to sign, yes?" Mei angrily clamped a manicured hand onto Ava's nearest shoulder, causing her daughter to wince.

"Yes, yes," the nurse said, shaking her head as if to shake away her surprise. She picked up a clipboard from a nearby table and handed it to Mrs. Magee. When Mei bent down to sign the release form, Ava watched the nurse study Mei, and then Ava caught the nurse staring at her own face. The nurse had looked away, embarrassed. She then took the form back and guided the boy to his cot.

"I've long since forgotten the nurse's name," she told Derek. "But I'll never forget that look on her face. It'd turned from confusion and disbelief to disgust."

He whistled. "Ouch. Your mom must've been *pissed.*"

"Yes. And I don't blame her." For once. "I can't imagine what that feels like—having someone adamantly try to give you someone else's kid."

"That's probably what families that adopt go through all the time."

"At least the ones that adopt children of a different race," Ava agreed.

She returned to picking at her sweatpants.

Derek tried again. "I didn't feel different until high school. Until then I'd only hung out with the nerds, and they never cared about race. I'd never really noticed that I look more Chinese than Russian. But then I began playing sports. I joined the football team, and some of the jocks were real asses. Pranks, like leaving greasy take-out cartons in my locker. They'd say that I was half smart because I'm half Asian. And then that I was half a man. Like my Chinese blood directly caused my inability to bench-press my weight. But I learned to ignore stupid people like that. The benefits outweigh the downsides, if you ask me. I mean, we know what real Chinese food tastes like, not the silly Americanized version."

"True. Most of my friends—most of yours too, probably—think Chinese food consists of fried rice, General Tso's Chicken, and dumplings; or they think I eat dog."

They lapsed into silence again.

"You know, Ava, that you can talk to me, right?"

She shrugged, disliking the turn of the conversation.

"You finally tell your mom about switching to the English major?"

Ava looked up, startled. "No. Why?"

Derek shrugged. "I thought maybe that's why I heard her say she was ashamed of you."

"No, we were just fighting about small things. The usual. I can't tell her yet."

"Why? Wouldn't it be better to tell her now so she can have more time to get used to the idea? You know, she'll be mad now, but by the time next semester comes around, she'll accept it. That's how my mom acted when I decided to play football."

Ava just nodded politely. But my mother's nothing like yours.

He sighed. "Why do you have to be so tight-lipped all the time?"

"Okay, so we're both mixed and probably share some experiences because of it. But don't discount individuality and personal experience. You don't understand, and you wouldn't understand. So stop trying to get me to explain my life story."

Derek looked taken aback by her outburst. "You know what? Fine. I'm your friend, Ava. I just want to help—we all just want to help. And I want to understand. I want you to *help* me understand so I can back you up. But if you're not interested, forget it, okay? I hope staying closed off works for you." He stood to leave.

"Wait," she said, looking down at her folded hands when he turned around. "I'm sorry I can't . . . can't help you help me. And . . . and I want to say thanks. Thanks for taking care of me on Halloween."

Derek paused. "Anytime, Ava—within reason. I'll see you in Asian American Lit. Good luck on the rest of your exams."

"You too." She watched the door swing shut behind him.

Ava went over to her laptop once more and continued where she had left off, on the seventh page. After rewriting the same sentence four times with increasing dissatisfaction, she slammed her computer closed and dove onto her bed. Derek had pinched a nerve.

She wanted camaraderie, she did. But her childhood raised too many hurdles. Ava hadn't learned how to leap over them; she never considered turning to others for help. Her troubles appeared to be a solo marathon. And even if she could run over her past, Ava still needed to shake the feeling that she—her very existence—was wrong. She'd always felt fragmented, dislocated. Limited by liminality. Sure, now most overlooked her Amerasian mix, but this seemed to cause more internal tension.

Professor Chen had begun helping her see that she could be more. More than a composite. But it remained a new concept, and their research sessions had been suspended for finals. So she still straddled two worlds. Non-suspecting, non-Asians tended to write her off as white. But even if she looked the part, she couldn't really play it—not convincingly. Asians recognized something of themselves in her: her name, perhaps some physical features, her mentality. Nonetheless, they never considered her "one of them." Neither group did, neither fully accepted her, both sides of her. Each thought too much of "the other" lived in her.

Chopsticks or forks? She used both—simultaneously, she *was* both. But she'd been raised by chopsticks.

With a sigh, she decided to break open the diary again. She pulled the envelope out from under her pillow. Ava found sleeping on *Lao lao*'s diary comforting. Her grandmother lived in her words, and in the diary she had the potential to love Ava in a way Mei could never be capable of. She took the pages out, thinking about her secrets. You want to tell Derek and Charlotte about your upbringing. About your real mother. At least, half of you does. But that would just complicate things more, even if she got them to believe her in the first place. She'd hidden for so long.

An invisible but indivisible Great Wall separated her from the people surrounding her. Entities composed the pieces of the Wall, the stones and tamped earth. She continually groped for their names. If she knew what to call these entities—these *things*—then perhaps she'd be able to identify their weaknesses. To seek out their true natures based on the power of knowing their names, their essences. To seek out the fissures in the Wall, where tiny spaces breathed between stone and earth.

Ava knew she was complicit in her own misery. How many opportunities had she been given during grammar, middle, and high school to tell guidance counselors that her back hurt not because she'd slept strangely, but because she'd angered her mother that morning by throwing out the bit of scrambled egg that had dropped to the floor? Too humiliating to admit such incidents aloud. She'd been vague in her explanation to Professor Chen for this reason. She'd known that her mentor wouldn't push her. Saying it into existence would cause others to react. To judge. They'd do whatever they felt necessary, all in the name of "helping." And then she'd be forced to face the consequences. So she left the Wall alone. She lived in fear, but she feared what stood beyond the Wall more: the unknown.

1967

I do not know if I can hold on. There is nothing to hold on to. Everything that was once certain has been taken away from me. Besides the humiliation of street-cleaning, the unrecognizable state of what we once called home, and my husband somewhere—in what condition I don't know—the baby haunts me. I try to hide my fear in front of Mei, but sometimes I cannot, especially at night. Although I never knew the sex of the child, in my nightmares it's a boy. His eyes shine the same shade of red as that woman's red scarf, that bitch who stomped on my baby's future. He speaks to me, moaning that I should've saved him, that I'm weak and a bad mother. I'm beginning to think he's right. He visits me on most nights, waking me from my straw bed. I spring up, sweating.

Sometimes Mei wakes with me. Since they took her father, I've made her sleep next to me. I say it's because I don't want her to feel scared, but in truth, I don't want to be alone at night. Anyway, when she wakes after I cry out, the poor child is confused. For a moment, all is forgotten; she asks for Dad. I don't have the heart to remind her of our tragic reality, so I say that he went to use the toilet and will be right back. Then I sing her to sleep, doing my best to mask my trembling voice.

Other nights, to put off the inevitable nightmares, I watch Mei sleep. She's so peaceful and lovely. On her seven-year-old face there are no marks of the Revolution; I feel like I am aging for her. I love her so much and tell her so each day. Disregarding Confucian custom, I try to show Mei my love, holding her, brushing her hair, telling her the legends my mother told me, teaching her about all the good that exists in the world. Good that she hasn't seen in these past two years. I watch Mei closely when she's awake, afraid she's been harmed by all she's witnessed, but she seems fine. It's a miracle I'm ever grateful for. I'm unsure if I'll ever see my husband again. So Mei has become my hope, my existence.

Jiao visits often. She brings her radio, which she's managed to keep as the Red Guard only searched her once. There's no longer any point in turning away from "black" family members. Since Guo's absence, we Lings have all been lumped into the black category. Our bad class background led to our being shunned.

But this morning Jiao came with a warning.

"I can't stay long," she said, pulling me and Mei into the bathroom. When they took Guo, they ordered me to share our once-private kitchen with the three other families in the building. The bathroom became the only place for private conversation.

"Something bad, Auntie?" Mei asked.

Jiao gently ruffled Mei's hair before returning her attention to me. "The Neighborhood Committee is coming after you. You'll be questioned repeatedly, daily, for as long as they want."

Swallowing hard, I pressed Mei against my waist. "Struggle sessions?" I asked, though I already knew what they were.

Nodding, she gently touched my shoulder. "Don't let them break you. From what I hear, they're ruthless. Don't admit to anything, even if they promise 'leniency.' They're lying; they have no mercy."

Mei looked up at our worried faces. Though she was growing fast, I lifted her up, balancing her on my hip. She reached up and tried to smooth my furrowed brow.

"How are your sons?" I asked.

A shadow of angst passed over Jiao's once sanguine face. She chewed her lips and then calmed her features.

"I must go, cousin." She opened the bathroom door and rushed out; I barely had time to thank her.

Two mornings later Jiao came again. I opened the door to find her bent over, panting.

"I . . . had . . . to run," she wheezed. I'd forgotten that she'd had childhood asthma.

"What is it?"

Jiao pointed at Mei, who'd snuck up behind me. "Let me take her to my place. They're coming for you now. I'll keep her safe."

I didn't have time to protest. Giving Mei a fierce hug, I sent her off with Jiao. Ten minutes later the Committee members knocked on my door. I silently left the apartment with them.

They brought me to Peking University. I bitterly entered a classroom I'd once held biology labs in. *Dazibao* and bright posters of Mao littered the walls. I knew that no room in the building had escaped propaganda. I'd heard that even the president's office had been looted. They posted a *dazibao* in his office, with his name on it—but the characters had been written upside down, and a big black *X* further damned him.

The Committee members stood, surrounding me, ordering me to sit. I couldn't believe that Guo and I had once supported the Communist regime. How had it become so brutal? I hardly remembered when the focus had been positive, on increasing steel production, on modernizing China. I looked at the cruel faces of neighbors I'd once been friends with, or at least civil with. When had things started regressing? Respect no longer existed, none for teachers, none for the past, and none for the human condition. Now, I thought grimly, China bleeds red for the sake of Mao's lust for power.

"Confess to your lies now, An-xiang, and we can spare you from severe punishment," said the secretary, a sweet smile belying the vengeance in her beady eyes. She was my first-floor neighbor, and had been since Mei's birth. Everyone knew her as the Stone Woman: infertile, she'd been unable to give her husband children. He dallied with other women, and Stone Woman always suspected Jiao to be one of his mistresses. It didn't matter that Jiao never involved herself in affairs with married men. Stone Woman believed what she believed and hated us.

"What lies?" I asked wearily.

The six members practically exchanged looks of glee.

"Lying, corruption, favoring students, capitalism, bourgeois ideology . . . ," Stone Woman listed, using her right hand to tick off the fingers on her left.

Again and again, I denied everything calmly. But during the second hour of the interrogation, when they accused me of lying about being pregnant to avoid punishment, I lost my temper. The demon-eyed baby boy appeared in my mind. I jumped up from my chair so forcefully that I knocked it backward.

"I had a miscarriage because of the brutality inflicted upon us during the first raid! Don't dare accuse me of lying about that! Who do you think you are? You're power-hungry, but you're just pawns in this game! Look at your—" They restrained and repeatedly slapped me.

When the session ended, early evening had settled in. They placed a heavy wooden placard around my neck. Escorting me back to the apartment, they forced me to beat a gong and chant out the sign's message.

"I am a capitalist monster," I droned, determinedly avoiding the gazes of familiar faces.

When I passed by Jiao's apartment, I saw Mei peering out from the window. I thought I saw her smile and wave. Distracted, I stumbled, tripping over my own feet. Stone Woman grabbed the switch she'd used on me earlier. She whipped my arm and though I winced, I kept chanting and resumed walking.

I used to be optimistic. I used to have faith. In community. In neighbors. In friends and family. But under this pressure . . . under threats, under violence . . . I've come to a frightening conclusion. The capacity for interpersonal cruelty is boundless. We will indict our uncles, aunts, cousins, parents, sisters, brothers. We will betray them if we think it'll bolster our own chances of survival. We'll do it because we buckle under the tumult. It's not always due to fear. There's desire: revenge, power, praise. We know what's right, what's just. But that isn't enough to stop us from doing what's wrong.

For a month, the sessions took place every other day. Each struggle session, the same. Baseless accusations, coaxing, threatening, beating, the chanting walk home. The last session hurt the worst. They humiliated me in front of the person I held most dear.

This time they brought me and three other professors into the university auditorium. They ordered us to stand on rickety wooden chairs. They placed placards around our necks. And then the head of the Neighborhood Committee shouted, "Airplane position!" I exchanged looks of misery with my fellow black-category professors. "NOW." We obeyed, bowing our heads, folding our bodies into the flat-backed position, spreading our arms out to the sides.

"Bring the family members in," I heard Stone Woman say.

I snapped up in shock. Jiao and Mei walked toward me.

"Back into position, reactionary hag!" The committee head kicked me in the shins. I wobbled, nearly losing my balance on the chair.

Again I bent over, spreading my arms. I will not cry. I will not show weakness. But then Mei came up to me, stopping five feet from my chair. My neck strained from the weight of the placard, but I managed to shift my head upward. To my dismay, I saw Mei bend down. She copied my position: her little back bent, her arms out.

"Mei, no, don't do that. You're just supposed to watch," I heard Jiao whisper.

Dropping my head in shame, I prayed that Mei would soon forget this. I tried to dream of the moment when she became an adult . . . when she could put all this behind her. But could she? I couldn't stop the tears. They silently fell to the auditorium floor, landing in front of Mei's small feet.

1968

Today is Mei's eighth birthday. During my trip to the market I bought her a red scarf, embroidered with the slogan "The East is Red"—the safest gift to get. I wish I had something extra special to give her, but I don't want to run the risk of buying something capable of attracting attention. During the last search, a Red Guard ripped off the head of Mei's porcelain doll, then taken the pieces. Seeing Mei's burning eyes, her fisted hands at her sides, I myself wanted to commit an act of violence. But there's enough of that already.

Now it's just me, Mei, and my cousin. Jiao has given up her apartment and come to live with us. She showed up at our door a week ago, her meager belongings at her feet. I won't ever forget the hopeless look on her face. She looked terrible, so pale, so thin. Her eyes were sunken and red.

"An-xiang," Jiao said tearfully, "may I come in?"

I quickly took her bags and ushered her in. Jiao took off her shoes. Mei came out of the bedroom and greeted her, apparently unaware of Jiao's fragile state. I've come to notice that while Mei displays incredible intelligence, more so than other children, she lacks social insight.

"Mei, could you take Auntie's things? Then wait for us in the bedroom. Auntie and I need to talk privately."

When I closed the bathroom door behind us, Jiao climbed into the tub and hugged her knees to her chest. She seemed oblivious to the dampness from my morning bath. I sat on the edge of the tub.

"Jiao, what's happened?"

In a guttural voice, still staring at her knees, she replied, "They left. To join the Revolution."

"Who left?" I asked gently.

"My sons." I leaned forward to catch her whisper. Suddenly she jerked her head up. "My sons!" Jiao shrieked hysterically. She broke into convulsing sobs.

I stared at her, aghast. "Are you . . . are you sure?"

I'd heard that family members, especially children and teenagers, sometimes renounced their elders to join the Red Guard. But I'd never really considered such situations; I'd brushed them off like all the other rumors. I'd sensed that Jiao's *dazibao* had been a source of distress for her sons. Before the Revolution, one had been in high school, and the other at Peking University. I hadn't seen them except in passing, but I'd thought they were just being selfish young men. I'd been sure they would wake up and see that their mother needed them.

"Of course I'm sure!" Jiao snapped. Swallowing gasps, she lowered her voice again. "Two days ago, they disowned me—publicly. They wrote their own *dazibao*, renouncing me. They said . . . th-they said, 'You're a disgrace; we don't want to be black like you; we disown you in the name of Chairman Mao and the Proletarian Revolution!'"

"Your own sons . . . ," I whispered in shock, stroking her greasy hair.

Jiao broke out into fresh sobs.

"Th-they even ch-changed their family name! Can't b-bear to be a-associated with Lings!" She took deep breaths, steadying her voice. "What's this world coming to? Utter betrayal, sons and daughters turning on their parents! And they think *I* dishonored *them*!"

"To be so unfilial." I shook my head. "At least . . . at least they didn't testify against you."

Jiao let out a bitter laugh, roughly rubbing her eyes. "No, but that's because they were elsewhere being revolutionary with their comrades. They would've. They would've spat in my face if asked!"

"Guo was right," I said miserably, handing her a handkerchief. "We should've gone to Nanjing when the whispers started. His parents could've taken us in. Beijing is the worst place to be."

"An-xiang. Don't bother. The past can't be undone." Jiao blew her nose.

"Ma! I have to pee." Mei opened the door and immediately went to use the toilet. When she'd finished, she opened the door and said, "Sorry, continue."

I almost wanted to laugh. But I composed myself and turned back to Jiao.

"I can't express how sorry I am. So long as we're physically able to, we will support you, no matter what. There will be no more familial abandonment. But I need you to promise me something."

Jiao looked up, folding the handkerchief. Her eyes were swollen and redder than before. For a second I thought I saw the red eyes of the son I'd miscarried. I shook my head, trying to exorcise the presentiment that came with the hallucination.

Jiao stared at me. "What is it, cousin?"

"If . . ." I cleared my throat and lowered my voice. "If anything happens to me, swear that you'll take care of Mei."

"An-xiang, don't say that; it might come true!"

"And if Guo ever comes back and I've been taken, I want you to replace me."

"I could never replace you."

"You don't need to marry him. I just need Mei to have two supportive parents."

"Why are you talking like this?"

"I need you to promise me!" I insisted.

For a moment, Jiao looked at me strangely. "Fine, fine. I promise."

Though I'm no longer subjected to struggle sessions, I'm making every effort to be invisible to Party eyes. I don't want Jiao to be forced to fulfill her promise, not if I can help it. I'll be lost if I'm parted from Mei. Right now she's playing outside with Jiao. I hope she isn't killing small animals again. First insects. Then rats and pigeons. I tell her that they aren't safe to eat, so she shouldn't kill them, but this hasn't stopped her. She's just trying to help me.

Aya, when did writing become so draining? I'm having trouble focusing, finishing a complete thought. When I was a professor, I wrote for days without tiring: letters, lab reports, poems when I became bored. But the laborious, daily cleaning that I do, in addition to my earnest efforts to home-school Mei, are proving to be too much. If I didn't have Jiao's support, I think I'd succumb to exhaustion.

No, I cannot create these excuses for myself. I must remember that this will one day be given to Mei, to her children. Words can teach, can heal. The power I believe writing can give still exists. And I must try to write, because I fear I'm losing my mind. I dare not tell Jiao about the hallucinations, though they're getting worse. The baby boy is more insistent now—he even visits me during the day. Sometimes, when Jiao goes to the market, I ask Mei if she can see her lost brother, crying out, yelling at me, accusing me. She doesn't answer, looking at me with wide black eyes, a confused lamb. I hug her fiercely and try to ward off the ghosts that lurk in my head. And the guilt. So much guilt! For being a poor mother. For losing the baby. For bringing Mei up in this dark, chaotic world. For losing my husband. For my inability to return Jiao's sons to her. For not defending myself and bowing to those who should've bowed to me.

1969

Where's my husband? Is he even alive? This is the third year without him. How is Mei already nine years old? I feel absentminded; I no longer have a sense of direction. Getting through the little tasks that make up a day seems an insurmountable challenge. I depend more on Jiao than ever.

I keep waiting for New China to collapse. But I think she will outlive me. May Mei safely live to see this chaos end. Or may she escape. But for now, my only purpose is to keep Mei safe. She's my guide, my living spirit, and the only tangible thing I have left. I hug her hourly because I am the one who needs comfort. I tell her that I'll always be there for her, but I'm beginning to doubt that I can keep this promise. Though Jiao says nothing, I think she can sense my deterioration.

I'm an awful mother. I've done a poor job of sheltering Mei. On the way back from a quick walk through the park, I let her drag me to the edge of a crowd. I should've known better. During these times, crowds never mean a good thing.

Mei tugged on the sleeve of another girl who looked close in age.

"What's going on?"

The girl looked down at Mei and then up at me. She decided to address the both of us.

"It's Grandpa Poet," she said, using the epithet the neighborhood had come to know the old man by. When we looked at her blankly, she explained. "His son was a counterrevolutionary. They executed him last night. This morning they forced Grandpa Poet to kowtow in the street. For hours. It looks like he just jumped."

Before I could grab Mei's hand and pull her away, she squeezed her way through the crowd.

"Mei, no!" But by the time I reached her, it was too late. She'd already seen.

Mei turned her attention from the mangled body to me.

With curious eyes, she asked, "The white mess is his brain, right?"

I nodded and began pulling her away. Mei followed, but I felt her body twisting; she insisted on staring at the mess.

When we escaped the crowd and resumed the walk home, she asked me questions that made me uneasy.

"What do brains feel like? Squishy? Did he die on impact? He committed suicide, right? What will happen with the body? Why'd he do it?"

Unable to continue to ignore her, I decided to answer the last question. "Mei, there's only so much a person can take. Remember the first time you boiled eggs?"

Mei smiled. "I kept the lid on and the water boiled over."

"When we're put under too much pressure and aren't given space to breathe, an escape valve, we become overwhelmed. We seek relief in different ways."

"So Grandpa Poet boiled over and jumped to his death for relief?"

"Exactly. But Mei, suicide's not the right way to find relief. We find relief in our loved ones." I abruptly stopped in front of our apartment. "Listen to me, dear daughter." I brushed Mei's hair away from her face and bent down to look at her startling black eyes. "Family is all that we have for sure. We must cherish each other. Now, I want you to be good for me, and forget what you just saw. Only remember what I've said."

I'm so afraid for her. Since that incident, I'm more determined than ever to protect her from harm. Never do I let her out of my or Jiao's sight. Now I don't let her outside alone. Too dangerous, I say. I tell her that she can see the sun from our door. Jiao and I bring her with us to work. I make her quietly recite the poems I've taught her. She avidly reads the books that no one confiscated; she finds learning fascinating and she's so bright.

Still I see my baby boy, and more often than ever. Jiao continually pulls me into the bathroom to ask me what's wrong. But I can't tell her the truth. It's the guilt, I know. The guilt chews at me. So much lost, and I could've prevented it. I should've tried harder. I should've fought my fears. My boy is right. I just pray that he chooses to curse only me. Leave my Mei alone, I tell him. Leave my cousin be. Spare my husband, if he's still alive. It's my fault. I could've saved us all.

I feel myself fading. Something's wrong. My boy, my boy! Do not cry! Don't be angry with me. The stories my mother used to tell me during the Ghost Festival must be true. I see more than my baby now. My maternal grandmother, whom Mei so resembles. Uncles, aunts, cousins who've passed away. My parents, though I haven't heard news of their deaths. I see my husband, but I hope this cannot be true. I fear I shall not last. Mei needs me; I must fight this. But no, I can't fight anymore. See, my baby, my demon-eyed baby needs me too . . .

Ava let a tear slide out of the corner of her eye before angrily flicking it away and composing herself. She flipped through the pages again. Surely there must be more. Where did Paul keep Mei's diary? What happened to *Lao lao*? What happened to her grandfather? Before more questions came to mind, she heard Charlotte's key in the door. She quickly put the diary back in its hiding place. Ava made a mental promise to herself and to the *Lao lao* she'd never known. She'd talk to her dad; she'd find out what happened. Ava resolved to piece together the troubled past she emerged from. She needed to look back before she could look forward.

Chapter Sixteen

"Any volunteers?" Professor Chen asked, standing by her large desk. Her multicolored streaks swayed as she scanned the room for a raised hand. Sixteen uneasy faces stared back at her. "Come on, I know at least one of you is just dying to present at this lovely podium." When still no one volunteered, she tried a different tactic. "Technically, this is your final. I can keep you here for three whole hours, you know; or if each of you presents for five minutes, we'll leave after eighty minutes. Tick-tock, students."

Ava stood up, presentation notes in hand.

"Alright, you take one for the team," Derek joked.

Taking her place at the wooden podium, she said to Professor Chen, "Derek elects to go after me."

"Excellent," Professor Chen replied, hiding a grin when Derek frowned. "Take it away when you're ready, Ava."

She took a deep breath and tried to ignore the fifteen classmates, the thirty eyes staring at her. Only five minutes; just get through it.

"The title of my paper is 'Eurasian Identity in *The Frontiers of Love*.' As we know from our reading, Diana Chang sets the novel in Japanese-occupied Shanghai, 1945. Chang narrates the stories of three half-Asian, half-European young adults: Mimi, Feng, and Sylvia. For better or worse, the three protagonists form different styles of being in their quests for racial and ethnic identity.

"Mimi, the youngest, suppresses her Chinese half and ultimately revels in the adoration of men, who view her as an exotic sexual object.

"Sylvia, Mimi's elder friend, shies away from flattery and tries to pay equivalent homage to her European and Chinese sides. She decides to break away from her relationship with Feng to become her own person.

"Feng, in an effort to solidify his Chinese identity, tries to discard his Caucasian half by working with communist revolutionaries. His efforts get Sylvia's Chinese cousin killed, and only then does he realize that his impulsiveness led him to lose self-agency and Sylvia's support.

"I know I've got two minutes left, so I'll sum up my thesis quickly. I argue that only after equally acknowledging the existence and intermingling of both the European and the Asian self can a Eurasian reconcile the opposing sides to form a unified identity. Therefore, I think that Diana Chang depicted Sylvia as a model of success. Um . . . thanks."

"Thank you, Ava," Professor Chen said from her seat at the back of the classroom. "I look forward to reading your paper. Save the clapping for the end, everyone. You're up, Derek."

Grudgingly, Derek shuffled over to the podium, glaring at Ava when she returned to her seat.

"I chose to write about masculinity in *Shortcomings*, the graphic novel we read. My paper is entitled 'Competing for a Piece of the Macho Belt: Why Asian-American Men Feel Pressure to Become Bananas.' As we briefly discussed in class, a 'banana' can be a metaphor for an Asian man who is 'yellow on the outside, but white on the inside . . .'"

When the last presentations were over, Ava stayed to talk briefly with Professor Chen.

"Go on without me," she told Derek.

"Okay. Oh, and Ava?" She turned to look at him. Derek paused by the door, smiling faintly. "Thanks for persuading me to take this class with you."

"Anytime. See you later."

"I'm glad you decided to write on *The Frontiers of Love*," Professor Chen said when she approached her desk.

Ava shrugged, sliding into a nearby student desk.

"Well, that's the only option that made sense. We hardly see anything of the mixed-race child in *Native Speaker*, let alone any of the other texts we read. Not that I didn't enjoy *The Frontiers of Love*," she added quickly.

Professor Chen laughed. "You know, it'd still be okay if you hadn't enjoyed it."

"I know, I just . . . actually, I wanted to talk to you about something else."

"If it's about the research, don't worry, I know you've still got exams. And I've got loads of papers to grade. We can even resume after the holiday break, if you like."

"I know. I'd like to resume after New Year's, but it's not that," Ava said, hesitating.

Professor Chen lowered her voice. "Is it your mother? Do you want me to talk to somebody for you?"

"No! Sorry, no. I still want to figure it out on my own . . ." Thinking of the diary, Ava continued, " . . . and I think I might be able to. But I wanted to ask you—I know I'm just a freshman and it's really early—about whether or not you'd consider . . ."

"Becoming your thesis advisor?"

"I—yes. How did you know?"

"Your honors dean told me that you might ask me. I'd be honored, Ava. You were a pleasure to have in class; I'm proud of how much you've grown over the semester. Besides, I'd be hopelessly behind in my manuscript if it weren't for you."

Ava blushed, unsure of what to say. "Oh . . . thanks, thanks so much!"

"Anything else?"

"Um, no. I've got another exam in an hour."

"Good luck. Once the semester is over and I'm officially no longer teaching you, I'll email you my cell number. Just in case you need to talk or text-vent about your mom . . . or anything else that bothers you. Don't be afraid to reach out to me. Okay?"

"Perfect. Thanks again, Professor Chen!"

"Next time we talk I'll teach you how to pronounce my first name. Look at my hair," Professor Chen said, holding up a white lock. "I don't want to be called 'professor' more than I have to be. And remind me to tell you the reason behind the multi-color dye."

Ava laughed and picked up her backpack. "I'll be sure to remember. Happy holidays!"

"You too, Ava. Take care of yourself."

"Of course." She opened the door and left her mentor behind.

During her walk to the lecture hall where she would meet Jason and take her Shakespeare final, she wondered how far she'd really come over her first semester at college. Sure, she'd made new friends and learned new things, but how much self-change could she claim? Ava's only triumph over Mei so far had been declaring as an English major—a secret triumph, one she feared her mother would strip from her. And, Ava conceded, she'd taken initiative in reading *Lao lao*'s diary; Mei didn't know that her daughter now knew some of the details of her childhood in China. What held Ava back, besides her own emerging self?

Silence, shame, and power. These ensnared her in Mei's firm grasp. Mei had raised Ava to be silent and ashamed, to respect her mother's power. Shame remained her default setting. Cartoon Dragon Lady or not, Amy Chua–tiger mother or not, or bits of both stereotypes and more, Mei had always been a constant. With a virtually absent father, whom else did Ava have but her twisted mother?

She wanted change, but now felt like the wrong time to bring it about. Yes, there'd be a time. Every day she felt closer, closer to naming the entities that solidified her Wall. But what never changed? Her fears of rejection, of asking for help, no matter from where. She shied away from all external forces: counselors, social workers, Professor Chen, her friends, and her father . . . imagining someone else involved in her situation seemed impossible.

Letting down the Wall, letting someone in—what if talking burned her, like the oil that splashed up when throwing onions into a wok on high flame? If she wrote it down—wrote down what disconnected her from others—like she'd written her thesis statement, it wouldn't be that hard. But saying it, *voicing* it, and then waiting for a verdict . . . she couldn't bear to think about that. It made her mouth dry up.

Besides, if she wanted to "equally acknowledge the existence and intermingling" of her American and Asian selves, she needed to talk back to her mother. In a meaningful way, with words that held knowledge. She still had doubts, succumbed to negative thoughts after particularly bad conversations with her mother; but she was building herself to a threshold, a crux of change. Asking for help would be cheating, in a general sense, but more importantly, she'd cheat herself. Until she enabled her *self,* until her ambivalence evened out, she'd silently survive.

"Hey Ava!" a familiar voice called.

She snapped out of her reverie and looked around for Kevin. He always made her laugh; she needed the lift now.

"What are you doing by our lecture hall?"

He looked around, pretending to be bewildered. "I must be out of touch! Since when did they change it from Dennis Hall to Jason and Ava Hall?"

"Really clever, Kev," she said, unable to hold in her smile.

"I'm all done, so I'm going to wait in the art museum while you guys take your exam."

"For *three hours*?"

"Nice try, Av," Kevin replied. "Jason told me that this is your third Shakespeare exam; you'll only have an hour and twenty."

"Where's Jason?"

"In the WC. Said he'd meet you inside, lassie."

Ava laughed. "They didn't have water closets in Shakespeare's time, Kev."

"Whatev. 'Least my British accent is better than Jason's. Now, off you go."

She nodded. "I'll give you that. See you after the exam."

Since she had reread the plays that had been assigned for the semester, Ava finished her exam in an hour. She and Kevin spent the remaining twenty minutes loitering in the hallway, waiting for Jason to finish.

"Ah, there's our fair Hamlet," he observed when Jason emerged.

"I'm a better blond than Kenneth Branagh, I'll have you both know. Now let's get out of here so winter break can finally start!"

They buttoned their coats up, put on their gloves, and headed out into the frost.

"What'd you think, Ava?" Jason asked.

She'd been half listening, already imagining the holidays with Mei and Paul. "About what?"

"I see she's already repressed her memory of the exam," Jason said to his boyfriend.

Kevin stroked his stubble with a gloved hand. "Ah, yes, a classic case of Freudian repression."

"I'm sorry, are you looking to relive your psychology exams?" Jason and Kevin made faces. "That's what I thought."

They continued the walk to Lockhart.

"We should do one last thing together before going home," Jason said.

Kevin nodded. "Just not Toby again. Walk in the park?"

Ava shivered. "Something warmer?"

"Dude, I've got it!"

"Should we be afraid?" Jason asked.

"Let's go swimming. University Way's got a heated pool."

"Oh yeah, I've been once," Jason said. "They've got a great patio pool."

Ava shook her head. "It won't work. They must be closed for exams."

"We'll see about that, Negative Nancy." Kevin whipped off a glove and used his iPhone to find out. "Ha! They're open till tomorrow at five."

"Let's go tomorrow after lunch," Jason suggested.

"But . . . but I don't have a swimsuit."

"No excuses," Kevin said. "Borrow one from Charlotte."

The next afternoon the five friends gathered at the L-shaped patio pool. In the shallow end, a group of guys played water basketball. On the other side, in two of the four lanes, an old couple swam laps.

"Hey Av, you gonna stare into space or join us?" Kevin asked.

Everyone else had already stripped down to his or her bathing suit. Charlotte, clad in a green bikini, waited next to Ava.

Jason called from the ladder. "Need encouragement?"

Ava shook her head. Unsmiling, she took off her oversized DU t-shirt. It's a black one piece. You're fully covered. Stop acting awkward or you'll draw more attention.

Once she'd joined them in the pool, Kevin gave her the once-over. "*This* is the bathing suit you borrowed from Charlotte?"

"Doesn't look like anything you'd wear," Derek said, splashing Charlotte.

"I . . . it's mine."

Kevin raised an eyebrow. "Thought you didn't have a suit."

"I misplaced it. I found it at the back of a drawer."

"*Ay, chica*," Jason said, "we'll need to get you something *más* sexy."

"Right?" Charlotte shook her head. "She's made for nothing but bikinis, but the girl's too damn shy."

"Is this the part where you say something about 'flaunting it'?" Derek asked.

"Goes without saying," Kevin replied.

Ava shrugged and sank into the water.

Jason shot Kevin a look. "Alright, let's leave her alone."

They alternated between messing around and lounging in the water. The conversation flowed onto the past semester and grade guessing.

Eventually all but two of the basketball players left. A freckle-spattered redhead and an Indian guy remained.

The Indian guy waved a mini basketball in their direction. "Jason, that you?"

"Hey, Brandon." They clasped hands. "Weird seeing you outside class."

"Ain't that the truth. You can use the other ball if you like."

Jason caught it. "Thanks."

The fivesome moved closer to the hoop and played a separate game next to Brandon and his friend. But they soon became more interested in talking than serious playing, resorting to passing the ball and throwing the odd shot.

Ava found herself drifting away from her group's conversation. The two guys were having a strange discussion.

"If you had to choose a chick based on race," the redhead asked, "what'd you go for?"

Brandon took a shot. "Dunno."

"What do you mean, you dunno?"

"That's weird. Really limiting." Brandon pointedly stared at his friend's hair. "Like what if you limited yourself to ginger girls?"

"Bro, you saying I should stick to my own kind?"

"I'm saying you can't limit yourself to *one* kind."

"I could. I'd totally do Asians only. They'll do whatever you want."

That comment caught everyone's attention. Derek and Jason exchanged eyebrow raises.

Brandon shook his head. "Oh, Mike. When'd you get an Asian fetish?"

"Since watching *X2*. That Asian girl with the claws, bro. Exotic, flexible. Bangin'."

"Nearly positive that chick's mixed."

Mike paused, considering. "No kidding? Maybe that's why she had tits."

Ignoring the warning glare Ava gave him, Jason turned to the duo. "Hey, essentializing isn't cool."

She gathered that Mike didn't know what essentialism meant. But it didn't seem like that'd prevent him from commenting.

"What's it to you, man?"

Jason squeezed the basketball. "I'm mixed. And two of my friends are half Asian."

Ava's stomach contracted, afraid he meant to reveal her and Derek. But Jason never glanced in their direction.

"Yeah, and?"

Her relief felt inadequate. Another feeling, an unknown one, detracted from it. Then she knew its name: disappointment. Part of her wanted recognition. This part wanted someone to call her out. Call her passing bluff. No. This part . . . *she* wanted to call her*self* out.

"And so I'm speaking for them. They'd be too nice to call you rude."

"It's not rude if it's the truth. How many curvy Asians do you know?"

Brandon cringed. "Mike, you're digging yourself deeper."

She saw Derek nudge Charlotte. "Probably best to leave now."

"No way," Charlotte whispered back. "I want to see this play out."

So did Ava.

"It doesn't matter how many curvy Asians I know," Jason retorted. "You're stereotyping."

Mike snorted. "And you don't?"

"I make a hell of an effort not to. How, you ask? I think before making generalizations that've been fed to me."

"You calling me stupid?" he asked, sending a small wave toward Jason.

"No, I didn't *call* you that."

The space between them shrunk to striking distance.

Ava looked for the lifeguard. His iPhone consumed his attention. Brandon seemed prepared to pull Mike back, but she couldn't be sure. Kevin, Derek, and Charlotte stayed in spectator mode. She remembered Derek's question. "What, so you bring it up yourself?" She remembered her response. And then Ava knew—

She cleared her throat. "I-I'm—I'm half Asian!"

Everyone turned toward her. The tension split. *She* made it split.

"Huh. What kind?" Mike asked.

She nodded, swallowing her resistance, her reticence. "I'm . . . I'm half Chinese."

"Really. You don't look like you're from there."

"I'm not."

"But didn't you just—"

"My mother's from China. So half my family. But I'm not 'from there.'"

Mike shrugged. "Well . . . you're hot for an Asian."

"That's not—on behalf of my . . . some of my people, I'd appreciate it if you'd stop fetishizing. It's disrespectful and . . . and creepy."

"You're overreacting. It's a compliment."

Ava crossed her arms. "If you want to like Asians, like them because you actually think they're attractive. N-not because they're different or . . . or fit your fantasy. That's degrading."

He blushed. "Whatever, babe."

"Oh, I get it now. You're so charming because the only action you get is from porn." She climbed out of the pool, her friends hooting their approval.

Chapter Seventeen

Ava's father would only come home for lunch on Christmas Eve. His flight left that night for Christmas day with his parents, brothers, and brothers' families in Seattle. When he'd bought his ticket a month ago, he also offered to buy Ava a ticket. The last time Ava saw her grandmother had been on the day she graduated from high school. Nevertheless, Mei turned him down. Ava must stay because Mei wanted to spend Christmas with her daughter. When Paul offered the easy solution of Mei joining, she still declined because flying petrified her. Ava bit back her observation that Mei overcame her supposed fear during her flight to America. Her father must've thought it unworthy of an argument, because he let his wife keep Ava for Christmas.

"What are you doing?" Mei demanded at 11 a.m. on Christmas Eve.

"What do you mean? I'm cooking moo shu pork for Dad, like you told me to. The mashed potatoes are ready and the ham will be done by the time he comes home."

"Stop."

Her mother put her hand on Ava's arm, preventing her from throwing the wood ear mushrooms and bamboo shoots into the wok. She reverently touched the typed sheet Ava had posted to the left-side cabinet door.

"This my mother's recipe. You must stick to it. Come, I show you how it's done. Chopped ginger goes in before anything."

Ava stepped aside. Maybe Mei respected one person. *Lao lao.*

"You didn't chop it fine enough." Mei moved to the counter and inspected the ginger. "Shut off the stove."

Ava adjusted the knob. The sesame oil in the wok stopped hissing.

"*Bai wen bu ru yi jian.* Americans have this phrase. Action better than words? Come, watch and learn."

She walked over and stood a safe distance away.

Mei laughed, a rich sound, like that of an erhu. "Closer, you can't see there."

Ava came close, expecting something. But her mother only minced the ginger with the chef's knife.

"How . . . how did you learn to chop so quickly?"

"Doing what you're doing. I watched nanny. And then Ma."

"You had a nanny?"

"Before the Revolution. We had to get rid of her when the gossip began. Turn the wok on again. Yes, high flame."

"What . . . what was your mother like?"

"Soft. Hand me vegetables," Mei said, stirring.

Ginger and sesame oil filled the air.

"Soft?"

Mei nodded, using two sets of wooden chopsticks to stir-fry the vegetables.

"Always feeling for others. Sensitive. That her downfall. Felt too much. What's that word?" she asked, taking out the spoon vegetables when they'd turned a gleaming green. "*Ruo shi*. Starting with a 'v'?"

For once Ava volunteered to fetch the Chinese-English dictionary. She flipped through until she found it. "Vulnerable, you mean?"

"*Dui*. Vulnerable. Weak. No way to be perfect when vulnerable. Why you think I push you so hard? Hand me pork."

Ava scraped in the raw pork she'd sliced earlier. The oil sizzled; bubbles formed and burst.

"Chinese cooking plays with flame. And preparation. Preparation is most important and consuming time. The cooking," Mei continued, tossing the pork, "is fast. Just need to finish the process. Don't want to underdo or overdo. Underdo and it's raw, woody or tough. Overdo and it's wilted or chewy." She lowered the flame and split open a slice of pork. The juices ran clear. "Chinese cooking is to be perfect."

The doorbell rang.

"Your father. You finish. Mix the eggs in with everything."

Ava slid the scrambled eggs, pork, and spoon vegetables into the wok. She turned the flame up and mixed while she overheard her mother talk to her father.

"Paul dear. How went the driving? You leave your luggage in the car? No, let's go to the dining room. Ava's busy with cooking."

Her father answered back cordially. She didn't know what kind of agreement her parents had made with each other, but she knew when her mother put on an act. Her father just sounded tired. She turned off the stove and added the finishing touches, minced garlic and a dash of soy sauce.

By the time Mei returned to the kitchen, Ava had dished the completed moo shu pork on a decorated serving platter, taken out the ham, and cleaned the oil that had splashed from the wok.

"Done yet? He's waiting with hunger."

"Yes," she said, wiping the sweat off her brow. Her mother carefully carried the dish to the dining room.

Ava found the carving knife and fork and brought them out with the ham. When she returned to the kitchen for the pot of mashed potatoes, she heard Paul ask who'd made the moo shu pork.

"I mostly cooked, but Ava helped," she heard her mother say.

An untruth, but Ava felt no need to complain, even if only to herself. Her mother seemed generous today. Mei almost always claimed to be the source of Ava's accomplishments. Any time her daughter "failed," however, the onus fell entirely on Ava.

After Paul carved the ham, the trio sat for lunch.

"*Man man chi,*" Mei said, passing a dish.

Any outsider observing the meal would have declared them a picturesque modern family. The well-kept, delicate-looking Oriental mother sat opposite the handsome, greying Caucasian father at the clothed dining table. Between them at one end, sat the non-threatening, Caucasian-looking beauty of a daughter they had produced. Indeed, from the outside, they looked neat and perfect. A model of successful integration, unified in all ways except those that mattered.

In reality, they only united in maintaining appearances. Each acted for another's benefit. As Ava and Mei knew, Chinese discipline was a private affair. Daughter and mother would be pleasant with one another, the latter more so than the former, around Paul, the outsider. The second Mr. Magee stepped through the door, Mei turned into Mrs. Magee, the kind, reverent, *faithful* wife and mother who obeyed her husband. As for Paul, he attempted to play the part of loving husband and dedicated father. Each sensed disingenuousness lurking beneath the surface, but individual secrets remained buried.

Though Ava knew her mother hated holidays—she hated conforming to capitalist American standards—Mei played hostess prettily.

"Dear Paul. How's work? New and exciting cases?" She spooned a dainty bite of mashed potatoes and slowly put it to her mouth.

Ava tried not to smirk. Her mother hated potatoes. Ava practically heard her think, "Curse foreign devils and their potatoes! These ghosts have no taste."

"The usual kinds, I suppose." Paul sounded distracted.

She picked at the slices of ham on her plate. Ava disliked ham, but her mother insisted Ava eat what she served. Be grateful—at least no chicken feet this time. "You eat what we're having or no food at all," Mei had told her during childhood. She quickly learned that her mother meant what she said. No question of preference, of taste. No questions allowed. Eating the Chinese way meant never wasting a single grain of rice.

"Ava, could you pass me the vegetables?" Paul asked.

She passed the food dish without making eye contact. She couldn't look at her father for a couple of reasons, the diary being one of them. Had he discovered its absence? She felt guilty for taking it without asking permission, but she didn't think he had a right to be angry. He promised it to her for her eighteenth birthday; it said so on the package. But she really wanted to ask him about her mother's diary. Ava ached to know more. To hear what Mei hadn't said in the kitchen, to see a part of her mother that she'd never seen before. What had little Mei been like; how had she thought? How had she reacted to her experience in the Cultural Revolution?

Mei pushed away her mashed potatoes and looked at them. After a beat of silence, she asked, "Paul. What time your flight is to Seattle?"

Paul finished his mouthful of moo shu pork and answered, "four-fifteen." He forlornly looked at Ava. "It's a pity your mother can't spare you. Grandma and Grandpa will miss you. Not to mention your uncles, aunts, and cousins."

Mei smiled tightly. "Well, they always can Skype with Ava. I need her here with me. A daughter a daughter all her life."

Please, whatever's sacred in this world, let this be inaccurate. She sometimes vacillated between wishing that her mother learn to atone and feeling driven to sever all ties. But her hope dwindled. Mei expected too much from her. Perfection could never be attained. Ava lacked *Lao lao*'s brimming capacity for empathy. But she'd never be as disconnected as her mother: there'd always be vulnerable spots in her. The liminal daughter forever in between.

"I'd better start cleaning up."

She stood and took plates to the kitchen. Ava dreaded her father's departure and chafed at confinement with her mother on Christmas Day. If Ava couldn't go to Seattle with Paul, she wanted to spend Christmas with Charlotte's family. Such a proposal suited Mei because her mother feared nothing from the Bells. The Bells, unlike Paul's family, lived within driving distance. But Ema would ask why she wanted to come alone—it'd be even merrier if Mei came too. Perhaps, Ava thought, the extended Magees knew something of the rift between her parents.

Her parents' voices drifted through the swinging door that separated the dining hall from the kitchen.

"Where you going, Paul? There's no need to help Ava in the kitchen. Children must serve their parents. Why you not leave early and beat traffic to the airport?"

"But it's only one o'clock. Besides, I haven't seen Ava since her birthday. I want to ask her how school is."

Moments later her father entered the kitchen . . . followed by her mother. Ava guessed that Mei followed out of fear that they'd conspire against her, two foreign devils against the native Chinese woman.

"So, Ava," Paul began, drying the dishes his daughter had already washed, "how'd you find your first semester?"

Mei poured herself a glass of port and sat on one of the bar chairs at the kitchen island.

"Yes. How you do on your exams? You get your final grades back?"

Ava appreciated that the kitchen island lay behind the sink; she could lie with her back to her mother.

"Cell bio neuro isn't an easy major . . . but I did get straight A's." She viciously scrubbed dried mashed potatoes from a pot to avoid her father's gaze.

"Like you should," Mei said, voice kitten-soft.

"I'm—" Paul shot Mei a look and revised, "We're really proud of you. But you're still enjoying college, right?"

Washing off the small mass of bubbles from the pot, Ava tried to forget the nights she spent drunk in an effort to rebel against Mei. She especially avoided thoughts of Dan, Halloween night, and Derek holding her hair in the ladies' room.

"It's . . . interesting. Just a lot of work, that's all."

"Don't work yourself to the bone, kiddo. Make some new friends, join a club or something. Remember, there's a social side to college."

Who are you to pitch your Western mentality? Your wife holds the power here. The Eastern approach is what I've got to pander to: college meant nothing but studying and exam taking.

Sure enough, she saw her mother frown. Mei put down her wine glass and stared at her daughter's side.

"Your dad's right."

Ava's eyebrows lifted, but when her mother finished explaining, she lost her surprise.

"You could do piano again. Davison must have many piano club."

"They don't even have one piano club."

Ava attacked the wok with her sudsy sponge. She'd never relive the fights she and Mei had over piano. Time only healed scars so much.

"No? You can create one," Mei said, with the encouragement of a parent taking away training wheels.

"Can't. Too busy studying. You don't want my grades to suffer for music, right?"

Paul momentarily held his dishcloth still. "No. She can't go back. It's still too soon."

"Only at sixteen," Mei protested. "It happened the once. Not even a phase. She's over it."

"No. She might be, but no. It could snowball again. When will you get rid of that piano?"

Mei took the dish he had stopped drying from his hands. "Your flight at four-fifteen. You now should get going. You can take leftovers to the apartment and drop off your car."

"Oh. Fine. Yes, and I've got to catch the train to the airport."

His wife took containers filled with ham, moo shu pork, and mashed potatoes from the steel refrigerator. Putting them in a plastic bag, she reminded him to refrigerate them immediately.

"Bye, Ava." Paul came forward to give her a hug. His daughter took a step back.

"Don't; I'll get suds all over your dress shirt," Ava said, holding up her wet dish gloves. She deliberately looked away from her mother's satisfied countenance. Her father settled for a kiss on her head.

"Bye dear." Mei walked her husband to the door. "Send my love to Seattle."

After New Year's, Paul went back to overworking and Mei used Ava for menial labor. She cooked, cleaned, did laundry, and ran errands for her mother. When Mei went out, Ava could never ask any questions. During her mother's absences, she completed task lists Mei had compiled that'd be "double-checked" when she returned. When Ava timidly fought back, she needed to be "put down." For punishment, Mei sent her to the basement—without the light, which Mei controlled from upstairs. Ava functioned with only a flashlight.

On one such occasion, six days after the start of the New Year, Mei told her to reorganize the basement bookshelves by height and color. Her mother thought up the consequence to address Ava's inability to sufficiently explain "twerking," which Mei had stumbled upon via Facebook.

"Shortest books on the left, tallest on the right. Lightest-colored books on the left, darkest on the right." Mei shoved her daughter toward the basement door.

"Can't I have the basement lights?" Ava protested. "They're still dim."

"When you were little, you always wanted to camp like other girls. Here your chance," she mocked, handing Ava a camping lantern and opening the door to the basement. "I go to speak for the animal shelter. When I come back, you better be done. I check good; you know my eagle eyes."

Ava waited at the top of the steel stairs, trying to avoid looking down. The staircase had no risers, and she feared the impossible: one misstep and she'd fall through the intervening space. When Ava heard her mother's heeled boots make their way out the door, she opened the basement door and peeked out into the hallway. The door was locked and Mei's car keys were missing. Safe to turn on the basement lights.

She descended back into the basement, fighting a shiver, her reaction due only partially to the lack of heat. With her mother gone, Ava could fetch a sweater to supplement the thin one she wore, but she used the cold as an impetus to work faster. Although Paul had bought the house eight years ago, and her mother had methodically renovated the rest of the house, the basement remained unfinished. Nothing warmed the stark concrete floor. Exposed beams and pipes formed the ceiling. In one corner, away from the steel bookcases, stood the water heater, guarded by dusty cardboard boxes that were filled with forgotten items.

Otherwise, a maze composed the entire basement. A maze of wide, tall, grey bookcases crammed with Chinese scholarly books, some brought from China, some collected in America. Six bookcases lined up like dominoes. A neat hoarder's nest, but a hoarder's nest all the same. Three bookcases housed Chinese books. Another bookcase held countless magazines, collected over the years from Chinese supermarkets in America. One bookcase kept newspapers, most yellowed, wrinkled, and faded with age. Finally, a bookcase filled with papers her mother had written and assignments completed during her studies at NYU. English only existed in this last bookcase.

Though Ava hated reorganizing books in the basement, she felt grateful that this time the task omitted picking out books for her mother. She couldn't read even a bit of Chinese, so she relied on her picture-recognizing skills—characters just looked like line art.

"I hate you, I hate you. Why do you torture me? What a sadist," she muttered to herself, surveying the books in one bookcase.

As she began reordering the books according to her mother's instructions, Ava wondered about the secrets Mei guarded. Had she really quit her PhD in East Asian Studies just a semester before completing the last year of the program, to have her daughter? Mei blamed Ava for this; Mei hadn't become a professor because of

Ava. Because of her existence. But the more she thought about her mother's explanation, the more it became an excuse. An excuse for what, though?

After reading *Lao lao*'s diary, Ava thought that the Cultural Revolution affected her mother more than *Lao lao* believed. At the minimum, Mei hadn't developed the discipline to follow through. The only things she finished now were her Chinese blog posts. She felt too restless to watch the Chinese news in its entirety. Maybe the real problem lay with Mei's youth. She never came to terms with her troubled childhood.

Mei witnessed so many damaging events, especially ones of personal significance: the humiliation of her mother's cousin, the destruction of her parents' house and heirlooms, the beating of her parents, the miscarriage, the last struggle session of her mother, the suicide of her neighbor. Not to mention *Lao lao*'s descent into madness. Mei could've quit the doctorate program out of fear, fear of someone forcing her to explain the revolution she'd endured—while teaching in the same occupation that'd gotten her parents into trouble. Her mother, Ava realized, moving on to reorder the next bookcase, might feel as unfinished as she did, except for different reasons. Mei's inability to confront her past paralleled Ava's inability to reconcile her split identity.

Perhaps this revealed another reason why Ava couldn't hate Mei outright, couldn't tattle on her mother. Mei fought her own demons, at least some of them summoned by the terrors she'd experienced as a six-year-old. Who'd stay the same after seeing parents beaten bloody? Who'd be normal after seeing a miscarriage firsthand? *Lao lao*'s entries indeed awakened Ava's sympathy, but she still craved an escape from her mother. Ava needed to get Mei's portion from Paul. Did her mother become vulnerable on paper? When she discovered the answer to this question, she could do whatever ended up being necessary, and without regret. Ava wanted her mother to acknowledge her adulthood and let her orchestrate her own life.

Finally, Ava reached the last bookcase to reorganize. She checked her phone: 3:38 p.m.; almost two hours had passed. Thankfully, Mei still hadn't returned. How ironic is it, Ava thought, that Mother rarely goes down to the basement. Though Mei filled it with her past, turning it into her underground, she always sent her daughter to do the sifting. The few knickknacks that Mei had collected also lined some of the shelves, guarding the books. A red scarf—from the Revolution? A samurai sword letter opener, from Ava knew not where, sheathed with an engraved cover. The snake belt Ava so feared, and a tribal-looking necklace composed of black beads and a few seemingly real dog teeth.

When she completed her task, another half hour had passed. Flashlight in hand, she bolted up the stairs into the lighted and warm hallway. Just as Ava closed the basement door, Mei opened the front door.

"How did the speaking engagement go? You convince people that their New Year's resolutions need to involve animal adoption?"

"I need you now to leave," her mother said, not even closing the door. She didn't seem angry, but her face looked flushed.

"What?" Ava almost asked "why," but the prospect of leaving captivity suppressed her curiosity.

"I can't stand you right now. You leeching my energy. What you are waiting for? Go!"

Without hesitation, Ava bounded up the stairs to her room and threw the bare necessities she'd brought home into her carry-on luggage.

"I'm timing you," Mei sang up the stairs. "You got five minutes until I make you stay for punishment."

In three minutes, Ava flew out the door and settled into her white Jetta. She left in such a rush that she didn't look in the rearview mirror, which she usually did—Ava liked to look back while driving away, smiling to herself at Mei's receding figure. So she missed the unfamiliar silver Lexus that pulled into the driveway.

Once she returned to Lockhart, Ava texted Professor Chen. "Happy New Year! I'm back at DU, ready to research." By the time she finished emptying the contents of her luggage onto her bed, Professor Chen had responded. "You eat dinner yet?" When Ava texted "no," Professor Chen replied, "How about hot pot, my treat? Meet at my office in 15 minutes?" She had no idea what a "hot pot" entailed, but she guessed it'd be spicy.

"Hi Professor Chen," she said. She hesitated before stiffly accepting a hug.

"Okay, lesson one for 2013. My forename is Li zhi. It's pronounced 'Lee jur.'"

"Lee jur," Ava repeated carefully. They began walking to the nearby restaurant, Sichuan Fire. The sun shone brightly, blunting the icy wind's force. The dusting of snow that had fallen on New Year's Eve had melted.

"Exactly. Unless we're among my colleagues, please use my first name. There's no need to make me feel older than I already do."

"How can you feel old when you've got hair like that?"

"Pull all-nighters with no repercussions now, Ava, but in another ten years, you'll dream of going to bed at 11 p.m. Careful, watch that icy patch."

They entered the restaurant, enjoying refuge from the bitter chill. A large fish tank joined the host's podium in welcoming customers. White and orange streaks marked each palm-sized fish, except for one. Red mottled this one's grey body; its fins looked like wings. Ava watched it bump against the glass before retreating behind a spiky plant.

Above, the strong lights left no room for shadows. Colorful lanterns hung from the ceiling, and scrolls replete with Chinese calligraphy shared the walls with watercolor paintings. On each table graced a miniature bamboo plant, resting in its small rock garden.

"*Jiaoshou*." Smiling until the wrinkles around her eyes deepened, the middle-aged hostess addressed Li zhi. She led them over to a table and provided menus. Flicking a glance over Ava, the hostess continued to speak to Li zhi in Mandarin. "Mixed-blood, am I right?"

"*Ayi*," said Li zhi, using the respectful "auntie" address as she and Ava shrugged off their coats and sat down. "That's not polite, and she doesn't understand."

Unaware of the content of the exchange, Ava studied the faces of the two women. The hostess looked curious, but Li zhi looked slightly annoyed.

"No *putonghua*?" the hostess asked in Chinglish, looking directly at Ava for the first time.

"No Mandarin," Ava said, gathering what the unfamiliar word meant.

"*Hao kexi, bu hui shuo zhongwen*!" The hostess frowned. She shook her head and walked away.

"What did she say?" Ava asked, confused, but sensing that she'd been unfavorably judged.

"She said that it's a shame you don't speak Mandarin," Li zhi explained. "Don't be offended, she means well. She reminds me of my maternal grandma. No English, always critical, but she secretly loves me and my dyed hair."

Ava looked over the laminated menu, grateful for the owner's attempt to provide patrons with descriptions in English, though they lacked proper grammar.

"What's a hot pot? I've never had it before," she confessed.

"Then we must order the Sichuan hot pot—it's a classic dish. It's basically a way of cooking. See this pot?" Li zhi tapped the metal pot in the center of the rectangular table. "This is where the magic happens. They'll put spicy stock in here and heat the pot. When it's brought to a simmer, we'll cook the protein and veggies ourselves."

"Like hibachi style, without the theatrics?"

"Exactly."

The waiter served tea and took their orders.

By the time Ava had tasted her first Sichuan hot pot and tea-smoked duck, she'd already revealed the contents of *Lao lao*'s diary to Li zhi.

"I haven't been able to talk to my dad about it, but I'll have to if I want to see my mother's entries."

"Why can't you talk to your dad?"

Ava took a sip of tea instead of answering directly.

"I . . . I can't say. It's because of my mother. When we were all together on Christmas Eve, I never got a chance to speak with him alone. It's more than that, though. It's all in my head, but she put it there . . . "

"She drove a wedge between you two."

Using her chopsticks to eat a piece of tea-smoked duck, Ava nodded. She took another sip of tea, desperate to talk about anything else, if just for a moment. Her eyes fell on Li zhi's multicolored streaks.

"I nearly forgot to ask you about your hair."

"My hair?" Li zhi paused, using serving chopsticks to slip a couple slices of taro root into the simmering hot pot.

"Yes, before winter break you said to remind you—"

"Right, the reason behind the colors." She prodded the taro. It'd become soft enough to eat. "Want to try one?" When Ava consented, Li zhi placed a slice into her bowl of rice.

"Soon after starting college—I went to Wesleyan—I began dating a girl named Shanti. She was half Indian and half Jamaican. She also became my first girlfriend. I waited so long because I'd felt responsible for my mother's passing."

"But you had nothing to do with her stroke!"

Li zhi smiled sadly. "I know that now. Still, blurting that I'm bisexual and then dashing off to catch the school bus probably didn't help." She cleared her throat before continuing. "I got home before my brother did . . . I found her, supine, on her bed. The doctors later told me that she died from an aneurysm about an hour after I'd left for school."

"That's . . . so awful," Ava whispered.

Li zhi pressed her lips together.

"Yes. I'm just glad that my brother and I were able to move in with my grandmother. I was sixteen and clueless. Anyway, after that day I tried to be straight. So that's why Shanti became my first."

Their waiter came by. "*Chi bao le ma*?" He looked at Ava and asked, "Full?"

"Yes, thanks."

Li zhi asked him to bring them the bill. She handed him her credit card when he returned, waving away Ava's offer to help pay. When he looked at the remaining food, silently reproaching her, Li zhi hastily asked if he could also pack the leftovers.

"Anyway, Shanti continually dyed her hair with henna. That New Year's Eve, we planned to celebrate at an off-campus party. A few hours before its start, Shanti insisted on buying more henna; she thought that her brown roots showed."

The waiter returned with Li zhi's card and the leftovers. She signed the receipt, said "*Xiexie*," and left with Ava.

"What color henna?" Ava asked, pulling her gloves on.

"Black," Li zhi replied, repositioning her grip on the bag of leftovers. They quickly walked toward the office; the sun had long set and the cold struck without mercy. "We held hands on the way to the store, like we usually did. It was only 8 p.m. when we got there, but the store stood across from a bar. A few college boys who'd already drank too much started shouting obscenities. When we entered the shop the boys called us dykes, and when we left with Shanti's henna, they followed us. They called her the 'n word' and me a chink. So we crossed the street, flipped them off, and speed-walked home."

"Were there other people around?"

"They just watched. No one intervened. We were lucky the boys were too drunk to pursue us; if the situation had escalated who knows what could've happened."

Li zhi and Ava crossed the street. They'd almost reached Li zhi's office building.

"I helped Shanti dye her hair that night and finally asked why she always dyed it black. She looked at me and said, 'So I'll look blacker and be accepted somewhere. Indians think I'm weird. It's like being half Indian doesn't count, and then I guess they're afraid because I'm also black.'"

"She must've been bullied a lot," Ava said. "One foot in each community, but unable to stand in either."

"Unfortunately. Why don't I drop you off?" Li zhi led the way to her black Ford Mustang.

"Is it out of your way? I can walk; I live in Lockhart, right on University Way."

"Nonsense. I have to pass there on the way to my apartment."

They got into the car. Li zhi cranked up the heat and put the leftovers on the backseat.

"Anyway, so that's when I decided to dye my hair," Li zhi said, changing gears to back out of the small parking lot. She waited for a car blasting music to speed by before turning onto the road.

"All the colors of the racial rainbow. Since my hair was already black, I only needed to add red, brown, blonde, and white. Shanti and I dyed my hair that first time. It didn't come out well; the dye was cheap and semipermanent. We made such a mess in the girls' bathroom." She laughed. "My RA yelled at us. It took an hour and gallon of bleach to clean up. Now I just get it done professionally. Turn right here?"

"Yes, it's faster that way. Do you tell people why when they ask about your hair?"

"It depends on the person."

"You ever miss your old hair?"

"Not really." Li zhi pulled into Lockhart's parking lot. "I'm used to it by now. I'll only change it back to black if racism ceases to exist."

"So you'll have multicolored hair in your nineties?"

"If I still have hair by then. I'm sure I'll be put into the latest *Guinness World Records*."

They laughed, trying to imagine it.

"Thanks for dinner and the ride," Ava said, opening the passenger door.

"You're welcome! Are you available to resume research this Friday?"

Ava stepped out of the car and bent down to look at Li zhi. "Yes, and Fridays will also work for me when the spring semester starts."

"Don't forget the leftovers." Li zhi reached back for the bag and passed it to Ava.

"Thanks! See you Friday." She shut the door, about to walk away.

"Wait—one more thing. When you need to talk again, remember that I'm just a text or call away, okay?"

Ava suddenly had an urge to cry. She silenced it. Swallowing hard, she nodded and smiled. She didn't trust herself to speak. Instead, Ava waved as Li zhi drove away.

Thanks for listening; you're the older sibling I never had.

Chapter Eighteen

Unfortunately for Ava, the mental harmony that Li zhi had given her was disrupted on the following Monday. Mei called; the internet had gone out. She summoned Ava home. The only consolation prize: Mei needed to leave, which meant no hovering or interference with the troubleshooting process.

After Ava had taken off her jacket, Mei slipped into her black rabbit fur coat—"no harm, sheared," she carefully told animal lovers. "I must to go to this fundraiser for my shelter. When I get back, the internet will be running. Or you stay here until winter break end. Your choose. Don't make this more of power struggle."

Fifteen minutes after her mother had left, she figured out that the modem needed a simple reboot. But before she could think of what to do with the remaining time, a notification popped up on the screen of Mei's desktop. Beneath the Chinese characters, an inept English translation: "Mix Beauty New Comment." Impulsively, Ava clicked on the notification box.

The notification brought her to its corresponding blog entry. Unable to read the Chinese comment, Ava clicked on the embedded video. She watched the four-minute clip. She'd never seen anything like it before.

While speaking in Mandarin, the woman in the video demonstrated how to use what looked like white liquid eyeliner or white-out. She cleaned her eyelid, used a forklike contraption to push her eyelid in, and then applied the white liquid to the crease she'd formed. After holding her eyelid against the line for a short while, she let go. Whatever she'd done made her eye look bigger. The video ended with a before and an after picture. In the picture to the left, the woman's eyes were small. In the picture to the right, her eyes were bigger. Still a bit confused, Ava opened up another tab and searched the internet for "Asian eyes."

She scrolled down until a website's preview caught her eye. "Asian eyes often have monolids (single eyelids, opposed to Western double eyelids), and some women are taking increasingly drastic measures to change that." Ava clicked on the website and read the article. Some Asian women, the article explained, used heavy liquid eyeliner to create the illusion of a double eyelid. Others used strategically placed, varying shades of eye shadow to create the same effect. Women who wanted more "natural-looking" results used glue or tape. Finally, women who wanted permanent change underwent blepharoplastic surgery, in which cosmetic surgeons created double eyelids for their patients.

Since when had this become a beauty trend? What's the purpose of trying so hard to create double eyelids? Just to look

Western? She returned to her mother's site, scrolling down in case there were other pictures. A picture of an eyeliner tutorial, a picture of an eye tape tutorial, and . . . *a picture of her own face*? Ava blinked in disbelief, but when she opened her eyes, a picture of herself still stared back. Her senior portrait from high school. She moved further down the page and encountered a series of snapshots that focused on different parts of her face. Her left eye, her right eye, both eyes. Her nose, her lips, her chin. Underneath each facial feature were small paragraphs in Chinese. She turned on the browser's webpage translator, fully knowing that she'd receive a messy translation. But she needed to gather some kind of idea of what her mother had written.

Underneath the pictures of her eyes, she read "these are eyes of my daughter's. See how clear there a double lid. They round and big because she is *Hunxuer*." Confused, Ava tried translating *Hunxuer*, but the translation repeated the same word back to her, thinking it English. Annoyed, she did a basic search and learned that it meant "mixed-blood child." How legitimate sounding.

The text under Ava's nose read "tall foreign-devil nose, not garlic-shaped or flat." Finally, by her chin she read "heart-shaped face, not round like mooncake." Questions fogged her mind. What? Why? She went back to her mother's main page and selected the beauty category. Ava clicked on beauty entries at random. They all focused on creating Caucasian or "mixed" looks. And many of Mei's entries featured pictures of Ava from her early to late teen years. She couldn't look anymore. But before she cleared her mother's browser history, she emailed the link to Li zhi. Ava trusted that her mentor would have something useful to say about it.

Covering her face with her hands, she finally put a name to what she felt. Revulsion. All her life Mei had mocked her, delegitimized her, treated her as less-than because of her Amerasian status. And all this time, while Mei simultaneously spat on her *Hunxuer*, her cursed *zazhong*, she'd used her as a . . . a model. Could it be true? That, for all her Western xenophobia, her mother wanted to *copy* her? Ava, the unnatural child she'd labeled bastard.

She'd always seen her mother as hypocritical, but this verged on insanity. Not to mention that Mei had broadcasted her daughter's face on the internet, without even pretense of permission. Those pictures were personal. Ava felt betrayed. No, worse than that. She felt like a twice-used, greasy napkin.

Did her mother participate in such beauty trends? Did she hide printouts of Ava's face around the house? The hair on her arms rose. Springing from Mei's roller chair, she headed to the master bedroom.

She opened the door slowly, careful not to disturb anything. Then again, did it matter if she did? If she found anything incriminating, perhaps it'd be time to demand an explanation from her mother. Toward the far side of the large room, in the corner next to the bathroom, stood Mei's vanity table. Ava sat down in the same seat her mother used to put on makeup and looked up at the trifold mirror.

Something stuck to the right-side mirror. She stood up from the cushioned bench and leaned over the table for a closer look. A printout, composed of six pictures that progressed linearly. Mei had written notes in Chinese above each picture; but it didn't matter that Ava couldn't read the characters; the pictures explained enough. Still shots from the eyelid-gluing video she'd just seen. By the last picture Mei had written in English, "see blog."

Ava looked into the two uncovered mirror panels and studied her doubled reflection. She stood up and then kneeled on the seat to see herself better. She avoided mirror gazing, but it felt about time to face her selves. She stared, hard. Did she recognize the Ava Magees that echoed her? Ava leaned closer. So did her doubles. Yes.

Yes, they were also her doppelgangers in appearance. Four pairs of round, blue grey eyes unapologetically glared back at the original Ava. Long dark lashes, dark auburn eyebrows and hair. A small, softly pointed nose. High cheekbones, a mole on her left cheek. Proportionate lips with a habit of smirking. A heart-shaped face, attached to a relatively long neck. How to evaluate the features of her face? With race in mind? Dissecting a face that way seemed unnatural.

Those eyes, with their double lids, clearly Western. So were those eyelashes, the color of that hair. The pointedness of the nose, so Caucasian, but its delicate nature, perhaps Chinese, like a China doll's. High cheekbones must be Chinese, but that mole Caucasian. The lips, who knew? That face shape, most Western. But that neck: the neck of a Chinese ballerina.

They stuck her on display. A showcase of the collision between East and West. A modern-day freak show, a guessing game. Let's break you down and then box you up as we see fit. Why do you say you don't like it? Look at you, so unique, getting so much attention! So desired. The latest commodity to be advertised to an even broader market audience. The best of a cross-cultural experiment, to be exploited with admiration. Was she really in a position of power and just hadn't realized it?

How wrong, these women weren't her! Ava stood up, tore down the printout, and scowled at her three reflections. They scowled back, mocking her mental anguish. She looked down at her hands, which gripped the table. The veins stood out against her light skin.

She could fight back. Get a perm. Do the opposite of what Li zhi had done. Dye her hair yellow. Or get a tan, wear chopsticks in black hair. But being one or the other failed her; she'd never fool herself. Ava Magee. Ava Ling. Two sides battling to control one body. Ava Ling Magee. Half white *and* half Asian. Indeed, Whasian. Both. Both, at the exact same time, all the time.

She wouldn't be able to change what others thought of her, how some might reject this racial multiplicity, how others might embrace it. But she could absolutely transform the way she thought of herself; *she* could shape the way she perceived herself. Hesitantly, Ava looked back at the mirrors. The women returned the look, eyes cautious, contemplative.

Ava checked her phone. Forty-five minutes had passed since Mei's departure. She'd be coming home soon. Ava wanted to battle her sometime, somewhere—but not in her mother's bedroom. So she re-taped the printout to the right-side mirror. Knowing she might not receive another chance to be in this room unobserved, she opened the drawers attached to the vanity. There were six total; three on each side.

Assorted cosmetics and makeup instruments filled the three left-hand drawers. She moved onto the right-hand drawers. The uppermost seemed innocuous enough; it just contained assorted false eyelashes, eyelid glue, and the eyelid fork she'd seen in the video.

But then Ava opened the second drawer. And found a section of her hair. Six inches long, kept together by an orange rubber band. She lifted it up for closer inspection. Using her free hand, Ava fingered her hair until she found the shortest layer. She drew the cut hair over to it and turned to look in the center mirror. The hair couldn't fit like a puzzle piece, but nonetheless confirmed her suspicions. Mei had saved the hair for two years.

She put the hair back and closed the drawer. Taking a breath, she opened the bottom drawer. Filled, filled to the top—with pictures of her, mostly of her face. She shivered. Swiftly, she pushed the drawer in and made sure everything else appeared as before. No more exploring. She didn't want to find anything else.

Chapter Nineteen

A scraping sound foretold the unlocking of the front door. Mei hastily stowed the golden wedding china before the door opened.

Leaning against the hallway closet, she asked, "How aren't you at work?"

Paul shut the door and shrugged off his wool coat.

"We just finished a case. Besides, I'm free to work virtually on Mondays," he said, holding his coat in his arms. He nodded at the closet. "May I?"

She continued to block the door. "No hangers more. Or space. Why you don't put it over a dining chair?"

He looked ready to argue, but instead made his way to the dining room. She followed, glancing at her watch. 4:45.

"What's that smell?" Paul asked. He drew out the leather chair at the far end of the table and sat down. Noticing the lotus-decorated burner on the lazy Susan, he leaned over to lift its lid. "It's like a . . . a sweet balsamic."

Mei perched on the edge of the chair opposite him. "Agarwood."

"Since when are you into incense burning?"

"I'm not. Not until recent. I hope you no staying for dinner. I have enough for myself only."

"No, I'll leave by then. Actually—"

"You need something from your office?" Turning the glass tray, she moved the ceramic burner away from him. She settled the lid. 4:48.

"Well, no. I wanted—"

"Then why you're here?"

"Let me *finish*."

Mei laced her hands together, resting them on the table.

"Anyway, I went over my finances today."

She fixed her eyes on him. "Our."

He paused before continuing. "The finances. My savings and stock market investments are stable. I've got a healthy amount in my 401k. Rossi and Esposito praised me during my last review."

"So? You can tell me this through the phone." 4:50.

Paul fidgeted in his seat. "It's a new year. Ava will be busy with the second semester soon. She'll be out of the way. Now's the best time. Don't you think we've put it off for too long? It doesn't make sense."

"You threatening me?"

"No. These are facts. It's time to face them."

Mei chuckled. "Facts? What about my daughter?"

"Our daughter. After it's over I can take care of her. Easily."

"Oh? What you know about parenting? Ah, all of a sudden silent. She hates you. She'll hate you more. She has enough pressure. Think this won't hurt her? *Fu chao wu wan luan*. When nest falls no egg is unbroken."

"I know the idiom. Don't patronize me."

She examined her nails. 4:52. "Our deal did work. Does work, too. One of your idioms: no fixing what's unbroken."

"*Jia xiang*. It's all pretense. I'm tired of pretending. Surely you also want to move on? Travel the world? Meet someone else? I'll be here for Ava."

Mei shook her head. "*Wu zhi wang shuo*."

"I'm not talking nonsense—"

"You talk about stable? People make assumptions. And what will Ava tell her employers? What will people think of her? At best, pity. At worst, think her needy, damaged. She needs togetherness. You want *gu rou xiang can*?"

"How would it be internecine strife? We have irreconcilable differences."

Mei gave him an empty stare. Most times she bypassed English words she didn't know, but this time it seemed important.

"*Shi bu liang li*," he explained.

She sat up taller. "All more reason to *qi xin he li*."

Paul chuckled, the sound like sandpaper on skin. "How can we work as a unit when we can't even handle each other's company?"

"Oh, Paul—" She let her eyes glisten. "We can . . . *po jing chong yuan*." Mei leaned over to touch his hand.

He yanked it away. "You can't put a broken mirror back together. That's the point. It's *broken*. You sweep away the pieces and throw it out. Then you get a new mirror."

"You want to sweep me out?" Mei asked, voice climbing an octave. "You want to bag me up and throw me on street for neighbors to see? After everything I make possible?"

"Don't be melodramatic. It won't be like that. And there comes a time when you can't care about other people. Other people aren't living this. We've never been a united front. I let you raise her. I let you have her childhood," Paul said, voice pregnant with reproach. "Your motherly duties are over. You're no longer needed."

"*Zhe hai liao de*! *Me*, no longer needed? You think you able to play daddy? *Ni, you ming wu shi – xu kong de baba* like your father!" 4:55.

"How dare *you*. My father did the best he could under the circumstances. And so would I!"

"You so sure? He had excuse. What you have? No war, born spoon in mouth!"

"Fuck. You," Paul said, quiet but clear.

Standing up roughly, he knocked back his chair. He picked up his coat but left the chair on the floor. Without another word or glance in her direction, he left the house.

Didn't even shut the door! Mei closed and locked it. Slipping her fingers through the thick blinds, she gently pulled them apart. She watched his Prius turn out of the Maplewood complex.

5:02. Good thing she'd done the time-consuming food prep that afternoon. Still, she'd have to concentrate to get everything ready. She only had fifty-eight minutes.

She used all four burners to speed the cooking up. Monitoring each dish, she thought about her fumbling husband. Paul displayed conventional intelligence, enough smarts to keep up with the bills, anyway. But he fooled no one if he thought himself able to best her. She knew every one of his weaknesses.

He accepted what others presented to him. Believed in people. Believed in ideals. In second chances. In "fair" treatment. Even when given the darts necessary to pin her to the wall, he'd never do it. He feared regret, feared hurting others. What a slave to remorse. Controlled by emotion. It never took much effort to shame him. She only needed to begin a sentence with "Ryan" and she won the game.

Some people's upbringing caused them to distrust. Others, like abused dogs, returned to the hands that both fed and beat them. Paul fell into the latter camp. He disliked the way she belittled him, the way she manipulated him. But he didn't have the balls to stop her. He had too many boundaries, too many codes of honor. And he didn't know how to apply what he practiced in law to his personal life.

The doorbell rang while she placed the dishes onto the lazy Susan.

She opened the door and relaxed into Mandarin. "Right on time."

"I brought fake flowers."

"Thanks for listening." She took his coat and hung it up in the closet.

"You're a most peculiar woman. I've never met anyone else who hates fresh flowers."

Mei led the way into the dining room.

"They're pointless. All they do is shrivel up and die. But manmade flowers never change. Timeless."

He shrugged and took a seat. "Whatever you say."

She smiled and uncovered the gold inlay stockpot. The scent of spices drifted up, blending with the agarwood incense.

"That smells amazing." He peered inside at the tawny contents. "Am I going to have to pick out pork?"

"I made porkless hot and sour soup," she replied, spooning soup into his bowl.

"You're so good to me."

"Too good."

"Oh please," he said, swallowing a spoonful. "You love me."

Mei paused, chopsticks hovering over the chicken lo mein she'd made. "You know I never do—"

"Sorry, it just slipped out. I didn't really . . . I don't expect . . . forget I said it."

She filled her own bowl and plate before resting the serving chopsticks on a saucer. They ate in silence for a few minutes.

"The soup isn't oily . . . The chicken's so tender. And the broccoli . . . even crunchier than my mother's!"

Mei nodded. She dipped a jiaozi into the soy sauce dish before slipping it into her mouth. If she hadn't filled it with shrimp and garlic chives, she wouldn't have known its contents. Everything tasted like nothing.

"I can't get over this lacquer table. Such painstaking, carved artwork! Mother of pearl, right?"

She sipped her oolong tea. "Mhmm."

"Ming dynasty design? Come on, don't you want to teach me?"

"Stop it and just eat."

"Okay. I'm . . . I'm sorry. Please, let's forget it?"

Mei got up and went to the bathroom. He knew better than to follow her. But she closed the door and locked it anyway.

She put down the toilet lid and sat on its padded cover. Resting her elbows on her knees, she closed her eyes. He shouldn't have said it, even as a joke.

They'd talked about this before. In bed.

"I love you," he'd said, reaching across the crumpled sheets for her.

Mei sat up, resting her back against the headboard.

He tried to hold her hand, but she withdrew it. "What's wrong?"

"Never say that again."

The darkness masked her expression. He rolled toward the lamp.

"Leave it off."

"But I can't see you well."

"I know."

"What, you think I don't mean it?"

She crossed her arms when he reached for her again.

"I'm serious. The time I spend with you . . . it's made me realize I didn't love my ex-wife. You make me feel . . . I've never felt this with anyone else."

"Stop it! Stop."

"Stop what?"

"Don't . . . you can't. Just don't."

"Don't?"

"This can't ever be more than this. You ask for too much. I can't give you that."

"I-I understand if you don't love me. You don't have to say it back. I'm fine with waiting."

"You don't understand. I won't ever. That's not . . . I'll never do that again."

"I'm not . . . I'm not your husband. I understand you more than he ever could."

"It's not about him," she'd said. "I . . . I grew up during the Revolution. I can't give you more. I can't ever give more. If you want to see me again, listen to me now."

Mei lifted her eyelids. She stood up too close to the wooden shelving, bumping it with her shoulder. A framed photograph fell down. She caught it and set it back on the shelf. Her daughter had the duplicate in the dorm.

Opening the door, she flicked the switch, throwing the Disneyland picture into darkness.

Chapter Twenty

Ava spent the first couple days back at Lockhart wallowing. Li zhi had recommended a documentary, *Never Perfect,* on blepharoplastic surgery, but Ava lacked the mental strength to watch it now. Instead, she halfheartedly watched *Friends* reruns and reread *Part Asian, 100% Hapa.* Most students, including Charlotte, Derek, Kevin, and Jason, enjoyed the rest of their break at home with family and friends. Only Ava's RA, Dan, whom she dodged with legendary avoidance maneuvers, and another student populated the first floor. The university itself slept, quiet and fairly empty.

After hating herself for indulging in too many doses of self-pity, she put on her coat, gloves, and sneakers. She intended to go for a walk, since the weather had warmed and melted the ice. She always enjoyed exercising, but more of the slow type: walking, lazy badminton, yoga—never anything intense like running or competitive like racing. Ava thought that her mother had beaten out her competitive edge. She decided to walk from University Way to the next-closest campus, Walter. Walking on the sidewalk, passing by cars, houses, trees, a park, a river, Ava's defenses no longer repelled the onslaught of her thoughts.

She searched for exit signs, but no matter where she turned, she found none. No escape from the unbearable relationship with her mother. No solutions, no answers to "how to deal." How to deal? With her distant father. With *Lao lao*'s diary. With Mei's elusive entries. And now, after finding literal and figurative *pieces of herself* dissected by her mother . . . what? What—who—is Ava? How could she even begin to ask for help, to seek solutions?

Unfathomable. No answer. No. Being miscategorized, misunderstood—or worse, not believed—debilitated her the most.

The unfairness, the anger, the hurt, the fear, the sorrow, they crossed and interwove, ensnaring her in an invisible, thick, sticky web. And they lined her Wall, further fortifying it. If she touched that Wall, it bound her, prevented her from moving, from hearing the sounds on the other side. From remembering that the other side even existed. She rarely cursed because her mother freely did. But, right then, Ava wanted to breathe deep and scream "Fuck." With each step, her frustration built. Random raindrops grew to a drizzle, then the sky burst. Cold, fat droplets pummeled her.

Ava turned around, intending to run back to escape the wetness. And then she turned around a second time and ran from shelter. The rain fell harder, pelting her, taunting her, unrelenting. Still, Ava ran. Soaked and hunted, she picked up speed, heart throbbing, lungs burning, driving herself forward over the wet pavement. With each step, she peeled off an internal layer.

Active molting. Scrape it away. Trepidation, anger, inferiority. Belly up, fresh skin out. Display your vulnerability—show yourself—no one's watching. Worse than stripping in front of a mirror. Full, public, mental nudity.

But it felt right. What's right is natural. I want to be . . . I can be natural. *Fuck* stares. *Fuck* silence. *Fuck* judgment. *Fuck* shame. Someday, I'll scream. Someday, I'll climb the Wall, balance on the border and shout from the top. I don't need you to be real!

Ava whipped past buildings and trees, focused on racing onward. Her body protested. She ignored its pleas. Push, push further. Embrace the pain. No more thinking!

Neither origins nor composition mattered. Doing transcended. Feeling. She owned a functioning body, and she used it. In charge. Left, right, left, right. Over and over. Again. Again. Simple.

When she reached Walter Campus, she stopped running. She sat in the middle of an empty sidewalk, folding her legs to her chest. I am here. You might not realize it. I'm here.

With half-closed eyes, she looked through her eyelashes. Cars whizzed by in the distance. Water seeped into every pore. Let go. It's safe to let go. She cried into her knees, hugging them.

No one noticed, and in this moment, Ava felt happy to be invisible. Everyone, her mother now included, apparently felt the need to look at her. Watch her. Inspect her. Dissect her. But they only stared at her surface layer. No one actually *saw* her. No one asked how she wanted to be seen.

Her tears mixed with rain, making Ava less conscious of the fact that she cried. Maybe the Revolution made Mei feel this way: misunderstood, on display, attacked, powerless. She had more in common with her mother than she cared to admit. After steeping for a while, she rose and ran back to Lockhart. Swiping her soggy self in, she puddled her way to her room.

She hung her soaked clothing up before taking a long, hot shower. When she came back to her room, exhaustion hit her like pelting hail. Her muscles, all at once, spasmed with shooting pain. She collapsed onto her bed, not caring that her damp hair wet her pillow or that dinner remained uneaten. But at the same time, she almost had a clear head, and damn that felt good. Ava fell into a nightmare-less sleep.

She awoke from her slumber to a relentlessly vibrating phone. Groaning, she stretched, struggling to sit up. Ava groggily grabbed her phone and peered at the bright screen. A text message from Julia.

"U bac @ DU?" it read. Good grief, Ava hated how Julia balked at spelling anything out in a text. It reminded her of Mei's way of spelling in English.

"Yes," she texted back.

"Party 2nite?"

Ava hesitated, looking at the clock, 10:50 p.m. She'd just showered and slept for a few hours. Did she want to go out?

"No thanks."

Julia responded immediately. "Y not?!"

"Way too tired."

Julia stopped texting and called. "Please? Come on! Don't be lame."

"Honestly, I'm tired, Julie. And I don't feel like drinking either."

"Well then don't drink! See, problem solved."

What, and you have no friends? Ava barely stopped herself from saying her thought. Instead, she settled for, "What about the friends you usually party with?"

"The bitches up and abandoned me."

Ava imagined Julia pouting over the phone. "Meaning your girlfriends went home for winter break, right?"

"Yeah."

"Why aren't you home for winter break?" she asked.

Julia became quiet and then Ava bit her tongue, realizing. They neared the anniversary of Mr. Bell's death. Of course, Ema and Charlotte hadn't expected Julia to stay home after the holidays.

"Sure Julie, I'll come out tonight, just for you," she said, guilty and resigned.

"Knew you would!" Julia crowed.

Ava cringed, already regretting her decision. "I'm not doing makeup or anything though; I'm just wearing an off-the-shoulder top and jeans. And remember, I'm keeping you company, which means I'll watch *you* get drunk. Don't expect a drinking mate."

"Fine, fine, whatever you want," Julia said.

Ava edged off her soft bed. Curse her guilty conscience.

"I assume you're going to come over?"

"Yup; I'll be over in about ten."

"Ten what? Hours, days, monkeys? What are your units?" she feebly responded, legs unhappy about standing up. If she wanted to run like this again, she'd need to ease into it.

Julia giggled and hung up.

In less than twenty minutes Julia and Ava walked to their partying destination, an apartment shared by two male graduate students.

Ava considered the neat brownstone ahead of them. "I'm impressed, but the ultimate question: is it as put-together on the inside?"

"Hell yeah, at least from what I've seen of it. The place isn't huge, but it's really modern and they've got cool gadgets. They look like they've done well for themselves, especially for philosophy PhD candidates. I've been here once before. They play good music and the guys are too smart to be sleazy. In fact, you might fit right in, little miss nerd."

"Well if you're right tonight, rhyme intended," Ava said, ignoring Julia's groan, "this'll be an upgrade from our usual venues."

They walked up the even steps and Julia rang the doorbell. A tall, black man with tidy, shoulder-length dreads opened the door.

"How may I help you ladies?" he asked, looking expectant.

"Kierkegaard, plus one," Julia said, twisting a purple curl.

He ushered them in. "Welcome to the abode I share with my buddy Tim. I'm Nick."

"Do you know who Kierkegaard is, or do you just know the password to get in?" Ava whispered to Julia.

"Yes, a Danish philosopher. You know, I actually go to most of my classes, thank you. I'm not stupid."

They followed Nick for a brief tour of the apartment.

"So the party's kinda separated." He pointed out each room. "We've got the potheads smoking it up in the walk-in closet, people who just want to talk and chill in the dining room, and the regular party people in the living room. There's a bar area in the living room; my man Austin can get you what you like. Bathrooms are by the bedrooms. You'll figure it out 'cause the place ain't that big. I'm gonna pop out to get more drinks. Enjoy."

"That's a T.V., alright," Julia said, admiring the monster of a flat screen television in the dining room when they peeked in.

"Ema would so disapprove," Ava remarked. She always insisted that food went with conversation, never "mindless tube-watching."

"Focus, Ava. I'm here to party, not think of my mother. Let's go to the living room."

With a wistful glance toward the dining room, she followed Julia. Every body part continued to ache, but her legs hurt the most.

They were both surprised to find people sitting, chatting and drinking, while others salsa danced.

"This is really cool," she said to Julia, not needing to scream to be heard.

"Where's the regular grinding? God, I need a drink. You want anything?"

Ava laughed. "A virgin iced tea, thanks."

Her legs demanded that she sit, but people swarmed the couch. She settled for leaning on a wall, watching the couples swivel their hips and spin.

Julia chatted up the bartender before ordering; by the time she returned with the drinks, Ava had already been twirled around by a couple of guys.

"You looked like you were having fun at least. How do you feel now?" She paused, thinking, and then gave Ava a drink.

"Thanks." She took a big gulp of her drink. Cloyingly sweet, but her thirst trumped taste. "A bit dizzy, but surprisingly less tired." For some reason, her legs had stopped bothering her, which probably meant that they'd kill her tomorrow.

"You're brave. I'm afraid of looking like an idiot or falling in these heels."

"Why don't you take your heels off, then?"

"Maybe after a couple of drinks, when I'm loosened up."

The night wore on. Ava danced more and watched a seriously uninhibited Julia try it out. But after knocking back her second iced tea, Ava began to suspect that her drinks contained alcohol. Her head spun, and not because of the salsa dancing. No wonder she felt dehydrated. Where . . . Julia? She slid down, seeking a solid floor.

"You okay?" asked a male voice from above.

"Mmm. Not really . . . I just want to go back to my dorm, but I can't find my friend." She strained to look up. No, too much effort. Head throbbing, giving up.

The guy crouched down. She turned to look at him. He had brownish hair and an attractive face.

"Why don't you call a friend? Let me help; is your phone in your pocket?"

"Yeah." Ava fished it out of her jeans. She stared at it, unsure she'd be capable of finding Charlotte's number in the suddenly complicated thing. "I think I drank too much, too quickly," she admitted to the kind stranger. What? Why tell a stranger that? Her filter had evidently left with her equilibrium.

"Let's see." He took her phone and scrolled through the contacts. "Who to call?"

"Charlotte."

He wore casual, brown lace-up shoes. Nice. Like him, she thought, closing her eyes and resting her head against the wall.

"Okay, it's ringing," he said. "Hi, Charlotte? Sorry, I know it's late. Do you want the phone?" He put it to Ava's ear.

"Lottie? I'm kind of drunk, but I swear, I thought my drinks virgins. Ha, that sounds weird. Um, you at home?"

"What the fuck, Ava? Where are you? You okay? I planned on returning tomorrow, but never mind; I'm coming to get you now. Who's that guy? Shit. Don't go anywhere. Stay put, okay?"

"We're at ten Peterson Street. I'll bring her out to you," nice guy said, taking Ava's phone back. "And she came with a friend?"

"Julia." Ava opened her eyes to scan the room again. There, across the room with her silly purple hair. Who wanted purple hair?

"Julia," he repeated. He listened for a minute before hanging up and returning the phone to Ava. "Charlotte's coming soon, okay? Hang tight for fifteen minutes; not too many people on the road at this time of night."

"You're nice," she murmured, resting her head on his muscular thigh.

"You're drunk," he said, gathering her silky hair away from her face.

"You live here?" Ava asked, unaware of how vulnerable she looked.

"Nope. I live a couple of blocks over. My older brother lives here though. I have to say, you're coherent for a drunk person."

"Heh, thanks. Julia over here yet? She's the one with the curly purple hair. Curvy, you know, and probably drunk-flirting with at least one drink in her hand. See her?"

Ava put her head back down and closed her eyes. She sensed the prelude to an especially agonizing hangover.

"Um . . . ," he said, scanning the room. "Oh, yes, I see her. Interesting choice of hair color."

His thigh felt comfortable. "By interesting you must mean stupid," she said, making him laugh.

Her phone went off.

"I think help has arrived," he said, picking up her phone when she made no move for it. "Yup. Charlotte's outside. Up you go."

"But your leg . . . it's so . . . nice," Ava protested.

He laughed. "'Nice' seems to be your go-to drunk word. Come on, you need to sleep this off."

After collecting Julia, who also protested, the trio went outside to Charlotte's waiting car.

"Julia, you idiot. Mom had to drop me off at your place and then I had to wake up Kathy to get our car keys! Way to treat Mom and your roomie," Charlotte scolded, helping Julia into the backseat.

Julia's eyes wandered, unfocused, but she looked serious. "You should've told Dad. He'd pick us up . . . he always picks me up from practice."

Charlotte momentarily stopped struggling with Julia's seatbelt to stare at her sister pityingly. "Julie, he's a bit busy." She clicked the seatbelt into place.

Nice Guy picked up a sleepy, drunken Ava and buckled her into the front seat, chuckling at her remark that he had "nice arms."

"Good luck to you, ladies," he said, saluting Charlotte. "You take care of that one, okay?" He motioned to Ava before turning back to disappear into the house.

"Thanks!" Charlotte called after him. To the out-of-it passengers in the car, she said, "I'm gonna bitch both of you out so much later, just you wait."

"Hello." Charlotte lifted her mug at an unhappy-looking Ava. "I hope you're not in the mood to throw up again."

"Mmm," she mumbled, lifting her head, which weighed more than the freight train running through it. Ava peered at the clock, clutching her pillow. Eleven in the morning. Her dry, swollen tongue stuck to the roof of her mouth.

"We need to talk, by the way," Charlotte said in a surprisingly decisive manner.

Ava frowned before burying her face into her pillow, hoping that doing so buried her shame. The envelope containing Paul's stapled sheets crinkled. She froze, but Charlotte seemed unaware.

"Take your time responding. I can wait. Also, we kinda live in the same space, just so you know."

Letting out a muffled groan, Ava adjusted her pillow so that it completely covered the envelope. She slid her small feet into slippers. Without a word, still frowning, she went to brush her teeth and shower. Twenty minutes later, Ava returned, her wet hair trailing droplets on the floor.

"About damn time," Charlotte grumbled, putting down the latest issue of *Cosmopolitan*.

"You wanted to say something?" Ava asked, practically kissing her knees to towel dry her hair.

"Yeah. To you, not your bath-robed ass."

"I don't need to look at you in order to hear what you want to say."

Charlotte shook her head. "You're such a guy sometimes."

"No, it's got nothing to do with gender norms. It's practicality." Ava turned right-side up and threw her towel on a hook to dry.

"Whatever. Stop deviating from the subject. We need to talk about you. Just sit, will you?" Charlotte exasperatedly motioned to Ava's bed.

"Fine. I'm sitting, happy now?" She crossed her arms in front of her chest. Ow, that hurt. She put her arms down. And regarding her legs, she'd unfortunately been right. The running plus the dancing? A terrible combination.

"No. Of course I'm unhappy. I think you've got a bit of a problem. Are you an alcoholic?"

Ava jerked back, immediately regretted the movement, and gingerly touched her temples. "What? Just because I drink doesn't make me an alcoholic. Besides, the majority of kids at Davison drink and I'd say most of them aren't alcoholics."

"Well, you can't say for sure, now can you? You drink like Julia. Tell me, do you think you have a 'normal' relationship with alcohol?"

"Probably not." Ava shrugged then flinched at the soreness. Okay, she thought. Her goal for the day: as little movement as possible.

"Ava, wake the fuck up! This isn't a game. Even if you aren't an alcoholic, you've been incredibly lucky. I've saved your drunk ass at least two times!"

"While I appreciate your freaking assistance—could you lower your voice?—it's unnecessary. I can manage myself, thank you."

"Oh really? What if that guy hadn't helped you last night? Actually, what if that guy had been a jerk? You could've gotten into real trouble. You don't even know his name, do you?"

"What guy? I stayed with Julia the whole night."

"Are you telling me you don't remember?"

"No," Ava said slowly, trying to think.

"What *do* you remember from last night?"

"Um. Spinning. Salsa. Yes. Salsa dancing and iced teas. Then dizziness and sitting down. And then your car." Literally, the only things she remembered. And the memories were choppy, like a stop-motion animation film with missing frames.

"No guy? Who helped you call me?" Charlotte prompted.

"No . . . wait. Maybe. Someone helpful, and . . . nice. Yes! I kept calling him nice. With muscular thighs, but that's neither here nor there. I can't picture his face." She closed her eyes, but still recalled nothing. "Or anything else about his appearance, actually."

"Well, I'm afraid I can't help you. I know he had brown hair of some sort and seemed to be good-looking, but there weren't too many lights. See what I mean? I think this qualifies as a blackout; Kev and I learned this in psych. This is getting dangerous, Ava. Why can't you recognize that? Why won't you listen to me?"

"I get it, I get your point; you don't have to be so . . . self-righteous. I hadn't planned on going out at all, I'll have you know. Julia guilted me into it. And I asked her to give me nonalcoholic drinks."

"Please, you know better than to trust Julia in those situations. You know better in general! How can someone so damn smart be so stupid?"

"Make me feel better, I feel great already," Ava said sarcastically.

Charlotte sighed. "I'm sorry."

Ava dropped her arms and stared at her bedspread. A few black marks stained the ivory comforter. Where'd they come from?

"Can I ask you a question?"

"You're going to ask it even if I say no, so go ahead."

"What's going on with the drinking? What are you trying to escape from?" Charlotte tried to get Ava to look at her, but she resolutely continued to stare at her comforter.

"I don't know," Ava lied, shrugging. More pain.

"I just don't understand. You're being so destructive and it makes no freaking sense! Av, you've got it all, everything anyone could ask for. You're smart, gorgeous, talented. You've got supportive friends and a wonderful family. You've always excelled; what happened to you? You know, sometimes I hardly recognize you."

That makes two of us, Ava thought. She said nothing at first, not even bothering to fight back, but Charlotte's silence insisted on a response. "I can't explain it."

"You mean you *won't*, and that's the difference. God, you can't even look at me. Look at me and tell me I'm wrong," Charlotte challenged. "Dammit, look at me!"

Of course, Ava couldn't bear to look at her.

"Stop. You don't know what you're talking about."

"So why don't you fucking tell me? I'm not a mind reader. We're supposed to be best friends! Sometimes you make me want to throw a pillow at you."

"There are just some things you keep to yourself; surely you'll agree with that." Ava finally looked up and boldly met Charlotte's eyes.

Charlotte turned away. "At least your father's still alive. You're just too lazy to demand attention from him!"

"Wow. I know you're hurting, but that's low of you. Things aren't always how they appear to be. Not that it's any of your business, but my parents are basically separated. I hardly see him. I exaggerated before. He doesn't always come back during weekends. And when he does stay over, he sleeps in the guestroom." She defiantly glared at Charlotte, whose mouth lay partially open. "Don't speculate when you have no idea what you're talking about." Charlotte looked ready to beg for forgiveness, but Ava held up a hand. "I think this conversation is officially over." She kept her voice soft, disregarding the tension in her jaw. "Please leave and let me change in peace."

Charlotte, stunned by the outburst, grabbed her coat and purse and left Ava alone.

Chapter Twenty-one

January twenty-second marked the start of the spring semester. Winter became vicious. Heavy snow had yet to fall, but barely perceptible ice slicked the sidewalks. Many a student literally running late to class learned this the cold, hard way. Still, the bus system worked fairly well because the roads themselves were kept clear.

Students resigned themselves to checking the weather before heading outside; throwing on jeans and a sweater no longer worked. In the spring and summer less than half of Davison University had air conditioning, but it more than made up for this inadequacy with the level of heat provided in the winter. Students quickly learned to layer; some classrooms felt like saunas, and most classrooms lacked a temperature control system. Some evil administrator controlled most of the classrooms in a given building.

Unfortunately for Ava, she sat in one of these classrooms learning about Medieval Poetry, her long sleeves rolled up past her elbows, sweating profusely. The professor, a tiny, middle-aged woman with a huge voice, excitedly plowed through an eight-page poem. Ava exchanged looks of sufferance with the attractive boy two seats to her right while attempting to follow along.

"Now, class, we'll break up into groups by poetic work. You'll work with a minimum of four people and a maximum of six people. As a *group*, you'll read the work—outside of class. No need to look so dejected! At the end of the semester, each group will present the work creatively. Since we'll be working on this all semester, I expect amazing presentations, you hear? Put on a play, shoot a movie, do something with art or technology. Just impress me.

"Dante Alighieri's *Commedia—Divine Comedy* is what you probably know it as—will be split up into three groups, with each group doing part of the *Inferno*, *Purgatorio*, or *Paradiso*. Once you get to working on the presentation, feel free to split up your group into smaller pairs; just be sure that each group gets a fair share of work. I'm circulating the sign-up sheet starting here. Pass it on down to the desk behind you and then over to the next row." The professor gave the sheet to the girl two seats in front of Ava.

When Ava received the sheet she signed up for Dante's *Inferno*. She had read and enjoyed it in high school. The circles of hell made her childhood seem like nothing to complain about. Mei never chased her with bees, hung her over a pit of fire, perpetually trapped her with weights, or shut her in ice.

Less than a week had passed since Ava gave up partying, but she resolved to continue throwing herself into fiction and research for Li zhi. And with the chilly state of affairs between Charlotte and Ava, the latter clung to these learning spaces more than ever before.

The next day she walked into U.S. Latino/a Literature for the first time. Professor Meier seemed to be in her seventies, but Ava noted nothing old ladyish about her. Although the height and build of the average American woman, she carried herself with innate stateliness. Her clothing also announced singularity. She wore a long-sleeved, knee-length black knit dress, paired with wool stockings and kitten heels. On the front of the dress ran, like a sash, a trail of embroidered, palm-sized applique eagle feathers. Her silver hair fell short, pixie style, which showcased the dream catcher earrings that dangled from her earlobes. Looking at her professor, Ava felt underdressed.

"*Bienvenidos*, welcome," said Professor Meier warmly.

"*Muchas gracias*," Ava replied, glad to have taken Spanish in high school.

She took a seat in the front row, toward the right side of the room. Only three other students were in the room, sitting in the third or fourth rows. Looking at the analog clock on the wall furthest from her, Ava noted that she'd arrived fifteen minutes early; class started at 1:10. She took out her phone and saw a text from Jason: "look thru the window in the door." Through the small window, Ava spotted a flash of shaggy blond hair. He opened the door, grinning at her.

"*Hola, Profesora* Meier," Jason said, sliding into the seat left of Ava.

"*Hola* Jason. *Otra vez*." Professor Meier smiled widely.

As Jason took out his notebook, Ava whispered, "How do you know her?"

"I'm a *mulatto*, remember? I know every Spanish-speaking person."

"Ha ha. And the real reason?"

"I'm thinking of doing a Spanish minor, so I'm taking her class for native speakers, which met earlier today."

Three more students filed into the classroom, talking amongst themselves.

Seeing that they only had five minutes until the start of class, Ava pulled out her own notebook. "You're a native speaker?" She thought that Jason had just taken Spanish in high school.

"Yeah, didn't I tell you? After marrying my dad, my mom learned Spanish. When I grew up, we spoke Spanish at home and

English outside. Your parents totally should've done that. With Mandarin, I mean."

Ava nodded. Her parents should've done many things.

"Okey dokey, let's get started," Professor Meier said, clasping her hands together. "I'm not going to bother taking attendance today, but next week onward you'll all sign a sheet for me. Anyway, I hope you've been able to access the syllabus online; I'll post readings on our course website. I'm teaching this in English, but if you want credit for your Spanish major or minor, you have to do all the written work in Spanish."

Leaning back on the front of her desk, Professor Meier scanned the faces of the eight students in her seminar. Ava noticed that she had unusual amber eyes.

"I figured that we'd begin by talking about our backgrounds, which will segue into the theme of this class. You've probably gathered that, race-wise, I'm not *latina*. I'm German, Dutch, and Russian. Now, I know what you're thinking. 'What's this white lady doing, being a Spanish professor?' Because, when I studied abroad in Barcelona during college, I loved it so much that I transferred there. After undergrad, I earned my postgrad degrees at Universidad de Guadalajara in Mexico."

A female student raised her hand. "Where'd you get your dress?" she asked, admiring it.

Professor Meier looked down at her attire. "Oh, this? I lived on a Mohawk Indian Reservation for a year. A tribe member made it for me."

Ava exchanged a look of awe with Jason.

"I had no idea," he mouthed to her.

When the students finished explaining their respective backgrounds in turn, Ava and Jason turned out to be the only ones of mixed-race. Caucasians and Hispanics composed the rest of the class. Still, Ava expected to enjoy the class; no philistines seemed to be present.

"Alright everyone, I'm going to let you journey forth a half hour early," Professor Meier said. "Read the articles I posted for next class. If you haven't yet gotten *The House on Mango Street*, *The Brief Wondrous Life of Oscar Wao*, and *So Far from God*, don't wait for an invitation from me to do so."

"Finally! I've figured it out," Jason said to Ava after they walked out the door.

"What?"

"Professor Meier looks like Helen Mirren! Except with yellowish eyes."

They walked to the nearest bus stop and waited for a bus from Irving campus to University Way.

"Um, I don't know who that is." Watching movies and television never made Mei's list of approved activities for her daughter.

"What, have you lived under a rock your whole life?"

Sort of, Ava thought, laughing with him.

"Helen Mirren's best known for *The Queen*." Jason pulled up a picture of the movie poster on his iPhone. "See?"

"Oh. You're right; they'd at least pass for sisters."

After letting two buses packed to capacity with students go by, Ava and Jason finally got onto a bus.

"This class will be awesome. I can feel it." Jason grabbed part of the railing that Ava held onto.

"Is that so?" she asked, raising an eyebrow. "How can you feel it?"

"'In the Air Tonight,' obviously."

Ava stared blankly.

Jason shook his head sorrowfully. "Let me guess, you don't know Phil Collins either, do you?"

"No idea. I only know old movies from visits to my grandparents. So nothing past Audrey Hepburn."

"My poor dear. Sometime Kev and I will pull you out from under that rock."

Before she could respond, her phone vibrated. A text from her father. "Can we talk?" Ava frowned. When she noticed Jason looking at her curiously, she explained, "Vague text from my dad."

Jason nodded. "It's probably 'cause it takes too much effort to explain over text. Parents just want to call you."

"On the bus now. What time works best?" Ava texted back.

Twenty minutes later, they got off the bus and she received a response from her father. "Please call now."

"Kev and I are going to the dining hall. Want to come?"

"Sorry, maybe next time. I've got to call my dad now."

"Want me to invite Charlotte so you'll have the room? Besides, aren't you guys still ice fighting?"

"Yes, actually. 'Ice fighting?' You just made that up." Worried what else Charlotte told him, Ava added, "Did she say why?"

"No."

"It's because of that party Julie and I went to last week. I shouldn't be drinking, yadda yadda."

Jason shrugged. "She'll come around. Until then, I get to use my neologism."

"'Ice fighting,' really. You think that'll catch on?"

"Obviously. Ice fighting, you know, the freeze-out, ignore-fest kind of fighting that girls do so well."

"If I had more time I'd word-slap you for that sexist comment. But I don't, so here you go!" Ava rumpled his hair. He yelped and she ran away, laughing.

"Never touch the hair," Jason called after her in fake outrage. "Just you wait. I'll get you back when you least expect it!"

She took out her keys just as Charlotte opened the door to their dorm room from the inside.

"Um. Hi."

"Hi," Charlotte said nervously, still holding the door.

Charlotte blocked her way inside. "May I? . . ." Ava gestured.

"Yes, of course." She stepped aside. "Uh, see you later, then."

"Later."

Ava put down her backpack and took out her phone. Charlotte slowly shut the door, expecting her to say more. But Ava focused on wondering what her dad wanted to say. She'd deal with her friendship some other time.

Her father picked up after the second ring. "Hi Ava."

She sank onto her bed. "Hi, Dad. Is it still okay to talk?"

"Yes, I'm taking a short break. I . . . hold on."

She heard a door, presumably the one to his office, click closed. Ava swung her legs restlessly.

"I read the diary entries. I mean, just *Lao lao*'s. Sorry, I should've . . . "

"No, Ava, it's okay. I'm glad you did. It's about time; I put it off for too long. Listen, your mother doesn't know—"

"I figured."

"I kept trying to talk with you about it, but you always seem too busy."

Ava swallowed guiltily. "Sorry about that."

"I have a lot to explain. It'll be easier in person. And I want to show you the actual diary. It's hidden in the house, in your mother's bedroom."

She noticed that her father hadn't called it "our bedroom."

"And you'll give me Mother's entries? You noted on the package that—"

Ava heard a beep. Her call waiting notification. "Wait, I think someone else is calling me." She looked at the screen. "Mother Dearest." Ava bit her lip to prevent herself from groaning in frustration. "Dad, I need to take it. It's Mother."

"Oh, okay." He sounded disappointed. "I need to get back to work anyway."

Realizing that this could be her only chance to talk to her father undisturbed, Ava said, "The next time I go home, I'll text you so you can come back too."

"But your mo—"

The beeping increased and then stopped. "When she's not there!"

Paul fell silent for a moment. "Then yes. When she won't be back for at least a half hour."

"Okay, talk to you then. Thanks, bye!"

"Good—"

Ava hung up, cutting him off. She called her mother.

"What taking so long?" Mei demanded. "It went straight to your voicemail."

"Sorry, I'd been—"

"*Bi zui*! I don't want your excuses. What's that shortcut?"

Ava almost looked at her phone in confusion. "Shortcut?"

"Pay attention. To select everything."

Ava looked at the ceiling in exasperation. "To select everything where?"

"Goddamn you. On the computer!"

Ava felt no sorrow at being unable to read her mother's mind. She imagined it a booby-trapped jungle. "Control 'A' on the keyboard."

"What?"

"Control—the button below the 'Shift' key. And the letter 'A.'"

"You useless. It didn't work."

Ava almost laughed in irritation. "Hold down the 'control' key, and then the 'A.' Did you do it?"

"Yes." Then Mei hung up.

"You're not welcome," Ava muttered. What had Jason said about helping her out from under that rock?

Chapter Twenty-two

On the tenth of February a knock interrupted Ava's reading. Putting down *The House on Mango Street*, she slid off her bed to answer the door.

"Oh, hi Derek. Charlotte's still at home. She'll be back after dinner."

He caught the door when Ava let go. "I know."

"Right, of course you do."

"I wanted to talk to you, actually."

"If you want to talk me into apologizing to Charlotte, you'll be wasting your time." She retreated into her room and Derek followed.

"No, I know better than to get between you two. What are you doing today?" He leaned on her bureau. "You going home to celebrate?"

Back on her bed, Ava asked, "Celebrate?"

"Oh, sorry, I guess that's rude of me. Happy Chinese New Year."

"That's today?"

"So you forgot, huh?"

"No, we never celebrated. My mother dislikes holidays. Which year is it?"

Derek made a hissing sound. "The year of the snake. Wait. Does that mean you've never eaten almond cookies?"

"Almond cookies?"

He shook his head mournfully. "I can't believe it. You haven't lived until you've tasted them!"

Ava laughed.

"You're coming with us. I don't care if we have to drag you."

"'We'?"

"My parents will arrive at the restaurant soon. Kevin and I are meeting them there. And now you're coming with us."

Ava opened her mouth, but she never got the chance to protest.

"Nope. This is happening. Trust me, my mom would've insisted anyway. Go get ready, and I'll knock on your door in five."

She took her phone off silent mode. She'd received text messages from her father and Li zhi. "Happy Chinese New Year!" from her dad. Li zhi supplemented the same text with Chinese: "*Gong Xi Fa Cai*!" Ava thanked both of them.

By the time she had brushed her hair and thrown on a red sweater dress and black leggings, Derek knocked on the door again.

Slinging her purse over her shoulder, she opened the door to find Derek and Kevin waiting expectantly. "Alright, alright, I'm ready to go."

Sunday afternoon blessed them with little traffic, so the drive to Edison took only fifteen minutes. Derek parked his Honda while Kevin and Ava looked up at the sign for the restaurant. Black Chinese characters stood out against a yellow background. Beneath them, in bold black caps, presumably read the English translation, "Gold Star."

Derek pointed at the restaurant's name. "Ma says they got the English wrong. The Chinese name translates to 'Golden Light.'"

"That's a fail," Kevin said, following Derek inside. "Av, why aren't you going bananas?"

Ava nudged him before they arrived at the table Derek's parents sat at. "That's actually a good thing. If the English is bad, it should mean that the owners are authentic Chinese."

"Hi Mr. and Mrs. Azarov," Kevin said. "Good to see you again."

Derek gestured to her. "Ma, Dad. This is Ava."

Mr. Azarov tried to smooth his dark, unruly hair. "Ah yes." His Russian accent was almost imperceptible. "Charlotte's roommate, right?"

She nodded and smiled, leaning forward to shake his hand. "*Gong Xi Fa Cai*." He also wished her a happy New Year. Ava turned, intending to walk over to Mrs. Azarov, but she beat her to it.

Without warning, Derek's mother pulled her into an energetic hug.

"*So* nice to finally meet you. Derek's told us so much about you." Mrs. Azarov pulled back to beam at a shocked Ava. "*Très belle*, just as he said! My daughters went to my parents' house, so we ladies must sit together."

"Ma!" Derek groaned quietly. "Stop, you're scaring her."

Mrs. Azarov defied all of Ava's expectations. She exuded beauty and shopped in the petites section like Mei, but the similarities ended there. Hardly any makeup appeared on Mrs. Azarov's face, and her updo looked rushed, like she'd put up her hair while moving. While everyone settled into their seats, she had a speedy chat with the waiter in Mandarin, ordering more dishes than the group of five would be able to eat.

Mr. Azarov pushed the appetizers to the center of the table. "Please, help yourselves."

Kevin used a spoon to take a dumpling while Ava used her chopsticks.

"What'd you get us, Ma?" Derek asked, taking a spring roll.

"*Tout*! Everything!"

Mr. Azarov grinned boyishly. "My wife went to boarding school in France. She knows all the romance languages, but French is her favorite."

Ava saw Mrs. Azarov reach out to her, so she refrained from recoiling when Derek's mother patted her arm.

"You see, Ava, my father became an official in the Communist Party, and I was his youngest, the only girl. He shipped me off to school so I'd escape the Cultural Revolution."

"Did knowing French help you become a flight attendant? Charlotte told me how you met Mr. Azarov."

Mrs. Azarov giggled and fondly looked at her husband, who engaged Derek and Kevin.

"It didn't hurt."

The food came out on blue-and-white designed china dishware. One, two, three, four, five, six dishes. Sa-cha beef with water chestnuts and broccoli, sesame chicken, eggplant with garlic sauce, squid with mixed vegetables, shrimp lo mein, string beans with bean curd.

"*Bon appétit*!" Mrs. Azarov passed the beef to her husband and then turned back to Ava. "Would you like some string beans?"

"Yes, please. Thanks, Mrs. Azarov."

"Call me *Ayi*. Do you know what that means?"

Ava nodded as she placed a few string beans onto her rice. "Auntie. *Xiexie, Ayi*."

Mrs. Azarov fully smiled, revealing dimples.

"So Ava," Mr. Azarov said, pausing to wipe sauce from his stubble, "why aren't you celebrating with your parents?"

Ava took a sip of tea before answering. "My mother isn't a . . . festive person."

Kevin tried to pick up a piece of sesame chicken with chopsticks, but only succeeded in chasing it around his plate. "So you're not gonna call your mom? Isn't CNY a big deal, like a Chinese Christmas?" He gave up and speared the chicken.

"Not all Chinese celebrate the same way," Derek offered, sparing Ava.

The waiter came by to drop off a small plate of Chinese desserts. Kevin took a treat but then looked at it in confusion.

Mr. Azarov laughed. "That's a pineapple tart. It's safe to eat, I promise."

At the encouragement of Derek and his mother, Ava took an almond cookie.

"Everything's delish!" Kevin sat back in his seat, content.

Mrs. Azarov's brow furrowed.

"He means delicious," Ava explained, smiling.

"And what year is this one gonna be?" Kevin asked.

"Year of the snake," Mrs. Azarov said.

"There's gotta be an app for that." Kevin whipped out his iPhone and began fiddling with it.

Mr. Azarov nodded. "What isn't there an app for?"

"Found it! Zodiac signs and what they mean. The year of the snake . . . blah blah, ah, the good stuff." Kevin began reading. "This sign is seductive and intelligent, capable of bending others to their will. Fortune-wise for 2013: don't take risky business deals, be wary of 'unexpected hurt,' whatever that means, and married people shouldn't have affairs."

Smiling slyly, Mr. Azarov said, "In Russian we call that *fignya*. BS."

They laughed.

"How about a toast?" Ava lifted her teacup. "To surviving the year of the snake!"

Chapter Twenty-three

Spring semester progressed quickly. Deadlines, midterms, papers, and long-term projects came due or fast approached. For the most part, Ava fared well, both in and out of her classes. Latino/a Literature had become her and Jason's favorite class of the semester. She continued to research for Li zhi; her future advisor had nearly finished composing the manuscript. But most remarkable: Mei's silence. Her mother hadn't bothered Ava since the start of the spring semester; and while such silence made her uneasy, she decided to take full advantage of the respite while it lasted. Her immobilized relationship with Charlotte, however, hurt. A month had passed since their last confrontation. As Jason observed, an invisible sheet of ice formed between Ava and Charlotte. Both girls felt terrible about arguing and saying hurtful things, and neither wished to bring the topic up again—partly out of fear of exacerbation and partly due to pride. So the best friends stayed distant friends.

But it hadn't all been for naught. Ava had abstained from "going out" since the last party. Unbeknownst to Charlotte, her reckless behavior—including the unintentional drinking— shamed Ava. She now deemed drinking a two-sided beast. She controlled how much she drank, but not the effects, from losing her stomach to blacking out.

She'd been drinking incautiously. Alcohol itself embodied no wrongs. However, she'd used it to ill effect. In succession, a drink or two created a buzz, a rosy spin on things. More, without pacing herself or listening to her body, drowned her—disempowered and victimized. Then she lost the escape. Alcohol seized control. Then the same things she sought to escape tormented once again. She'd thought drinking would help her forget the Wall. Help her repress herself, erase what she hated, purge what she feared. She wanted to feel untouchable. Untouched by pain, stress, vulnerability—any and all of those facets that limit humans, which make humans . . . human. For a brief moment, drink set Ava free, but the moment always faded; illusion yielded to the degraded reality of a failed escape.

Ava wanted to embody the triangular tattoo that Jason had showed her before the start of their last class.

"Is that permanent?" Ava asked, pointing to the back of his neck. To combat the heat, Jason had stripped down to his t-shirt; during this change she caught a flash of the tattoo.

"Indelible ink, baby." He grinned.

"I didn't know you had a tattoo!"

"Really? But I showed the crew at the same time . . . oh. You went home that weekend."

"Well, what is it?"

Jason gathered his hair into a small ponytail. "Move my collar down so you can see."

Gently, she pulled on his shirt. Three cursive words, in black ink, formed a triangle. Serenity, Courage, Wisdom.

"It's lovely. May I touch it?"

"Go for it, but it's not going to feel different from the rest of my skin."

Ava traced the word triangle with a forefinger. Up Serenity, down Courage, across Wisdom. Setting his shirt to rights, she asked, "This refers to the serenity prayer, right?"

Jason dropped his hair. "Yup. Kevin and I got tattoos together for our two-year anniversary. His dad started pushing therapy again—you know, to 'fix' his gayness—so I came up with the idea."

"He has the same one?"

"No, actually. His goes down his side," Jason explained, demonstrating with a hand. "It says 'This, too, shall end.'"

"Isn't it 'pass,' not end?"

"Kevin hates that word, remember? We also shouldn't like it 'cause we're mixed."

Ava smiled. "I'm impressed. Most people our age don't get informed tattoos."

"We're not like most people, Ava. We're more like Oscar Wao. God, I love this book," Jason said, tapping the cover of *The Brief Wondrous Life of Oscar Wao*.

"You mean we're lost, confused, and everyone thinks we're losers?"

Jason shifted his glasses down to look at her directly.

"No, we're outside tradition. People judge us for being different, but we hold true to ourselves. *Sin duda*, we believe in our cause, even when we're mocked."

Ava looked at him admiringly. "But what about belonging?"

Professor Meier bustled into the room and began setting up for class.

Jason lowered his voice and leaned closer to Ava.

"Fuck belonging. You can't change your background. But you can sure as hell change your mindset. Be bold! Strip off your masks. Belong to yourself, *mujer*. Be your own Whasian."

Ava replayed Jason's advice. Belong to yourself. Be your own Whasian. What had she tried to prove via the partying? Becoming a playgirl clashed with her aspirations. Be my own Whasian, she thought to herself.

Later that week she carefully trekked over the frozen ground to the library to meet some classmates from her Medieval Poetry class. She looked forward to the meeting because she enjoyed reading Dante's *Inferno*, but also because the attractive guy who sat near her in class, Flynn, had joined her group. Ava infrequently spoke with him, but when they did speak, he always offered something intelligent or amusing. She'd been humbled by his intelligence. At first glance Ava had pronounced him to be good-looking and therefore obnoxious, stupid, or some combination of the two. After all, the attractive guys she encountered during parties led her to these assumptions. Derek, of course, didn't count. He felt like a brother, and he'd officially become Charlotte's boyfriend.

Ava arrived at the University Way library. Peeling off her gloves, she headed for the group's usual meeting spot, the comfortable reading couches striped with Davison's school colors, red and white. She expected to find at least half of her group already on the couches, but at 6:15, she appeared to be the only on-time member of the six-student group. After swiftly walking around the couch area and finding no familiar faces, Ava took off the rest of her outerwear. Getting comfortable on one of the longer couches, she took out her book.

But instead of reading, she found herself staring at the stripes on the couch. Red and white. Mei would've loved the red, a Chinese good luck color, but hated the white. Ava disliked the overbearing red but loved the white because her mother hated it. She supposed it fitting that the stripes lay side by side. Such opposing colors deserved their own space. If one color crossed over or bled into the other, mixing diluted the opposition. Then again, given her mother's secret obsession with her . . . maybe Mei would agree that some of the most interesting colors were mixed. Ava frowned to herself. That disrupted everything. Overturned the simplistic view she had of her mother. Mei couldn't also be complex. They needed to be opposites. She must not share mentalities with her mother. She wanted nothing derived from her, no resemblance.

Disturbed, Ava returned to her book. She'd only finished a stanza when a familiar voice read aloud, "'I submit!'"

Ava started, fumbling with and nearly dropping her book. Looking over her shoulder in the direction of the voice, she found a laughing Flynn.

"Hope you enjoyed my panicked show."

He grinned and came around to sit on the couch. "I'd say sorry, but I'd only half mean it."

"Jerk."

"Glad to be thought of so lovingly."

"Did you just get here?"

She concentrated on bookmarking her place, careful to avoid his eyes. Those eyes were the color of rich Colombian drinking chocolate. He never shied away from direct eye contact and Ava found his gaze unnerving.

"Nope. I've been here since six, in the clear-walled computer room. Rachel and Ben aren't coming; he just texted me. You have the twins' numbers?" Flynn leaned back, propping his feet on the nearby coffee table.

Ava pursed her lips and stared at his feet before answering. "Yes; let me check my phone. And really? Must you put your at least slightly wet sneakers on the table?" What a boy. She turned to the other side of the couch.

When she took her phone out of her coat's inner zipper pocket, she felt Flynn slide over and swiftly put his legs onto her knees. Ava promptly stood up. She gave him a cross look, biting her cheek to keep from smiling. Thank goodness she'd decided against wearing her white jeans; he would've gotten them dirty.

"You're no fun," Flynn teased, finally sitting normally. "You know, *we* never exchanged numbers."

Ava threw back the bait. "The other girls are on their way; they said they'll be five minutes."

She scrolled through her phone, continuing to read her text messages. One from her father, the usual "How are you?" They still hadn't found a chance to meet at the house. Deciding to text a longer answer, Ava blocked her mother's word about their father-daughter conspiracy—"unnatural." "A bit stressed, but okay," she texted back. Thankfully her mother didn't know how to text. If she could text, Ava would surely have been inundated with angry messages. Enough. No thinking about Mother until doing so became absolutely necessary. Still, she had a misgiving that Mei's silence wouldn't last for too much longer.

"Guess that's what happens when we've got twins and a couple in our group," Flynn said, finally succeeding in getting her to look his way. "We lone wolves are the only ones who show up and show up on time."

"Mmhmm," Ava agreed, still focusing on her phone. She sat back down on the other side of the couch. The boy distracted her, and she had no time for distractions. Too many complications in her life.

She sent Li zhi a text. "We're reading Junot Diaz's novel in Meier's class. I'm loving it!" Only a minute passed before she received a response: "Glad to hear it! What do you think of the mom?" Ava smiled to herself. "A Dominican tiger mom," she texted back. Li zhi asked, "Did you ever read *Battle Hymn of the Tiger Mother*? Chua is tamer than your mom, but I'm sure you'd find moments to relate to." Ava replied that she hadn't, and thanked Li zhi for her offer to lend the book to her when they next met for research.

Flynn tried again. "You know, I don't bite. Unless you ask for it, that is."

Luckily the arrival of the twins spared Ava from responding to this strange statement. Apparently Flynn liked to flirt one-on-one. So if not stupid or truly obnoxious, he must be one of those Casanova types. And she wanted nothing to do with that either.

They had assigned each other large portions to read outside of group sessions, so after an hour they finished reading and discussing the *Inferno*. The next session would entail actual planning and brainstorming for the final project, but at least they completed the first step. While Flynn and the self-proclaimed "Barbie twins" talked, Ava packed up her things and prepared to leave. Her phone read 7:22 p.m. No wonder her stomach complained of neglect. Dining hall food bored her, but she hated to be the sad person eating alone at one of the crowded cafes or restaurants in the area. Everyone looked at you, and Ava preferred to be the observer, not the observed.

Ordinarily she'd have texted Charlotte, Derek, Jason, or Kevin; but she and Charlotte still stood on shaky ground and the guys now seemed to be taking Charlotte's side. Derek, as part of his boyfriend duties, supported Charlotte. Kevin and Charlotte shared an affinity, and while Jason and Ava shared the same kind of rapport, he supported his boyfriend. She disappointed herself by allowing a month to pass without really attempting to win her best friend back, and Charlotte proved to be just as stubborn. So she remained alone.

Mournful but resolute, Ava buttoned her long, royal blue wool coat before cinching its belt around her waist.

"Flynn, we're going to eat at the dining hall. Want to come with?" she heard one of the twins say.

"Nah, I already ate. I'm just going back to my apartment. Thanks though."

"Oh, that's such a shame. Rain check then!" And with that the girls made their way slowly toward the door, lingering in the apparent hopes that Flynn would walk them out. Ava felt secretly pleased when he didn't. Instead, he walked back into the computer room.

She wrapped her silky white scarf around her head, picked up her backpack, and headed toward the automatic exit doors. Ava felt a tap on her shoulder. She turned to find Flynn.

"Hey, Grace Kelly. You eat yet?"

"No, why?"

"Have you been to Rumpelskillet? It'll be crowded, but we can probably get a table there. I'm good friends with the owner's son."

"Didn't you just say that you'd already eaten?" Ava asked, raising an eyebrow.

"A slight exaggeration. The twins annoy me. So how 'bout it? The food's good and inexpensive."

She hesitated, not wanting to seem too eager. "Sure. But I've never even heard of the place. Where is it?"

"Probably 'cause you're a freshman." Flynn grinned when she gave him a scowl. "It's a couple of blocks away from University Gym."

"Lead the way then, oh wise one." She motioned for him to step in front of her.

They ventured out into the unforgiving winter air, backpacks in tow.

"So are you a junior or senior?" Ava speed walked to keep up with his long strides.

"Neither. Sophomore."

"You sure fooled me," she said. She'd been comparing him to her RA, Dan. An ill-advised comparison, she realized.

"Probably not hard to do," Flynn teased, making Ava roll her eyes. "To be fair though, it's probably the height. I'm 5'11" and you're what, 5'2"?"

"A gross miscalculation," she huffed, arching her back against the weight of her backpack. I'm 5'5," an inch taller than the average American woman, thank you very much."

"Same difference. You're still fun-sized."

"I'm just going to ignore you until we get to Rumpelstiltskin or whatever it's called."

"Rumpelskillet. Aren't you an English major; don't you pay absurd attention to words?"

"I am. And it's not absurd. Your point?"

"So you're supposed to love plays on words. I'm doing engineering and even I know that!"

They arrived at the small restaurant and Flynn charmed the hostess for a table. Ava took the chair opposite him, facing the window. Every so often she saw students rush by, gripping their winter gear tighter around them, desperate to reach their destinations.

"Engineering? Then why are you taking Medieval Poetry?" she asked after the host seated them.

"So what? Does that mean that I'm disqualified from taking it? Have you got something against engineers interested in English? Are you an engineer-ist?"

Ava laughed. "Easy now with the machine-gun questions! No to all of them. It's just surprising; that's all."

"Surprising that an engineer isn't complete shit at the study of English lit.? Admit it. I saw that part of your thought process."

"Maybe. Maybe not. And what a cheesy rhyme."

"Hey, Flynn. This your latest girl?" Ted, the owner's son, expectantly stood at their table. He put down two waters and gave Flynn and Ava menus.

"Absolutely not," she blurted, feeling her cheeks turn pink. She hastily became absorbed in the pages of the menu.

Flynn took his coat off his chair, and before she could protest, took hers too.

"I'll put these away."

He stood up, giving his friend a "shut up and follow me" look. They walked over to the coat rack.

Though Ava couldn't hear their conversation, she watched them with interest. Flynn said something while he hung up the coats. Ted raised both eyebrows and replied, a skeptical look on his face. He seemed to be berating Flynn. Annoyed, Flynn shot something back. Ted nodded in her direction and clapped Flynn on the back.

On their way back to the table, she thought she heard Ted say, "If she's special, don't fuck it up."

Ava hid behind her menu to keep from smiling at Flynn's response: "Stellar advice."

"So that's me," Flynn said, sitting down. "But you never answered the question."

"What ques—" Ted started to say, about to give Flynn a hard time, when he received a kick to his shin. "Right, *that* question." He winced and rubbed his leg.

Peering over the top of her menu, Ava watched the rest of the interaction with amusement, which had just been heightened by Flynn's kick.

Ted glared at Flynn. "Well. I'm either working here or studying for organic chemistry and its friends. Nothing new. What'll it be, bro?"

"That sucks. Uh . . . my usual is fine," Flynn replied, handing over the menu.

"And for you, miss?"

She peeked out from behind her menu and asked, "What about your New England clam chowder?"

"Oh yeah, it's homemade; you won't regret it," Ted assured her.

"Okay then I'll have that, thanks."

After he left, she looked out the window at the brightly lit campus and asked, "So you come here a lot?"

"Tell me when the window responds to you," Flynn said.

Ava reluctantly looked in his general direction. "I'm obviously speaking to you."

"Not familiar with standard human communication, eh? Interesting."

She silently took out her hair tie and swept her layers into a bun, inadvertently emphasizing her cheekbones. How could she tell him that direct gazing rattled her?

"I come here every so often. I didn't purchase a meal plan; I prefer to cook myself."

"I suppose that's impressive," she conceded. "Most sophomores survive on packaged noodles, junk food, and the dining hall."

"Well I'm not like most sophomores, just like I'm sure you consider yourself different from most freshmen."

Ted came back with a tray full of hot food. "Enjoy."

After he left, Ava stared at her giant soup bowl.

"The clams are already dead and cooked, I promise," Flynn said, putting hot sauce on his barbeque chicken sandwich.

"It's just a great deal of soup. I don't foresee myself eating more than half of it." She stirred in the parsley sitting on top.

"Smaller people have less space. Take it home then."

"I've got it under control, thanks, *Dad*. I'm perfectly capable of—"

Flynn chuckled, putting his hands up. "Alright, alright, I believe you. It's like you're looking for a fight."

"Sorry. I can be defensive."

"Just a tad." He held his forefinger and thumb nearly together, smirking when she gave him an annoyed look.

They finished what they could of their meals over banter and some thoughtful conversation. Flynn offered to pay but Ava resisted, intending to treat him. To Ted's amusement, they fought over the small bill until he insisted that the pair split the bill as he had other customers waiting.

They left to meander in the direction of Lockhart Hall, ending up discussing their group project and what each thought of Dante's *Inferno*; they'd both read it before Medieval Poetry. Finally outside Lockhart, they lingered, idly chatting despite the unrelenting cold.

Then Ava's phone rang, destroying the calm of the night. She shook her head sadly.

"It's my mother. I have to take it."

When it rang again shrilly, Flynn took out a pen from his pocket. "Hand," he commanded.

She cautiously put a gloved hand out, palm up as if to receive the pen. Flynn shook his head, chuckling. He swiftly took off her glove, flipped her hand over, and printed what she supposed to be his number.

Quickly slipping the glove back onto her hand, Flynn said, "See you, Ava." He waved before crossing the street.

Her hand tingled. She watched him go before picking up the phone. Taking a deep breath, she greeted her mother.

"I tested you, Ava Ling," Mei seethed from the other line.

Ava swiped into Lockhart. "What are you talking about?"

"You failed the test."

"I still don't know what you're talking about."

She opened the door to her room to find Charlotte absent. Ava felt torn between relief and disappointment. For a few moments, she loitered in the doorway, looking at the darkened room. Their things loomed unfamiliar in the dark.

"It precisely twenty-eight days since last we talked. No calls for twenty-eight days. I knew it; you never be trusted to report back to me!"

"What? I've been busy with schoolwork and starting the spring semester off right." Thinking about Li zhi, Ava added, "And I'm researching for my molecular bio professor."

"Lies, excuses. You never called to see how I'm doing and if you can help me. You even didn't wish me a happy Chinese New Year! Selfish bitch, I taught you better."

Ava slowly exhaled away from her phone, resisting the impulse to hang up or scream back. She'd come so far, but her mother would erase her progress again. Turning on the light, she saw that Charlotte had left a note on her bed.

"Spending the weekend with Derek at his parents' house. Will be back Monday morning; see you then," it read.

Great. So she couldn't even use Charlotte as an excuse to stop talking.

"Have you be listening to me?"

Crap. "Yes," Ava lied.

"Quiz. What did I say now?"

"'Quiz. What did I say now.'"

"Don't play English words with me! You know what I mean."

"Um . . . you said that I hadn't called you to check up on you."

"Wrong!" Mei said gleefully. "What else comes new? You have the attention span of a spy."

"A fly. 'The attention span of a fly.'"

"Shut the fuck up, *hutu dan*. You didn't get my approving of your schedule. This your first semester choosing classes by yourself. I must be involved; *I'm* paying for your schooling!"

"No you're not. My education is fully paid for through a scholarship. You're paying for my housing," Ava corrected. Technically, her father paid for her housing and had real control over the purse strings, but she knew better than to bring that up. "And you never told me I needed to get your approval."

"You supposed to *know*. I'm still paying. I must choose classes with you. You no want that? Then teach many piano kids to pay for your dorm. Not so easy now, ah?"

"What do you know about the classes I need to take, anyway? Guess what? I'm an English major; you're awful at English!"

She put a hand over her mouth, aghast. All this time she'd been lying so effectively. To lose it like this—utterly pathetic.

A goose-bump-inducing silence.

"What's this?" Mei's voice, a still river. Ava braced herself for the inexorable flood. "*Feihua*! An *English major*? What happen to pre-med? You *lied* to me. English? You might better be a whore! What job you will get? There no money, no future, no honor in that degree—"

"That's not true—"

"Shut up, dare you interrupt me. You wish to make nothing of yourself and make me look stupid? *Bu yaolian*! My reputation matters. Dare you shit on me, dare you! You're coming home. *Now*."

"I'm sorry! I planned on telling you. There are respectable jobs for English majors, even outside teaching! Let me explain, please."

"You drive home now or you really be sorry. *Quan shan jie e*. Easy or hard, you know. Challenge me. You know I always keep my words." Mei sounded calm again, voice firm and sure. A chef's steel knife.

"I'm sorry, I said sorry. Can't we just talk this through?" Ava knew that once she left Davison, all semblance of emotional equilibrium died. She'd be at her mother's mercy. Mei understood mercy in the same manner she understood privacy.

"*Gouzazhong*! No, mongrel dog. No exceptions. No excuses. I carry my word. Come home now. I must teach you, again. You refuse? You know I'm a tiger. I lash out and you face issues. Easy or hard, easy or hard. I expect you home in thirty minutes or under. Hear this ticking? I'm timing you."

Ava's phone echoed when Mei hung up.

Despite the slippery road conditions, she managed to make it back to her parents' "Maplewood Estate" in twenty-five minutes. Now she just needed to summon the valor to step out and face her mother, no easy deed. But waiting longer never made matters better. It just made her more nervous, so Ava rang the doorbell at 9:28 p.m.

"You almost late," Mei snapped, practically wrenching the door open.

"I—"

"Don't care for excuses, in." She pulled her daughter's arm until she reluctantly stepped into the house.

"You look like shit," Mei said, circling Ava after shutting and locking the front door. "At your age I twice as *piào liang*. Your hair look stupid. And your skin, you ghost . . . "

Calling up the memory of her mother's blog entry on beauty, her saved hair, and the pictures of her face, Ava let the insults tumble to her feet. She hadn't found time to watch the documentary Li zhi had recommended. But the trailer for *Never Perfect* had been a helpful overview. Striving for physical beauty linked to striving for perfection, and the clash between Western and Eastern ideals made the quest impossible.

"What's this?" Mei seized Ava's right hand, studying the line of numbers.

Internally she cursed herself. Flynn's number. She'd entered it into her phone, intending to wash off the ink, but had forgotten. Obviously too late now.

"It's the number of a classmate; we work on a group project together. I didn't get a chance to wash it off."

"The girl never hear of paper? Stupid attracts stupid. Wash it off and then come upstairs to my office. Hurry up or you'll have to organize the book basement tonight instead of this weekend." Mei spun on her heel to head up the stairs to the second floor.

This weekend? Dread settled in Ava's stomach. Three whole days of her mother? No, especially not now. Her recess from her mother had opened her mind to a world beyond the Wall, a world that never included Mei and her choke collar hold. She felt like one of those leashed children she and Charlotte had once seen while walking in the mall. They'd been horrified, but the parents strolled along casually, like they walked their dogs, not their children. After washing off Flynn's number, she trudged up the stairs, mentally cursing her mother every step of the way.

As Ava approached Mei, she thought of Derek's mother. Effervescent, earnest Mrs. Azarov. She played dog to Mei's cat. The two Chinese women united only by their country of origin.

With her back facing the doorway to her office, Mei stood with her toned arms on her slim hips. At fifty-two, she still obsessed about her image. Since Ava had started college, she'd noticed that her mother put even more effort into perfecting her physical appearance. Mei also wore makeup more often than she used to. Like she planned to reclaim her Mrs. New Jersey title, though Ava saw no actual evidence of this. Perhaps she just imagined things.

"About damn time." Mei pointed to the wooden chair she'd pulled up next to her computer chair.

"I had to scrub it off," Ava explained, sitting down.

Still standing, Mei returned her hands to her hips. "*Bi zui*! You never get anything useful to say. You're a burden. You know, you so lucky to have me. *Wang en fu yi*? Think you allowed to deny me, reject me? *Lie to me*? What you are without me? Nothing, less than shit! Where you be without me?"

She looked down at her feet so her mother missed the anger in her eyes.

Mei used her palm to smack the top of Ava's head, hard.

"Pay attention. Answer the questions! Where you be without me?"

Ava didn't know. Probably much happier. "Nowhere," she whispered dutifully.

"Louder. Again; *look at me*!"

"Nowhere." Ava fiercely bit her cheek to check her temper. If she bowed and did as her mother dictated, she increased chances of escaping sooner.

"Glad you realize that. Now give me all your passwords for school," Mei ordered.

"*What*?"

"Are you death and dumb?" She knocked on her daughter's head.

"No, I am not *deaf* and dumb," Ava replied coolly.

"Then do what I say!" Mei pointed at her computer screen.

"Why?" she asked, barely masking the anger that clawed up her throat.

"Because I say so; I'm in control. To humiliate you! I always must teach you lessons, even at this age. Pathetic."

"That's student privacy. I-I can't share my passwords; I'm not supposed to!"

What would she do with the passwords? Mei could ruin her academic career; she didn't know how to use Davison's online systems.

"I don't give fucks about your precious privacy. You think Mao cared about privacy? I never had privacy. You don't deserve it."

"But you don't even know what to do with them!"

Mei abruptly left and went into the master bedroom. Ava heard a drawer jerked open and the shuffling of materials. Her heart rate escalated. Powering back down the hall, making too much noise for a diminutive woman, Mei returned with the object that haunted many of Ava's nightmares. Her mother must have recently brought it up from the basement; Ava wished it'd been forgotten.

"Remember? *Shé*. Happy Year of the Snake."

Her mother fondly held the withered snake belt by its intricately detailed metal head, the circularly carved patterns giving the metal a bumpy feel.

Did she remember? Its marks were written on her body with invisible ink; the ink had seeped into her bloodstream. Parts of her body tingled, remembering their connection with the belt.

The first one she could recall: six years old, running around at an after-school picnic, back when Mei at least had fake friends. Ava tripped and tore her white stockings. Not paying attention to her scraped knee, she ran to her mother and unwittingly asked—in front of said friends—"I tore my stockings by accident; are you going to hit me later?" Mei had used the snake to strike Ava down when they got home, bruising her other knee.

Seven, when she lied about taking the Chinese medicine chewable, covering it up with a tissue in the trash. When her mother found it she snapped the braided part of the belt over Ava's behind seven times, one for each year of her life. Then she'd dragged her over to the long bathroom mirror, where Mei pulled down her pants, forcing Ava to look at the marks.

Eight, a "B" on a Spanish quiz.

Nine, for not moving her fingers fast enough in a piano piece. It became even harder to move hurting, swollen fingers after.

Ten, for threatening to tell the school counselor that she thought Mei a monster.

The violence continued. The years flickered by. Eleven, twelve, thirteen, fourteen, fifteen. She no longer remembered what had provoked the punishments. The events that led up to the violence were never important. Only Mei's black sinkhole eyes as she taught Ava "right" and the nights she spent silently crying into her pillow, dousing it in salty misery. And then the nights she learned how to prevent herself from crying.

Three years since the last beating. Ava supposed Mei found other methods easier. The wax and the bag. The feeding. The pool. All the Chinese medicine. Then the cursing, the ridiculous tasks. After all, physical punishment required exertion on the part of the punisher. Or maybe because Mei had discovered nail tips and didn't want to break them. Whatever the reason, Ava had been glad of it. The pain hurt the least. Humiliation and fear did her in.

"Okay. I'll write the passwords down on a sticky pad and show you the websites."

"Always the threats." Mei laid the snake belt on the carpet. "If you just listen," she said, pulling her daughter's ear, "there be no need for them. But you don't learn. You never learn. Spoiled ghost girl."

What Mei intended to do with the passwords, she still couldn't imagine. Her mother only knew how to blog and use email.

"You must wash all laundry next. I got three weeks in the laundry basket."

She stood up, knowing Mei expected immediate action, but her mother stopped her.

"Don't think this over. I'm just starting."

Mei backhanded her daughter so hard she needed to shake out her hand.

"That only part of what you deserve for lying. What this about studying English?"

Ignoring her burning cheek, Ava looked up and defiantly met her mother's bottomless eyes.

"I don't want to be a lawyer, doctor, engineer, scientist, or a money-making machine. I'm just a freshman, but I know that I'll value my work with an English degree. It's my degree. My life, *my* choice!"

Mei slapped her again, the same cheek. She felt one of her mother's false nails scrape against her jawline.

"*Zhao da*. You deserve beating! You think this your life? You think ownership? Half-breed bitch. Dare you, you want to shame me and your ancestors? *Wen ming gui fan*! Where your respect? You never make something of yourself that way."

She returned her gaze to her feet again.

"Change your major back."

Jerking her head up, Ava gasped, "What?"

"Do it now. I know you can online."

Slowly, she shook her head. "I can't. I . . . I won't."

Mei glowered at her daughter. "You right. It's your choice."

She picked the snake belt from the ground and carefully placed it on Ava's lap. A quiet promise.

With quivering hands, she typed in the Davison website for declaring majors. Dropping the English major meant dropping everything it stood for. Ava's self-determination, her newly acquired self-knowledge, her friendship and research with Li zhi. Her mother wanted to take the "Wh" out of Whasian.

After logging in, the website stated, "You have declared as an English major." She hesitated over the "Change Major" button, but the subtle weight of the snake forced her to click.

"What you are waiting for? *Sanba*. Pick cell bio!"

You will not cry. You will not cry. You will not let one tear drop. Ava selected cell biology neuroscience and hit "OK." She'd find a way to fix this. Just a momentary capitulation. This caused no permanent damage.

"Good." Leaning down, Mei snatched the belt off Ava's lap. "Disobey me again, dare lie, and I make you wish you never born. I'm your mother. Your father's too busy to give a shits about you. *I* own you. You do what I say. Never forget that!" She finished by spitting in her daughter's face.

Ava sat still and quietly took it. Took the insults. The rage. The spit. Only react if you're able to handle the counter-reaction. She couldn't yet. Her voice felt half formed. But I'm getting there. You can't stamp me out. You can't tame me. I'm not an object. *I have feelings*. Yours may be deficient, but you have some of them. I see the desperation in your eyes, Mother. You should be afraid.

Mei's cell phone rang. Ava saw the name "Li Wu" pop up on the screen. Her mother lunged to the computer desk for her phone, picked it up, and said "hold on" into it. Covering the microphone with a manicured finger, Mei barked "laundry now" at her, shoving her out of the computer room and closing the door.

Weird. "Li Wu"? And since when did Mother have anyone to talk to? No, who cared? She dismissed her curiosity. Purposefully ignoring the eyelid-gluing picture on her mother's vanity, she went to the master bedroom's bathroom to wash off the spit. Looking in the mirror, Ava inspected the laceration from her mother's nail. She touched a finger to the skinny, inch-long cut, drawing a light smearing of blood. Funny how you could be humiliated in front of a party of one.

Lugging the heavy laundry basket up the stairs to the laundry room on the third floor, she tried to think of something to suppress her anger. She had just shared a nice dinner with a seemingly interesting guy. Ava could talk to Li zhi about what to do about her mother and the change of majors. She could change her major back to English, but the Davison passwords presented a problem. If she changed her passwords, she'd have to face her mother's wrath.

She thought she heard Mei laugh over the phone. Ava leaned over the stairway's oak bannister to make sure she hadn't hallucinated. Yes, that'd been laughter. How strange; her mother continued talking to this Li Wu person. A fairly late call, too. Who—

"You not starting the laundry yet!" Mei shouted up the stairs, jarring her back to attention.

"Working on it!"

She frantically threw tailored pants, shirts, skirts, and a couple of male dress shirts into the washer. Her father must've stopped by and forgotten to take his laundry back to his apartment in the city. She threw the rest in, adjusted the appropriate knobs, and poured in detergent before letting the machine do its work. There, now it rumbled her productivity. Did Paul also know Li Wu? Maybe she'd ask him when they met at the house to go over the diary. *If* they met at the house. Ava found it difficult to imagine a time when Mei would be out again.

Moments later, her mother bounded up the stairs. She braced herself for a continuation of the violence, but Mei said, "That enough. Go back to your dorms now."

"What?" That sounded too good . . . and her mother seemed almost . . . mellow.

"Enough! Get out of my way. I had enough of you; don't make me tell you twice," she said, waving her hands in front of Ava's face.

Ava almost wanted to thank her mother and smile gleefully. She maintained her composure, dipping her head in thanks. It took a fair amount of self-control not to sprint away. Instead, she calmly went downstairs, collected her things, and left. Strange; her mother never acted impulsively. As she approached the sanctuary of Davison, she decided that she didn't care.

Chapter Twenty-four

Paul clicked on his daughter's Google+ profile. For once, the video icon appeared green. Online. Sunday night seemed an innocuous time to call.

He sent her two video-chat invitations before she answered.

She'd twisted her hair into a high bun. The way Mei used to wear hers, back when she kept her hair long.

"Dad?"

"Hi Ava."

"I didn't . . . since when do you know how to use Hangout?"

"Looked it up online."

She moved her laptop screen and became a floating head. Her attention appeared to be directed elsewhere. She must have another window up.

"I wanted to talk to you. And see your face."

He heard typing.

"Oh."

She looked off to the side. Then down. Everywhere but at him. He noticed the bags under her eyes. Their shadows gave her a haunted look.

"Something the matter? You seem . . . "

"Tired. Stressed." Ava shrugged. "Nothing new."

"No, it's different. Do you want . . . why don't we talk about it?"

She appeared to be reading something onscreen. Her voice flattened. "Talk about what?"

"What. Uh, what you're feeling."

"Talk about my feelings?" The ghost of a smile flitted across her face. She meant to mock him.

"I know. I know how hard it is. You feel pressure. You feel a need to live up to expectations. But that doesn't mean . . . "

"How does your job relate to my stress with—with school?"

"It . . . I'm not talking about the firm. I'm talking about family pressure. About struggling to make parents proud."

He heard clicking. More typing.

"What do you mean? Family pressure? *Your* parents?"

"Well, not Mom—not Grandma. Ryan. I mean, Grandpa."

The typing stopped. "Grandpa? Grandpa, who loves Jelly Belly?"

"Yes. He used to be . . . unapproachable."

She glanced up. Almost met his eyes. "Because of West Point?"

"Not really."

"The war, then? I thought he never talked about it."

Shut your fucking mouth, boy. You don't know what I've seen.

"Not directly. I—we stayed out of his way. He became either numb or irritable."

"Did he have PTSD, then?"

Paul shrugged. "During the Second World War . . . I don't think they had a name for it."

"But I haven't . . . he's always been quiet. But not unkind."

"He never sought a diagnosis. Never sought help. Things were different then. And he'd been a Depression kid. He grew up expecting hard times. The point is, Ava, that seeking help carries no stigma."

She raised her eyebrows. "You mean there's less stigma now than there used to be."

"What? Oh. Yes, but stigma must never prevent us from doing what's right. Mental health is just as important as physical. You shouldn't use your mother as a model. She's also been through too much."

She went back to her other window. "What are you saying?"

"Don't shut your loved ones out. I just want . . . I don't want piano to happen again. You can't ignore your mental health."

The typing, the clicking, the scrolling stopped. Ava's jaw clenched.

"My mental health."

He tried to sound soothing. "You need to remember—remember the alternative coping mechanisms?"

"Those sessions didn't do anything. *Nothing* applied to me."

"Maybe . . . maybe you weren't open to them. Maybe they weren't right for you then. You don't have to talk to me. What about Charlotte? Or someone from school?"

She shook her head. "Listen, I get that you don't know how to be a dad. So why don't you stick to doing what you do best?"

"You're out of line, Ava. I try my damnedest. *You* always cut me—"

"Stop pretending you care. Why don't you be real, for once? Say what you really mean. These halfhearted attempts . . . they're worse than not being in my life at all."

"Is this late teen angst? You're saying ridic—"

"Am I, though? You know, Charlotte's jealous when I get texts and emails from you. Cards with money. Like any of it means anything, takes any effort. 'Just checking in. I'm always concerned.' You do it when it's convenient. You're full of it. I wish you didn't try anymore!"

Ava hung up before he thought of anything to say. Paul waited for his heart rate to level before calling back. Three tries before he conceded to the notification "AvaLMagee@gmail.com is unavailable."

"Goddammit!" He snapped down the lid to his laptop.

Mei's voice reverberated in his head. *What you know about parenting? She hates you. Ni, you ming wu shi – xu kong de baba!* No, he felt too much to be hollow. But he apparently shared Ryan's capacity for delivering pain. He felt bloated with self-loathing.

Pacing in front of his world clocks, Paul began ruminating. Over and over, like a hateful song on loop, he replayed the video-chat conversation. In each new rendition, he recognized more and more of his failings. Hurting his daughter seemed to be his specialty. His only child. She interpreted his distance, his lack of transparency in the worst way. She believed he thought of her on an occasional basis, that he never considered her a priority. That every move he made, every plan he composed revolved around everything and anyone else. So much dirty laundry lay between them. He and Mei continued the pile. Their fault, but mainly his.

He stopped in front of the LA clock. Seattle shared time with LA. He'd be interrupting dinner, but he decided it necessary.

"Ryan, turn it down! Someone's called. Hello?"

"Mom. It's Paul."

"What a pleasant sur—"

"Could you talk away from hi—the living room?"

"Of course. Ryan, I'll be in the sitting room. You know, actually wearing your hearing aids helps with that."

The sounds of *Hogan's Heroes* died down as his mother moved to the front of the house.

"Should I steel myself for something? Is everyone okay?"

Paul sank onto the corner of his bed. "Everyone's fine. I just, I wondered . . . knowing what you know now, would you have married him? If you could make the decision again?"

"Yes."

"That's it? No doubt?"

His mother exhaled. "Paul, you're not asking the right question. I'm the mother of four successful men. Without your father I wouldn't have my sons. Without you I wouldn't have grandchildren."

"But you could've married someone else, someone without . . . "

"Baggage? We've all got baggage, son. It just weighs on us differently. Besides, if I'd married someone else, I wouldn't have you. I'd have different children. But we can play the 'what if' game forever. What's this about, Paul? Has she done it again?"

"No. I don't know. Does it matter?"

"You're still young. There'll come a time when you only see what matters. When you'll think—really reflect—on what you've done. Who you've been. And what you've left behind."

"Legacy, you mean?"

"I say this with love. Don't be like your father. There's more to life than law and order."

"JAG isn't even close to what I do."

"I know; I always listen to my sons."

"Sorry, Mom."

"We can't change what's happened. Wishing we could, imagining alternatives gets us nowhere. If you're forever looking back, you'll never see what's right in front of you."

"Do you . . . do you remember that banner that used to hang in the room I shared with Mickey?"

She laughed. "I'm seventy-nine; do you expect me to remember that? Describe it to me."

"It had black calligraphy. 'Children learn what they live.'"

"Oh, yes."

"Do you believe that?"

"You're far from childhood, hun."

"Do you think it's true?"

"To an extent. But I believe more in the power of change. In learning to expand the base you've been given." She paused. "Your father's come a long way. Give him a little credit."

"Why? He never gave me any."

"So you'd like to repeat his missteps?"

An ambulance wailed by his apartment.

"I thought so."

"I . . . I don't know where to go from here. How to find recourse."

"That's the trouble with habits, isn't it? Start by being honest. Talk to Mei again. Pull up divorce papers. Talk to Ava. Be clear about your intentions."

"Even if it's not reciprocated?"

"Especially if it's not."

"But what about—"

"Letting you watch *Father Knows Best* was the worst thing I ever did to you. Let go of the perfect family. It never existed."

"Mom, you don't understand. If everything I've done achieved no good, then—"

"I never meant that. You haven't failed. You're not a failure. You've simply been running a marathon with no finish line."

"I . . . I guess this is where you say I should've listened to you."

"Listen to me now. Make this last effort. But whatever happens, you owe Mei nothing else. If you're going to worry, think about your daughter. Ava's an adult now. She doesn't need you. Either of you."

"I'm beginning to see that."

His father's voice warbled through the background. "Clara? Clara, *The Producers* is about to come on!"

"Sorry, Mom. I've kept you too long."

"No apology necessary. It's been too long since our last chat."

"My fault. Thanks . . . I'll call you when I've got more of a handle on things."

"You're welcome. And Paul?"

"Yes?"

"Don't be so worried about breaking the cycle that you create a new one."

Chapter Twenty-five

Charlotte unlocked and opened their door.

"Came back early to talk . . . ," she trailed off, taking in the state of her roommate.

Ava lay stomach down on her bed, staring out at nothing with red and puffy eyes. She had moved the garbage bin just beneath her bed, and it overflowed with crumpled tissues. A number of tissues littered the floor surrounding the garbage; Ava hadn't made much effort to aim.

Charlotte let the door click shut, abandoning her luggage by it. She climbed onto Ava's bed, silently pulling her best friend into a hug. A wilted Ava made no move to push her away, just closed her eyes. Charlotte rocked Ava slightly. For a while her uneven breathing remained the only sound in the room.

"You know, opening up hurts less than keeping it all in. Trust me, I know. Want to tell me what's wrong?"

Ava opened her eyes and stared across the room, not attempting to respond. She wanted to let everything out in a deluge of words, but she felt tears coming on instead.

"What's really been going on? I know I've been missing something, but I can't help if you don't tell me anything. Let me help, please?"

To Charlotte's surprise, Ava started sobbing. She froze, never having seen her cry.

"That's it, let it out, let it all out," Charlotte said soothingly, continuing to hug her.

After Ava had finished and cleaned up, Charlotte attempted to talk again, but Ava unexpectedly beat her to it. The passwords and the stripping of her English major had been the teetering point. The video chat and its aftermath sent her over. And then the shame, the self-loathing.

A dreadful vision had come to her. If she continued to acquiesce, continued to let others and her parents define her, she'd be stifled into a ghost. She hated her abstract existence. She wanted to be tangible. To carry a felt presence like the women she admired, Li zhi, Professor Meier. Ava wanted to be recognized, seen, and heard. She *needed* to create an alternate ending for herself, one in which her mother no longer held control. One in which the Wall no longer relegated her to interminable seclusion.

"If I tell you everything that's bothering me, old and new secrets, will you a) promise never to tell anyone—I mean *anyone*—and b) believe me?"

"This sounds like the lead-in to an unpleasant story. But yes, I promise."

"Well, for starters, my mother . . . is . . . a crazy bitch, at least to me." Ava watched confusion take over Charlotte's face. "I-I can't . . . I don't know how to begin. It's . . . unsettling."

"What do you mean?"

Ava fell silent for a few beats, collecting the wind-blown pages of her thoughts.

"I've always defined myself against my mother. Sometimes against my Chinese half—through English. Words as weapons. Language as a wall. And here I am . . . struggling. Struggling to even form words!"

"Relax, then. You're forever putting pressure on yourself. I always freeze up when I do that. Just let the words come when they're ready."

She drew in a ragged breath. "But what if they don't come? Compared to force, words *do* nothing."

"Um. Elaborate a bit more?"

"My mother . . . she hurts me. She uses me. Doesn't love me. Resents but needs me . . . you don't believe me. Remember how I asked you to believe me? Now's the time." Ava retreated from Charlotte's reach.

"No, no, it's not that I don't believe you . . . if you could explain . . . I don't know, with examples, that'll help me out."

Where to even begin? Too many instances to remember, let alone detail. She didn't want to overwhelm Charlotte.

"She used to hit me . . . and stuff. Now she mainly belittles me and curses at me. When she wanted to punish me . . . she'd use a braided snake belt. The head of the belt looks like a metal head of a snake. Trust me, the metal leaves bruises. Being whipped with the braided part isn't fun either. Following so far?"

"Wait, wait. We're talking about Mei here. Mrs. Magee, right? The same Mei who cooked Ema enough meals to last two weeks when Dad died? The one who always jumps at a chance to brag about you?"

"See, I knew you wouldn't believe me. You see her as Mrs. Magee, the living China doll. That's not who she really is." How come people needed to "see" to believe? Someone's word, written or spoken, never meant enough. Never stood alone. You couldn't just say you were bleeding, you needed to turn to the side: look, I'm oozing red.

"No . . . I'm just having a hard time imagining this. H-how? Why?"

"I have no conclusive answers. She doesn't abuse substances, if that's what you're thinking."

"So she's a closet tiger mom?" Charlotte asked.

"Sort of? She's not entirely a dragon lady either. She's more of a . . . serpent. Manipulative. Silently striking, that kind of thing."

"Not that I'm complaining . . . but what brought this on? Why tell me now? I've been asking you what's wrong since last semester."

Ava hugged her sides, staring at her marked ivory comforter. At the black smears that remained even after she'd repeatedly scrubbed it.

"Because . . . over the years I built this Wall. I mean, I picture it that way in my head. It keeps other people away, at a safe distance. The Wall's impermeable, made of complex things, negative feelings, I guess. Most times it's all I see, but lately I keep thinking about what's beyond it. You're confused. I'm making no sense."

Charlotte shook her head. "I get the analogy. What makes no sense is its existence. You realize that it works both ways, right? Sure, you never let anyone in. But at the same time you never get out. Think of the Berlin Wall. The Mexico–U.S. barrier. You're cutting yourself off, preventing yourself from receiving other opportunities."

"I know that now. It's distorted my thinking. I started—what I need . . . I need a better way of finding release. I can't slip out of this cycle, and I realize that she won't ever change. If I let her, she'll never leave me alone. Thursday night she made me go home. I let it slip that I declared as an English major."

"Less than thrilled, huh?"

Despite her sorry situation, Ava looked up, letting out a small laugh.

"No, she didn't applaud my bravery and tell me to follow my dreams like your mom. Instead, she slapped me—the cut by my chin is from one of her nails—and threatened me with the belt." She tilted her chin up for Charlotte. "So I had to give up my Davison passwords. Then she made me go online and change my major to cell bio neuroscience."

"God. I . . . I don't know what to say. How does she hide this from everyone? She's the spokesperson for our animal shelter! No one would believe it."

Ava smiled grimly. "That's the point. She knows that. And I've always been too ashamed to say a thing. Only during last semester, I spoke to Professor Chen about it. We kind of mutually shared secrets. Other than that, my mother's even alienated me from my dad."

Charlotte frowned. "That's why, when we fought . . ."

"I lashed out at you without meaning to. My parents have a secret between themselves. They act like they're a couple in public and in front of me, but they haven't been for years. It probably relates to my dad's apartment and the new house. Things got weird after his firm promoted him. He worked all the time. Until the estate agent got him the apartment, he came back really late. I'm nearly positive he slept in the guestroom. I found his pajamas there. Then he got the apartment, and came back on most weekends. But he'd only sleep over on Saturday nights."

"Didn't you visit him? I thought you stayed over every weekend for a while. I joined you once . . . we stayed up all night, listening to ambulances and cars."

Ava nodded. "But then my mother ruined it. I-if I say this . . . this *never* leaves this room, okay? I couldn't even tell Professor Chen. I've never . . . never said this aloud."

The weight of this responsibility seemed to worry Charlotte, but she nonetheless replied, "I won't ever tell anyone unless you ask me to."

Clearing her throat, Ava began, "After I came back one weekend, Dad helped me bring my bags to the door. As usual, he gave me a hug and kissed the top of my head. He got in the car. I waved, he waved, he drove off. Then I lugged my things inside. She waited. She'd been watching from a window."

Mei had crossed her arms in front of her chest. She stared at her thirteen-year-old daughter as if seeing her with new eyes. "How you find it?"

Taking "it" to mean the visit, Ava replied, "Fine. A bit windy in the city." She dropped her bags on the floor. "Um. I'm going to go unpack now."

Her mother stepped to the side, blocking Ava's path down the hallway.

"You know what *xiao qing ren* means?"

Wrinkling her brow in confusion, Ava said, "Of course not."

"Little lover. Tell me, how long you been fucking your father, *xiao qing ren*?"

She felt herself turn white. "*What*?"

"Why else he want to see you every weekend?"

"Because I'm his daughter!"

Ignoring Ava's outburst, Mei had icily continued, "That's why he choosing you over me, isn't it? Because you're half ghost. It's like fucking himself. Well go ahead. *Cao ni ba*! Fuck your father."

The telling had been too disturbing; Ava returned her gaze to the stained comforter, mortified.

"Holy *shit*." Dumbfounded, she repeated the curse. "Your mother's fucking *psycho*!"

Ava nodded.

"I felt so sick, I didn't even bother arguing anymore. I just ran up the stairs to my room. Since that day, I haven't stayed over at his apartment." She looked up, eyes glistening with unshed tears. "Th-the worst part is, I became afraid it'll come t-true!"

"Oh, Ava . . . " She grabbed one of Ava's hands and gave a reassuring squeeze. "She planted it in your head. I've seen your dad with you. He loves you like . . . like mine loved me. Normally. You're his daughter; of course he wants to see you. No threat of incest involved."

"I-I know." Ava roughly swept away the tears she'd let escape. "I couldn't help it. I still avoid . . . being touched by him. No hugs especially."

"Listen to me. It's all in your head. *She's* in your head. You've got to rely on your reason. You're letting her poison your relationship with your dad!"

Holding her forehead in her hands, Ava whispered, "It's so hard. She makes me think that *I'm* the one in the wrong. That I'm the problem."

Charlotte slowly pulled her into a hug. "Ava, this is all your dad wants to do. He just wants to comfort you."

When Ava had calmed down, Charlotte gradually sought more information.

"Um. So I guess your dad has no idea that Mei accused you?"

She shook her head. "No way. That's why I couldn't tell anyone; no one knows her the way I do. She's an expert manipulator; she knows whom to tell what and when."

"Good Lord. I'm afraid to ask, but . . . what else has she done to you? Whatever you feel comfortable telling me, of course."

"Um. Well, remember when I suddenly got choppy layers?" Ava held up her shortest locks for emphasis.

"Yeah, a couple of years ago. Before school pictures, right? You said you were tired of your hair being the same length. Why, that a cover-up of some kind?" Charlotte reached out and gently reexamined Ava's hair like it would tell the truth.

"She held me down and cut off a chunk of my hair. Then I had to pay to get it done in choppy layers, telling the stylist that 'my hand slipped while holding scissors.' She's made me keep it this way ever since. To remind me."

"What the hell? So basically, your mother sadistically abuses you."

"I think that 'abuse' is harsh. I mean, when I think of child abuse, I think of parents starving their kids or throwing them down the stairs," Ava said, shrugging. "She doesn't do anything illegal. Hitting your child in the name of discipline may be wrong, but it's not illegal. Plus, that's an American view of childrearing. In China, hitting is a common method of parental discipline."

"Don't make excuses for her! Ava, she's been living in America, not China. There's a sliding scale of abuse, but your mom treats you like shit and that's what counts. That's not how you raise a child. I don't care what your cultural background is."

Ava grimaced, clutching her sides. "I have nightmares sometimes, or what I guess I'd call flashbacks. Something in the day will trigger an unpleasant memory."

"Oh, like when you woke up screaming but denied the gravity of the nightmare?" Charlotte shot her a look of disapproval.

Ava nodded. "I didn't—couldn't—tell you. I've been so used to carrying it around solo, you know? Dealing with it . . . telling you this is new and . . . scary."

"And so you let it eat you up inside instead? That why you started drinking and partying?"

"I guess. I mean, I knew that she'd never approve of it, so I sort of did it to spite her. Thing is, I also spited myself in the process."

"So you used alcohol to escape. But after the hangover your past still exists. Drinking will never change that. You've been self-sabotaging." Charlotte swung her legs over the bed. "Hold that thought. I need to pee."

Ava watched her step into the bathroom.

"What the . . ." Charlotte swung open the door and peeked her head out. "Why are there bloody tissues in the toilet?"

Oh, no. Ava swallowed. "What?"

Charlotte repeated the question.

"Oh, that! It's only . . . I just." Ava coughed. "Gah, words! It's nothing. I got a bloody nose. Didn't want to throw them out in the bin. Appropriate disposal methods and all. Sorry, I must've forgotten to flush. I expected you to return tomorrow, remember?"

Charlotte wrinkled her nose. "I thought you'd gotten your period. You know how blood makes me feel."

"I'll get rid of it now. Relax. Just pretend you didn't see."

"Nah, I need to get over it anyway. Blood is blood."

Ava grabbed a tissue and blew her nose.

"Yes. To paraphrase Monty Python: it's just a surface wound."

Chapter Twenty-six

"*Nepantla.*"

Professor Meier paused for further emphasis, looking dramatic in her red lipstick and red-and-white-patterned poncho. After erasing "2/27" from the chalkboard, she wrote the word in loopy cursive. "The space in-between. Where every immigrant is, and where every diplomat claims to be."

Ava mechanically copied the term into her notebook.

"That's so us," Jason whispered to her.

She forced a smile. It felt like squeezing juice from a prune.

"Keep this idea in mind for the rest of the semester. Now, the majority of you will work in groups to analyze part two of *The Brief Wondrous Life of Oscar Wao*. I'll call up one lucky student at a time to discuss final paper topics."

Breathe. How many more minutes until the end?

Professor Meier raised her eyebrows at her quiet, still students.

"Please, don't bowl me over with your enthusiasm. What must I do to seize your attention? Come in wearing a flamenco costume?"

The sooner you cooperate, the sooner you get to leave, thought Ava.

A few girls sat up, interested. One asked, "Did you ever do flamenco?"

"Did I ever. When I lived in Spain I performed with a flamenco dance company. My dresses still fit me." Professor Meier smiled nostalgically.

"Will you dance again?" another student asked.

"Perhaps *un día de estos*."

Twenty minutes left. Cut that in half. Ten and ten.

"Everyone, order yourselves into groups of two or three people. Ava, since you signed the attendance sheet first today, how about you be the first to consult with me?"

She eased out of her seat and perched on the chair across from her professor's desk.

"So, I know it's early yet, but in my experience it's best to think about final papers well in advance. I dislike reading last-minute papers written by sleep-deprived, coffee-charged students, and I don't think students should do that to themselves anyway."

Trying to evade Professor Meier's amber eyes, Ava said, "I think I know what I want to do."

Professor Meier smiled. "I'm not surprised. You always come to class prepared."

Not always. But this time she knew what to say.

"I want to write about Latin American female identity. A little while ago I came across this novel called *Cantora*. It's about a Mexican-American woman's quest for self-discovery and the familial secrets she uncovers during the process."

"Sounds interesting! I look forward to seeing what you come up with."

When class ended Jason and Ava rode the bus back to University Way. For once, they managed to snag themselves seats.

"Hey. What's eating you? You've been really . . . subdued."

"Nothing. Just tired. And sore. Slept on the wrong side. What do you think you'll write about?"

Jason appeared unconvinced, but he let it slide. "I'm going to compare *mulatto* and *mestizo* passing as white, you know, to gay men passing as straight."

"That sounds like it'll be an intense paper."

"*Sí, muchacha*. It's going to take some research. But it means a lot to me, so I'll love every minute of it. Speaking of research, how's it going with Li zhi?"

Ava tried to smile. "It's over."

"You don't want it to be."

"No. But there's nothing else for me to do. I've contacted everyone and photocopied everything. She's asked me to read over the manuscript when it's complete, but that won't be until the end of the semester."

The bus lurched to a stop as a daring pedestrian ran across the street. They held onto their seats.

"So you don't see her anymore?"

"No, I still do. Just not as often. And outside of the office. We meet up for coffee or food and catch up. Lately she's been teaching me some Mandarin. In fact, I need to stay on till the student center; I'm meeting her there." Her phone vibrated. Two texts: one from her father and the other from Flynn. She tapped on Flynn's name. A picture text popped up.

"A smile!" Jason said, giving her a nudge.

"Ahh," she groaned, bending over. "Sore side!"

"Crap, I'm sorry. You okay?"

Ava straightened up. "Yes, fine." She held out her phone. "Look at this picture."

Confused, Jason asked, "What's funny about an aerodynamics worksheet?"

"Look again. Hint: there's a typo."

"Oh. 'Airodynamics.' Ha ha?"

Ava texted Flynn back. "You can't appreciate it like I can. He's been sending me picture texts of typos since we started texting."

"What's this boy's name? Where did you meet him again?" Jason's eyes narrowed.

"Flynn. He's from my Medieval Poetry class. Don't get your boxers in a twist; he's just an acquaintance."

"That's how they all start off," he began, but a new text message spared Ava a lecture. "Kevin and the swans want to grab late lunch." The bus stopped by Lockhart. "We'll see you later, then?"

"The swans?"

As he got up to join the crowd heading off the bus, Jason said, "Charlotte and Derek. Kevin's idea. Swans mate for life, and he thinks they will too. Besides, they look really good together."

The bus pulled in front of the student center. Five minutes early, Ava waited for Li zhi in the lobby.

Her phone reminded her of the unread text message from her father. Like a bee unsure of whether or not it could carry more pollen, her forefinger hovered over it.

"I'm sorry about the way our last conversation ended. I want us to work things out. I've been looking into divorce procedures. My colleague got sick, so I've taken his place at the SU law conference. I'll fly out of Seattle on Sunday morning. We need to talk, but we better do so in person. Let me know next time you're home and Mom's out. Love you."

Divorce. Divorce would change everything. Right? She saw Li zhi approaching the automatic doors, so she settled for a basic reply: "Thanks for letting me know. Will do."

"So, from your succinct texts, it seems we've got a lot to catch up on," Li zhi said after Ava greeted her. They went upstairs to a student-run café.

They bought coffees and secured a small table some distance away from the noisy students.

"I finally told Charlotte."

"I'm glad. Don't you feel better?" Li zhi tucked a blonde lock behind an ear.

"Yes and no. Complaining only helps so much." Ava opened the lid to her coffee, letting some of the heat escape.

"It's not complaining. What your mom subjects you to isn't like getting served a cup of cold coffee. You've been suffering. And it's about time that you shared that. Trust me, that's how I got to be level-headed. I talked through the silence with friends. Don't underestimate the power of friendship."

"Do you really think it's that simple?"

Li zhi stirred a packet of sugar into her coffee. "It can be."

"You always seem to have the answers."

Laughing, Li zhi shook her head. "Hardly. I've just been around for a dozen years longer."

They were quiet for a moment, enjoying their coffees.

Looking at Li zhi intently, Ava said, "Yesterday one of my professors cancelled class. I spent the time watching *Never Perfect*."

"Oh? And what did you think?"

"It's the best documentary I've ever seen. The segments on Whasians really resonated."

"Whasians?"

Ava let out an embarrassed laugh. "Slang for Amerasian. Charlotte introduced me to it. I used to hate it . . . but it's grown on me."

"If it feels right, don't be ashamed of it." Li zhi smiled. "Did the film give you a new perspective on your mother's blog?"

"Well, I still think what she did is disturbing . . . "

"And you have every right to."

"But now I think I can guess her thought process. She has double eyelids, so that's not her problem. But she'll always be seen as Asian." Ava sipped her coffee. "Maybe she doesn't like that because of the Revolution. Or maybe she subconsciously bought into the new ideal."

Li zhi raised an eyebrow. "You mean moving toward racial uniformity, the fetishization of multiracial women?"

"Yes, being 'cosmopolitan.'" Ava recapped her coffee. "Actually, I need your advice on something else."

She inclined her head. "Tell me, and I'll do my best."

When Ava finished summing up her problem with the involuntary change of majors and the update from Paul, Li zhi looked at her thoughtfully.

"You don't have to worry about your major yet; we can easily change it through the online system. And you're a freshman, so it's expected that you'll switch your major once, even a few times. What you need to worry about is your mother. It seems to me that she's a really destructive force in your life. I'm glad your father realizes he should prioritize you, but you can't depend on a divorce. That'll probably make her more desperate. And I know you plan to move to Seattle after graduation. But if you don't face her beforehand, nothing's going to change. She could also move there, who knows?"

Ava's eyes widened. She hadn't thought of that possibility.

"The point is, Ava, that running away won't solve anything." Li zhi softened her voice. "If you want to become your own person, *you* need to diminish her influence. Yes, I think you should tell your father everything, and when you do that is for you to decide. But first you need to talk to her. About *your* childhood and the hurt she's caused you." She paused to drink her coffee.

"I need to be agentive. Own my problems. Avoid creating more."

Li zhi nodded. "You need a lot of change. Too much change can be overpowering, though, so deal with one problem at a time."

"You're reminding me of this novel I read for Latino/a Literature. It's called *Cantora*. The protagonist is mixed like me, except *mestiza*. She's curious about her origins, so she learns about the lives of the female relatives she's close to. A lot of the novel is about the past and familial, long-kept secrets."

"Sounds pertinent to you. What happens to her in the end?"

"She becomes one with her past and thinks she knows herself. She's so . . . sure. It's like all her identity confusion disappears." Ava drank more coffee. "I enjoyed the novel, but the ending felt . . . easy."

Stirring her coffee with a straw, Li zhi said, "See, in novels, as in movies and all other art forms, there has to be an end. It's expected, and we usually find it comforting. We don't need to see what happens after the finish. In life—sorry if this is macabre—the ending is death. What leads up to it are varying degrees of struggle."

Ava stared at her sanguine expression. "That'd be more effective if you'd lowered your voice, frowned, and wore a black robe."

Li zhi grinned. "When possible, I like to be cheerfully pessimistic." Her iPhone buzzed. Dipping into her jean pocket, she turned off the reminder. "Unfortunately, I've got to go. I have to teach my night class."

They got up and discarded their trash. When they'd reached the bottom of the stairs, Li zhi leaned forward to give Ava a hug.

She backed away, apologetic. "I don't—I've got a cold. Want to avoid passing it on to you."

"No worries." Li zhi dropped her arms. "Stay strong, *mei mei*. Don't be afraid to pursue change. And never be afraid to bother me. Oh! I almost forgot to give you something." She shuffled through her tote bag. "Ah, here it is." Li zhi handed her a hardcover book.

Ava ran her hand over the white jacket cover. A red square framed the white-lettered title, giving the square an East Asian, seal-like effect.

"*Battle Hymn of the Tiger Mother*," she read. "I completely forgot about it."

"I almost did too. If nothing else, I'm sure you'll find it entertaining. When it came out she received a fair amount of backlash for 'vicious parenting,' but Chua seems to be critical of herself. If nothing else, she does a great job of revealing Chinese foibles. Read it while you figure things out."

Ava slipped the book into her backpack. "*Xiexie*. For everything."

Li zhi smiled. "No need to thank me. Your accent is improving, by the way. We'll have you speaking like a Mainlander yet!"

Chapter Twenty-seven

His mother must be out. A gaping vacancy hovered in place of the Oldsmobile Cutlass Ciera. Paul continued through the garage and found a note posted to the inner door. In her distinctive curvy script, she'd written on paisley-bordered paper. "I'm at Marge's for the book club. Dad might be working on that Seahawks puzzle Joanne gave him for Christmas. Be a dear and try to avoid picking a fight while I'm gone. I'd like to see your father make it to 92."

He took off his shoes and crept into the living room.

Ryan had fallen asleep in his La-Z-Boy recliner. He snored, his mouth an open bucket. Paul could almost hear his mother's reaction: "What's he trying to do, collect raindrops from a leaky ceiling?"

The History Channel featured a special about the Great Depression. Paul shut the television off. Ryan didn't need to learn about it. It defined his childhood.

Ryan appeared to have completed fifteen percent of the puzzle on the side table. Paul made out part of the crowd and the beginnings of the Seahawks end zone. He shifted the puzzle aside. Placing his briefcase on the couch, he took out his laptop, careful to avoid disturbing the divorce pamphlets. Paul turned it on, forgetting that he'd left the volume on high. It announced its awakening with the delicacy of a trumpet.

"I'm up, I'm up!" Ryan sprang forward with the vigor of youth.

Paul caught him before his ninety-one-year-old body crumpled.

"What's happening?"

"Nothing. It's nothing. It's just me. Paul."

Ryan rebuffed Paul's offer to help him back onto the recliner. "I'm not a cripple."

He shoved his Clubmaster eyeglasses further up his aquiline nose and peered up at his son. The clouds in his blue eyes cleared. They widened in alarm.

"Paul? It can't be. Paul?" he hollered, pulling his son by his dress shirt.

Paul cooperatively sank his knees onto the carpet. Waking Ryan up always triggered consequences. "Yes, it's Paul." He tried to lift the crooked fingers from his placket front.

Ryan resisted relinquishing his grip. He shook the cloth he'd captured.

"You're not Paul," he rasped. "He's dead."

"What are you talking about? It's Paul. Your son. I'm right here."

"You're lying." Ryan shook his head. "You can't be Paul."

Paul tried removing Ryan's fingers one by one. Each time he removed a finger and moved onto the next one, Ryan slipped the previous finger back into hold.

"Ryan, let go. I don't have time for this. Don't you have better things to do? Work on your puzzle. Watch a war movie."

"You're a liar! Paul's dead. He's dead! I saw him dead on Omaha. And Mick and Chris and Phil . . . ," Ryan began crying, " . . . and Tom and Bruce and Henry. B-but especially P-Paul . . . one of eight. Team eleven LCM we're hit. Paul? *Fuck off don't touch him.* PAUL! No, no, no. I'm the only o-one. G-goddammit, the only one."

He dropped his son's placket front and curled into himself, head on his lap.

Paul bounced upright. Listening to Ryan snivel, he stared at the shrunken man, as familiar with his father breaking down as with menstrual cycles. Conceptually, he understood it. But witnessing it . . .

Ryan's voice swelled and broke like an unseen tide. "I don't want to be left! What now? All I see . . . no forgetting. P-Paul. Oh, Paul! I wrote your m-mom . . . they've given me another t-tent mate."

He couldn't prevent himself from remembering a time when their positions had been reversed.

The evening of October sixteenth, 1981 found Paul sobbing on the floor of his parents' living room. Grief rolled him up like a snail retreating into its shell.

Bottle of Rainier Beer in hand, Ryan nudged his son with the tip of his leather loafer.

"Get your scrawny ass up, Paul. We get it; you're in touch with your PMS. Cry over your sore tits elsewhere."

Paul raised his head, ignoring the ice behind Ryan's eyeglasses. He wiped his bloodshot eyes with the sleeve of his black suit.

"Aren't you g-going to ask what's w-wrong?"

"Jesus fucking Christ. You really do want to hold my hand."

"I just . . . just came back from P-Pearl's f-f-funeral."

Ryan stormed over to his recliner and hunkered down onto it.

"And I just came back from court-martial."

Gulping down a hiccup, Paul glowered at his father. "P-Pearl. My g-girlfriend. Her *funeral*."

"I know; Mom told me." Ryan took a swig of beer. "What you want me to say? 'Tough break, kiddo'?"

Paul climbed to his feet, hands clenched at his sides. "D-do you always have to be an a-asshole?"

Ryan raised his beer bottle at him. "D-d-d-do you always have to be a cunt? Or are you overcompensating for Pearl?" He shook his head. "Fifty feet over a railing at a Stones concert. You were too busy listening to 'Start Me Up' to save her, weren't you? Just let her fall. I can't imagine dying on the Kingdome's parking lot. Can you?"

Paul charged at his father, but Ryan moved faster. Crack! He backhanded his son. The force of the blow sent him staggering back.

"You little shit. Look! You made me spill beer on Mom's carpet."

He recovered. He found himself walking up to him. He felt his fist rear up.

Ryan sneered, placing his bottle on the coffee table.

"Go ahead. I dare you. Give it your best fucking shot. *Maybe* I'll need to take a step back."

His fist drew back. But then Paul caught a glimpse of himself. Thrown back by Ryan's eyeglasses. He dropped his hand.

Chuckling, Ryan picked his beer up again. "Knew you didn't have the balls."

"I'll never become you."

"We all knew that the second you came out." He drained the bottle.

It took great effort for Paul to hold the tears in, to regulate his breathing. But he did.

"When you were seventeen," he said quietly, "your father treat you like this? You have a reason for being a bastard, or is it a congenital condition?"

"Shut your fucking mouth, boy. You don't know what I've seen."

Paul had nodded at Ryan's Rainier Beer. "The bottom of lots of bottles."

"Get the fuck outta my sight before this one smashes your zit-oozing face in."

The voice of Paul's mother jolted him back to the current moment. "What on earth is going on here?"

"Ryan's having a . . . a fit."

She raised her eyebrows at his choice of words. Like a doctor preparing a child for a shot, she bent down, drawing Ryan's hand toward her.

"Ry, dear, it's Clara." He remained hunched over, crying in silent shakes. "How can I help?"

Moving faster than a nonagenarian should've been able to, Ryan snatched off his eyeglasses and threw them. They landed on the carpet, still intact, five feet away.

"Well that's as definitive an answer as we'll get, I'm afraid. Best leave him be for a few minutes." She turned her attention to her son. "Come with me into the kitchen, please."

Paul sat down across from his mother. The wrinkles on her face, though fine, were many, like a sketch that hadn't been smoothed out.

Tucking a wavy grey lock behind her ear, she pulled in an unsteady breath.

"Since Christmas, your father's been having more night terrors. And flashbacks. We went back to sleeping in separate beds."

"Have you taken him to the doctor?"

"You already know the answer to that question."

"Of course you did." He watched his mother's face droop. "Bad news?"

She cleared her throat. "Vascular dementia."

"Dementia?"

"Early stages. Some studies have found links between PTSD and dementia."

Paul frowned. "And I'm sure other studies disproved those same links. Besides, no one ever officially diagnosed him with PTSD."

His mother sighed. "Naming's often the last step toward identifying. Anything unnamed still holds power; no need to name it to know it's real. Paul, honey, you know this. Why do you think the mere sight of you irritates him?"

"Because I'm the youngest and therefore the weakest?"

She reached for her son's hand. He let her rest her fingers over his.

"I made a mistake, I know, letting him name you after his best friend. You became a reminder of his loss. He'd been last in line—"

"When the German artillery hit their explosives. I know. We've all heard the story."

"Yes, but did you ever realize how much he blamed himself for it? Paul traded places with him. His birthday fell one day before your father's. Apparently he'd made a joke about seniority and went ahead. A minute later the explosives detonated. This may or may not be true—your father told me during one of those drunken states—but he remembers taking cover and looking over at Paul. The smile had been ripped off his face."

"Good God."

Paul's mother shook her head. "Your father never did go to church again."

"Clara?"

They returned to the living room.

Ryan had moved to the couch. He studied the Seahawks puzzle. "Sit down."

She sat down next to her husband.

"You too, on the other side," Ryan said to Paul.

He pursed his lips but followed the order.

For a few minutes they watched Ryan work. He wouldn't accept help but seemed to want an audience. Grumbling, he tried to find a home for a particularly odd-shaped puzzle piece.

"So Paul," his mother began, "when are we next going to see—"

"Ava?" Ryan cut in.

"And Mei," she added.

"Uh, that depends—" Paul began.

"On Ava's schedule, no doubt," Ryan finished.

"Don't forget about Mei," his wife scolded.

"I'm not." Ryan fitted the puzzle piece into place and held onto the table to stand. "Next time we'll only see Ava." He bent over something on the recliner.

Paul leaned forward. His briefcase.

"Oh? Why is that?" she asked. "Have you recently become an oracle?"

Scowling, Ryan turned around. "I'm senile, not crazy." He held up the booklet like a scorecard.

"Thinking of Breaking it off? DIVORCE: What You Need to Know."

Chapter Twenty-eight

The second week of March arrived, and spring midterms fast approached. Davison students had been lulled into a false sense of complacency during an unexpected break due to a snowstorm. Professors with long commutes found major highways impassable. The bus system shut down. Many assignments were cut out completely or condensed and due through Davison's online methods. But, knowing that for most classes midterms composed a considerable portion of a final grade, students dusted off unopened books in an attempt to make up for being irresponsible. Davison students knew how to party hard, but they studied hard too.

At the dorms, quiet hours were in full effect. In Lockhart, doors that'd normally been propped open to allow students to pass easily from one side of the hall to the other stayed closed. Bulletin boards advertised "Pizza studying parties," as well as tips on how to prepare for exams. Programs that most students never attended were colorfully displayed: "Try Yoga!" and "Free workshop on how to stress less!" Many students tried their own coping methods with varying success: participating in group study sessions, drinking outrageous amounts of coffee, smoking, getting no sleep, sleeping too much to avoid studying, or crying to their parents.

Couples spent less time together enjoying recreational activities and communicating in general. Charlotte and Derek shared no classes but were disciplined enough to study for their separate exams in the same room, ignoring each other until "designated break time." This kind of set-up never worked for Kevin and Jason, so they studied separately and met up to quiz each other. Since Derek and Charlotte used his room to study, Ava studied alone in her room. She had no problem concentrating, which she supposed she could thank her mother for. Mei used to sit behind Ava at her desk and watch her work, only allowing her to take timed bathroom breaks.

Consequently, Ava finished preparations for all six of her exams while everyone else just started to study or write papers. Half of her exams were take-home papers given out early, and she'd already turned them in even though they'd be due a week later.

Back from having dinner at the dining hall, she meant to re-peruse her class notes on Dante's *Divine Comedy*, but then her phone buzzed. A text from Flynn; they'd been texting often.

"Want to study for Medieval Poetry? I'm done with my exams except for that one. We engineers do stuff early."

"Sure. Where?" Ava replied.

"How about my place? You can finally see it."

His place? Charlotte would probably disapprove, but Ava agreed anyway. She began walking to Flynn's apartment once he texted her his address.

Ava didn't think she'd been to this part of campus before, but the off-campus apartments she passed seemed slightly familiar. Then again, much of the housing, both on- and off-campus, looked similar. They all incorporated some kind of red bricks.

Her phone read 7:30 p.m. Except for the streetlights, darkness reigned. The days had of course been getting longer, but Ava felt unable to tell the difference. She longed for the summertime, but not the summer. Going back "home" . . . what a dreadful prospect.

After avoiding several sneaky patches of ice, she arrived at Flynn's place about ten minutes later. His studio appeared to be part of a high-rise apartment complex, and it looked upscale. He'd told her that he lived in his one-room studio alone, an uncommon living situation for undergraduates. Ava wondered how he afforded to do so. His part-time job couldn't be paying him that well. She texted Flynn that she'd arrived. Moments later he opened the door.

He grinned. "Don't know how to buzz in?"

Unwilling to admit that she in fact did not, she silently followed him inside.

"I'm on the third floor. You able to handle taking the stairs?" Flynn called over his shoulder as they headed into the small lobby.

Ava sprung up the stairs before him.

Amused, he didn't attempt to overtake her though his strides were clearly longer.

"You made it!" he teased, making her scowl.

Flynn opened the door and led her in, revealing a compact but modern-looking apartment with dove-white walls and pseudo-wooden floors. Geometric lighting hung from the ceiling.

"You can take off your shoes and leave them by the door. It's not much space-wise, but it's all I need really."

He showed her a closet with sliding doors, a Queen-sized bed that peeked out from behind a partition, a black computer-desk station that seemed to be part of the living room, and a small couch.

"On the other side of the living room is the kitchen, which looks the most impressive, in my opinion. And the other side of the kitchen leads into the bathroom," he said, motioning to the shiny steel appliances, black granite countertops, and the slightly ajar bathroom door.

"Charming," Ava announced after looking her fill.

Flynn shrugged. "It's a bit overpriced for just this; but my mom insisted on it, and she's paying. And it's in a good location, so that also doesn't hurt."

"Wow, that's awfully nice of her." Is that what "normal" mothers did?

"Eh. I guess," he said unenthusiastically.

Ava could take a hint. "But don't you get lonely?"

"No. I have people over to make up for it."

He didn't look like he wanted to elaborate, so she switched the subject again. "So you're done with most of your midterms?"

"Yup. I just have five classes. Besides our class, I'm only taking classes for my major." He walked over to his dark brown couch and sat down.

She continued to stand.

"You just going to stand there? If you don't like my couch, sit on one of the chairs by the kitchen counter."

"Oh, right." She sat on the other side of the couch, facing him.

Flynn chuckled at the distance Ava had placed between them. "I shower, I promise."

Because she'd been continuously thinking about her "major" problem with her mother, Ava asked, "Did you choose your own major?"

He gave her a confused stare. "As opposed to what? Picking it out of a hat?"

"No, wise guy. As opposed to someone else choosing it for you."

An incredulous expression settled onto his face.

"If I have to spend four years of my life studying my ass off for a degree that's supposed to set up my future, I'd better like it. My life, my choice of major. Why, did someone choose yours?"

She shifted on the couch, tucking her legs beneath herself. "I chose the English major, but I'm running into some . . . complications. I'll figure them out eventually."

"I'm sure you will."

"Are you being sarcastic to annoy me?"

Flynn's eyes widened. "No, I'm serious. I can tell it's important to you. You seem like a capable person. Flaky people don't have their shit together like you do."

Amused, Ava said, "Oh? How would you know?"

"From experience. I used to be unreliable. Rebellious, even."

Draping her arm over the couch, she lifted an eyebrow. "What, but now you're a changed man?"

Flynn grinned. "Not really. It's hard to straight-up explain . . . see, I've got this theory."

"Oh really? Let's hear it, then."

"People are like apples."

Ava laughed. "Like apples? Strange comparison."

"Hey, I didn't finish! It'll make sense when I do. Hold on." He leapt up from the couch and went to the kitchen.

"We're supposed to be studying!"

He opened the refrigerator and rummaged through a drawer.

"Who are you kidding? You're the one who sidetracked us first!" Flynn took a paring knife from a drawer, holding whatever he had retrieved behind his back so she couldn't see.

"What are you doing?" She hadn't smiled so much in a while.

"I'm going to demonstrate something." He returned to the couch and faced her, sitting cross-legged. "In my hands," Flynn began dramatically, "I have a knife and . . . an apple!"

Ava glanced at the shriveled red fruit. "I see that. Don't tell me you're going to perform a magic trick."

He shook his head. "I'm not cheesy. Anyway. As I said—"

"People are like apples."

"Yes. See, we've got an outer skin. And it can be bruised, like this apple. Think of the skin as representing our quirks. Let's say you don't like the way I brush my teeth. You think I do it too fast. This quirk of mine, you see it as a blemish, a bruise. Following so far?"

"Somehow, yes."

"My fast teeth brushing upsets you. So, to make you happy, I slow down." Flynn cut off the dented, bruised part of the apple. "I get rid of the bruise," he said, giving it to Ava.

Wryly, Ava bowed her head, cupping the brown piece in a hand. "What an honor."

"I changed a small, easily modified habit for you. But what if you hate my ideals? You hold beliefs in conflict with mine."

He cut the apple in half, revealing a rotten core.

She wrinkled her nose.

Flynn laughed. "See? You're repulsed. You think my insides rotted. My core beliefs aren't changeable. You can't save a rotten apple. So when you ask me if I'm a changed man, my answer is still 'not really.' I just changed my habits, not my beliefs."

She looked at him in amazement. "When did you think this up?"

He shrugged. "Over time. It's the product of a string of failed relationships."

"Sometime I have to introduce you to my friend Jason. He's a philosophy major. I think you'd get along well."

"I'm game. Garbage," Flynn said, holding out his hands for the bruised piece he had given her.

She watched him walk to the kitchen. He threw the discards in the trash and rinsed the paring knife. Admiring his physique, she considered him. By this point, she thought she actually liked him. People are like apples, Ava thought to herself, smiling. An analogy she would remember. No forgetting him, either. But she had misgivings about connecting with someone who had relationship trouble. Please, you're one to talk, she scolded herself, thinking of her parents. Besides, Ava thought when Flynn sat down again, she speculated about a hypothetical situation. What if he just wanted to be friends?

He gazed at her. Feeling awkward, she searched for something innocuous to talk about.

"Did I tell you? I'm halfway done." Ava looked over the couch, out the nearby window. She stretched her legs straight out onto the couch, feet nearly touching his legs, marking her side.

"Oh, and what are you done with?" he asked, continuing to stare at her. Flynn laughed when she shifted uncomfortably and declined to meet his eyes.

"Midterms for a renaissance class, an anthropology class, and a journalism class. I finished their take-home midterms early. Three sit-downs remain," Ava said, eyes roving from his tousled, chestnut hair, to the window that overlooked the edge of Davison campus, to a poster of U2 on a wall.

Do not look at his eyes; do not look at his eyes. Too warm and brown.

"Cool. Well, want to get down to business?"

"What?" she asked, snapping her head back to focus on him.

"Your book or mine? Studying, remember?"

"Yes, of course," she said, mentally shaking herself. "My book? I take copious notes in the margins."

Flynn grinned. "No surprises there. If you sell that book the person buying it will be in for a treat."

"Yes, even more so since the book is used. The person who had it before me also took notes. Whoever gets it next will own a note gold mine." Ava reached down from the couch to retrieve her book from her backpack.

They studied for a solid hour, quizzing each other on key historical dates, important terminology, and the poems they'd read, as per the detailed syllabus. Then they decided to take a break from Medieval Poetry.

"Do you like wine?" he asked, getting up from the couch to stretch his legs.

She shrugged. "I haven't really had it. They only serve jungle juice at the Greek houses. And how'd you get your hands on wine? Aren't you still underage?"

"By seven months and three days, but who's counting? I got my brother to get it for me, but he charged me double for it. Jackass."

Ava laughed, gathering her longer layers and tossing them behind her shoulders.

"So you want to try it?"

"Sure."

He selected a bottle of red wine from one of his black cabinets, along with two elegant wine glasses.

"Impressive, actual wine glasses," she said, watching him from the couch.

"What, you thought I'd use Solo cups? Or that we'd just drink from the bottle? Give me some credit. I'm a tad classier than the majority of our fellow underclassmen."

"Dreadfully sorry. How presumptuous of me!"

"You want a sarcasm war? 'Cause we can go right here, right now," Flynn joked, setting the bottle and glasses on the living room's coffee table.

Ava shook her head, opting to sit on the floor, closer to the coffee table.

"Are you rejecting my couch again?"

"What's this obsession you have with your couch? No, I'm on the floor to get closer to the wine, therefore lowering my chances of spilling it."

"Kneeling, how Japanese of you," Flynn said, joining her.

She shrugged. "Actually, I think my mother's family in China did that too."

"So you're half Chinese?" he asked, surprised.

"Yes. My dad's the white one. Irish and Italian, except more Irish. You can't tell?" She studied him closely, trying to gauge his reaction.

He shook his head. "Not even after you've pointed it out. But that's cool. Quite a mix of cultures. I'm jealous."

"Really? Why?"

"Personally, I think white people are boring. I'm a mix of a bunch of European cultures: English, German, Irish, Italian, Polish, a smattering of Spanish. My ancestors came from all over the place. Because of that, I've never really had a connection to anything. But you've got just enough of a variety. Ties to two opposites, the East and West. Cosmopolitan."

Flynn poured wine into the glasses.

Ava said nothing for a minute.

"What's up?" he asked, handing her a glass.

"I've never thought of it that way."

"Oh? And what way have you been thinking?"

She took a sip of her wine before answering. Slightly bitter with a hint of berries. Definitely better than downing jungle juice.

"Um. That it's better to be entirely white, at least in America. I feel like my mother had to work twice as hard to be accepted here, but that must also come with being an immigrant. We learned about this in a couple of my classes. When you can easily be placed into the broad category of 'other,' you need to fight to . . . to not necessarily fit in—because that might mean you lost a part of yourself—but to coexist."

Flynn placed his glass on the coffee table. "That probably goes with everything, not just race, ethnicity, and culture, you know? If you're noticeably different, you encounter problems. So many possibilities for difference. If you've got a different orientation, religion, political or ethical belief, a disease, illness, or disability . . . you can't take your rights for granted. You feel compelled to mask the part of yourself that's different, that threatens the people in the majority."

"I guess so. That's kind of depressing." She drank more of her wine.

He shrugged. "Only for now. I doubt that it'll stay that way for long. Think of the last census. The face of the American population is changing. Why do you think Republicans seek the elusive 'Hispanic vote'? Obama points to a shift. Soon you'll outnumber plain guys like me. But for now, without some sort of hierarchy—even an unfair one—there'd be no sense of order. No guidelines on how to divvy up resources. You know, economics and shit," he said, making her laugh.

"I guess it's partly our responsibility. With no antagonistic force, there's less pressure to innovate and create meaningful change. Surely, some injustice or suffering is necessary to make us stronger, to allow us to understand each other. Maybe we just need to get angry and demand acceptance." She felt the wine start to go to her head.

"What, like Black Power except . . . except what?"

She laughed. Finally she could comfortably use Charlotte's term.

"I call myself an Amerasian, but 'Amerasian Power' is a mouthful. My roommate, Charlotte, calls me a Whasian . . . "

"Whasian Power. Sounds interesting. I'll drink to that." Flynn and Ava clinked glasses.

They continued to talk, branching off into different topics. Neither of them paid attention to how much wine they'd consumed until Flynn looked down.

"Uh, did we just drink most of the bottle?" he asked her, examining the low wine level.

"Probably. But, to be fair, you'd already opened it. Did I just giggle? Gross!"

He laughed. "Oh, the effects of alcohol. You drink a lot?"

He seemed pleased that she stopped actively leaning away from him.

She shrugged a shoulder; shrugging two felt like an unnecessary amount of effort.

"Used to drink more. Used to party. Now I've cut down on the drinking and don't party."

"Why no partying?" he asked, watching Ava skim the rim of her glass with a forefinger.

"Well, I last went out during winter break. My friend—sort of, anyway, she's my roommate's older sister—pressed me to come out since all of her party friends went home for the holidays."

"Oh nice, so she used you, the next best thing?"

"I don't know, maybe. Anyway, I really didn't want to go. Too tired. But she made me feel guilty, so I told her I'd go on the condition that I abstain from drinking. She didn't seem to care, not even enough to make fun of me, so we went to this grad student's apartment. What street . . . I think it started with a 'P.'"

"Pierce Street?" Flynn suggested, but Ava shook her head.

"No, it has something to do with Narnia . . . no, that's not right. Neverland. Oh, Peter Pan!"

"Peter Pan Street?" he teased, dodging a playful tap.

"No, no. Peterson Street!"

"I see. So I'm guessing you ended up drinking that night?"

"By accident. Julia, the girl I went with, brought me a virgin iced tea. I guess she paid no attention or the bartender forgot, because it must've been spiked with alcohol. I danced salsa, which I'd never done before, so I got really thirsty . . . "

"Uh-oh. How many drinks did you end up having?"

"Two full Solo cups, and I downed them," she admitted. "I think I blacked out bits of that night, because I don't remember things in a neat sequential order. Hate being unable to remember. I want experiences, good and bad. I want to *live* every moment.

Anyway, it's like someone made a puzzle of that night, shook it up like a tossed salad, and put it back in my head."

Laughing, Flynn said, "You really are an English major, even when tipsy. You just used two different types of figurative language to describe one thing."

"Whatever, Mr. Apple Theory. You know what I mean. Ugh, I hate when people say 'you know what I mean.'"

He grinned. "So what else do you remember, or is that all?"

"Um . . . no, there's a bit more." Ava bit her lower lip in concentration. "This guy . . . "

"A guy you danced with?"

She shook her head. "When I felt dizzy and weird, I sat down by a wall. And this guy . . . he seemed really nice. I think I told him that too many times."

"What, that you found him nice?"

"Yeah, he stood next to me and asked if I needed anything. And then I think he bent down to help me call Charlotte. I rested my head on his thigh, which I cleverly deemed 'nice.'"

Flynn whistled. "Oh, risqué," he said, prompting an eye roll from Ava. "So you never saw his face or got his name?"

"No, and he could've been my soul mate," she said dramatically, putting the back of her hand to her forehead in a fake swoon and drawing a laugh out of him.

"Actually, I'm not proud of that night. Now when I need to cope with my mother, I run." Crap, how had that last sentence slipped out?

"Coping with your mom?" he asked, raising an eyebrow.

Somehow, she found herself telling him more than she had planned. About the name-calling, being forced to change majors. She glossed over the root of the reason behind her shaky relationship with her father. Ava also failed to mention the blog or *Lao lao*'s diary—too personal. When talking about the physical violence, she omitted the basement and the snake belt; but she gave enough details to cause Flynn to say, "No offense, but your mom's a little crazy."

"None taken." Ava shrugged. "What can I do? And it doesn't help that my dad's a workaholic. They're on bad terms. I think he really bought the apartment in the city so they'd be separated. Cheaper than getting a divorce. I guess." Most likely her mother would fight a divorce, thinking it would tarnish her reputation.

"That sucks. If it makes you feel better, my mom's an ice queen."

"I'm sorry. Why's that?"

Flynn shrugged. "She's a dentist and runs her own practice, so she's really busy. But when she's not working, she tries to recapture her youth. She doesn't talk much to me or my brother. A live-in nanny raised us. Now she throws money at us, hoping that's all we want from her. That's why I have this apartment. She doesn't give a shit about me; she's all about reputation. She can afford to pay for this, so she does. And she doesn't want me living in a house or room with people who are less fortunate."

"My dad tries to compensate for his absence with gifts, and my mother throws money at me sometimes."

"Money instead of affection." He shook his head. "I also think my mom's a man hater . . . probably because my dad left after I was born. Since then she's never dated a guy longer than a month, let alone thought of marrying again. I think that's why she doesn't like me or my brother."

"Screwed over once, so take it out on the whole sex?"

The wine allowed her to boldly lean her head on Flynn's shoulder, which he didn't seem to mind.

"Yeah. It seems like it's her hobby to get a guy to fall for her. Then she manipulates him, and when she's done or bored, she kicks him away. The few times I've gone home and seen a guy, she's asked him to leave, never even introducing us. It's like she wants to prevent the two worlds she dislikes colliding. I don't think she's cut out for parenting."

Ava's head slid off his shoulder to rest on his thigh. He slowly ran his fingers through her silky hair, roots to ends, staring out at nothing.

"That's awful. Our mothers are opposites: mine's about control, but yours seems to be about distance."

She closed her eyes. It felt strange to be handled so gently, yet it reminded her . . . of something. To avoid becoming annoyed at herself and ruining the moment, she tucked the feeling away, intending to deal with it later . . . if she remembered.

"Yeah." He looked down at her tranquil face.

"You staring at me?" Ava asked grumpily, feeling a pressure bearing down on her. She opened her eyes, turning her head to fix a glare on him.

"And what if I am?" Flynn challenged, lifting a dark bronze brow.

She used her hands to push herself up and off his leg. Sitting up and turning her body to face him, she pursed her lips in mock annoyance.

Ava parted her lips, about to berate him, when he swiftly leaned forward and softly kissed her—once—before pulling away.

She closed the space between them and unapologetically kissed him back, lacing her fingers through his dark, coppery brown hair. Flynn started, her bold response surprising him. Then he rebounded, drawing her closer and playing with her reddish brown locks.

Ava's hands slid down his back, caressing every angle, every muscle, feeling the hair on his arms rise.

He lightly pulled back, meeting her heavy eyes. "I think . . . I think we should stop." He took her hands and carefully placed them in her lap.

"Mmm?" She finally met his dark brown eyes. Why stop when they were having so much fun?

Flynn gathered her hair away from an ear so he could whisper into it. "We're kinda drunk, and I want to talk to you about something."

"So?" Ava said lazily, dragging out the word, shivering from his soft touch. "Talk to me later." This—he—felt fitting. For once, she acted without anger or despair. Without the dictates of the Wall. This would be different from Halloween.

"But I don't want to ruin this."

"Ruin what?" she asked, slightly more alert.

"Well . . . what we could have," Flynn said.

"What we could have," she echoed, bolting upright. No. The Wall slammed into her. Too much.

"What? What's wrong? What happened?"

"Um. I need to leave." What they "could have"? She needed space to breathe. She needed to reset the divide. She headed to the door.

"Wait, what's going on?" He reached out for her hand but ended up grasping her wrist.

She turned back, and for a split second, Mei replaced Flynn. Mei, grabbing her wrist before dragging her down the hallway. Mei, in the basement, restraining her wrists. Frightened, though she knew it'd been her imagination, the wine, or a combination of both, Ava jerked her hand back. She'd touched a snake, mistaking it for a stick.

"Don't touch me." She jerked the door open and scampered away.

Chapter Twenty-nine

Ava ran back to Lockhart. Confusion choked her, obscuring her thinking, but running provided a clearing antidote. The soft sounds of her shoes and the soon steady beat of her heart soothed. So she fled, hair flying behind her, free. And in that moment she could pretend, believe in this alternate existence. Free. Free from her past, free from her fears, and from the Wall she'd built in reaction to both.

'"What we could have"' echoed in her head, each word the sounding of a gong. Even if Flynn meant his words, they sounded awfully heavy. Trusting someone with your feelings . . . too risky. I can't let you lift me up. No letting you drop down. You need to stay on the other side. For your safety. For mine. If you really knew me . . .

You'd never accept me. You can do better. I'm unworthy, unfinished. Scratched, defective, scarred. Damaged goods in hiding. Too many issues. Too much baggage. I can't let you see. No, the Wall must remain. No passing it on. But no keeping it in without . . . 'what we could have.' What did that mean? How to interpret such a vague, futuristic statement? And we. Not you and I. Not you plus me. We. Togetherness.

Nearly at Lockhart, Ava realized what she'd forgotten. Her purse, of course. No wonder her person felt lighter than usual. Excellent! It held her cell phone, wallet, and keys. Her wallet carried, besides her credit and debit cards, her license and school ID card. Should she go back and face Flynn, tail between her legs? No, impossible at the moment. She thought she spotted Charlotte's curly halo by Lockhart's front doors.

"Ava?"

Relieved, she jogged over. Once safely inside their room, sitting on their beds, Charlotte began a scolding session.

"Now I'm going to cut this short because it's late already and you've got that exam tomorrow afternoon. But seriously, you need to get it together!"

Ava gave a small shrug. "I know, I shouldn't be out so late, or have forgotten my purse."

"Well yes, obviously. But moreover, you need to start putting more trust in people!"

"What are you talking about?"

"Remember the night you went to that grad student's party and blacked out bits of it?"

"Even if I couldn't remember, you'd never let me forget it."

"Come on, what are best friends for? Anyway, how did I pick you up?"

"Are you *quizzing* me?"

"No, I'm trying to stir your memory. You called me, and somebody helped you."

"Yes . . . a guy."

"I believe you used a certain adjective to describe him," Charlotte said.

"Right. Nice. I leaned on his nice leg . . . " That's what had felt so familiar.

"What?"

"Nothing." That must've been what he'd wanted to talk to her about. Odd. No, irritating, that he'd spent two months trying to find the right segue. She supposed he wanted to avoid telling her through a text. But he could've called.

"That guy's Flynn, right?"

"Yes. He just called me—with *your* phone—to say you forgot your things at his place. And that you ran away, freaked out for no apparent reason. But I'm sure you had a reason, even if it's weird."

Ava looked away. "He indicated interest in something with me."

"Gasp!" Charlotte feigned a look of horror. "You mean, like a *relationship*?"

"I guess," Ava said, unamused. "It's . . . it's disturbing. Relationships . . . balanced relationships, involve physical and emotional sharing. Giving and taking. Willing to try something that holds no guarantees. I can't do the emotional stuff."

"Balanced relationships. God forbid you participate in such a healthy thing." Charlotte shook her head.

"Whatever." She shouldn't have drunk so much wine; her head throbbed. "I'm going to get ready for bed. We'll figure this out in the morning."

Yet, once in bed, Ava had trouble sleeping. She wished she could rewire her mind and destroy the negative associations with relationships. Because being with Flynn, kissing him . . . made her feel normal. He could've been her new normal, her anchor. No, that's wrong. *She* needed to be her own anchor. To break apart her Wall. And she couldn't be with Flynn—with anyone—until that occurred. At the moment she felt weighed down. Weighted by the bonds of her past, which constantly reminded her of the reasons for her defenses. She reverted to fear, to uncertainty, to anger and suspicion. She never cared for excitement or drama. If normal meant boring, if it meant stability, she yearned for it.

But she couldn't move forward until she finished examining the past, her roots. And that meant finishing the rest of the diary entries, learning about the mother she'd never known. Ridiculous, she knew, but she couldn't stop hoping to be enlightened by the remaining entries. Ava wanted to confirm that she'd find nothing worth saving in Mei. Only then could she put an end to her mother's interferences. As Jason had said, *sin duda*. Ava wanted to be without doubt. No hypotheticals, no regret. What if I'd only . . . This, along with the Wall, prevented her from telling her father, from asking Li zhi to help her *do* something. Get a grip. That isn't the solution. She needed to take action on her own. Alone. A solo marathon. Eventually, while trying to forget the events of the hectic night, she fell asleep.

Despite getting fewer than six hours of sleep, Ava woke immediately, sitting up in bed so quickly she saw stars. Only 8 a.m., but no way she'd go back to sleep. She had had a nightmare—not a memory this time—and though the details had already evaporated, the fear held on, tenacious as ever. She had dreamed of Mei attacking her in the creepy book basement. Mei had bashed her over the head with Amy Chua's *Battle Hymn of the Tiger Mother* and yelled, "I'll show you what a tiger mom can really do!" Ava recalled nothing else, but she didn't want to risk falling back asleep into the same nightmare. So while she waited for Charlotte to wake up, she began reading the book that had graced her nightmare. To face the tiger, you must know it, she thought to herself semi-seriously. Ava longed for the day when Mei would be forced to turn around because her daughter had caught her tail.

"Mmmm," Charlotte groaned when she woke two hours later. "Up already?" she asked, stretching.

"Yes, I read a book Li zhi lent me; and then I studied some, but I think I'm done. I don't want to over study."

Charlotte nodded in agreement. "God, I hate mornings. Your exam's from four to seven, right?"

"Mmhmm. It shouldn't take the full three hours. Especially since I'm prepared."

"That's good. I'm going to get dressed and stuff, and then we're going to the dining hall for breakfast."

At breakfast Charlotte seemed more awake.

"Eat some of your breakfast and then we'll talk. Eating is important on exam days," she ordered, pointing to Ava's half-full plate.

"Yes ma'am," she replied with a mini salute. Sometimes Charlotte sounded just like Ema.

"So what's your deal?" Charlotte asked after Ava had eaten her scrambled eggs.

Confused, she raised an eyebrow in question.

"Flynn, I think, is a great guy. Not only did he take care of you the night you first met, but when you became friends, he didn't tell you about it," Charlotte said. "He could've used it to play the hero, tried to impress you. I don't think he's your typical college boy, you know?"

"I guess. It turned too real for me to handle."

"Because he told you he liked you? Did he just tell you that randomly?" Charlotte asked suspiciously.

"So we may have made out beforehand," Ava muttered, looking down at her plate.

"Ha, I thought so. Eat your toast."

"I don't want to."

"Well, that's all you did?" Charlotte asked.

"Yes, yes. If you must know, he stopped it."

"Well, then he seems sincere. I approve. He made the conscious effort to be a gentleman. So why'd you run out?"

"He grabbed my wrist when I turned to go and . . . promise not to think I'm crazy?"

"Oh excellent. I love when you make me promise when I don't know what's coming next. Sure, I promise."

Ava leaned closer and dropped her voice. "I kind of hallucinated my mother for a second."

Charlotte didn't respond for a moment, contemplative. "Do you think you might have some emotional issues?"

Ava crossed her arms. "Care to explain?"

"Promise not to get mad at me?" Charlotte challenged.

"Touché. Fine, I promise."

"I spoke to someone at CSAPS about you."

Ava blankly stared.

"The counseling center."

"You *what*?"

"Chill out! I made sure never to use your real name."

Ava eyed Charlotte warily. "Go on . . . "

"I did it about midway through the month we were fighting. So before I knew the shit Mei had done to you. Anyway, I called up the office and explained what I'd noticed. The woman gave me some possible lengthy diagnosis that I can't remember. But she did agree that you have trust issues. I don't even think you trust yourself, honestly. Beyond the defense mechanisms you've built to deal with Mei, I think your mind is rebelling. You don't usually remember all the run-ins you've had with her, right?"

"No. But lately it's like I've been having unwanted flashes down memory lane."

Charlotte nodded. "Exactly. I think your mind has repressed the most traumatic experiences you've had, but now, maybe because of the added stress of college and everything else, your brain is bringing them to your attention."

"Say what? Try translating that psychology-speak into lay-people terms. English major, remember? Kevin and Jason took that class with you, not me."

"Then you know semantics. Think about it: what's the difference between the mind and the brain?"

"Um. The mind has something to do with consciousness and perception, while the brain deals with neurological processes?"

"You get a gold star!"

"You pet my head, and I'll bite you." She glared at Charlotte.

"Not in public, Av," Charlotte joked.

"So you think that, to protect me from going insane or something just as bad, my mind repressed my worst memories?"

"I mean, this is armchair psychology on my part, but I think so. And now, maybe you've had too much, so your mind's protection is cracking. Freshman year, the college transition . . . all that's really stressful. You're having hallucinations, nightmares, flashbacks. And in turn, this stresses you out further and even more unwanted memories spill out."

"Interesting. Like a shaken-up bottle of unopened soda, just bound to explode." Ava finally took a bite of her cold toast, and regretted doing so.

"Perfect analogy; Julie and I did that all the time when we were kids. Ruined quite a few shirts," Charlotte said, making her smile. "Also . . . have you ever considered that you might understand your mom more than you think you do?"

"Mother. I only call her 'Mother.' Any other variation is too endearing. And what do you mean by that?"

"Well from what you've told me, she likes control. And she wants to be right. She's mentally strong, and has a bit of a temper. Ever consider that you share some of these same qualities with Mei? *And* you've both had broken childhoods."

"Excuse me?" Ava nearly hissed.

"Do *not* take this the wrong way. Think about this for a moment. Why do we fear certain people? Part of it has to do with a fear of likeness. We're afraid of being like the person we fear and dislike the most. Of course you're not your mother; of course you're not exactly like your mother, but consider that you might've picked up a thing or two from her."

Ava took a deep, shuddering breath, pressing a hand to her forehead like it'd keep her from lashing out in defensive anger.

"So you're saying that I try to control as much as I can in my own life . . . to fight the fact that my mother tries to control me, and so on?"

"Yes. We talked about this in one of my classes. It's scapegoating, which involves demonizing another person or group. Part of what lies beneath scapegoating is fear, fear that the alien person or group resembles you. And so those who scapegoat accuse scapegoating victims of crimes they didn't commit, just out of fear. Your mom may accuse you of being a bad daughter because she subconsciously considers herself a bad daughter. It's probably crossed her mind that she could've done something to save her mother or her sibling. So how does she reconcile that? By taking it out on you. It's kind of like me and my dad. When I learned that he'd committed suicide, I felt so angry. How dare he throw his life away, whether or not cancer would kill him anyway?"

Ava quieted, always unsure of what to say whenever the late Mr. Bell arose in conversation. But she knew it'd be unreasonable for her to be angry at Charlotte for comparing her with Mei. Whether or not Ava agreed, Charlotte tried to help, even using the discovery about her dad's suicide to illustrate her point.

"But after some reflection, I know I had no right to judge him so harshly. I mean, I still think suicide is a sin, probably because I've been raised Catholic, but I don't hate or dislike my dad for what he did. On some level I can relate to his decision. Self-euthanasia is kind of a noble thing to do. I'm sure he hated suicide as much as I do, but when faced with his difficult situation, he changed his mind. Sometimes your beliefs change when they're tested. If I'd been in his place, I could've made the same decision. Maybe doing what he did made him weak, or maybe not . . . sorry, I got sidetracked. This clearly has nothing to do with my example."

Charlotte pushed her tray away and stared at the grainy-patterned table.

Ava hated seeing her friend uncertain. *She* should be the uncertain one. Feeling the need to take Charlotte's mind off her troubles, Ava reluctantly steered the conversation back to her own.

"You're probably right—about Mei and me. I think my worst fear is becoming her."

"You could never. You'd never let that happen, especially since you're so aware of it. But if you do start to go haywire, I'll be the first to tell you."

"Gee, thanks. That's just what I wanted to hear." Ava faintly smiled. "You know what's funny?"

"What?"

"This morning I continued reading that tiger mom book Li zhi lent me."

Charlotte furrowed her brow in confusion. "That's funny? I thought everyone ragged on that author for evil Asian parenting."

Ava thought back to her dream this morning. "I'll show you what a tiger mom can really do!" dream-Mei had shouted.

"Well, some moments are kind of funny. She can be a humorous writer, but that's not my point. The most controversial name Chua called one of her daughters was 'garbage.' Reading that, I actually laughed out loud."

"You've got a weird sense of humor."

"No, think about it. My mother has cursed at me in two different languages, saying things that'd make a nun faint. And the worst Chua can come up with? 'Garbage.'" She grinned.

"Ava." Charlotte shook her head. "That's not funny. That's just sad."

"No, you just have a white-person sense of humor. Ema obviously raised you the Western way. Ready to go?"

"I like the Western way. The worst my mom tried to do? Overfeed me!" Laughing, they put their trays away and walked up the stairs to leave the dining hall.

They headed out into the mild sunshine.

"Know what I'm really dreading?"

"What?" Charlotte asked, squinting slightly.

"Talking to Flynn before or after the exam."

"I'd be worried about looks from classmates." Charlotte giggled. "Guys don't usually give girls purses."

Ava groaned.

"You'll manage, I'm sure. You're Ava Magee. You always do."

"I love how you say my name like I'm somebody. Like that means something."

"Hey, Negative Nancy. I'll have none of that, especially not before an exam. You are somebody. Sure, you may not yet know *who* you think you are, but everybody's somebody to someone else. And guess what? You're my somebody." Charlotte went to give her a loving poke.

Ava jumped away, startling her, and then chuckled. "I never expect your jabs."

"Sorry, didn't mean to scare you."

Half an hour before the start of her midterm exam, Ava set off for her Medieval Poetry classroom, stomach twisting. She regretted eating. Pulling her coat's belt tighter around her waist, she reviewed key terms in her head in an attempt to distract herself.

Before leaving Lockhart to go to her own exam, Charlotte had told her that if she wanted to test out being with Flynn, whatever that meant, she still could. According to what he'd said to Charlotte the night before, Ava's weird behavior hadn't scared him off.

Could he help her become more comfortable in her skin? She didn't know, and the unknown bothered her the most. She foresaw the safer, easier option, which involved forgetting about Flynn, even figuring out a way to sabotage things further to ensure that he would forget her too. But that would mean that her mother had won, right? That she'd given her enough negative reinforcement to continue being self-destructive. To forever sequester herself behind the Wall.

Ava arrived to a classroom already half-filled with a mix of calm and panicky students.

"Quickly sum up the *Inferno* for me. I only read an online summary of it—two weeks ago!" she heard one student urge another.

She took her usual seat. From the corner of her eye she saw Flynn look in her direction. Would it be better to talk to him before or after the exam? Oh no, too late. Breathe, look normal. Crap, she didn't know what that meant.

"I think this is yours," Flynn said, placing her purse down on the desk in front of her. "Your mom called twenty times between 3 and 4 a.m., by the way. I obviously didn't pick up. I think she left a few messages. And you got a text from your dad. Listen, I know—"

"Why didn't you tell me sooner? That we'd met at the party? I had a right to know."

Looking cornered, he slid into the seat next to her. "I . . . I didn't want to influence you. I wanted to see if you could like me for me . . . not feel obligated to like me because I became the 'nice guy.' So, selfish reasons, really. I'm sorry."

Ava's irritation evaporated. Surprise took over. After an awkward pause, she thanked him for her purse. "I'm sorry I ran out like that."

"I'm sure you had your reasons. Do—"

"You should probably get back to your seat; it looks like the exam is about to start."

Flynn nodded. "We'll talk some other time, then."

The ability to concentrate under pressure never left her. When the exam started, she put everything unrelated to Medieval Poetry on pause. She completed the exam and double-checked it, handing the test in with an hour of exam time remaining.

"Thanks, Ava," her professor said. "Remember that in place of a final exam is the final project, okay? Make it fun!"

Great. Even if she decided to leave things the way they were, she'd still have to work with Flynn because they were in the same group. And if the past indicated the future, they'd be doing most of the project themselves. Ava headed out the door, glancing back for him. He'd already left.

Outside the classroom, she checked her phone. She decided to look at her dad's text message first. "Isn't spring break coming up? Think we can meet at the house then?" Looking at her call log, Ava saw that Mei had indeed called twenty times. She'd left eleven voicemails. Shoving a gloved hand into a pocket, Ava used her other hand to listen. Cursing in Mandarin, cursing in English, threats, threats. No surprises so far.

Just then her phone rang, and without thinking, she picked it up.

"Listen, *sanba,*" Mei spat into the phone. "Who you are to ignore me? Know what? I'm outside your dorm."

"What? Why?"

"Because you disrespect me!"

"But I have and have had exams!"

"Fuck everything but me. *I'm* the most important part in your life. The most important relationship of your life! And you're going to prove it. You coming home *now.*"

"What? I have two more sit-down exams; both of which are tomorrow! If I don't go, I'll fail them automatically!"

"I don't give shits. A mother is the most important person in a child's life."

What to do? She'd partly defined herself through her schoolwork. Triage. Ignoring another cursing rant, Ava texted Jason that she'd miss their final due to a family emergency. Then she texted her father back. "Going home today. I'll text you when I know she'll be out." After sending the last text, she returned the phone to her ear.

"I'll make you sorry for this! For punishment, you come home early for spring break. That teach you to care for your mother first!" Mei barked before she left Ava listening to emptiness.

Chapter Thirty

Querida Ava,

According to my attendance sheet, and the exam packets that I have in hand, you never showed for my Latino/a Literature midterm. I am writing this email because this is extremely out of character for you. You are one of my best students; you always come to class, participate, and turn in incredibly intelligent work early. Is everything alright? Jason informed me that you are no longer on campus because your mother needed you. Davison's policy allows students to take a make-up exam due to a family or medical emergency. I have a feeling that something serious happened to prevent you from taking my exam. As of right now, your interim grade is a C; as you know the midterm and final paper are weighted more heavily than quizzes, attendance, and participation. Please contact me with an explanation. I want you to take a make-up and I want you to succeed.

—Professor Meier

Dragged home as Mei had promised, Ava finished reading the second email regarding her outstanding exams and cringed. What could she do? Say, "Why yes, some*one* happened to prevent me from taking two midterms. Who is that someone? My mother, of all people! She picked me up from my dorm a day before the start of spring break, fully knowing that I'd miss my last midterms. And better yet, this is her punishment for me. Punishing me for what? I don't really know; she says it's because I'm an awful daughter and that it's about time I suffer so I can 'learn a lesson.' Is a legitimate excuse, according to Davison standards, 'crazy mother punished daughter by preventing her from taking midterms'?"

Evidently this would be a hard fix. And no one could clean up the mess but Ava herself. No chance of asking her mother for help or for a delay in the punishment. Showing desperation encouraged Mei to worsen Ava's current situation, and she knew her mother enjoyed making matters worse. She compromised by emailing her professors vague, succinct statements: "I am afraid that at the present moment I cannot fully explain my situation, but due to a family emergency, my mother needed me at home. I wish to make up the two midterms I missed, and, hopefully, I will soon have the proof the university needs to be offered make-ups."

Perhaps this could've been prevented, or at least delayed, had Charlotte not been taking an exam when Mei collected Ava at her dorm. Despite her past threats, Mei never made a scene in public. She maintained face. "Oh Mei, you're so beautiful. It's like you haven't aged since winning Mrs. New Jersey. Mei, you're so fit! What's your secret? Ava's so successful; can you give me parenting advice? You're so kind, speaking on behalf of the animal shelter. How do you do it all, you're such a supermom!"

The start of Ava's spring break consisted of obeying her mother's snappy orders, but she did get some respite when Mei randomly left the house without saying where she meant to go. When she left for the first time, Ava first texted Li zhi. "Forced home. Could you tell Prof. Meier that I plan on taking a make-up?" Li zhi responded almost immediately: "Are you okay?" Ava bit her lip in anger. "No. You were right; I can't let my mother control me forever. How dare she screw with my exams! I've had enough." Li zhi texted back, "Don't worry; I'll make sure she doesn't. I'll talk to your professors. Let me know if I can do anything else."

Then Ava texted her dad with updates on her mother's comings and goings, and Charlotte to keep her roommate from doing anything drastic. After the third time Mei left, Ava began seriously wondering where she went. It couldn't be the gym. Her mother had cancelled her membership a few months ago and bought more gym equipment for the house. She didn't have real friends, only acquaintances. Her mother thought she didn't need friends; she believed them too hard to maintain and therefore not worth it.

Unfortunately, neither Paul nor Ava discerned a pattern in Mei's erratic errands. The first time Paul came back, Mei returned within ten minutes of leaving. He had no choice but to act preoccupied: he put some of his laundry in the hamper and then receded into his study to work, leaving for the city before being forced to have an extended conversation with his wife. The second time he returned, however, Mei remained gone for some time. Paul called his daughter into his office.

Leaning against the doorframe to her father's office, Ava said, "It's already been twenty minutes. I think we'll have enough time to talk."

Paul shifted in his chair nervously. Though they'd finally conspired to find a moment away from Mei's watchful eyes, he seemed unsure how to begin talking to her.

"I'm sorry this took so long—" Ava began, when her father still said nothing.

"No, *I'm* sorry."

They weakly laughed.

"I'm sorry I didn't show you my translations sooner; for some time you've been old enough to know the whole truth." Paul glanced at his door like he expected Mei to appear. "See, your mother and I had a small wedding. My family and the people who were our friends at the time attended the ceremony. Your mother told us that no one from her side could attend. I know now that I should've paid more attention to this. But during the reception, the one and only time I've ever seen this happen, your mother got completely drunk."

"How?" Ava tried and failed to picture Mei drunk.

"She played a drinking game with Uncle Mickey."

"Ah."

"Anyway, that night she showed me the diary and told me about its entries. She'd never talked about her family before. Whenever I brought it up she completely shut down. She always refused to reveal any kind of information other than the fact that her family had endured the Cultural Revolution."

"And so you knew that if you actually asked her for it, under ordinary circumstances, she'd never give it to you?"

"Exactly. Anyway, as luck had it, she didn't remember showing it to me or telling me about it. The next time she met with friends, I read it. The originals were in Chinese, of course, and over a period of time I translated them into English, knowing that they'd be important someday."

She thought of the creased package labeled "Lao lao/Mei diary, 1966–1970," still under her pillow at Lockhart. "Why were they separate?"

"I forgot to take *Lao lao*'s sheets with me when I settled into the apartment. I'd translated them at different times."

"Can I keep *Lao lao*'s entries, or is that your only copy?"

"Go ahead and keep it, and the duplicate of Mom's. I've got others back in the city. Anyway, you should read the rest of it—your mom's entries."

Paul reached into his briefcase and pulled out the rest of the copy. He handed the stapled sheets to her. "Wait. I have to show you the original diary. I don't know how much longer Mom will be away, but it shouldn't take too long for you to look at it."

"Where is it again?"

"Her bedroom." He beckoned her to follow him.

Ava couldn't believe that such a significant personal, historical artifact had been hiding in this house for eight years. She followed him to the master bedroom and then into the bedroom's walk-in closet. Paul pushed away some of Mei's clothes to reveal a silver wall safe.

She watched, intrigued. She'd never known of the safe's existence.

"How do you know the code if she told you before we moved here?" She placed the translated entries onto her mother's bureau.

"I helped your mother install the safe. She wrapped up what she wanted to store away, and then I set the code. It's a . . . a memorable date and it's never been changed."

Frowning, her father punched in the code and then opened the door. He took out a red-and-gold brocade pouch, envelope-sized, and handed it to her. "Go ahead, open it."

Briefly caressing the silk, she unbuttoned the pouch and removed its heart. *Lao lao*'s little red book.

"This is it?" It reminded her of a pocket-sized dictionary. Chinese characters were imprinted on the plastic, faded red cover, and beneath the characters lay a small star. But she had no idea what the title read.

"The cover translates into 'Quotations from Chairman Mao Tse-Tung.' You probably expected something more substantial, but they made them cost effectively. During four years, the government ordered a record-breaking 720 million printed. These book pamphlets—otherwise known as 'little red books'—were distributed during the Cultural Revolution."

"So *Lao lao* wrote diary entries in a communist propaganda book? That seems illegal."

"These books were like the communist bible. Some people refer to it as the 'Chinese Bible,' actually. The government required everyone to have them and even memorize the quotations. *Lao lao* wrote cryptically in the margins, in classical Chinese, in case they inspected the book. Your mom followed suit." Paul pointed out the hand-written characters while Ava gently flipped through the thin pages.

Seeing that a great number of pages had clearly been ripped out, she remembered what her father had noted on the back of the diary package: "Incomplete translated copy of original. Sections missing from original, likely lost/ burned in Cultural Revolution. Find out from Mei someday."

Looking up from the worn white thread that held the remaining pages together, she asked, "How much is missing?"

"Most of it, unfortunately, because of your mother. Only sixty pages remain. From what I've gathered, this book's a third edition, so it's supposed to have 270 pages. And that's not considering the possibility of extra material."

"What kind of extra material?"

"They sometimes included extra propaganda. 'Latest Instructions,' for example, provided more quotes from Mao."

She reverently touched the marginal, faded black ink. *Lao lao*'s ink.

"Did Mother destroy the rest of it?"

"That's what she told me on our wedding night. After her mother died, Mei burned whatever she felt too blasphemous or incoherent. *Lao lao* really lost her sanity by the end. And then there's a chance Mei lost pages when she emigrated."

Evidence of history and its layers. Lived and rewritten. *Her* story, Ava thought, in awe. She held a two-faced book. Communist writing on one side, the side open to the world, dissenting comments embedded inside. This book, this bifurcated book, had survived Mei's childhood, adolescence, and adulthood to travel with her to the States.

"How long did it take for you to translate this?"

"The translation went quickly; I'd recently completed Chinese language classes. I only needed to research the time period and the characters I couldn't recognize. But I had to time everything around your mother's abs—"

Hearing the front door open, Paul and Ava froze.

"Go, go," he whispered. "No getting caught. Hide her entries while I take care of locking up!"

Why did her mother have to break up everything? For the first time in five years, she'd bonded with her dad. Grabbing the papers from the bureau, she rushed upstairs to her room with cat-quiet strides. Ava hid the stapled sheets underneath her bed and then dashed to the laundry room. Dad must've finished up; she heard him go downstairs and greet Mei in soft tones. Taking out the clothes in the hampers, she shook with excitement. That book . . . what a link! A link to her Chinese roots. And underneath her bed hid the finale of the entries she'd read and reread. Finally, finally she could—

"Don't do the laundry now," Mei said from behind her.

Ava almost jumped. Do not look at her face; you might give something away. She looked at her mother's feet.

"Be dear and help me with dinner; your father's staying to eat before heading back to New York," Mei continued. "What you doing, standing there like a cow in the road? Get downstairs."

Ava mumbled an apology and went downstairs. At least her mother behaved herself while her father stayed there.

Paul left straight after dinner, afraid of making Mei suspicious. By the time Ava finished cleaning up, an hour remained before midnight. She still couldn't believe that, hours earlier, Dad had shown her that little red book. That little red book had been used to oppress the Chinese, but *Lao lao* told the truth inside. *Lao lao*'s testimony had been written in the margins, but it shunned marginality. History may often be written by the majority, but the minority could—should—also have their say.

Ava felt heartened. She could learn to pass parts of herself down, too. Memorialize your experiences. In the telling, whatever way you choose to do it, you'll make a difference. You'll reach out and touch a life, even if it's only one life. Write it out. Write it over, under, beside. *Believe* in your right to write. Defend it, even in secret. In hidden rebellions.

Mei usually stayed up until at least 2 a.m. writing blog posts, so Ava went to bed in the hopes of waking before her mother. She didn't want to risk getting caught reading the translated entries. So Ava stared at the ceiling, wishing for the morning to arrive.

Chapter Thirty-one

1970

Ma used to write in this. She wrote this for me and her hypothetical grandchildren, so I guess it's only fitting that I end this. I have no one to write to. No way am I having children, and writing to ghosts is a waste. I guess it doesn't matter. No one will read what I write. I'm not even sure why I'm writing. Boredom makes you do strange things.

After four years, two years since my school opened again, my father has come home. He's different from what I remember: stone-faced, bone-thin, and silent. And old, older than his age. Tan, overbaked. Deep lines furrow his face. He looks like old leather. We struggled to recognize each other. When he came home we hardly believed it. Ma's happiness threw her into a mania; Auntie needed to calm her down. When Ma got like that, she became incoherent, as she'd been of late, babbling about superstitions and ghosts. I'd tried to tell her these things weren't real, just stories our ancestors created to scare us. Pain meant reality; hadn't the Revolution taught her that? Pain held substance. Something you could hold onto. Something that held onto you.

During Dad's absence, Ma deteriorated. She became increasingly paranoid, telling me that the Red Guards were forever watching us and that my brother floated around, haunting her. Auntie and I didn't know what to do. For Ma, imagination became indistinguishable from reality. Reality: I have no brother; I have no siblings.

But I couldn't tell her this. It'd remind her of the night everything changed. Ma had been screaming and Dad had been crying. I couldn't pull myself away, so I helped clean the mess. Blood everywhere. Thick, wet, warm. It terrified them, but fascinated me. So did the white mass that came out, the other part of the baby. If Dad hadn't thrown it out, I would've kept it. Later, when I saw Grandpa Poet's brains, I thought of Ma's would-have-been baby. So strange. So interesting, how life ended and began.

Anyway, I never understood what Ma constantly went on about. I see no ghosts nor believe in such nonsense. And then her love for me grew to be suffocating. She channeled all the love that'd gone into growing that baby into loving me. She told me she did everything for me in the "name of love." Too much love, and when I complained she heaped on more, like bringing firewood to extinguish a fire. Ma never let me go anywhere without her "guidance," as she called it, even the bathroom. She waited outside the bathroom door until I finished. Auntie tried reasoning with her, but Ma wouldn't listen. Perhaps she couldn't listen. Regardless, I felt glad when I returned to school; at least then I could play outside. She always said she protected me. A lie. The truth? She choked me.

It's been a week since Dad came home, and four days since I found Mother.

That morning Dad went to work in the alley, sweeping the streets. Auntie went rag-picking and foraging for paper to recycle. Ma stayed in bed, unwell. I missed school to take care of her.

After making breakfast and tea, I brought both to her room, like a filial daughter. I found her hanging by her neck, choked by a coiled rope. Ma looked like a broken doll. She kind of reminded me of the Japanese doll I'd once had, the one the Red Guard decapitated. I put down the tray and softly called for her, not really expecting a response. Of course, I didn't get one. Her neck bent at an odd angle, like a snapped twig. For a moment I stared, finding beauty in such distortion. Then I walked outside and found Dad, who, devastated, confirmed my suspicions. Mother had hung herself to fly with her ghosts.

The lead-up to the cremation blurs in my mind. All I remember is that Auntie and Dad cried a lot. I tried to cry, too; I knew they expected me to, but I couldn't.

On the way to the crematorium, I walked between Auntie and Dad. Remembering the conversation I'd overheard between Auntie and Ma, I felt out of place. Would Auntie hold true to her promise, stay with us? Would she marry Dad? Did I want her to? Auntie had been right about one thing: she'd never be able to replace Ma.

When we arrived at the crematorium, I knew not to expect a traditional memorial service. Chairman Mao made clear that suicide is a selfish, criminal, counterrevolutionary act because it disrespects one's country. I find this amusing because his policies have caused many suicides during the Cultural Revolution. So we couldn't wear mourning bands; they denied us funeral music. We weren't even allowed to have a private viewing room.

I watched the careless crematorium worker dump Ma's body onto a white cart. Before I got a better look, he threw a wrinkled white sheet over the body. His motions reminded me of the hurried way I sometimes made my bed. I looked around. Three other families paid respects to three other bodies on white carts.

"Five minutes before cremation," the worker barked before shutting the door. When he'd left, we drew closer to Ma. Dad and Auntie held hands. Auntie gently grabbed mine. They bowed their heads in respect and closed their eyes, just like the other three families.

I closed my eyes for a moment, but I couldn't concentrate. In the near distance I heard sounds from the private rooms. Funeral music. Muffled howls and sobs. My eyes snapped open. I probably only had three minutes now.

With a flick of my wrist, I shed Auntie's loose hold. Rushing forward, I flung back the sheet. I wanted—no, I needed—to see. The thin sheet slid to the ground, exposing Ma. Dad and Auntie were shocked motionless.

Ma's eyes had been closed. Her skin, ghost-white. A smaller, shorter white sheet had been wrapped around her torso and lower half. Her knees stuck out, and her calves looked skinny, like stripped chicken drumsticks. Before anyone could stop me, I reached out and touched her arm. It felt icy and stiff. I sensed Dad move toward me. Quickly, I pried open the hand closest to me. Possessed by who knew what, I roughly held her hand in mine. I bent down near her dead ear.

"You told me that suicide's not the way to find relief," I whispered, unable to summon a single tear. "You lied. How could you?"

Dad cautiously placed his calloused hands on my shoulders, trying to coax me back.

"Mei. Enough. There are other families here. You're making a scene. She can't hear you anyway."

I shrugged him off and reached for her. He wanted a scene? Then I'd give him one. Seizing Ma by her shoulders, I violently shook her empty shell.

"How could you lie to me?" I yelled.

Then I let Dad pull me back to Auntie. When the crematorium worker came running, I looked over at the other families, defiantly staring back at them.

"Control your wayward daughter," the worker demanded, angrily re-covering Ma's body. He carted her out the door, wheels screeching.

We left the crematorium without another word. Auntie's suppressed crying filled the silence between us. When we'd walked about a hundred feet, I paused, looking back. Auntie and Dad stopped too, silently waiting for me.

The dirty brown chimney towered into the sky like a morose, roofless pagoda. I thought of The Legend of the White Snake, the story Ma loved to tell me. The traditional ending is happy; the snake spirit recovers her human body and reunites with her human husband. But in the alternate ending, the Buddhist sorcerer monk captures the snake spirit, forever imprisoning her in Leifeng Pagoda. Suddenly, thick black smoke billowed out of the chimney. I wondered when it would be Ma's time to burn.

Ma must have gone mad. That's what I decided when I walked home from school one day. Had she felt herself go crazy? Or had the madness just seized her in that moment? I guess I miss her, even the way she followed me around like one of those stray dogs. Halfway through my walk, I spotted something furry moving in the tall grass. A stray.

The small dog reminded me of a guardian lion, which didn't make much sense because it had medium-length, straight hair all over. Black, and severely matted hair. Only the reddish brown tufts of hair sticking out of its batlike ears were smooth. I walked up to it, and it looked at me with marble-shaped brown eyes.

"Abandoned?" I asked. It wagged its tail, eager for the attention it'd once received. Harmless.

I found myself picking it up. It squirmed, trying to wriggle away, but went still upon learning that my grip never wavered. I flipped it over, holding it like a baby, and noted its sex. Female. I meant to put it down and go on my way until I felt something wet on my leg. It peed on me!

The stupid animal soaked the bottom of my uniform. I looked about, but saw no one around. When I put it down on the grass, the dog resumed thumping its tail. It looked up at me, expectant. Kneeling down, I massaged its back until it lay down for me. With one hand I pet it, and with the other I felt around in my backpack for the fist-sized rock I carried with me.

"You're so stupid," I cooed. Its tail thumped the ground. Taking the rock in my other hand, I brought it down on its little head. It screamed on impact but the cry cut off; I'd dealt a fatal blow. Standing up and out of the way to keep blood and urine off my clothes, I struck a couple more blows for good measure. The dead grass drank the blood, a blood different from Ma's miscarriage. I inspected my work. The rest of the body remained in good condition; only the head had been affected. I saw its skull peeking through the bloody black fur.

Feeling much better, I wiped my stained rock on grass untainted by red. Looking at the body, I wondered what to take from it. It died in messy disgrace. Its head, unrecognizable, like Grandpa Poet's. The meat meant nothing to me; I never enjoyed eating dog. What about its teeth? What it would have bitten me with if it had been smart enough to defend itself. So I took my pocketknife and cut out its four canines. Easy enough because they were already loose. Eventually they would've fallen out by themselves. I decided to take the carcass back with me and bury it.

Dad and Auntie weren't there when I arrived home, so I worked in peace. I'd planned on digging a hole in the backyard, but halfway through, my shovel struck something. Digging further than I'd intended, I unearthed the family belt Ma had hidden a week before the first visit from the Red Guards. Brushing the dirt away from the head of the belt shaped like a snake, I smiled. I put the belt aside and buried the lifeless body of the stray. Then I went inside and washed. First the beautiful belt, then the four canine teeth, then my soiled uniform, then myself. Wrapping the teeth in a napkin, I decided that I'd take them with me to America, along with that belt. Perhaps I will fashion the teeth into a necklace someday.

Though I'm only ten, I know I'll be able to get out of this hole. In America, I've heard teachers whisper, you can study anything. Do anything. Be anything. No Communism, just openness. There, in the beautiful country. It's a place to start over, if that's what you want. Escape your past. Become someone new, change countries like clothes. And I will. Just as precisely as I extracted that stray's teeth.

What had Ma been thinking? Writing your reflections down in this little red book is stupid. You can't learn anything, go anywhere with it. No one cares to look at it, even if they discover that the cryptic notes are diary entries. I'll be different. Ma let herself go mad. I'll study hard to leave this sick place and go to America, no matter how long it takes. I'm through with writing. From now on I must do.

Ava turned the page, but found nothing else. Just fourteen pages of half-sized sheets. She couldn't even . . . she didn't know where to begin. Her mother, the charming spokesperson for their local animal shelter. The ultimate hypocrite. Full-time liar, one-time dog killer. Ava's intuition had been vindicated. Nothing worth salvaging in Mei—not as a mother, for sure.

Perhaps there'd always been something lacking in Mei. *Lao lao*'s suicide, the cremation service, these seemed to be snapping points. But still. Who *kills* a harmless stray dog? And so . . . so coldly. Forget empathy. There hadn't even been sympathy. Mei felt no remorse during the killing, when she beat the life out of the dog. No pity when she stared down at its blood and brains. Nor when she extracted its canine teeth. And no regret when she buried it. Ava looked at her locked door, thinking of Mei in her second-floor bedroom. What kind of sick woman had given birth to her?

When she successfully stopped imagining the death of the dog, her thoughts veered to the other macabre descriptions. *Lao lao*, a broken doll. An empty shell on a white cart. Ava shivered and rubbed her arms.

What had happened to *Wai gong*, her grandfather, and "Auntie" Jiao? How much, she wondered, had Mei's childhood influenced the person her mother had become? Had Mei been predisposed to lacking compassion? Ava felt more unsettled than ever. How had her father stayed married to her mother after reading the diaries? Did Paul think his wife had changed? Had he stayed to maintain appearances? Why had he never confronted her? Too afraid to? How dare he leave her with this serpent of a woman! If he'd been present, if he'd made an effort, everything would've been better. What had her father expected, that Mei miraculously recovered from everything she'd experienced as a child? Moving to another country didn't mean that the move erased the past—it just lurked in the background.

Ava's stomach growled. Her room clock informed her of her usual breakfast time: 9:00 a.m. She slipped the papers under her mattress. Ava would deal with those ghosts later. Still in her sleepwear, she unlocked and opened her door, intending to go downstairs and make breakfast. As she approached the stairs, she glanced at the wall. When they moved into the house eight years ago, Mei had begun artfully arranging family pictures diagonally upwards, in chronological order. Each step you ascended to get to the third floor, a picture and a period of time ascended with you.

Eight years desensitized Ava; she'd long since ignored the photos. But this time when she glanced at the wall, she saw the pictures. Images from the past. A past she now knew something about. At the top hung a photo of the family of three, taken during Ava's high school graduation, not long after she'd given her valedictorian speech. Nearby hung her senior portrait, the picture Mei painstakingly examined on her blog. For a moment, Ava visualized her image being used in an empowering manner: her face on display in the book she'd received for her eighteenth birthday, *Part Asian, 100% Hapa*. A Whasian among Whasians.

Taking a step down, Ava recognized a picture from her last piano recital, a year before quitting. Fifteen years old. After she played, the announcer asked, "Whom can you thank for your pianist abilities?" Due to her fear of public speaking, Ava said the first answer that came to mind, "My piano teacher." Just before the well-meaning announcer took the picture, Mei pulled her aside for a tongue-lashing. "Dare you not mention my contribution! If I never pushed you, you still be musically retarded! Just wait until your father leaves. Next time I make you think before on purposely undoing me." And so Ava stood between her parents and glumly smiled for the camera. Remembering the secret humiliation, her hunger dissipated.

Ignoring her embarrassing toddler pictures, she only paused for a moment at the picture taken shortly after her birth. When Charlotte had first seen the photo, she remarked, "What an Asian baby!" Indeed, Mei's genes then reigned supreme. The thin clump of ink-black hair on the center of Ava's head, the tiny slanted eyes, the nearly nonexistent eyebrows, these had been dominant, visible indicators of Mei's racial contribution to her. Paul only slipped into Ava's misty eyes and her skin, which had been ghostly pale.

Below her baby picture, a picture of her parents at their wedding, surrounded by Paul's many Italian and Irish relatives. With no Ling relatives present, Mei stuck out like bean paste on a white tablecloth. But still she smiled, looking comfortable. In her Western heels, she stood taller than her typical height of 5'3." Looking fiercely pretty, she wore a traditional Chinese red brocade dress. Her thick black hair, elbow-length then, dangled in loose coils. She'd stained her lips. A red slash, like the wound of a slit neck.

Ava skimmed over the picture of a yet unmarried Mei, taken during her undergraduate years at New York University. She managed to look glamorous and elegant in a simple knee-length beige wrap dress, posing in a scenic part of campus. Her straight black hair flowed down her shoulders, and she softly smiled. Ava knew without looking what Mei's eyes looked like. Black and hard. Obsidian, and capable of darkening when she flew into a fury.

Toward the landing of the stairs hung the pictures Ava sought. They used to be meaningless black-and-white images of

Chinese grandparents she never knew. Now they became more. There were only two photos on display; she hoped that more survived the Cultural Revolution.

The picture that captured Mei standing with her parents, Ava knew, had been taken in 1966, one month before the Revolution. Paul had told her that much. She took the picture down and held it in her hands. Her well-dressed maternal grandparents, *Lao lao* and *Wai gong*, looked like they'd just come from teaching at Peking University. It'd been Mei's sixth birthday; she wore a special dress to commemorate the occasion. Everyone stood woodenly erect. No one smiled. Although the family stood within reach of each other, none of them touched. A proper Chinese family.

Once, a childhood Chinese friend of Ava's told her a "joke" that related to Chinese stoicism. He said that the reason many Asian kids' heads are "shaped funny" is because parents never played with their babies or rolled them around their cribs. Western parents did and this is why Western children have round heads. As Charlotte would've said, this held no humor, just misery.

She came to the final picture, taken following *Lao lao* and *Wai gong*'s marriage. They were dressed in Western wear: *Lao lao* in a white wedding gown, a veil on her head and a bouquet in her hands, *Wai gong* in a dark formal suit. Ava knew that they first met at Peking University; theirs had been a love match. But they didn't look like they married for love. They stood close, shoulders brushing against each other, and they didn't look aggrieved, but again, no smiling. Still the stiff body positioning.

Silence, secrets, and stoicism. According to this Chinese doctrine, Mei never almost had a sibling. *Lao lao* never miscarried during her fourth month of pregnancy. The Red Guards never desecrated the Ling home. They never carted *Wai gong* away to be reeducated in the country. No struggle sessions ever occurred. *Lao lao* accidentally broke her neck. If culture forbid talking about such things, if culture pretended that they never happened, had they ever really happened? Willful denial turned everything into a palimpsest. Familial events, national history, written over by silence. What Great Famine? Millions dying? No, just leaps forward.

If you kept quiet about the bad things, the unfortunate things, how were you supposed to learn? You'd never be able to truly reconcile your past and work toward a better future. And so you'd never be able to become anything more than a two-dimensional person. Ava tiptoed past her mother's still-shut door, then down the rest of the stairs to the first floor.

When she entered the hallway, the doorbell rang. Afraid her mother would wake, she dashed to the door. No one there. Looking down, she found a UPS package addressed to her mother. She brought the small package inside and locked the door behind her. What could it be? Too small for a book. Maybe jewelry. Since when did Mei order jewelry? She mistrusted online shopping. Ava looked, but the sticker with the sender's address had been scraped off. Maybe there were more details inside, but she dared not open it.

Reconsidering the wisdom of breakfast in her sleepwear if Mei awoke early, Ava went back to her room to get ready for the day. Did this have something to do with Mei's cultivated appearance, her outings? Ava's suspicions that she kept missing something increased. She couldn't remember her mother behaving this way before. As she cooked breakfast—"Chinese-style eggs" Paul called them because she scrambled them with soy sauce—her thoughts again turned to Mei's disconcerting entries. A surprising idea formed. Although her mother had been exposed to so many traumas, an outsider would never be able to tell. Mei hid her past, hid her vulnerabilities, her deficiencies, so . . . so immaculately. Her defensive shell, like Ava's Wall, seemed impenetrable. In this way, Ava realized, *she* became like *her*. Except instead of lashing out at others, she lashed at herself. Instead of blaming others, she blamed herself.

Mei came downstairs at 10 a.m., took her package, and headed up the stairs without a word or glance at her daughter.

Is she tired of me? Of seeing fragments of her reflection in me? Tired of looking at my foreign face? Can she tell that I know her secrets?

Moments later her mother returned downstairs dressed in gym clothes, holding her favorite Louis Vuitton keep-all. She wore jade earrings Ava had never seen before.

"I don't want your eggs; put them away. I'm going out and when I come back I expect all laundry done."

Ava stared at Mei, unable to stop herself from picturing her mother crushing a dog's head.

"You *listening*?" she asked threateningly, taking a step toward Ava, who backed away.

"Y-yes. I'll do the laundry."

Relieved to have her mother gone, she went upstairs. Sifting through the clothes, she created three piles, more out of curiosity than anything else; she'd eventually run them all together. One pile for her own clothes, another for her mother's, and the smallest pile for her father's. She nearly tossed a man's dress shirt into

Paul's pile when an unfamiliar scent caught her nose. Holding the shirt by her face, she inhaled, closing her eyes. It smelled like . . . a cedar tree . . . mixed with lemon or some other citrus fruit. Her father never wore cologne.

Ava lay out a shirt she had seen her father wear, and then lay the aromatic shirt on top of it. They didn't match up. Paul's shirt looked shorter and a bit wider. She filed her observations away for later use. While the washer worked, she responded to the recent texts she'd received from Charlotte, Jason, and Li zhi.

"I'm okay," Ava replied to Charlotte's "Why haven't I heard from you today?!" text.

"You sure? If she goes crazy bitch on you I'll call the cops!"

"Haha thanks, but so far she's done nothing illegal. Also, Dad gave me the rest of the diary. I can't explain over text, but I guarantee you'll be shocked when you see it. How's spring break? You hanging out with Derek?"

"That sounds ominous. We can talk about it later. Break's good; I'm helping Derek's mom cook now. :) Oh and I know it's none of my business, but too bad. I told Flynn that Mei kind of kidnapped you and that you're going through a tough time."

"WHAT?"

"Relax, he totally understands. And from what I can tell, is still really interested. Just to let you know."

"I don't know whether to thank you or yell at you," Ava texted back. She moved on to the texts from Jason.

"I told Prof. Meier what u texted me. She email u yet?"

"Yes. Thanks! I'll explain some other time."

"*No hay problema*. Hope the emergency isn't serious."

Finally she scrolled through Li zhi's texts.

"I explained to Meier and Hines; they'll give you make-ups when you get back from break. Don't worry, I stayed relatively vague. They trust you."

"You're my academic savior!" Ava replied.

"Hardly. I'm just doing what I can. Let me know if anything else happens. Like if I need to contact anyone else . . . "

"I'll keep you posted; I'm going to confront her later. Time for her to let go of me."

"Be careful, okay? I'm nervous for you."

When she finished reading the text, her phone rang. To her surprise, the incoming call came from her father.

"Dad?"

"Ava. Is Mom around?"

"No, actually; she left about half an hour ago. How did you know?"

"I didn't. Just a . . . lucky guess," Paul said. "Did you finish reading?"

"Yes, this morning, before she got up. I don't know what to make of it. *Lao lao*'s suicide, the murdering of that poor dog . . . " Why are you still married to her? How did you let her raise me? You *abandoned* me! But Ava couldn't say any of this aloud. Not over the phone.

"Well, your mother's come a long way. Look at how normal she is now, how American."

"Right," she said. Normal. No, Ava thought she could safely conclude that when Mei had moved to America, she brought her sickness with her.

The washer stopped. Ava took out the wet clothes and put them in the dryer, shouldering the phone to her ear.

"And, you probably don't remember this, but she took her anger out on you when you were two. I stopped her and put an end to it; I told her she couldn't treat you that way in America."

You thought that by just telling her "no," you "put an end to it"? Did you really think that, because she'd moved to America, she stopped being Chinese? That your domineering wife would offer no resistance to Western norms? Ava said nothing. She knew that if she spoke, the truth would erupt in anger. Not unlike the way Mei raged at Ava over the phone.

When a good thirty seconds had passed without a response from his daughter, Paul asked uncertainly, "Ava? You still there?"

She exhaled. "Yes."

"Oh. You were quiet for so long I thought I'd lost you."

You lost me a while ago, Dad. "I'm processing all of the laundry," she replied in a clipped tone.

The front door opened.

"Ava? Come down here and clean my boots," Mei yelled.

"That her?" Paul asked.

"Yes, the monster beckons," Ava whispered. "I've got to go." She hung up as he said "Wait!"

She put her phone in a jean pocket, glanced at the dryer to confirm that it ran properly, and descended to the first floor.

"Lazy bitch. What took you so long?" Mei snapped, unzipping her leather boots and sliding them in Ava's direction before slipping her feet into her silk slippers. She went to the living room and dropped her Louis Vuitton bag onto a couch.

"I checked on the laundry," Ava explained, stooping down to retrieve Mei's boots.

She looked over at her mother. It appeared, from her clingy black sweaterdress, that she went out to lunch after the gym. Wait a second . . . the gym? Mei had cancelled her membership months ago! Just when Ava thought that there were no more secrets, more surfaced. How much did she really know about her mother? What lay beneath Mei's many masks?

"No excuses. And clean the slush floor too," she said, walking by and pushing Ava's shoulder, throwing her off balance. "You so deserve it," Mei said, laughing when Ava fell on her butt.

She got up, refusing to be provoked, and fetched a couple of paper towels. Next time she'd be the one to deliberately provoke.

"I'm going to take my shower, and when I get back we go down to the basement. You wait for me down there," Mei called over her shoulder as she headed up the stairs.

"What? Why? I didn't do anything wrong!" Ava protested. She wanted to confront Mei above ground.

"Discussion done."

"There was no discussion. There never is," she muttered bitterly, scrubbing the floor. With every scrubbing action she felt her resolve build. She'd no longer be treated this way, like some poor damsel in a fairy tale. She'd grown stronger than that. Mei became twisted because she'd let herself get that way. People are like apples. Mei let her bruises eat through to her core. She rejected intimacy, rejected help. Ava faced a Wall. Mei lived in her own country. She allowed the awful circumstances of her childhood to define her. Ava refused to follow her mother down that path. She must break the cycle.

She put off going into the basement, waiting until she heard her mother open the bathroom door before descending into the hateful place. She turned on every light, but shadows still lurked in the corners. What a dungeon. Her mother's dungeon. While she waited for Mei to join her, Ava walked through the aisles formed by the six bookcases. The aged Chinese books were still arranged by height and color. Nothing had changed since the start of the New Year. She forced herself to confront the creepiness of the mazelike aisles and the unfinished basement. I am a child no longer, she told herself.

Beyond the artifacts placed on the shelves in front of the books, something drew her attention. Horrified, but unable to stop herself, she walked up to the upper shelf of a bookcase, standing on her tiptoes to see better. Wedged into a corner, behind some books, lay her old Raggedy Ann doll, its yellow dress faded. Dust clung to the red hair made of yarn. This doll, with its black-stitched eyes, with its lips threaded into a smile. Her old source of comfort. Hearing footsteps, she turned away from her childhood and found her way back to the steel stairs.

"I locked your laptop in my safe. I saw you email your professors, you try to fix your missed midterms," Mei said, descending.

"Why'd you do that?" she asked, anger seeping into her voice. Her mother knew no bounds. She stood a few feet away from her.

"Because I know it bothers you. Because you dared took a class on the *amigos* that mow our lawn!" Mei shook a forefinger at Ava's face.

"It's actually about—"

"You lucky I no know how to work your emailing system all the way. I'd email them back and tell them the truth. That you on purposely missed your exams and can't make them up. That you fail."

She slowly closed the gap between them.

Ava resisted the urge to back away.

Mei began pacing back and forth in front of her. "You never know your own mind. I do. And I only want what best for you. *Jin shan jin mei*. Better over good enough. I never afraid of asking for perfect."

She nearly laughed. "You've only wanted what's best for *you*, what makes *you* look good. But you're slipping. You want to sabotage my grades? How does that reflect your status as mother to a 'perfect' daughter?"

Mei stood still. "*Pihua*. Bullshit!"

"I'll get my laptop." Ava crossed her arms. "I'll change my passwords and change my major back to English. I don't need to listen to you anymore!"

Her mother resumed pacing. "What? You dare? Dare you disobey me! *Guilao*, ghost girl. You reject me, you reject the Chinese in you!" Her black eyes burned.

"No, I'm just tired. Tired of shutting up. You never listen to me and I think it's time you did." Although Ava's voice remained steady, her knees shook. Stop shaking, stop it. You need to pull yourself together and . . .

"*Zazhong*, bastard child, look at you! Where your face? *Bu yaolian*? I'm your fucking mother! I never have to listen to you. *You* must to listen to *me*."

Mei strode forward and slapped Ava with enough force to make her stumble back.

She regained her balance and fully straightened her spine.

"My face? You want to talk about *my face*? Then tell me about your beauty blog. How you dissected pictures of me on it. How you keep photos of me in your vanity. And that you've kept the hair you cut from me. For *two years*." She leaned toward her mother, savoring the stunned look on her face. "You're obsessed with my appearance. So yes, let's talk about my face. What, do you want to be my twin? Look just like me?"

Mei regained her composure. "You wish! I only care because everyone find you so curious. You a show."

"So you think *I'm* what people want? All these years, you called me 'mongrel,' 'bastard,' and all this time you *envied* me?"

"Watch out, *gouzazhong*." Mei jabbed her sternum. "Know your place. *Gui xia*! Show your respect. Kowtow in front of me!"

Ava returned Mei's gaze. "With all *due* respect," she said evenly, knowing that her mother wouldn't get it, "no."

"*What*?" She slapped her other cheek.

This time Ava took the hit without moving. "No. I'm not kneeling before you anymore!" Heart racing, she resisted the urge to reciprocate the slap. She wielded something better than brute force: she wielded words.

"You *sick* me!" Mei's voice cracked. "*Buyaolian de dongxi*!"

Arms akimbo, she retorted, "*I* sicken *you*? How dare you. You bring shame to all of China!"

Mei raised her arm to strike again, but Ava caught her wrist.

Enough. "Don't. Touch. Me," she said icily.

"You dare?" Mei screamed, but her voice waivered with something that sounded unfamiliar.

Ava finally recognized it. Uncertainty.

"I dare do what?" she asked, just loud enough for Mei to hear. "I turned eighteen in October, remember? *This is America*. I'm an adult now. In the eyes of the law, school, society. You don't own me. Not anymore." She continued holding onto her mother's wrist. "You know what your problem is? You defined yourself through *me*. And look where it's gotten you! Why can't you look at yourself, for once? I'm more Chinese than you are. You're a serpent!" She lifted her mother's wrist, holding it in front of her face. "This the hand you used to murder that stray dog? You're *repulsive*."

Mei's eyes widened in shock. "Wh-what? Let go or I . . . I call the police," she hissed.

"So call them. And I'll tell them about *you*. About how controlling, cruel, abusive, and crazy you are, and always have been since I can remember. About how you've hit me for no reason, force-fed me, stomped on my back, and more that I've probably blocked out. How you call me names, treat me like I'm less than human. I'm more human than you'll ever be. *I* have compassion!" She pushed her mother's hand against her own heart. "Feel—it beats. Yours is half dead!"

Mei jerked her hand away, breathing hard. "You want to bring up secrets? Fine! *You* the one I should've miscarried! A son, lost for you!"

Ava shook her head, grimly smiling. "Nice try. That happened to *your* mother."

Slowly, tucking a stray lock of hair behind an ear, Mei seethed, "Ma no knew the sex of her baby. I did. Five months, *I* lost a son. Just ask your father. He never tell you, did he? He wanted me to keep it secret from you."

"What? You're making this up." But Ava didn't speak with conviction. Had the cycle repeated? Had there been *two* miscarriages?

Mei smiled triumphantly. "Just like how he wanted me to pretend that we not separated. You sabotage my life! We wanted a son! If he survived, we wouldn't have another child. We wouldn't have *you*." She seemed to be remembering; her eyes momentarily shifted out of focus. "You supposed to be a worthy replacement, another son." Mei glared at her. "If I could trade you for him, I would!"

Ava wanted to press her hands against her ears and curl into herself. But she ignored the desire to fold.

"*Lao lao* and *Wai gong* would be ashamed if they saw you now! And if what you say is true, then you've got no right to dictate to me. You have no right to control me. I can be as unfilial as I want! You want to drag me through the dirt?" Hands clenched into fists at her sides, Ava pulled out the worst insult she'd learned from Asian American Literature. "Then you're more unfilial than I am! Doesn't Confucius say that failing to bear sons is the worst?"

"Y-you. You . . . fucking whore bitch. *Cao ni zuzong shiba dai*! Ungrateful. You dare, you dare! I *own* you," Mei yelled, lunging at Ava.

She feinted away.

"You don't own me," she said, her voice gaining strength. "I may be like you in some ways, but that's because *I'm what you made*. I'm just a reflection of my upbringing. A screwed up one, by the way."

Mother and daughter circled, facing each other. Who stalked whom?

"But unlike you, I won't use it as an excuse. Yes, I know, I know all about *Lao lao* and your childhood." Pulling at her white shirt, Ava said, "And guess what? I'm *your* ghost!"

"*Ni zai jiang shen me pi hua*! *Qu nide*! Shut the fuck up! I take everything away from you!" Mei put her hands on her ears, covering them.

Her mother looked ready to cry in fury. "You know, I'm actually in a better position than you now. I've got more leverage."

"Shut your whore mouth!"

"Ha! See that's the funny thing. *You're* the whore. You're cheating on Dad with what appears to be a younger, skinnier guy . . . 'Li Wu' is how he's listed in your phone." Ava spoke with confidence, but prayed she supposed correctly.

For a moment, Mei looked surprised. Then she quickly composed herself. She smiled, a black ray of sunshine. "You no proof."

"A couple of his shirts, which reek of cologne. Plus those jade earrings you're wearing. I bet he's Chinese." Mei's lack of denial seemed evidence enough. "So really, I can ruin you. I'll tell Dad, and I'll tell everyone you know. And your worst fears will come true: you'll lose your face and your honor and all of your precious Chinese values. And it's about time, because you're a hypocrite."

"I always knew you try turn on me. *Ni bu xiaoshun*. You ghosts never know to serve elders. You must always bow to me, no question!"

Ava stared at her mother disbelievingly. Mei's face flushed so red the color appeared to bleed down to her neck.

"I've served you all my life. You just never learned to appreciate it. You've never appreciated *me*. Charlotte's mom is more of a mother to me than you could ever be. And I'm done. I won't put up with your . . . twisted ways. This is how you treat your own flesh and blood? Do you think *Lao lao* would be proud of you, if she lived today? Want to talk about shame? You're a disgrace to your mother's memory! She'd be *ashamed* to call you daughter."

Mei's hands trembled. "You think you so smart with your fancy English arguments. Mongrel ghost, you be nowhere without me!" She leaned forward, reaching for Ava.

Anticipating the movement, Ava darted away.

"That's it! I'm telling the world about you, but first I'll tell Dad!" She ran forward, down an aisle.

Mei followed her. Chasing her down another aisle, she yelled, "Like I care! You ghosts deserve each other. Go tell your dad! I knew you just a father fucker!"

Ava stopped running and faced her mother. Her hands, at her sides, curled into fists. Suppressing the need to pant, she shouted, "Shut up! You think everyone's as obsessed with race and perfection as you are. My father loves me. There's nothing abnormal between us! You're the abomination; how could anyone ever love *you*? You're so selfish. Guess what? You're not the center of the universe. Surely, Mao taught you that?"

"You demon *zazhong, zhao si? Pin ge ni si wo huo, yu si wang po*—fish dies or fishing net breaks!"

Her mother charged at her, tackling her into a steel bookcase, knocking her head into one of the steel shelves. They shook the bookcase before colliding on the hard ground. A few books rained down on them. The corner of a hardcover sliced the skin above Ava's eyebrow. Before she recovered, her mother used the fallen book to whack her across the cheek.

She shook her head and blinked, trying to shake the sudden pain. When she stopped seeing stars, she put a forefinger to the cut on her forehead. Blood marked her finger. Then Ava focused on Mei. And froze. A hallucination? The samurai sword letter opener . . .

Kneeling over her daughter, Mei firmly held the hilt in her hand.

"Dare you accuse me, be so self-righteous!" she screamed. "My past mean *my* business! Think you accuse me and get away with it? Think I'm a demon, a *mu laohu*? I show you what a real tiger mom do!"

Mei lunged.

Ava rolled. Dodged her mother's strike. Ripping her phone out of her pocket with sweaty hands, she smacked the "emergency dialer." Mei pinned Ava before she spoke. She shoved the phone away.

"Nine-one-one, what's your emergency?" an operator calmly asked.

"Help! She's trying to kill me," she screamed before her mother pressed a palm to her mouth.

"Hello? Ma'am? Where are you?"

"Fucking bitch! You be so lucky," Mei muttered, squeezing Ava's side. "No, I'm going to make you kowtow. You kiss my feet and beg for mercy!"

"Fuck you, you psycho," Ava tried to say through her hand.

"I teach you, *gongfu ba quan, huo yan xie shen*!"

Mei no longer paid attention to the operator's distant questions. As she'd done at the age of ten, she raised her other arm and brought it down. At the same time, Ava bit her mother's hand. She rejected the idea of playing dead and allowing herself to be carved up.

"*Ta ma de*," Mei cursed, snatching her hand away. Her surprise caused her other hand—the one holding the knife—to fall with force.

Ava's eyes widened as she felt the teeth of the blade slice her upper arm open.

They stopped struggling for a second and looked down, the sight of bright red blood mesmerizing. The thin laceration curved down, about four inches long. Ava expected it to hurt more—the wound seemed deep—but she dimly supposed that shock blocked her pain.

The front door opened, snapping mother and daughter out of the inertia they shared. They looked toward the basement door.

"Somebody help me!" Ava screamed, pushing her mother off her. Mei let go without a struggle.

As Ava used her uninjured arm to push off a bookcase and stagger over to the stairs, Mei sank onto the concrete ground. She let the knife slide to the floor, its blade dipped in blood. Mei looked down at her hands. Her left hand: untouched, nails still perfectly manicured. But her right hand: awash with the stain of blood.

Ava turned back. Compulsively, Mei looked at the ceiling. For a second, Ava wondered if Mei saw her mother's ghost hanging there.

"Ava? Are you in the basement? What—?"

Paul opened the basement door and spotted her dripping arm. When he rushed down the stairs, he continued past his daughter to his wife.

Seriously? Holding her throbbing arm, Ava turned to look at her parents. And then she understood. Her mother had turned the blade on herself.

"Drop it, Mei." Paul shook the hand that held the knife. Blood spat onto the floor.

"*Fang kai*! I won't go. I'll die before," she babbled. "Think you can lock me? *Fang shou*! You can't . . . I won't go, won't go—"

"What are you talking about? Drop it before you make things worse. What've you done; have you gone crazy? Stop this! The police are here."

"Police! We're coming in!" Ava heard from above. In the background, her mother appeared incoherent.

A dark-skinned policeman stormed down the steps, gun drawn. He walked over to her parents and said fiercely, "Ma'am, drop the weapon and put your hands in the air! Sir, please step away."

"Miss?" another officer said, appearing beside Ava. She glanced over and saw that a young policewoman had addressed her. "Why don't you come upstairs with me? No need for you to see this, and," the officer continued, looking at the blood staining Ava's white tank top, "you need care."

"Actually," Ava replied, instinctively pressing her hand to her bleeding arm, "I do need to see this. Give me this second. She's been terrorizing me for eighteen years."

Paul stepped to the side. Mei, warily watching the policeman's ready gun, carefully placed the miniature samurai sword on the concrete ground, in the small puddle of Ava's blood. While the policeman kept the gun aimed at Mei, the policewoman by Ava walked over and cuffed Mei. Though she kept her body still, she turned her head to look at Paul.

"I hate you all; I curse this country," she spat in Mandarin.

Before Paul could respond, someone else answered in English. "Then why'd you come here?" Everyone turned in astonishment to look at the African-American policeman. Putting his gun away and firmly grasping one of Mei's restrained arms, he said matter-of-factly, "Chinese parents adopted me." He switched to Mandarin and told Mei that she had the right to remain silent.

Chapter Thirty-two

"How are you feeling, Ava?" Paul asked, leaning over his daughter's hospital bed.

She shrugged and then winced. The cut stung.

"I'm okay. It's just that the numbness is wearing off." Ava looked down at the cut Mei had made, black stitches now snaking down her upper arm.

Her father's greying brows bunched up and his eyes tightened with worry. He cleared his throat a couple of times.

"Listen . . . I know it probably doesn't make up for anything, but I'm sorry."

She sat still and waited. The pitiful look on her father's face irritated her. And the pain in her arm only bolstered her impatience.

"What . . . what did she tell you, down in the basement?"

Ava laughed harshly, surprising him. "That's the wrong question. 'What didn't she tell me?' is much better."

Looking pained, Paul drew a poorly padded hospital chair to her bedside and sat down.

"Did she . . . did she tell you about the miscarriage? Her miscarriage."

"Don't worry, she made that plenty clear. That you two only wanted a boy. After the miscarriage, you hoped I'd be a boy, and you were disappointed. From the beginning, all you never wanted."

Paul reached out to touch his daughter's hand.

"Don't touch me! That's my injured arm anyway."

He folded, unfolded, and then folded his hands, finally settling them on his lap.

"Not want you? How could you believe that?" Paul asked softly.

She exhaled. "I don't. Not really. But I need you to say it. Aloud."

"The only part that's true is that she miscarried a boy. Like how *Lao lao* supposedly miscarried a boy. I grew up with four older brothers. We competed for Grandma's attention. I went to an all boys' school. Boys are ordinary for me. Please don't misunderstand; her miscarriage upset me terribly. But not because we'd lost a son. I felt grief for losing a child at five months."

Ava studied her father. He seemed sincere.

"I've never been able to understand the Chinese hang-up on having sons. Daughters are extraordinary. When you were born . . . " Paul shook his head as if still amazed. "The best night of my life. You were—still are—the best thing that's ever happened to me." He stared at the railing around Ava's hospital bed and smiled. "My God, I just remember thinking, I now have a baby girl. And not just any girl, but a girl derived from two cultures. What a precious gift, a blessing. Not just to us, but to the world."

She blinked away tears. "I'm not that special. It's not like I'm a messiah."

"You are that special, but you're not a messiah. You're my little miracle."

"Then how come you left me with her?" Ava whispered.

He took a deep breath. "I . . . I don't know how to be a father. All I know is that I've been a bad one. Sure, I provided for you. But I purposely became a blind workaholic: blind to my work obsession and blind to my absence at home. When things fell apart between your mother and me, I tried to deny my disappointment. No, my devastation. I became numb. I threw myself into my work. If I didn't see the problem . . . if I felt reasonable doubt, or any doubt at all, then I disregarded it. I'd made a life plan. But I never considered the power of feelings and situations to change plans. It's . . . it's no valid excuse, but that's what Ryan . . . Grandpa taught me to do. Never admit defeat or own up to weakness. Never display uncertainty.

"And . . . and I thought that I could get over the injustice she'd put me through by helping immigrants gain citizenship, one case at a time. Selfish of me. I never realized how I neglected my own daughter, who, despite whatever garbage your mother told you, matters to me most. I put complete trust in her, thinking she'd never hurt you again. She'd promised not to so remorsefully, and I believed her. I *wanted* to believe her. Too badly. I let it cloud my judgment. Just like when I took my vows believing that she'd never cheat on me."

"Wait, what?" Ava tried to shift up in her dinky hospital bed with her uninjured arm. "What do you mean? You know that she's cheating?"

"What?" Paul's head snapped up. "You mean she's cheating now?"

"Um. At least, I'm nearly positive she's cheating. Those times she went out, I think she went to see him."

Paul paused, considering. "When you were ten, I learned she cheated on me with an Asian American. A Cantonese man named Hui."

"Not another immigrant?" Ava asked, surprised.

"I'm not sure. He might've been an integrated immigrant like your mother."

"Integrated? She hates America."

"No, she doesn't hate America. She probably just says that when things go against her. See, your mother tried to give up her immigrant status after marrying me. She only cared about fitting in. The American fashions, the food, the materialism. She'd never been a communist, never believed in Mao, for reasons you now know. It's been thirty-one years since she came to this country. She's American. If she went back to China now, she'd never recognize it. She's changed too much, and it's changed too."

Her father exhaled. "The day I found out about Hui . . . that same day I called the house about my promotion to partner. Do you remember?"

"I mean, I remember talking to you on the phone . . . right, and then I left for my piano lesson. When I got back we went out to dinner, but nothing felt celebratory. It felt . . . "

"Awkward. Because while you were out I found . . . them." Paul cleared his throat. "And then you walked in on the end of our argument. I decided against divorcing her because I wanted to give you a stable home environment. Better than I had. So we tried to keep our separation a secret from you."

Bitterness rose again. "I knew," Ava said, thinking of his pajamas in the guestroom. "I didn't know the details, but I still gleaned the general idea. I'm sorry, you wanted to give me a what?"

Confused, Paul repeated himself. "A stable home environment. That's what helps a child grow."

"That's . . . coming from you, that's absolutely absurd!"

Paul stared at his daughter, silenced.

"Where have you been these past eight years? You *abandoned* me. I lived in fear. What stable home environment?" She chuckled angrily, remembering the strategic ways Mei had hit her. Ava never lifted her shirt for anyone to see the odd-placed bruises her mother inflicted. "It's a miracle that I'm not more screwed up. Mother's psycho. What do you think you walked in on earlier? A tea party? And you knew something. You knew about her past, the Revolution, the hanging, the dog murder!"

"Wait!" Paul leapt up and drew the curtain around Ava's hospital bed.

"Listen to me," he pleaded. "I thought she'd changed. Perhaps that's just what I wanted to see . . . A dog is one thing. Dogs in China aren't worshipped like they are here. I couldn't imagine her being capable of really hurting you. Her own child. If anything, I believed she'd come after *me*. Defame me, ruin what I'd worked for. Turn you against me. I thought that by staying away, I did the necessary, best thing. For you, for the whole family."

"You thought wrong! You helped her drive a wedge between us."

"Trust me, I regret it. I mean, I should've known . . . but you should've told me."

"How could I tell you? If *you* were scared of her, why couldn't you imagine that I'd be too?" Ava cried. "Why didn't you just get a divorce?"

Springing up from his seat, Paul began pacing.

"I contemplated divorce. But I feared losing you! She would've done, said anything to keep you. She told me she'd plead her case as a battered, devoted mother and take you away."

Ava shook her head. "You're a lawyer. And you'd just been promoted. You could've exposed her lies, fought and won!"

He ran an unsteady hand though his greying hair. "My specialty is immigration. And I didn't want to gamble over my daughter like that. You're not my job. You're my *child*."

"Why didn't you do anything the second I turned twelve, then?"

"Nothing . . . nothing seemed wrong then."

Lowering her eyes, Ava asked, "What about sixteen?" She rubbed her itchy side.

Paul stood still. "I thought . . . ," he began, eyes following the movements of her hand.

"That I faked it, caught up in teen angst? Wanted to create drama?"

"No! God, no. I'd been distracted. With work. And with Uncle Mickey visiting. The scare Ryan had at the doctor's . . . I thought the ultimate problem lay with piano. That she'd tried to make you a virtuoso. And it . . . and playing, the playing hurt you."

"No. It happened . . . I think I wanted help."

"If things were so bad with her, what stopped you from telling me?"

Biting her lip viciously, Ava said, "You were never there."

"I stayed away, but what about the times you visited me? Why not tell me then? Why did you stop visiting, stop responding to my attempts to reach out to you?"

Because Mother tainted our relationship with her appalling accusations. "Same reason you call Grandpa by his first name."

"That's . . . that's different."

"Is it?"

"I . . . "

"Fine! It's because of fear."

"That's it? That doesn't jive with your argument that I should've gotten a divorce."

"Save your tactics for the courtroom. This is just a family drama." Hugging her side, eyes trained on the white bed sheets, she decided to come out with it. "It's because . . . because she accused us of incest."

"Wh-what?"

"I'm not going to repeat it." She turned her head away from her father.

"*Incest*?" Paul whispered incredulously. He sank into the chair. "How could she . . . how could she even come up with that?"

"What can I say? You married a monster."

But Paul no longer listened, trapped in the unfathomable.

"On what grounds? A father's love for his daughter?"

"You know," Ava began, reaching for a subject she felt more comfortable discussing, "I can't believe you thought she'd actually listen to you."

He looked up. "What?"

"When you called me to talk about her part of the diary. You said something about how she punished me and you put a stop to it."

"I really thought I had. That I'd convinced her of alternative teaching methods. Nonphysical discipline. You were only two . . . and you put your hand in the toilet after she'd told you not to. To 'teach you,' she said, she took a belt that she'd inherited, the head of it shaped like—"

"A snake?"

Paul stared at his grown-up daughter, startled. "You remember? I threw that thing out after I found she'd used it on you . . . "

"Surprise, surprise. She must've salvaged it from the trash then, because I've always been afraid of that belt. She stopped using it later. After we quit piano. She no longer needed to use it to get me to play perfectly, at any rate." The anger faded from Ava's voice. Her face calmed. Exhausted, she resorted to stating facts.

"God Ava, I've failed you," her father said, covering his face with both hands. His shuddering shoulders gave the only indication that he'd begun crying.

She thought she heard him mutter, "You pathetic fool. You created a new cycle."

Or he continued the old one. The anger and resentment she'd caged for years spied weakness in a wire. An outlet. Those feelings wanted to charge, to wound, to bloody his tears. To give him a taste of their captivity. She opened her mouth but his whisper interrupted.

"I failed and hurt you." He crumbled onto his knees, arms shielding his face like a boy who'd scraped his knee. "I'm so . . . so ashamed."

Bitter feelings vindicated, Ava felt the presence of *Lao lao*. Soft emotion. Sympathy. Learn to forgive. Neither of them remained faultless.

"You know what, Dad? You didn't fail me. You'd only have failed me if you hadn't come home earlier today."

She didn't believe that, but she wanted to make her father feel better. Ava held the conviction that, even without outside help, she would've been able to handle her mother.

She believed in the words she'd thrown at Mei. *Lao lao* had been right: words, when wielded well, could be everything. Now Ava understood why Li zhi found solace in poetry, in words. When she'd excoriated her mother, she felt like a person of substance. It hadn't mattered that Mei thought her Amerasian child a freak show. All of Mei's curses bounced off her. She'd turned her mother's underground, a place that'd always caused uneasiness, into overground. By rejecting Mei's denouncements, Ava discovered fortitude that she hadn't known she possessed. It'd been inside her all along, latent, waiting to erupt.

Rubbing his eyes, Paul slowly slid his hands away from his face to look at his daughter. She faintly smiled at him, so far away from the girl who'd clung to her Raggedy Ann doll. Sometime during his absence, without his help, she had learned to fend for herself. She didn't need him like he needed her.

He took a tissue from the nightstand and blew his nose. "You've done good without me, you know that, right kiddo?"

"Come on Mr. Lawyer, you know it's 'done well,'" Ava joked lightly, her smile widening.

Her dad looked at her like he meant to figure her out. Weird. But how would she figure out the father who had missed so much? In a way, Mei had brought father and daughter together again. But neither knew what to do about the reunion.

He returned the smile, though it seemed pained. Ava suspected his past still burned him.

"I owe you big. If you want to backpack through Europe this summer with Charlotte, I'll pay for you both. I'll . . . "

He trailed off when Ava vehemently shook her head. Because of her stitches, she couldn't move her arms freely, but her head felt free enough.

"That's a terrible idea. How can we fix what she helped break by continuing to avoid each other? Let's do something fun. Some cheesy father-daughter mini-vacation or staycation. Tell me about your experiences studying at NYU while we toast marshmallows over a fire. We could go to the movies or a museum. We can start over and talk about the past when we're ready."

Paul agreed, pleasantly surprised.

Her father seemed to be reaching for words that hadn't formed. Perhaps he wouldn't blame her if she'd chosen to forever distance herself from him. Neglect could've done that.

"Always knew you were smart, but forgiving too? I'm not worthy." He exaggeratedly bowed in front of Ava.

"See? You know how to be a dad. You've got the cheesy jokes completely mastered!"

Paul smiled for a moment before sobering. "I must attend to unfinished business between your mother and us. Ava, would it be alright with you if we didn't press charges? But it's your choice."

"Press charges? Oh, right," she said, realizing that Mei's fate remained undetermined.

"I know you're angry with her, and rightfully so, but I know the process. It's long and painful for everyone."

Ava wanted to curse Mei to the depths of a psych ward or even prison, if possible, but out of unmediated anger. The anger she received from her mother, the anger that poisoned Mei's mind. No need for vengeance, especially through such a public method; it brought out the worst in people. Distance, receiving support, learning to forgive, gaining closure. These things were worth pursuing. More than anything, she wanted her mother completely out of her life.

"What about getting a restraining order instead?"

"Yes. I also thought that I could have a heart-to-heart with her. Give her some money and ask her to go far, far away and never to come back. The good news is that she's afraid of the law."

"More importantly, she's concerned about her public image. If she can get off without a record or whatever, she'll take that kind of deal."

"Well, I'd better get going." Paul began to stand.

"Wait," Ava said, ashamed that she'd nearly forgotten to ask, "what happened to *Wai gong*, to Jiao? Any chance they're still living?"

Momentarily sitting back down, he shook his head. "I seriously doubt it. I don't know for sure, of course, but logically . . . "

"I see." She tried to flatten her disappointment. "Where are you going now?"

"Down to the station to make sure our statements are in order. And then I need to settle things with your mother and call up people who owe me favors."

"But what about me? Can't I recuperate elsewhere? I only have stitches," Ava complained.

"No, I'm asserting my fatherly authority," Paul joked. "Seriously though, you're staying tonight. I want you to rest and I want you out of the way until Mei's gone. I'm not going to run the risk of you becoming collateral damage. But it's late; I really need to go."

"Fine, fine. I'm going to be so bored here." Sickly green curtains surrounded her and she didn't want to watch reruns on the static-dominated television that hung from the ceiling.

"Hospitals aren't boring; you're just in a boring wing, but you won't be bored for much longer."

"What do you mean?" Ava asked suspiciously.

He smiled. "I've got to go."

"Come back here and answer the question or I'll . . . I'll get out of this bed!"

Her father walked away. A passing nurse said, "Oh no you won't, honey."

Ava closed her eyes. So many other things to think about. She needed to make up her midterms, change her passwords, switch her major back to English, and talk to Li zhi. Then, of course, she needed to think about explaining this to her friends. She'd have to vary the amount of detail she gave away.

Then came the truly unknown: how she'd live life after Mei.

"Miss Magee? You have a visitor." The nurse opened the curtain to reveal Charlotte.

"Ava!" Without thinking, Charlotte practically leaped onto her, squeezing her into a hug.

"Child, she just got stitches. Save some love for later," the nurse said before leaving them.

"Okay, you heard her, get off. My arm. Charlotte, my arm hurts!"

Charlotte backed off, brushing a couple of tears from her face. She scanned the parts of Ava uncovered by the white hospital sheet.

"You had me so worried. I couldn't believe you'd been taken to the hospital. Your dad did the right thing, calling me. You obviously need company."

"It's nice to see you. Now could you let go of my hand? I'm going nowhere, trust me. The nurse out there already knows of my desire to escape."

"So," Charlotte said, eyes continuing to hunt for the injury, "are you ready to talk about what happened? Your dad specified nothing on the phone. He just said that you and your mom fought and that you're in the hospital."

"Lottie. Stop being so ginger. I'm not a doll. Since you obviously don't have the nerve to ask, the stitches are *here*, dodo." She turned on her right side.

"*Shit*." She stared at the long, curved line of fresh stitches. "Why do doctors always use black thread for stitches?" The contrast of the black stitches against Ava's light skin startled.

"No idea; I'd shrug, but that requires both arms. Come on, it's not that bad. Cheer up, you look like you've seen a ghost."

"What do you mean, 'it's not that bad'? It's terrible! Mei *did this*?" Unable to contain herself, Charlotte leaned on the bed railings to further examine Ava's arm.

"It could've been worse, I'm sure. We argued for a while. I spilled some secrets, so did she. We traded insults and I must've really gotten to her, because then she came at me with a knife. She got the upper hand—no pun intended—and cut me. Then Dad came and the police followed. The end."

"What? Is that how mothers in China end arguments?" Charlotte asked in disbelief.

"Um. Not to my knowledge. I think Mother's a . . . special Chinese woman. *Oh*, but that reminds me. I never told you about the rest of the diary." Finishing the story of her mother's childhood had given her the strength to fight Mei. No more vacillating, no regrets; she'd been able to face her mother, alone, on equal footing.

"Naturally, you were too busy getting stabbed. Um . . . sorry, too soon?"

"Actually, after trading insults with my mother, I don't think I'll be easily offended again. I'll never again cringe at your use of 'Whasian,' that's for sure."

Charlotte grinned. "Whasian love! I knew you'd come around."

"And then," she continued, "I have to tell you about the ludicrous stuff my parents kept from me. *For years*. You'll never believe the skeletons they've been hiding. I almost don't myself."

"You know, it's hard to believe you've been stitched up. What, did they give you a shot of adrenaline instead of anesthesia?"

"Be quiet and sit down," Ava said impatiently. "I just want to talk to you, no holds barred."

"Why do I have to sit?" Charlotte protested. "That chair looks uncomfortable. I hate hospital furniture."

"Mother's entry requires sitting. Trust me."

Warily, Charlotte dragged the chair Paul had vacated to Ava's bedside.

"Alright. Spill the nasty details."

Ava narrated Mei's 1970 diary entry, staying true to her mother's words—as they'd been translated via Paul, anyway. As she expected, Charlotte became disturbed.

"It's like karma had it in for her. I mean, at five—"

"Six," Ava corrected.

"Fine, at six she watches commie freaks beat her parents, and then sees her mom's gory miscarriage. Then life gets even better: her mom goes nuts, and after her dad returns she finds her mom hanging. To be honest—and I don't mean to discount the grotesqueness of the torture—I'm not surprised she took it out on that helpless stray dog. Anger management issues, much? No wonder she's fucked up." Charlotte quickly looked at Ava. "Er, no offense."

"No offense to be taken." She leaned forward to get a glimpse of a nearby wall clock.

Charlotte gently pushed her back. "Oh, no you don't, sickly one. No moving! If you're looking for the time, it's 9 p.m."

Defiantly, Ava sat back up. "I'm not an invalid. Don't write me off because I have a cut."

"Touchy. Well, at least you've regained your old spunk. I hated when you were drunk or depressed."

"Well, to be honest, I didn't enjoy those times either. But I think that once the legal nonsense passes, and she's out of my life for good, I can rebuild. Because you know what? I'm okay."

Yes, Ava had an unusual family background, even for an Amerasian. Mei's psychopathy obscured her daughter's already complex identity. Her violence mixed with Confucian values, her racism with contradictory ideals of beauty. But now that Ava understood her mother's conflicts, she recognized her own. She could discontinue the legacies of trauma that she inherited.

Ava began to form a panoramic view of herself. Her Chinese side, her Caucasian side—the two sides together. She may not feel as Chinese as she felt Caucasian, but she'd take steps to change that. Li zhi had informally begun introducing her to Mandarin, but Ava wanted more. If she wanted her Chinese self and her American self to be commensurate, she needed to actively become Chinese. And her father could help. This summer they could vacation in China, maybe visit Peking University, and trace the Ling roots before they'd been tainted by the Revolution. Find out what had happened to *Wai gong* and Jiao and visit wherever *Lao lao*'s ashes could've been scattered.

"You going to get that?" Ava asked, nodding at Charlotte's vibrating jacket pocket.

"Yes," she said, picking up the call. Charlotte turned on her speakerphone.

"We allowed to come in now? We've been waiting in this room for ages," Derek complained.

"Oh please. What are you going to do when you have to wait for a kid to be born?"

"What? I'm eighteen!" he protested.

"Not now, obviously. But it's never too early to practice patience."

Groaning, Derek muttered, "I'm too young for patience. Can't we just visit now?"

Charlotte turned to Ava. "Well? It okay if the boys come visit?"

Ava looked down at her white hospital gown and blanket. Her hair must be a mess and she knew she looked like she'd been spun around a washing machine a few times. Sure, she wore her obligatory white. But with her mother out of her life, she no longer needed to be in mourning. She no longer needed to be a ghost. When she could try clothes on without pain, she decided, she'd look into colorizing her wardrobe. Best to keep this from Charlotte: she didn't want her wardrobe to be invaded by varying shades of pink.

"Sure, why not? It's not like I need to impress anybody."

"You've already impressed him, no worries." Charlotte went back to her phone. "Derek? Yeah, you can come. Actually, why don't I come get you?"

Already impressed him? What did—ah, matchmaker Charlotte. Charlotte came back with Derek and Flynn. When she'd said "boys," Ava thought she'd meant Kevin and Jason. Ava shot her a dirty look, which Charlotte pretended not to see.

"So . . . ," Derek began.

"How're you feeling?" Flynn asked.

Ava wanted to hide under her blanket. Embarrassed to be seen this way.

"Well enough. How is everybody's spring break?" Pretend this is just another conversation. They could've been hanging out at the dorms or someone's house. What did each of them know, anyway? She didn't think she'd care if both Derek and Flynn knew the muddy details, but "So did you know that my mother has violent tendencies that were likely promoted by childhood trauma, and that earlier today we fought and she came at me with a knife?" seemed like an inappropriate question given the present circumstances.

"Uh. Just hanging out with Charlotte, you know," Derek said.

Flynn cleared his throat. "I've actually been doing a bit of programming work for a company."

"I thought you were an engineering major," Ava said, glad Flynn played along.

"Yeah. But since when does that preclude computer programming on the side?" he challenged. "Besides, I'm an electrical and computer engineering major."

As Ava threw a retort back at Flynn, Derek whispered to Charlotte. "You know, I don't think we're needed anymore."

Charlotte smiled at their bickering. "Yup, I say my work here is done," she whispered back. In a normal voice, she said, "Hey Av, Derek and I have . . . somewhere to go. Text me when you're ready to meet up."

"Where . . ." But she'd already left, holding hands with Derek. Bemused, Ava glanced at Flynn. "Well . . . "

"I guess I'll sit." He took what had been Charlotte's seat. "Want to tell me what really happened? If you want to," he quickly added.

"It's okay. I have a feeling I'll be a lot more . . . relaxed from now on." Had she made everyone walk on thin ice for her, like how she'd walked around her mother? That needed to change. The Wall must disintegrate. She'd learn how to be open, and with whom. Flynn seemed like a good person to start trusting. And so, bit by bit, she let go of her secrets, sharing her burdens with someone who cared, who wanted to share the weight.

It became late, but no one had checked in on them. He ended up in bed next to her, by her uninjured side.

Flynn rolled over, resting on his side to better see Ava.

"So if your dad knows Mandarin, how come he never taught you? I can guess why your mom wouldn't, to keep you in the dark or whatever, but why not your dad?"

She frowned at the ceiling. "You know, I only recently thought to question that. We discussed that in my Latin American class before midterms. Most immigrants actively decide whether or not to teach kids their native language. Take my friend Jason. He's half Spanish, half African American. Both his parents know Spanish; they raised him in a bilingual household."

"But which language does he know better?"

Turning her head to look at Flynn, she replied, "Jason's fluent in both. They taught Spanish at home, and he learned English at school or whenever they left the house."

"That's useful. He'll definitely get a job. But wait, what about your dad?"

"That's the odd thing. The other option is to purposely avoid teaching your kids the native language, to avoid 'tainting' their English. My dad didn't do that either. I guess he never made the decision, never thought about it. Maybe he didn't have time. It took him nine years to make partner at his law firm."

Flynn raised his eyebrows. "What, so he neglected his daughter in the meantime?"

Ava winced. "Trust me, it's still a sore subject. Let's talk about something else."

They fell quiet for a few minutes before he spoke up again.

"Do you wish you could've met your—how do you say it?"

"*Lao lao*, though I'm sure my accent is terrible."

He studied her lips and repeated the word, trying to sound authentic. "Don't worry; I'm sure mine's worse. Would you want to meet her, if you could?"

Finally Ava forced herself look into Flynn's eyes, fighting the urge to look away. She couldn't continue to shun connections with other people. "Of course I do. I'm sure that if she'd been given the chance, she would've been a loving grandma. And I don't think she would've cared, Chinese customs or not, that I'm her granddaughter, and a mixed one at that."

He smiled. "Who cares? This is the twenty-first century. You're a Whasian and that's cool. Fuck the haters!"

Ava started to smile, but froze when they heard footsteps. "Quick, pretend we're asleep!"

The nurse peeked in. "Teenagers will be teenagers," she muttered and left.

When they were sure that all nurses and doctors were elsewhere in the hospital, the pair opened their eyes.

"You know, it's kinda three in the morning. We should sleep for real," he said, lightly resting his chin on her right shoulder. She agreed, and soon fell asleep holding his hand.

In the early hours of the morning, Flynn said goodbye to her and drove back to his apartment. He thought he'd make a better first impression if Mr. Magee didn't find him sleeping next to his daughter in the hospital.

Though she hadn't gotten much sleep, Ava felt well rested. Lighter, free. If Paul figured things out with the police, maybe these feelings would stay. After rejecting the poor excuse for breakfast offered her, she anxiously waited for her dad's arrival. He came into her curtained room looking drained.

"You sure you want to go home? We can go to my apartment. Or you can go to Charlotte's."

"No. We need to go to the house. It's ours now. I'm not going to live in fear."

After following proper hospital exit procedure, they left and Paul drove them home.

"Everything okay? You seem on edge," Ava said, noticing his hunched shoulders, his furrowed brow.

"What? Oh, yeah. I just hope your mother is going to hold up her end of the deal, that's all."

When they'd stopped at a red light, she searched her father's face. The bags under his eyes were more prominent than usual.

"What exactly did you get her to agree to?"

Raking a hand through his uncombed hair, Paul said, "A detailed domestic violence restraining order. All contact will be prohibited and she can't come within a hundred yards of you. But that's not going to be a problem."

The light turned green.

"How so?"

"I bought her a plane ticket. This morning the police escorted her to the house to collect her things. She should already be on her flight."

"Flight to where, Dad?"

"Sorry Ava, I'm tired. Apparently to California, where . . . where her lover lives."

The street signs began to look increasingly familiar. They were only a couple blocks away from the house.

"So she confessed?"

Turning into the Maplewood complex, Paul nodded gravely. "I'm afraid so. He used to come here on business. Then he came back for your mother. Apparently they met online."

"I'm sorry."

He shrugged. "I didn't enjoy hearing about it, but I don't love her anymore. Haven't for some time." Smiling faintly, he glanced at Ava. "We'll get on fine without her."

They'd get on better, at least. Her father pulled into the driveway.

"When will you divorce?"

"After the restraining order goes through. I want to concentrate on putting you at ease before anything else."

When Paul parked they took a moment to stare at the yellow house.

As they got out of the car, Ava joked weakly, "Well, at least we know she didn't set fire to the place."

"Your mother is many things, but never an arsonist. Let me go first, okay?"

He opened the door and cautiously stepped into the hallway.

The house echoed its emptiness. No dangerous objects appeared to ready to attack them. Upon closer inspection, they found, to their great surprise, that everything associated with Mei had been taken. Her computer, clothes, shoes, jewelry, pictures of herself, and pictures of her parents. When they walked up the stairs that led to Ava's room, they were startled to learn what Mei had done to their family pictures. The pictures were still in their frames, but she must have momentarily taken them out. They'd been cut; she'd slashed herself out of them. In the master bedroom, the safe lay empty, the little red book gone. No more vanity. She tried not to think about what her mother had done with her hair, with her pictures.

All remnants of Mei, except her largest pieces of furniture, were neatly gone. Like they'd never been there. Like *she* had never been there. But Ava knew what the real test would be.

"Dad? Can you help me inspect the basement?" she asked timidly, heartbeat already speeding up. If her mother had left a nasty surprise, it'd be in the basement.

"Of course. Let me bring a flashlight."

With a big camping flashlight in tow, Paul flicked on the dim basement lights and led the way down the steel stairs.

They found the basement stripped too, except for the ugly steel bookcases, still placed in maze format. Every book, every magazine, every Chinese relic. Gone. No NYU papers, no red scarf, no snake belt, no bloody samurai sword letter opener, no dog teeth necklace. Ava half expected Mei to charge out with the snake belt or worse, but after making their way through the maze of bookcases, they declared the basement empty.

Father and daughter stood next to each other, looking at the now clean spot of concrete that Mei had attacked Ava on.

"You know, we should finally finish this basement," said Ava.

"Finish it?"

"Yes. She left it unfinished. The one room she never cared about maintaining. We'll fix it up. Get rid of the bookcases, put in a carpet. Install heat." Take away the reminders of what happened here. Take the basement back from her mother for good.

"That sounds like a solid idea. We could paint the walls too."

Just as Paul suggested they return upstairs, away from the cold and depressing room, Ava spotted the one object left behind:

Raggedy Ann. Retrieving it from a dusty corner, she brushed it off. The doll's stitching appeared to be coming apart, but otherwise looked whole. To toss or to take? Mostly she wanted to throw it away, as if by doing so she could purge some of the pain her mother had caused her. But then Ava thought that she should keep the doll. A reminder of what she'd endured. Of whom and where she came from. A memento.

"Did you find a note or an artifact?" Paul asked before walking over and seeing the doll. "Good God, that's Mom's baby shower gift to Mei; she sewed it herself!"

"Really? Speaking of Grandma . . . I want see her. And Grandpa." She passed the doll to him.

Turning Raggedy Ann over in his hands, he nodded. "Yes. Grandma especially missed you during Christmas. Not only do you watch old movies with her, you help clean up. If I can swing more vacation days, I'll go with you. But you're definitely going."

"Are we going to tell your family? About . . . everything?"

Paul frowned at the doll. "I don't think so. Grandma's turning eighty in August. Ryan's on a slow decline. No need to risk giving either a heart attack."

"Maybe just say that you're getting a divorce. If you can't take off work, I'll tell her."

They headed up the stairs, debating the best course of action. When they reached the hallway, Paul shut off the lights and locked the door to the basement. The rest would be dealt with later.

Chapter Thirty-three

"Step on up, ma'am," the TSA officer said, summoning her with his blue-gloved hands.

Mei rolled her new Pégase 55 carry-on luggage to his podium. She handed him her driver's license and boarding pass.

"Off to the Golden State, eh?"

"Yes."

He returned the documents to her. "Line all the way to the left. Next!"

She stood at the end of the long line. Far too many people. Everyone seemed to be traveling with someone else. And families, of all kinds, in different stages. Babies. Children. Teenagers. Young adults. Most mothers, even the Asian ones, were in worse shape than she, rolls of fat apparent beneath ill-fitted clothes. Wrinkles, white-streaked hair, no makeup. Mei focused on the strangers in front of her.

A white woman in her thirties made faces at a baby strapped to its mother's back.

The petite mother, speaking in Tagalog, leaned down to scold her other child, a little boy.

"How old is your baby?" her husband asked the father.

"Eighteen months," he said, rubbing his red beard.

The wife stopped playing peek-a-boo and turned to the father. "She's precious. And what stunning blue eyes!"

"Will she grow out of them?" the husband asked.

"Maybe. Her brother did. It's not like my wife has a variety of color in her family."

They chuckled and moved up in line. The mother now comforted her crying boy.

"How'd you meet?" the wife asked.

The father smiled. "Strangely. I crashed my motorcycle."

"She your nurse?" the husband guessed.

"My surgeon, actually."

They moved to the luggage belt and Mei lost the rest. Not that she wanted to hear. No, she didn't. They might laugh now, gaze with fond eyes, but that'd change. They only shared pretend understanding. Even if the wife had a perfect past, too many differences lay between them. Too many trials would arise. And gaps. Gaps in style, in mentality. They'd use their vulnerabilities against each other. Best, safest to stick to your kind. To your skin folk.

She took a bin and placed her purse in it. Her shoes followed. The big-bellied man next to her lifted her carry-on onto the belt.

"Workout more," she said, smiling.

"Excuse me?"

"You know, for health."

"Humph." He bent down to take off his loafers and didn't look in her direction again.

Ungrateful white pig. Advice meant more than thank you.

When she passed through security to the waiting area, she called him in California.

"How are you doing? Is everything going as agreed?"

Her driver's license slipped out of her outer purse pocket. It stared up at her. The snapshot of her face. The name. Mei Ling Magee. For a moment she said nothing.

"Mei? You there?"

"Yes." She retrieved it, zipped it away. "We board in forty minutes. Everything is as planned."

"Your things are already here. You sure you don't want me to pick you up?"

She caressed the monogram canvas of her carry on. "I'm sure."

"I'm . . . I'm glad you chose me. You won't regret this."

"I never have regrets. Regret is for those who care about the past. I only look forward."

What would she do about her name? Her initials?

"Let's look to the future," he agreed. "What idiom are you thinking of now?"

"None."

"Bamboo grows after the rain? New ground must be broken? I know. Push out the old to bring in the new."

"I have to go. Someone—someone wants my seat."

"Oh, then—"

Mei ended the call. She sprung up, taking her luggage with her to the bathroom.

A grandmother wearing a red wig approached her. "Dear, are you okay?"

She escaped into the handicapped stall, locking herself away from the prying eyes of foreign devils. This country possessed no hard-earned beauty. Everything stolen or superficial. Splaying her manicured fingers on the stall's wall, she pressed her cheek against it. Cool against her burning skin. Like the stones of the Great Wall in autumn, her earliest memory.

Had she become a Four Old, something to be torn down in a revolution? Which one? Culture, Customs, Habits, or Ideas? More than one? All? Shards of Ava's voice ran through her head, piercing, stabbing holes in her perfect veneer. *You bring shame . . . repulsive serpent . . . what would . . . you made me . . . twisted ashamed . . . see you . . . now your ghost . . .*

Should she have joined her mother?

"United Flight 1966 to San Francisco, now boarding all Star Alliance members."

Mei unlocked the door and wheeled out her carry on. She stood in line behind the group of first-class passengers.

Nonsense, stop thinking nonsense. Regret, remorse, loss . . . these stemmed from doubt, a lack of conviction, a weak will. Fracture. Incompletion. Faults. You must choke your weaknesses, choke them until nothing but strengths remain. Until reaching perfection. Perfection meant wholeness. Meant order. It meant flying above criticism. Becoming harmonious.

She refused to be purged. Refused to let her past dictate her future. Review the old to know the new. That's what they said. But that saying . . . too old. Obsolete. Too messy. She thrived on order. She held herself above her perpetually mixed up daughter. Ava remained too diluted to imagine perfection, to reach out and touch it. It made her faulty, and she'd been so from the beginning, born female—an ever-growing inkblot on Mei's existence.

Her daughter deserved the blame for any troubles she'd had. But none of it needed to be acknowledged. Cut the ties. No. What ties? Within Mei existed her own country. She lived in an invulnerable wilderness. Untouchable. Above connection. All she needed she'd find within herself.

Mei allowed the attendant to scan her boarding pass.

In first-class, she stowed away her Pégase 55. Sat down. Stared out the window, at the wing of the plane.

Never vulnerable. Always a survivor. *Zi li geng sheng*. Self-sustaining. The power of self-regeneration. She didn't *need*. Never needed anyone but herself. Nothing left to fear. She could handle anything. She would.

Chapter Thirty-four

Two weeks later, Ava's life seemed to be coming together. With her father's and Li zhi's help, and the police statements, she'd been able to complete her two make-up midterms, even managing to do well on both. The restraining order blocked access, and the troubling dreams became more infrequent. No more Mei. Ava had her freedom.

She met with Li zhi to have their first sit-down discussion since before spring break. *Battle Hymn of the Tiger Mother* in one hand, umbrella in the other, she walked through an April downpour to Li zhi's office.

Ava raised her hand, about to knock, when Li zhi opened her door.

"Perfect timing! Why don't you get settled? I'm going to get us some coffee," she called over her shoulder, already striding toward the lunchroom. This time her multicolored strands integrated into two plaits.

While Ava shrugged off her trench coat and shook out her umbrella, Li zhi returned with two steaming cups of black coffee.

"I finished the tiger mom book," she said, nodding at the hardcover she had placed on Li zhi's desk. "Don't worry, I kept it dry."

She accepted the cup Li zhi offered.

"Oh good. Though I never worried." Smiling, Li zhi swiveled her chair to face Ava. "Did Chua give you some perspective on your situation?"

She raised one side of her lips in a half-smile. "At times. I could somewhat relate to the piano incidents, but compared to my mother, Chua's a kitten."

They laughed lightly. While Li zhi sipped her coffee, Ava sobered again.

Placing her untouched cup down on the nearby table, she said, "Today's Mother's birthday. She turned fifty-three."

"You okay?"

"The weird part is . . . I think so. I have regrets, but that's good . . . I think we've convinced ourselves that regret is something to eradicate, but it isn't."

Li zhi nodded. "There's a Confucian saying, *qian shi bu wang, hou shi zhi shi*. We remember the past to understand the future. Regret lets us discover what's important to us."

"Yes, I think regret is useful. A tool. A barometer that helps us to measure out future change. Helps us determine how to adjust for a better way of living. I know I must still work through lots of things, especially with my dad, but I've never felt better. Today's a reminder of how much relief I felt—still feel—when she left."

"That's nothing to be ashamed of, you know. Especially after what you found out . . . and how she told you. I can't explain how terrible I felt when you filled me in. I should've called your father sooner."

Ava, about to sip her coffee, set her cup down again. "When my dad told me how he knew to come home, I suspected you. No need to feel bad. You helped bring us together!"

"Still, when you texted me about confronting her, I knew she'd lash out at you. I just never imagined . . . "

Gesturing toward her stitches, she said, "I'm actually glad it played out the way it did. That I faced her. On my own. The police were right behind my dad. I planned on saving myself. You just sped up the process. Thanks for that."

"You're welcome, but you're right. When it came down to it, you knew what to do." Li zhi paused, coffee cup in hand, and contemplated Ava. "Not to get sentimental like an American, but I'm proud of you."

"Thanks? Why?"

"When we first started doing research, I saw parts of myself in you. But the truth is, I'd never have been able to carry on like you did. *And* you juggled school at the same time. Few students could do that; I can hardly believe you're only a freshman. Where will you be senior year? You might take my job!"

They laughed.

"You know what you have?" Li zhi continued. "Quiet strength. Never lose that."

Ava felt embarrassment, but for once it held no ties to shame.

"*Duo xie*. I can't thank you enough for your help."

"*Bu yong xie*. Students like you are why I got into teaching in the first place."

"Do you think . . . I believe I want to double major."

Li zhi put her now cold cup of coffee down. "You changed your passwords and switched your major back to English, right?"

"That's the first thing I did when I got on a computer. But I'm thinking of also majoring in Chinese. To get in touch with the language I never got the chance to develop, you know."

Beaming, Li zhi nodded. "I have a few friends in the Asian studies department. They're great instructors. I trust that you'll pick up the Mandarin quickly."

"So you think it's a good idea?"

"Ava, never mind me. What do *you* think? It's *your* college degree."

She searched for a feeling. "I think . . . it feels right."

Li zhi chuckled. "Well, since it's registration week, you couldn't have picked a better time to decide."

"Actually, I'm already registered. Half my classes for next semester will be for Chinese." Ava smiled. "I just wanted to be reassured that I'd made the right decision." From now on, she wanted to devote equal attention to both parts of herself.

Rain and wind defined the next day. Because both of their umbrellas had blown out, Jason and Ava dashed to the building where Latino/a Literature took place.

"*¡Dios mío!*" he said as they burst through the doors.

They wiped their feet on the large black mat and struggled to close their broken umbrellas.

"I feel like a wet dog," she complained, squeezing her soaked hair.

Jason vigorously shook his head in Ava's direction.

"Hey!"

They settled in the classroom just in time for class to begin.

Professor Meier set her sturdy umbrella on the floor. She unbuttoned her rose-colored trench coat. A black silk shawl with embroidered floral designs draped over her burgundy turtleneck.

"*Estudiantes,* I hope you're enjoying our last novel." The shawl's tassels swayed when she took *So Far from God* from her tote bag and placed it on her desk.

"But before we discuss the first chapters, let's revisit the theory you read before *The Brief Wondrous Life of Oscar Wao*. Anyone remember the hero's journey?" Professor Meier sat down, surveying the room. "Looks like you've got some fierce competition, Ava."

Ava turned around. She grinned when she found that no one else had raised a hand.

"Well. You said that it's cyclical, like in *The Odyssey*. The hero leaves home, has adventures, and dies in some way or another. If the hero hasn't literally died, he returns home and tells his story to the community."

"*Muy bien*. Now, someone else tell me why the hero needs to tell the community about his adventures. Ava can't be the only one who stayed awake for that lecture!"

Jason raised his hand. "Because the hero returns wiser. The community learns lessons from him. And then they go out to have their own adventures, avoiding the mistakes the hero made."

"Yes. That's what Campbell argues in *The Hero with a Thousand Faces*. Great book, by the way. Put it on your bucket list, along with Homer's works. Anyway, as we continue on with Ana Castillo's protagonists, I want you to think about the 'hero question': 'what in me has to die so that I can thrive?' How do the characters in Castillo's novel handle setbacks and struggles; what do they do to change themselves? What personal insecurities do they kill to become fully formed heroes?"

That Thursday in mid-April, after her last class, Ava decided to drive back to the house that she and Paul were going to make a home. Without her mother, she walked into the house without fear. As for her father, there'd no longer be a need for his Manhattan apartment. He no longer had a wife to avoid; he only had a daughter to make amends to. They planned on building a father-daughter dialogue, especially over the summer.

At the moment, no logical reasons existed for her to be home. After all, she had everything she needed back at Lockhart. But she came home to try something she hadn't done in years. Her father remained at work; she'd planned it this way. She wanted to be alone. After closing and locking the front door, she went into the living room. And there it stood, covered in black taffeta, still collecting dust. For the first time in two years, she lifted the cover and put it aside.

Two years and Mei's absence had given her enough distance. Ava returned to the baby grand piano with fresh eyes. Oh, how she fought her mother, how she *hated* playing. Her mother felt that true Chinese excelled in academics and the arts. Master of all except sports, which never mattered. At fifteen, Ava had been cultivated. A skilled pianist, easily able to play all the hard classics without sheet music. But, at sixteen . . .

She pulled the bench out and silently sat on the front half of the seat. Such a handsome instrument. She lifted the keyboard cover like she lifted a baby. Reaching out, Ava swept her fingertips across the engraved gold brand, "Steinway & Sons." The piano still appeared in top condition: its ebony finish gleamed and the cover had protected the piano from dust. She kicked off her flats and felt the cool pedals with her bare feet. She hit middle C. Unexpectedly in tune. Taking a deep breath, she softly began playing the étude Mei once made her play for four hours straight. Ava remembered playing until her hands cramped up, wishing she were actually playing—in the park, like her classmates.

She thought she'd cut all piano knowledge from her mind, but her fingers knew exactly what to do. She closed her eyes and played Moonlight Sonata. That'd always been her favorite piece, though less flashy than some of the Chopin pieces she'd learned.

The first movement felt the most poignant; when she played, the notes became her lamentation. She mourned the loss of the mother she never had. She mourned the grandparents she never met and never could meet. When Ava finished, she skipped the cheerful second movement, progressing onto the storm, the third and final movement. She forced up everything that had upset her: being called a chink during recess in the third grade, the many episodes with Mei and her obsession with Ava's looks, the unsettling diary entries, the family secrets, Paul's neglect and willful denial, the way people judged her, the way she judged herself. She used all the pieces that composed her to pound out the third movement, using more ferocity than Beethoven had likely intended.

When Ava finished, she curled up on the piano bench, spent. She felt like she'd run for miles. Hands sore, heart caught in her throat. How long would she have to wait until she reached personal harmony? Until she no longer needed any remnants of the Wall? Would her life make more sense after graduating with a dual degree? When Ava spoke both languages, when she *thought* in English and Chinese, would each side recognize and understand the other?

Maybe then she'd be able to forgive her mother. But for now, the entries—and talking about them with her dad—diminished a lot of the anger that she repressed. Learning about Mei's parents also moved Ava closer to feeling less resentful toward, less confused about her mixed heritage. Coming from two seemingly incommensurable cultures would never be easy. It'd always require a balancing act. A new definition of splitness, the right kind: balancing and accepting differences. Because Amerasians deserved a place in this world. Sometimes that place would be challenged, but everything worth celebrating must be defended.

Ava began the drive back to Lockhart. Her phone vibrated. At a red light she checked it. Flynn had texted her: "How about hanging out this weekend?" She quickly replied, "Sure, driving now. I'll text later."

When she returned to her room she discovered a note from Charlotte: "Gone camping with Derek's family! Would've invited you, but you hate dirt on your whites. (Don't bother texting: sucky reception.) See you when the weekend's out."

After spending a majority of the day alone, she'd looked forward to Charlotte's company. As if on cue, Ava's phone vibrated again. Flynn's response.

"And by the way, I'm also free tonight. If you're not doing anything, come over and save me from boredom. No need to text. Just show up."

Welcome news. Ava had a feeling she'd be staying the night, so she packed pajamas and a toothbrush into her backpack. When she arrived, she confidently buzzed Flynn's apartment.

"For the third time this week, no, I did *not* order Domino's pizza. That's Joe in the apartment nex—"

She laughed into the intercom. "Want to let me up? Don't worry, I'll leave the pizza for the raccoons."

"Ava?" He sounded pleasantly surprised.

"Let me in before I change my mind and get something to eat."

"Alright, alright."

Hearing a buzzing sound, she tried the door; it opened. Halfway up the stairs Flynn greeted her.

"You got lucky. I just finished cooking dinner, so you get to eat without having done any prep work."

They made their way to his place.

"You poor thing. Slaving away in the kitchen. Must be hard, living by yourself, hmm? You can't order anyone to make you a sandwich."

She dropped her backpack by his closet as he shut the door behind them.

"Please, this is Jersey. If I asked a girl to make me a sandwich, I'd get beaten up."

They laughed and walked into the kitchen.

"Ah, looks like shrimp and peppers with pasta," Ava said, peering into the pan and pot sitting on the electric stove. "Fresh basil? Impressive."

"Well, I know I've done something right when the food's recognizable. Now out of the way! Man in the kitchen."

He gave Ava a gentle tap, dodged her not-as-gentle smack, and started mixing the food together.

Ava watched him from the counter, smiling to herself.

"Av, could you grab me a couple of plates? They're in the cabinet next to the sink. No, not that one. The other . . . yeah that's it."

She took down the dishes and set them on the stovetop counter.

"I'm serving you first, so tell me when to stop."

She held a plate up to the pot and he began doling out food.

"Stop. Stop!"

"God, that's it? You bird." He served himself as she set her plate down on the kitchen counter, which also served as a small dining area.

"Shut up. Large stomachs aren't for everybody."

Flynn wisely decided to listen. He brought his food over and moved his chair to face Ava.

"Oh, we forgot about drinks. I'll get them if you tell me where to go." She hopped down from her chair.

"Well . . . we can do wine. But *just* a glass this time."

Ava grinned, fetching the glasses and pouring red wine into them. She put their drinks on the high counter and climbed back onto her chair.

"These chairs are great. Look, I'm so high I can swing my legs!"

Flynn watched her lips. He leaned forward to kiss her smile when she took her glass and raised it, clearly expecting him to do the same.

"What are we toasting?" he asked, picking up his glass.

"Um . . . to moving on from the past," she decided.

They clinked glasses and took a celebratory sip.

Ava took a bite of Flynn's dish and chewed thoughtfully, knowing that he waited for a reaction.

"Well . . . I don't know how to say this," she said, suppressing a smile, "but it's kind of awful."

"That's not true!" He gathered a forkful of food to taste for himself.

Unable to contain herself, she laughed at him.

"You little liar! Cruel, just cruel."

"Do you have no faith in your cooking skills? I can't believe you fell for that!"

"I'll get you back later," he warned.

"Seriously, though, it's really good," Ava said, taking another marinara-infused bite.

"Nope. Apology not accepted."

They continued eating.

"So what'd you do today?" Flynn asked, having just told Ava about his standard Friday routine for the current semester: going to work, doing homework, and cooking dinner.

"Well, I went to class, general psychology, and then I went home," she said, moving ziti around her plate.

"Want to go into more detail than that? I mean, I told you I swerved to avoid a squirrel on the way back from work. No near collisions with small animals during your drive?" he joked, trying to smooth out the furrow in her brow.

Ava put her fork down and slid back into her seat.

"Nothing eventful in psychology; a lecture as usual." She began to swing her dangling legs. "Then I drove home. Unlike you, no foraging animals ambushed me. But when I got home . . . I found myself walking to the piano."

"When was the last time you played?"

"Until today, two years ago."

He gave a small whistle. "That's a long time. Because of your mom?"

"If you mean did I quit because of her, then yes." She absently rubbed her side. "She made me start piano lessons on my third birthday. She used to make me play for hours without a break, and if I messed up, if I faltered or missed a note, she'd hit my fingers with whatever she chose to use. Most times she struck with chopsticks."

Ava stretched her arms out on her lap. Looking down, she flexed her fingers as if they still felt sore.

Flynn seemed uncertain of what to say. He reached out and cupped her hands in his larger ones.

Ava stared down at their hands for a moment.

"So I uncovered the dusty beast and played the étude I'd always screwed up."

"And without her hovering over you, you played it right, didn't you?"

She nodded. "Then I played Moonlight Sonata. Not exactly a great segue, but my hands just—"

"Took over? Muscle memory at its best."

"Yes. It felt . . . exhilarating, actually."

"You know, when you get bored with me you can always play my keyboard," Flynn said, gesturing toward the instrument that took up a corner of his living room.

"Finally! I'm only interested because of your keyboard anyway," she said, withdrawing her hands from his and pretending to get up.

"I knew it. Everyone uses me for my keyboard."

They paused for a moment, looking at each other.

He looked about to lean in. She'd never kissed sober.

"Did I tell you?" Ava leaned back in her chair. "When she left she took all her things. It's kind of eerie. Like she'd never been there."

Flynn followed her cue and sat back in his seat. "Where's she now?"

"Apparently in California, with the guy she's been having an affair with."

"Has your dad started the divorce process?"

Ava nodded. "He promised her more money if she cooperated, so they'll do divorce mediation. It'll take less time, I think only two months. They won't need to go to court."

"Well that's good. You won't need to testify then."

She held back a shudder. "Thank goodness."

After finishing the last of his wine, Flynn asked, "Do you know what she's going to do?"

Ava shrugged. "Maybe she'll get a job or finish her PhD. Or just use her boyfriend. Honestly, I'm not interested in even speculating."

"Perfectly understandable."

She focused on the black granite countertop. "But I do wonder what she did with my pictures."

"Your pictures?"

"She'd always belittle me for being mixed." Ava fiddled with the stem of her glass. "'Mongrel dog,' et cetera. Verbally, she'd always hold her 'purity' over me. I found that she'd kept pictures of my face. On her blog, in one of the drawers to her vanity. And a small section of my hair that she'd cut off two years ago. Because I'd quit piano."

Flynn stood up and held out his hand. Ava stared at him.

"Come on, let me help you down."

She reluctantly took his hand, frowning. "Where are we going?" she asked as they headed through the kitchen.

"To the big shiny thing in the bathroom. Come on, stop pulling back. You're more stubborn than my brother's golden retriever! This is for your own good."

He flipped on the switch and the bright lights came on.

Ava stood in front of the faucet and crossed her arms, glowering at his amused reflection.

"What are you doing?"

"This is me ignoring your death stare. Now look at yourself, will you?" He pushed her forward until she drew as close to the mirror as the cabinet allowed.

"What?"

"You heard me. No questions, just look. *Trust* me," he said, pointing to the mirror.

"Fine, I'm looking, now what?"

"What do you see?"

"Me, looking annoyed. Any other brilliant questions?"

"You're not trying. You know what your problem is? You're looking, not seeing yourself. That's what your mom did. She looked at the different pieces that you're physically made of and thought she saw you. People will always try to nail you down.

She's Chinese. No, she's white. But you can't change the way others look at you, so stop trying to."

Flynn moved Ava's hair away from her face, putting it behind her shoulders.

She hugged her sides.

"Let me tell you what I see," he continued, looking at her reflection. "I see a face every girl loves to hate. Why? Because you're more than hot. You've got a double-take face. You're not someone to be skimmed over. People feel compelled to stare at you for a reason. You're more than half Chinese and half white. You're . . . indefinite, complex. Embrace it; you're lucky. You were born having already won the battle over the typical."

"What would you say . . . " Ava stared at Flynn through the mirror. "What if I . . . " She tried again. "What about my scars?"

He bent down, wrapping his arms around her stomach.

"What about them? Everyone's been through something. We're all scarred."

Here, a chance to continue digging under the Wall. To crawl—to drag herself between earth and stone—through to the other side. To stand, marked and naked, squinting into the sun. Warm me or burn me . . . You don't have to do this. You don't have to realize that this is an opportunity. So many flaws, faults, shortcomings. Open wounds that wept in her head. She feared that if she reached out, she'd find no hands. She'd find turned backs. Leave your damages alone. Ava exhaled. She knew she must try. Needed to call her worst self out.

"No, I mean literally."

"We've got those kinds of scars too."

She swallowed hard, decided. Courage! It needed to be done. The last barricade. She began pulling the hem of her shirt up.

Flynn dropped his arms, uncertain.

Ava lifted her shirt over her head and let it drop onto the floor. Her white bra made the contrast worse. The severe lights exposed her. Arms up, she turned so that her left side faced the mirror. Then she turned so it reflected her right side.

"These kinds?"

" . . . the fuck," he whispered, staring. First through the mirror. Then at her flesh. "How could she do it?"

"My mother . . . she didn't."

"Then . . ."

She fixed her eyes on her fallen shirt. She repulsed him. No one wanted these faulty goods. What'd she expect? They were raised, hypertrophic. The lines on her left side had settled into whiteness. A bone-colored white, but luminous against her pale skin. The ones on her right, tea rose.

She'd never *felt* so much before. Stripped of all defenses. The entities of the Wall screamed at their exposure. Insecurity, fear of failure and rejection—on display like tormented trophies.

"Now you see how . . . how far from perfect I really am. I'm built of flaws."

"Ava. Hey," Flynn said, voice soft. "It doesn't matter. Look at me?"

Slowly, she lifted her gaze. His eyes were soft, too.

"It doesn't change how I feel. I just want . . . " He nodded at her right side. "I'm guessing those are newer. Is it over?"

Ava blinked rapidly. "Yes. It's . . . it's really over."

"Can I?" he asked, arms out in offering.

She nodded.

He enfolded her into a hug, resting his chin on her hair.

"I wish you hadn't."

They stood there for a moment. She closed her eyes.

"The old ones . . . that's how I managed to quit piano."

"And . . . and the new ones?"

"Months ago. When I . . . I couldn't hold it in anymore."

"Hell."

"Exactly." She drew away, held his hands in her own.

"That's not—I'm sure you know—healthy. You didn't . . . didn't respect yourself. You deserve better. You're worthy of better."

His eyes spoke. They said sympathy.

She forced herself to meet those eyes. "I felt . . . of all things, lonely. Divided from everyone by the wall of my loneliness. Alone in my flaws."

"In moments of despair, I think we forget about networks. There's no need to remain alone: a whole network of people cares about us. You're far from flawless—we all are. It's a burden we share. Together. And knowing that is enough. It's enough to live on. But it doesn't matter if I say it, does it? *You* need to believe it."

What Ava needed to do now? Continue breaking down the Wall. Win the war within herself. In time, she hoped to see in herself the things he saw. But, as she saw herself reflected in his eyes, she became sure that Flynn meant and believed what he said. That she owned the right to reach out, to grab hold of offered hands. To feel more, to be of substance, to continue seeking full sketch. She kissed him. For once, she needed no words. He understood. He wasn't Amerasian. He hadn't hurt himself. Somehow he understood.

Chapter Thirty-five

Ava walked into her dorm room Sunday night to find Charlotte already there.

"Hi, and where have *you* been?" Charlotte asked with a grin.

"I spent the weekend at Flynn's. How was camping with the Azarovs?" she put her backpack down next to her bed.

"Oh, no you don't. You're not getting away with that vague of an explanation. I can't believe you didn't tell me!" Charlotte shut off the rerun of *Psych*.

"I seem to remember you leaving a note saying *not* to text you. Something about no reception in the big bad wilderness." She wanted to talk about Flynn, but she also wanted to make Charlotte work for it.

Unable to contain her grin, Ava unpacked with her back to Charlotte. She put her laptop on her bed, then her pajamas, a change of clothes, and her toothbrush.

"Ugh, you could've tried texting anyway. Since when have I been able to stop you from doing anything?" Charlotte stopped complaining when she spotted something on Ava's bed. "Is that a red t-shirt I see?" She hopped off her bed to investigate.

"Yes. So?"

Ava smiled to herself as she put her laptop on her desk. She'd been wondering how long it'd take Charlotte to notice that color had been introduced into her wardrobe. About time: she'd gone shopping with Kevin ten days ago. Charlotte had been too caught up in schoolwork and Derekland to notice.

"It's not white or blue. But more importantly, it's not white! How long has this been going on?"

She went over to Ava's bureau.

"For a short while. Hey, did I say you could go through my drawers?"

"Of course not. But this change requires confirmation," Charlotte said, gasping at the full spread of colorful clothes. Blue, green, yellow, maroon, tan . . . "Oh my God, is this a *pink* camisole?" She held the camisole up to Ava, who came over to watch.

"Don't worry, that's the only pink item I bought. In my defense, it's Kevin's fault. He insisted on helping me shop."

"I'm speechless. What happened to the white obsession?"

Ava refolded the camisole and put it back. Closing the drawers Charlotte had opened, she said, "I let it go. Time to move on. I'd only worn white to spite my mother anyway." She kicked off her shoes and sat on Charlotte's bed.

Moving a hot pink pillow, Charlotte sat next to Ava. "What? How did your mom find white offensive? It's so plain. Or if you want to think religiously, it's the color of purity. And wedding dresses."

"Not in Chinese culture. My mother didn't wear a white wedding dress. It's a death color, the color of mourning. White is their black."

"Seriously? That's weird."

"It's only weird because white's not the color you associate with mourning. Obviously, white's usually the color of ghosts. The Chinese can be really superstitious about ghosts."

"Oh. I thought you tried to use clothes to become invisible."

"I never thought of it that way; but, yes, I probably wanted to be invisible."

"Wait, did that piss off your mom?"

"Maybe, but she never showed it. Too wrapped up in trying to . . . erase me, I guess, to notice." But Mei noticed in the basement. "I forgot to tell you . . . before she cut me, know what I said to her?"

"What?"

"I'd been wearing a white shirt, so I waved it at her and yelled, 'I'm your ghost!' Theatrical."

Charlotte laughed. "A loud, furious Ava. I bet you gave her a real fright."

Ava agreed, but thought she might've scared herself more. She hadn't known she could be that fierce, but perhaps a fierce streak wasn't something to eradicate. It could prove useful in certain situations. Her phone vibrated.

Charlotte raised her eyebrows. "And who's that from?"

"Oh, it's just Flynn."

"Right, just. And you're just beaming. Come on, spill."

"You first. I've been talking ever since I got back. So you made an expedition into the great outdoors with your boyfriend. Did you camp in tents or a cabin?" Ava asked, making an effort to tune down the brightness of her smile. She felt—dare she think it?—content. This relaxed state seemed strange, but she foresaw herself getting used to this kind of serenity.

"Please, his entire family chaperoned it. His younger sisters look up to me. Derek and I kept it G-rated; we only held hands. We camped in a cabin that Mr. and Mrs. Azarov rented for the weekend. *So* many bugs. See? Nothing more to tell. Now, back to your *un*-chaperoned weekend—look at you, you're blushing!"

"Shut up. We had fun. He made dinner, we cleaned the dishes together, and we even played a duet on his keyboard."

"Riiight. That's *all* you did, the *entire* weekend."

"Oh, and we also slept together." Flynn had been the first guy she'd literally slept with.

"Yeah, I'm sure you did a lot of 'sleeping.'" Charlotte smirked.

"Naturally. He has a memory foam mattress."

"So what now? Are you official?"

The one subject they'd avoided. "No. Although I think I actually wouldn't mind being his, what's that word you use?" Ava joked.

"Uh oh. You're not his girlfriend? So he could be seeing other people? Just this once, I think you need to listen to *Cosmo* and 'define the relationship.'"

"It goes both ways. I could also see other people. But I don't think he is, though I've gathered that he's never been one to define relationships."

"Perfect. The two noncommittals get together and decide to continue being afraid of commitment."

Ava grabbed one of Charlotte's pink body pillows, hugging it to her middle. "Stop worrying about it. We'll figure it out sometime. Figuring out what you want is easier said than done."

"Speaking of figuring things out . . . over break I told Mom about Dad's letters."

"Why didn't you tell me sooner?"

Charlotte nodded at the scar on Ava's arm. "You were dealing with plenty of your own drama."

She shrugged. "Well, how did Ema take it?"

"Really well, actually. I mean, after the crying. She said she'd denied the suicide because we found no note. So of course I felt terrible giving her three! But she didn't go hysterical. After she read hers, I offered mine. She turned it down, though, and Julie's too. Anyway, I think she'll finally be able to move on now. She still sleeps in his t-shirts, but she's considering dating. Apparently I'm supposed to give her advice on that front." Charlotte shuddered.

"Maybe you can extend your advice to my dad. He's dropped hints about dating after the divorce."

For a moment they looked at each other, considering. Then they dissolved into laughter.

"Nah," Charlotte said. "That'd never happen."

When they quieted down, Ava asked, "Wait, what did Ema decide about Julia's letter?"

Charlotte pulled a face. "She wants to give it to her later. Wait until Julia's more 'stable,' whatever that means."

"It's hard to determine what's best for others. Ema's right. Just leave Julie be, at least for now. What's important is your relationship with her. And Ema's relationship with Julia. Trust me, you've got to work with what you've got."

"Yeah . . . " Charlotte yawned. "God, what time is it?"

"I hate you for passing that on," Ava said, yawning herself. She looked at her wristwatch. "11 p.m. We should go to bed so we can get up for class."

"Morning classes on Mondays. Who came up with that sick idea?"

"Can you believe it?" Charlotte asked Ava. "After tomorrow's finals we'll be done with freshman year!"

They headed out to University Way for the last day of classes. Though early May proved breezy, they didn't need sweaters.

"Yes, actually. I feel way older than a freshman."

"Seriously. I'm so glad you're okay. And that the divorce and all that legal stuff went through. Hopefully your mom will someday get hardcore help."

"Thanks. Not regular help, hardcore help?" Ava asked, smirking.

"Obnoxious. At least you make life interesting. Speaking of interesting things, I took the liberty of texting Flynn and inviting him to meet the guys."

"What? How'd you get his number?"

"I have my ways."

"He's coming to lunch with us, then?"

Charlotte nodded. "We're all meeting at 1:30 at the dining hall."

Ava groaned as they approached the building where their respective classes were held.

"It's going to be terrible. You've been yearning for a double date, haven't you?"

"Maybe. I also invited Kevin and Jason. All of us haven't gotten together in so long."

"Even better. So it'll be like a triple date, except we're the odd ones out." Everyone else would be so touchy-feely. Charlotte and Derek, Kevin and Jason. They loved holding hands in public.

"Well who decided to avoid defin—"

"This is me going to class and ignoring your stupid *Cosmo* tips."

"Define the relationship," Charlotte called as Ava walked through a pair of swinging doors.

While Ava waited for class to start, the scar on her arm caught her eye. It began to lose its stark darkness, but its shape still resembled a snake. She found the imperfection suited her. She'd never forget what it meant to her. In a way, the snake freed her; it eased some of the damage. Ava had become a different type of snake than her mother, and her scar served as a permanent reminder. A snake scar in the Year of the Snake. Lucky, no?

When class let out, Charlotte and Ava walked over to Flynn's apartment. The three of them made small talk while walking to meet the others outside the dining hall.

"So Derek—you met once or twice when you visited Ava—is my boyfriend. He's also Whasian. Sorry, Amerasian," she hastily amended, glancing at Ava.

Ava shrugged. "I'm okay with it, remember? Amerasian, hapa, Whasian. They're all synonymous."

"So that's why they look alike. Ow! Just a joke," he protested, having received an elbow into his side, courtesy of Ava.

"I know. I found it that funny."

Charlotte smiled at the exchange. "No, Derek's half Russian. Plus, he looks more Asian than Ava. Anyway, you'll also meet Kevin and his boyfriend, Jason."

Tobias Dining Hall came into view. Ava received a text. "Jason's nearly there." She nudged Flynn. "Avoid debating with him, okay?"

"There's nothing wrong with a healthy debate."

Charlotte laughed. "No, but you'll be arguing until the building closes. I recommend listening to Ava—in this case."

"What are you trying to say? That I usually give bad advice?"

Flynn jumped in. "Look, Derek's in the lobby. Let's go talk to him."

Soon after they joined Derek, Kevin and Jason arrived. Introductions were made and hands shaken before the couples swiped in and went downstairs. Everyone intermingled in the buffet line. Jason and Flynn talked to each other. Charlotte and Kevin caught up, which left Ava and Derek with each other.

"So how are things?" she asked Derek.

"Good."

"And when will you pop the question to Charlotte?"

Derek fumbled with his tray, nearly dropping his utensils. "Say what?"

She laughed. "Relax, I'm only kidding. Charlotte mentioned that your family keeps speculating that you two will get married after college. And that the idea freaked you out."

Derek righted his tray and his dignity. "Right. Of course."

"At least your family loves her, right? Imagine, they could've hated her. That would've been more of an issue, no?"

"Yeah. Actually, when Mom first met Charlotte she seemed sort of concerned. I think she wanted me to date an obedient Chinese girl."

"Oh. What, like those mail-order brides? I'm unsure that many strictly obedient Chinese girls exist anymore. At least not American-born ones. You remember Li zhi's hair, don't you?"

He smiled. "Like I'd forget."

"I think she started a trend. A few of my Chinese classmates either have multiple piercings, tattoos, dyed hair, or a combination of all three."

They laughed.

"So. Flynn seems cool. At least, he did when I talked to him at the hospital."

They piled food onto their plates. "He is. I'm glad you approve."

"Who said I approved?"

"I can read you like you can read me," she said.

"So not at all?"

"No, you've actually been fairly accurate. You knew I had problems before most people. I responded by being a jerk. And I'm sorry about that."

"Apology accepted. I shouldn't have pushed you to tell me then anyway. Bad timing."

They joined the others at a round table.

"Talking trash about me, hmm?" Charlotte asked as Derek sat down next to her.

"He'd never dream of it," Ava said, watching him smile at his girlfriend.

"And that's why stem cell research could be the key to finding the proverbial fountain of youth," she heard Flynn say to Jason.

"Hey Av, let's get drinks," Kevin suggested. "What'll it be, guys?"

After requests had been made, she stood up with him.

"Well, well, looks like you got quite a catch."

They filled up glasses and slowly walked back to the table.

"How can you tell?"

"He's smooth. Jason liked him immediately, and you know how judgmental he gets. And he obviously adores you. I see the way he looks at you."

Kevin stopped talking just before they set the first batch of drinks onto the table.

They turned back to get their own drinks.

"How does he look at me?" Ava asked.

"Like you're a goddess."

She laughed. "Stop being dramatic."

"Fine, if you insist. But I can tell he appreciates you and all your quirks. So don't eff this up."

"Unfair. Why would I screw it up?" But they'd already made it back to the table.

After a pleasant lunch the group left the dining hall, still talking. Ava surveyed her friends. They could be the set-up for an offensive joke. "Two Whasians, a gay *mulatto,* a gay hipster, a white chick, and a white guy walk into a bar . . . " Some people might see them that way, and Ava could try to change that. So long as she saw herself outside of the labels, she wanted to try. Her comrades would help. Because Ava had earned one of the things she'd wanted out of freshman year: "real" friends.

Chapter Thirty-six

During the second reading day, Ava met Flynn at his apartment to take a break from studying. They'd successfully presented their cartoon mini-movie interpretation of selected sections of Dante's *Inferno,* and with their opposing majors they had no academic reason to meet. So they met to talk: about her expectations for doubling in Chinese and English, Mei and Ava's break from her, Flynn's vague relationship with his mother, his friends at work, about the faster maturing process that the combination of life and college put students through. About their hopes for the future.

They'd been about to resume studying when her phone rang.

"Hi, Dad. What's up?"

She made a "shh" hand gesture. Ava hadn't yet brought Flynn up to Paul. She had no idea how to do so. She and her father found talking about the weather difficult, though they began to get better and build a rapport. But to talk about Flynn? Ava needed to figure that out soon. She wanted to see Flynn over the summer and had promised herself that she wouldn't lie to her father again, including lies of omission.

"I know you're hard at work studying—"

Hearing Flynn scoff in the nearby distance, Ava threw a small pillow in his direction, hoping that he'd stop making noises. Luckily it seemed that Paul hadn't heard.

"Actually, I'm on a break right now. I'm about to go back to studying, though."

"Well, this'll be quick. I have good news. First, I wanted to propose a summer vacation plan. Something to motivate you to study hard. Not that you need the motivation, but . . . "

She sensed his struggle and tried to put her father out of his misery. "Great idea. What about China?"

"That's exactly . . . exactly!"

"We could visit Peking University and maybe find where *Lao lao* used to live. And do the tourist things too," Ava said, excited. Surely someplace existed for commemorating the victims of the Cultural Revolution. She'd get an early start on learning Mandarin, easing the transition into her language classes next semester. Just being in China would be inspiring. Ava would meet the country of half her origins. The half that she continued getting to know.

"The good news," Paul continued, "is that *Wai gong* and *Lao lao*'s cousin Jiao still live."

Ava nearly drop her phone in surprise.

"Ava?"

"Really? But you seemed almost positive . . ."

Paul cleared his throat. "I thought a lot about what you said in the hospital. So I did some digging. *Wai gong*'s alive; he retired from teaching just a decade ago. He married Jiao."

"That's unbelievable. Did he get back his post at Peking University? How old are they now?"

"Yes, he eventually resumed teaching at Peking. He's eighty-seven. Jiao's eighty-five."

"Eighty-seven and eighty-five! Then we must see them this summer. What kind of condition are they in?"

"Healthy, as far as I know. They live in Hong Kong now. I've already made contact. They're eager to see you."

Ava's voice rose in excitement. "And then, when I go to Seattle I'll have lots to entertain Grandma and Grandpa with."

Paul laughed. "First let's figure out China. Then we'll worry about my parents. How about we go the month of June? I can even teach you some Mandarin while we're there, and you'll be so immersed you'll have no choice but to pick it up."

"June? Um, I think there's—" nothing going on for me during June, she'd been about to say, when Flynn shook his head "no" vigorously.

"Uh . . . let me check my calendar. I'm going to put you on hold for a second, okay?" After her father agreed, she muted the call. "What're you so emphatic about?"

"I planned on telling you this later, but I want to take you somewhere during June. June ninth. So go after then," Flynn said.

"What do you mean, 'take me somewhere' on June ninth?" Ava gave him a penetrating stare.

"It's a surprise. I'm taking you into the city. And don't bother asking Charlotte; I haven't told her the details on purpose. Go after June ninth. Please? It's a once-a-year event that I have no control over."

"Fine, fine. Now be quiet; I'm taking him off silent mode." She disliked surprises, but Flynn looked strangely earnest. Ava unmuted her phone.

"Sorry, Dad. It looks like I'll be busy during the beginning of June. How about we plan for mid-June or July? Are you looking to buy tickets now?"

"Not right now, but soon. Probably next week or the week after. I need to notify the firm that I'll be away."

"Wait, can you even be away from the firm that long? You're a main partner!"

Paul chuckled. "I haven't taken a vacation day in *years*. They owe me. Plus I'll have email access in China, no problem. Alright, we'll work out the details soon. I'll let you get back to studying."

"Sure. And Dad? Thanks." She hung up and gave Flynn a wary look.

"What? Why are you looking at me like I'm a criminal?"

"Because you look like you're up to no good."

"I think you'll like this surprise. Trust me. I haven't let you down yet, have I?" Flynn asked, sitting next to her on the couch.

"I guess not," she conceded, and grudgingly let him give her a kiss.

"Mmm. Responsive as stone, I see. You leave me no choice . . . ," he said, tickling her into a laugh.

"Al-alright! I raise the white flag, enough tickling."

"I'm not going to stop until you agree to let me surprise you *and* you kiss me back."

"Okay, okay," Ava gasped. "You drive a hard bargain."

"Now, raise your right hand."

"You've got to be kidding me."

"I can resume the tickle torture, you know."

She unenthusiastically raised her right hand.

"Repeat after me. I, Ava Ling Magee."

"I, Ava Ling—how do you know my middle name?"

"I didn't say that. You're breaking your oath already and we've just started! I, Ava Ling Magee, solemnly swear . . . "

Flynn had clearly been hanging out with Charlotte behind her back. She repeated after him, giving him an annoyed look.

" . . . to allow Flynn Will Davis . . . "

" . . . to allow Flynn *William* Davis . . . ," she said, receiving a similar look from him.

" . . . to take me to New York City on June ninth, no questions asked."

Ava wanted to argue about the last condition, but decided it wouldn't be worth it.

"And kiss." Flynn motioned like he ended a scene in a movie. So they did.

"Back to studying. I only promised *one* kiss. Get away, or I'll take my books and study back at Lockhart. If we get enough studying done, I'll stay over as planned."

She took out her studying materials and ignored his pathetic attempt at a pout.

"We're DONE!" Charlotte shouted. She pulled Ava onto her bed and they jumped on Charlotte's stripped mattress.

Ava grinned and gently bounced. "Only three more years to go." Where did she see herself in three years? As a successful student fluent in Mandarin, she hoped. A woman confident in her abilities. A woman without a Wall. A woman unashamed of her past, comfortable in her scarred, mixed-race skin. With her mother no longer in her family pictures, Ava looked forward to discovering who she could become, one day at a time.

Charlotte stopped jumping and made a sour face. "Ugh. Maybe more for me; I think I'll need to go to grad school."

"Supposedly, it'll pass quickly. But first we'll have summer."

Charlotte brightened. "Yes, the sun, the beach, the ocean!"

Ava grimaced. "You'll be doing that with Derek, then. You know I hate the beach. Besides, I'll be in China during July."

"You'll only be gone during July. By the way, you need to email me when you reunite with your grandpa and cousin. That's so exciting!"

Ava smiled. "I know."

"But it's only mid-May. Until your trip, I can drag you to the beach all the time."

"Remember, Flynn has something planned for me on June ninth."

Charlotte snorted. "Please, that's one day. Unless you'll be devoting most of June to hanging out with him. And forgetting about your best friend."

"That won't happen." It couldn't happen without lying to Paul, anyway. She still hadn't talked to Flynn about where they stood.

Julia walked in and saw them standing on the bed. "What are you doing? *Now* who's being immature? Come on, Mom's waiting."

Ava climbed down from the bed. "She's right. We really need to get out." She joined Julia in the doorway.

"Wait!" Charlotte pleaded.

"Jesus, Char," Julia said, "don't tell me you're going to cry. It's an empty room!"

"Shut up. We need to take a last look!" Charlotte motioned to the unfamiliar room.

Their bedspreads, things, and decorations were gone. Over the course of freshman year they'd individualized their sides of the room. It'd been the home they'd shared together. They'd just settled into their college lives, and now they had to leave.

"She's like a girlfriend sending off her sailor boyfriend," Julia muttered.

Ava, on the other hand, felt ready to start anew.

"Haven't you read any Greek myths? You're *never* supposed to look back." She wanted to leave the room that her mother had stormed into, the room in which she'd been yelled at. Next year, in the on-campus apartment she and Charlotte had signed up for, Ava would set up her room the way *she* wanted it.

"Come on, you've looked long enough. Julie's right; it's just a bare room. We've got everything that made it special with us. Let's *go*." She urged a mournful Charlotte ahead of her and then let the door close for the last time.

Once they said goodbye to their RA Dan—Ava said farewell faster than Charlotte—they wheeled their luggage outside, where their parents waited. Ema and Paul had been animatedly talking. Paul helped Ava put her baggage into the trunk of his tan Toyota Prius. Instead of offering to help her sister, Julia studiously began texting.

"Ema, let me take care of that; I insist. You need to rest your back, remember?" Paul said, lifting Charlotte's baggage into Ema's dark blue minivan. "Alright, you're all set. We'll be seeing you, I'm sure." Paul and Ema kissed on the cheek.

Charlotte, Julia, and Ava exchanged looks.

"Well, ladies, don't you want to say bye?" Ema asked. "Though we're only ten minutes away. I'm sure you'll see each other next week at the latest."

To Charlotte's surprise, Ava gave her a gentle hug. "Thanks for everything, Lottie," she whispered in her ear. Charlotte squeezed her in response, for once not caring that she'd been called Lottie.

Ava nodded at Charlotte's sister. "Have a good summer, Julia."

"You too, Av. I'm sure I'll see you when my lease here is up."

Both families got into their vehicles and began to drive home. Ava looked back at Lockhart. She imagined herself last September. Standing outside, looking up, Wall perfectly in place. Being impenetrable. Feeling shut in. Fearing, but also longing for connection and a chance to belong. Hoping to find solace, freedom, and independence here.

Where are you from, really? Let me answer you, in the same breath. Nowhere; Everywhere.

Chapter Thirty-seven

"Bye Dad," Ava said, passing by his home office, leaving to do goodness knew what in the city. Flynn waited outside.

"Your friend's here already?" Paul asked, taking off his glasses and walking her to the door.

"Yup. Gotta go!" Ava wrenched open the door. She sensed her father come out with her. "Walking me out's unnecessary, really."

"You think I'm going to let you leave with someone who's a stranger to me? You forgot your purse."

Ava inwardly groaned.

"That's a muscle car." Paul said, frowning at the two-door, engine-red Camaro.

"So?"

"This boy one of those trust-fund types?"

"Dad!"

They fell silent when Flynn walked over, back extra straight.

"Mr. Magee, I'm Flynn Davis. It's nice to finally meet you."

"You've got a firm handshake," Paul said, more at ease. "Any tattoos or piercings?" he asked, ignoring Ava's pointed stare.

"No to both."

"Drugs? You smoke or drink heavily?"

"Nope."

"Good. So you can't tell Ava what you have planned for the day, but what about me? Concerned father and all."

"Da-ad." She cringed in embarrassment.

"No, your dad's right. I should explain myself."

Paul smiled. "A cooperative young man, I like that. Ava, why don't you wait in his car? Come, let's get out of hearing range."

She reluctantly walked over to the fancy-looking car and opened the door. Momentarily, she stared at her father's moving lips, but read nothing. She sat in the car and took out her phone. Li zhi picked up on the third ring.

"Hey, Ava. I'm glad you called."

"Hi, Li zhi. You said you wanted to tell me something?"

"Yes, it's something you should think about during your trip to China: studying abroad."

"Studying abroad?"

"Davison has a relationship with Peking University. Recently I had a conversation with one of my students; she's a global ambassador."

"Sorry, what's a global ambassador?"

"A former study abroad student who promotes studying abroad."

"Oh." Ava watched her father cross his arms and attempt to tower over Flynn. She imagined him asking the typical intimidating question, but with the oratory skills of a lawyer: "What, young man, are your intentions with my daughter?"

"When you've taken three semesters of Mandarin, you'll be eligible to study abroad in China," Li zhi continued.

"That'll put me in the second semester of my junior year."

"Many students study abroad during junior year. And, if you so choose, you can study at the same university where your grandparents taught."

"That'd be . . . novel." Her father firmly patted Flynn on the shoulder. With his back to her, Flynn's reactions seemed muted. But she thought she saw him flinch.

"Exactly. I think it'd be an edifying experience for you. I'll write one of your letters of recommendation if you want."

"Where would I be without you? You're the best mentor I could ever ask for."

Li zhi let out an embarrassed laugh. "Thanks, but I'm sure you'd be successful without me. Just keep studying abroad in mind when you visit the university, okay?"

"I definitely will. Have you finished your manuscript yet?"

"Ugh. Almost. I just need to finish commenting on *Never Perfect*. Do you still want to read it over?"

"Absolutely. Feel free to email it to me when you're ready."

"Alright. I'd better get back to it. Shall we meet up before your trip?"

Her father's hand still gripped Flynn's shoulder. "Yes, please text me when you're free."

"*Zai hui*, Ava."

"*Zai jian*."

When she hung up, Paul and Flynn walked to the car. She opened the door. Leaning on the doorframe, she asked, "Dad, can't you be done?"

Her father smiled at his daughter. "Almost." Stopping in front of the driver's side, Paul shook Flynn's hand again. "Treat her right, now. I have friends in high places, son."

She also heard her father mention driving extra safely due to precious cargo. "So embarrassing," Ava muttered.

Flynn smiled weakly and nodded. "Of course. And don't worry, we won't be back too late."

Escaping to the Camaro he and his brother shared, he looked relieved to have his shoulder and hand back. Ava waved at her father while Flynn pulled out of the driveway.

"It must be the car," he muttered.

"What?"

"This car. It's kind of sporty. And bright red. I think that's why your dad gave me the third degree."

Ava laughed.

"Go ahead, laugh at my misery."

"That's what I'm doing."

"I'm stopped at this light, you know. Which means I can safely tickle you . . . "

"Hands on the wheel, mister, or I'll sic my dad's legal hounds on you!" she teased, but Flynn frowned.

"Were you on the phone?"

"I called Li zhi. She wanted me to think about studying abroad in China."

Flynn glanced at her. "When would you go?"

"Spring of junior year."

"You've got to do it."

"Tired of me already?"

He pulled into the parking garage. "No, I just think you shouldn't pass up the opportunity. No one—I mean nothing—should hold you back. I wish I could study abroad, but I can't because of my major."

Ava smiled to herself. She knew she'd go, and she felt glad Flynn wouldn't try to stop her. No more being held back, not by anyone. Including herself.

During the hour-long train ride Flynn declined to tell her about the surprise, so they slipped into a comfortable silence. To pass the time, she looked around at the other people riding the train. She noticed a group of middle-aged women sitting together, talking rapidly in Spanish. A frazzled mother and her redheaded children. A couple of girls who looked at least two years older than Flynn. Some other couples sat nearby, young and old, but she and Flynn appeared to be the only interracial couple.

Sooner than Ava expected, they arrived at New York's Penn Station. Flynn held her hand as they walked through the station with the crowd. She ignored the voice that said "this is weird." Because while holding hands with Flynn felt intimate . . . it never felt wrong.

When they reached street level, he pulled out his smartphone.

"Okay, so we need to take the subway, make one transfer, and then walk to our destination."

"Want to tell me more than that? How can I trust that you won't get us lost?" she asked, on her tiptoes, trying to peek at his phone.

Flynn raised his phone out of her view. "I did my research. Now let's go; it's already 3:30 and the event started half an hour ago."

They took the subway. When they got off at the 1st Avenue stop, they began the walk to Solar One.

Flynn laughed. "Stop trying to walk ahead of me; I'm the one with the directions."

Ava slowed down. "Sorry. I just want to cut down on our lateness." She caught her reflection in a shop window. The skirts of her red-and-white-flowered sundress bounced. She gasped.

"What? What's wrong?" he asked, alarmed. They stopped walking for a moment.

"Am I dressed appropriately? I completely forgot to ask about dress code!"

Flynn chuckled. "Don't be ridiculous. I'd have told you if you needed to dress up. It's completely casual. Now, we turn right here and walk for a bit longer. It's supposedly next to a gas station."

They soon arrived at a large open walkway that ran next to the East River Waterfront. A few midsized white canopy tents stood by the riverside. The rest of the tents stood by the street side, in front of an overpass. A larger tent provided shelter for a DJ and his equipment. About a couple hundred people milled about. Young or old, they looked diverse, with skin tones of all colors. Ava spotted at least ten other Amerasians. Fascinated, she looked around for a sign, for an indicator of what they celebrated. "LovingDay," read a black sign with white lettering.

"What is this?"

"It's the annual Loving Day event in New York. This is their ninth celebration. The event always takes place around June twelfth, the day the Supreme Court outlawed Virginia's ban on interracial marriage. I mean, I know it doesn't directly affect you since we didn't have that kind of law, but I figured it could be special—"

"Flynn? Shut up and let me thank you. I can't believe you did this for me!"

"You're welcome. Now instead of standing here watching, let's go check it out." He smiled when she practically bounced over to the volunteers manning the welcome booth.

"Happy Loving Day," a bronze-skinned woman said.

"Thanks, you too." Ava appreciated the contrast between her bright green eyes and tan skin. The woman had wildly curly hair and a warm smile.

"Why don't we walk around counter-clockwise? That way you see all the booths," Flynn suggested.

One of the first booths they came across offered pamphlets that explained the concept of Loving Day, and what it celebrated.

"This is what I talked about with your dad."

"Oh, that's what took so long. You talked about a legal case."

Flynn frowned. "No, what took so long came after that, when your dad decided to roast me."

Picking up a pamphlet, Ava read about *Loving v. Virginia*, the Supreme Court case she'd never heard of. Mildred Jeter Loving, an African and Native American woman, and Richard Perry Loving, a Caucasian man, left Virginia in 1958 to marry in Washington, D.C., where interracial marriage hadn't been prohibited. Shortly after their return to Virginia, they were arrested. To avoid prison for marrying one another, the Lovings left Virginia and agreed to remain elsewhere for twenty-five years. Fortunately, they fought their exile, hiring an attorney affiliated with the American Civil Liberties Union. After a legal battle that lasted more than four years if you counted their indictment, the Supreme Court unanimously struck down Virginia's anti-miscegenation laws, finally giving the Lovings peace.

They passed a table where children made arts and crafts. Mixed children of varying backgrounds and ages drew everything from simple art, like peace signs and rainbows, to detailed pictures of interracial couples kissing.

"How'd you find out about this?"

"My brother majored in history and philosophy. When I told him about you, he mentioned the court case. Then I searched for *Loving v. Virginia* online and stumbled upon the Loving Day website. I thought you'd like it because they're all about celebrating mixing. Mixed dating and marriage, mixed children. Look at how many Amerasians are here. Turns out you're not so alone after all."

Ava smiled and shook her head. "You, Flynn Davis, are . . . surprising."

"In a good way, I hope?"

"Most definitely in a good way. Now let's dance." She pulled him into the small crowd of dancers.

During a fast song he spun her around. Unprepared, she stumbled into someone at the edge of the crowd.

"Ow!" cried a woman with cat-eye makeup.

Ava turned to her. "Sorry! You okay?"

"Sure. It's not like I need my toes."

"My fault," Flynn added.

She pushed a blonde dreadlock out of her face. "Why are you here?" When she received no response, she rephrased. "Like who are you here for?"

"Who are we here for?" Ava asked.

She fiddled with her black nose hoop. "Yeah. I'm here for my boyfriend. He's Blasian. Like Tyson Beckford."

"Nice mix," Ava said.

The woman nodded. "I know. Who're you supporting?"

Flynn put his arm around her waist. "I'm here for her."

Her eyebrows flew up. "Oh?"

"I'm Whasian."

"Huh."

Ava couldn't resist. "Whasian. Like Kristin Kreuk."

"Well, enjoy the event," Flynn said.

They escaped onto the dance floor.

"Nice comeback."

She grinned. "I know."

When a slower song played they hugged each other and swayed in place.

"So, Ava. Am I now allowed to refer to you as my girlfriend?"

"You mean you want to be more than my supporter?"

Flynn laughed. "Yeah."

She pulled away to meet his brown eyes. "Did my dad put you up to this?"

"No, though he'd probably approve."

"Were you building up to that this whole time?"

Flynn shrugged. "Maybe. It's not hard to think about. Look at all these couples. If they can be happy together, why can't we?"

"Mmm. Sure. I guess this means we're dating for real now."

He smiled. "Guess so."

"Whatever are you going to do without me for the month of July?"

"Video chat you *every day*. Just kidding. Only when you want to. I'll miss you. Don't go forgetting about me when every Chinese guy you meet worships you."

They laughed.

"No, I've already got my guy right here." She gave him a kiss.

When they had danced enough they stood in line for hot dogs. They ate them while leaning on the railing that separated them from the waterfront.

Enjoying a passing breeze, Ava looked out at the diverse crowd of people in front of her. Loving Day. It felt like the people photographed in *Part Asian, 100% Hapa* stood, danced, and walked before her. Loving and celebrating, together, the fact that they were so different. They displayed their own faces, their own voices. But this time they existed off the page, off the record. They lived and breathed, three-dimensional. And so lived Ava.

She turned back to Flynn. He'd helped her see beyond her mother's desecration of her image. Beyond the harm she had done to herself. And while she felt grateful to him, she knew she never needed him to feel complete. Because in truth, she wasn't complete—and didn't need to be. She would remain unfinished; the cursor that followed her name perpetually blinked. *Qian shi bu wang, hou shi zhi shi*. She grew out of her old mistakes and flaws. Created new ones, forever learning. Rose up, reborn out of many former selves. Living, breathing, human art in progress.

Yes, Ava would never have a fixed identity. Some days she'd feel more Chinese than American, or vice versa. But she was, and always would be, both. Hapa. Mixed. Halfie. Hybrid. *Hunxuer.* Amerasian. Whasian.

Ava. Ava Ling. Ava Ling Magee—more than just a term. She couldn't be looked up in a dictionary. She wouldn't be confined, she'd struggle and ebb and flow as it suited her. She existed outside boundaries. Between them. Unlimited liminality. Ava smiled at Flynn and he returned the smile.

Professor Meier's question resurfaced. "What in me has to die so that I can thrive?" The compulsion to fulfill unattainable expectations. Her mother's quest for perfection. Self-shame. Her fear of connecting, of how others saw her. She needed to uphold seeing herself above all else. She would continue learning to accept herself for who she was. Who she had become. Turning, she looked out at the waterfront, admiring the seemingly endless skyline. Her possibilities, she realized, were open to her own interpretation.

Preview of "The View From Here" by Joy Huang Stoffers

At 6:10 p.m. Charlotte's Global Warming class let out. She stepped into the December air and pulled her red scarf tighter, trying to avoid the unkind touch of the wind. Tonight she'd drive home to take care of the cat. Not the most exciting way to spend a Friday night, but she preferred a night at home to one in a frat house. She missed the smell of Mom's cinnamon sticks.

Charlotte opened the door to the faded blue Honda Civic she and her sister shared and threw her backpack into the passenger seat. Her breath lingered like fog. While cool air blasted through the vents, Charlotte pulled out her phone. She texted Derek. "There's a lipstick stain on my steering wheel. What was Julia doing last time she had the car?"

Derek lived across the hall. Like most students on campus, they participated in the "Save-us-son from Davison" meme, texting each other about strange sightings of people dressed up in gorilla suits, ragging on faults in Davison bureaucracy, and complaining about the annoying classmate who never read but constantly asked for help. Then conversations became more personal. And then flirtatious. Charlotte thought her interest reciprocated; but she refused to be the first to act, especially because of a recent discussion.

They'd been rocking out to the latest version of Guitar Hero when he asked about her best friend. Charlotte told Derek how she'd awkwardly confronted Ava about her excessive partying. And then he steered the conversation in an unexpected direction.

"You know, I used to like Ava," Derek said casually, banging on the drum controller.

Charlotte paused, stealing a peek at him. His face gave nothing away. "Um. No, I didn't. Since when?"

"I guess not long after school started. That's why seeing her . . . like that on Halloween ruined it for me. I realized I shouldn't like someone who refuses to accept help, can't communicate. Emotionally speaking, she's high maintenance—all those repressed feelings need to come out sometime. And I don't want to be around when that happens."

She set down her guitar controller. "I know she's got . . . things to work through, but that's harsh, no?"

Derek concentrated on the animated television screen. "No offense to her. I mean, I have some of those problems too. Probably only liked her in theory. But I think . . . if we got together, we'd slowly drive each other nuts. Maybe it's a half Asian thing."

Charlotte had long since neglected the game. "Oh? How so?"

"Oh right, you're white and clueless."

"Hey! Jerk."

"Ignoring problems or hiding them—that's classic Asian style. I'd thought Ava was whitewashed, but now I'm not so sure. She looks white, but I think she's inherited some typical Chinese character traits. Come on," Derek said, handing the guitar controller to her. "You know, it's no fun playing by yourself." And so they returned to their game, with Derek at ease and Charlotte confused.

A notification from her iPhone refocused her attention. Derek's response: "Everyone drives with their mouths now. Where've you been?" Charlotte held her hands up to the car's vents. The air passed for warm. "Stuck in the nineties, obviously. Driving now, ttyl," she replied. Fastening her seatbelt, she pulled out of the parking lot.

At a red light, Charlotte turned the radio on. She sadly smiled, recognizing Dad's favorite Billy Joel song, "Just the Way You Are."

In the corner of Charlotte's heart pulsed a terminal ache. The intensity of the ache depended upon how often something triggered the connector. That connector, like a bell pull, led to the source. The Bell. Father Bell. She covered the bell pull of memories with mental cobwebs. She avoided thinking about them, calling them. That first year, she'd continually failed. Every place, every person yanked the connector. The bell rang so often she feared she'd lose her equilibrium. That the ache would eat her insides until she became an empty shell. But she'd learned to coat the bell with dust.

Now the ache, awakened by the song, surged. It pulled the bell. Snippets of memory, like moth's wings, escaped. Dad, dancing with her and Julia. Mom and Dad singing the song during karaoke night. Watching and listening to Dad play it on his saxophone. She breathed through them, breathed until the hurt lay down and rested its head on its claws.

Charlotte could hardly believe that two weeks remained before she'd finish her first semester of college. Her dad would've been so proud of her.

In eight more days, the three-year anniversary and its shadows would pass over them. As usual, Julia would ignore it. She hurt the most. Dad never failed to support her, through soccer, through softball. As a child and teenager, Julia lived for sports; their father never missed a game, even taking off from his accounting job to be there. He loved Charlotte, but he and Julia had automatically understood each other. They'd spoken the same internal language. Charlotte and her mom understood each other in the same manner.

Half an hour later, Charlotte pulled into the crooked driveway of their redbrick house. Stripped bare of its leaves, the maple tree out front looked tired. As tired as the Bell's home. Mom tried to maintain it, but Do-It-Yourself projects had always been a hobby of Dad's. But like old jeans, the worn appearance grew on Charlotte. The steadfast vulnerability of the broken doorbell, the slanted gutter, the rusty patio swing, the garden that wilted no matter the season. Unlocking the door, she greeted Goldfish, their orange cat that enjoyed swimming.

"Meow to you too, Goldie," Charlotte said as the cat rubbed against her jeans.

She brushed off her jeans before remembering the irrepressible nature of cat hair. Putting down her backpack on their saggy leather couch, she scanned the first floor. A stack of half-graded papers scattered over the dining table. Charlotte organized them into two piles. Mom still held true to her word to never grade with red ink as "nasty red marks potentially destroy a child's self-confidence"; she'd used a green pen instead. There were still dishes in the sink, something Charlotte never saw growing up. "Cleanliness is critter-less," Mom used to joke.

After cleaning and giving Goldie some catnip, Charlotte realized she'd forgotten to bring the mail in.

"Away! You know you're not allowed out when mom's not home," she told Goldie when the cat tried to sneak outside.

After retrieving the mail, Charlotte sifted through the envelopes. Junk mail, junk mail. Coupons, a ShopRite flyer. An early Christmas card from her paternal grandparents, who'd retired to Hawaii. The annual anonymous bereavement card. Disturbed, Charlotte slid that envelope behind the others and put the mail on the kitchen counter.

Almost three years of annual cards. Almost three years since the day he'd chosen to leave them. She found herself wandering over to the locked door next to the hallway closet. Dad's office. Forbidden territory.

She knew what lay beyond this barrier. All traces of him, from him. Pictures and video recordings. His books, his art, his music, his work. Almost all of his clothes. They'd collected these remains from the rest of the house and hoarded them in his office. They'd wanted no reminders. But there were consequences for their absence. For the ache Charlotte dulled, for the dusty bell. The idea of Dad disintegrated. No longer seen in flesh or image, they relegated him to the transience of memory. Each day she persevered in failing to remember, she became better at forgetting. Forgetting the pieces that'd once composed Dad.

Even though Julia remained at school and Ema was in Chicago, Charlotte furtively looked around. Mom thought no one knew where she hid the key. She wanted to avoid stirring up the depression that Julia had sunken into following his death, and if Julia couldn't know, neither could Charlotte; Ema believed in equal treatment of her children. Mom only visited the office on the anniversary of his death. As she'd once explained it to Charlotte: "one day of wallowing is acceptable."

Retrieving the key from the bottom of the cookie jar filled with teabags, Charlotte unlocked the door. She twisted the knob and pushed. The hinges screeched from disuse. Guilty but resolute, she walked up to the threshold and flicked on the light.

She slowly surveyed the sacrosanct office. The room smelled stale from disuse, but otherwise seemed the same. Dad's scratched-up oak wood desk—which he'd made with his "bachelor-crafty hands"—still proudly stood against the wall that faced the door. Under the desk, in its stand, sat Dad's saxophone. If she touched it, she knew her fingertips would be smeared with dust. His grey-wheeled chair had its back to the desk, as if he'd spun out of it quickly with every intention of returning. His sketches remained in the frames Ema had put them in: landscapes, his two daughters, his wife, and even the cat decorated the walls. Against another wall stood the bookcase he'd also built over twenty-five years ago. It housed a multitude of books: scholarly, science fiction, classics, and Do-It-Yourself.

Charlotte remained in the doorway, still shocked. Three years, three years. She'd been in the tenth grade, in history class. Her teacher received a call from the main office and immediately summoned her. She needed to leave class and visit the school counselor. He refused to elaborate. Though nerves consumed her, she listened to his instructions; she kept the questions in her head. Did she forget to hand in an assignment? Did she fail the last test? Did Julia skip a class?

The last thing she'd expected was for the counselor to take both Julia and Charlotte by the hands and say that Mr. Bell was in the hospital. Later, they discovered the disturbing details. Doctors tried to save him, but he'd "passed on." Even worse, police ruled it a suicide. He'd pulled his car over on Route 1 and then jumped into the Raritan. Julia became all emotions, especially at the hospital with Mom. Screaming, cursing, crying. Charlotte just felt numb, cold all over. So sudden. And ten days before Christmas, too.

Despite what everyone else had concluded, Charlotte and her mother refused to believe that he'd committed suicide because of a secret depression. Charlotte still refused to believe that. The Bells had never been in debt, Dad and Mom had enjoyed a happy relationship; he'd even liked his job. Charlotte knew something else caused his death, something they'd overlooked.

Because none of it made any sense. He'd always put family first. Following his death, Charlotte became preoccupied with the causes of suicide. She'd immediately ruled out alcoholism and drugs, as her father had been a devout Catholic and chose, like his parents, to abstain from both. Her tentative conclusion: Dad had succumbed to a mental disorder he'd managed to hide from his family. But that still seemed an unlikely explanation.

Wiping off her damp cheeks, Charlotte turned to leave the office when Goldfish leapt onto the bookcase, knocking a stack of books over.

"Shit, Goldie, look what you did! Shoo, shoo, out. Oh God, what order were the books in?"

She began fixing the damage. Mom would be so disappointed if she knew that Charlotte not only knew the key's hiding place, but that she'd used it to invade Dad's shrine of an office.

Let's see . . . *Do-It-Yourself Repairs* used to be on top. Then *Great Expectations, The Complete Works of Edgar Allen Poe . . .*

During her shuffling and reordering, a scrap of paper slipped out from between the pages of *The Hobbit,* which Dad used to read to her. Charlotte hesitated for a moment before picking it up.

Acknowledgments

So many people helped me breathe life into this novel. I wish I had the space and memory to thank you all here. 感激不盡, *gan ji bu jin*, I cannot thank enough.

The dynamic duo at Harken Media, Robert and Sheila.

Barry, Rick, and Paul for being extraordinary thesis advisors who willingly suffered through multiple drafts.

The friends who became my cheerleaders: Amanda, Brittany, Cassandra, Caroline, Jayne, Jean, Jennifer, Larissa, Marissa, Mel, Nikki, and Sarah.

Photographer and friend Mariana.

Friend and mentor Mekala; Professor Persin.

The "intrepid" staff at the Rutgers University Press, especially Peter, Katie, and Brice, who offered to read an unpolished draft.

My parents and the best friend who happens to be my brother. 我愛家人, *wo ai jia ren*, I love my family.

About the Author

Mariana Klinke

Joy Huang Stoffers was raised in East Brunswick, NJ, by a Taiwanese mother and a Caucasian father. At the age of six, she wrote, illustrated, and promptly recycled her first short story. Since then she dreamed of becoming a novelist. She holds a BA in English from Rutgers University and an MA in Creative Writing from Newcastle University.

Join Joy at **www.joyhuangstoffers.com** for a short story bonus about Ryan Magee, "What Happened on Omaha Beach."

CPSIA information can be obtained at www.ICGtesting.com
Printed in the USA
LVOW11*0309201115

463463LV00003B/3/P